Rebel

Bernard Cornwell

REBEL

HarperCollins*Publishers*

HarperCollins*Publishers*
77–85 Fulham Palace Road,
Hammersmith, London W6 8JB

Published by HarperCollins*Publishers* 1993
1   3   5   7   9   8   6   4   2

Copyright © Bernard Cornwell 1993

The Author asserts the moral right to
be identified as the author of this work

A catalogue record for this book is
available from the British Library

ISBN 0 00 223719 9

Set in Goudy

Printed in Great Britain by
HarperCollinsManufacturing Glasgow

Rebel is for Alex and Kathy de Jonge, who
introduced me to the Old Dominion

PART ONE

1

The young man was trapped at the top end of Shockoe Slip where a crowd had gathered in Cary Street. The young man had smelt the trouble in the air and had tried to avoid it by ducking into an alleyway behind Kerr's Tobacco Warehouse, but a chained guard dog had lunged at him and so driven him back to the steep cobbled slip where the crowd had engulfed him.

"You going somewhere, mister?" a man accosted him.

The young man nodded, but said nothing. He was young, tall and lean, with long black hair and a clean-shaven face of flat planes and harsh angles, though at present his handsome looks were soured by sleeplessness. His skin was sallow, accentuating his eyes, which were the same gray as the fog-wrapped sea around Nantucket, where his ancestors had lived. In one hand he was carrying a stack of books tied with hemp rope, while in his other was a carpetbag with a broken handle. His clothes were of good quality, but frayed and dirty like those of a man well down on his luck. He betrayed no apprehension of the crowd, but instead seemed resigned to their hostility as just another cross he had to bear.

"You heard the news, mister?" The crowd's spokesman was a bald man in a filthy apron that stank of a tannery.

Again the young man nodded. He had no need to ask what news, for there was only one event that could have sparked this excitement in Richmond's streets. Fort Sumter had fallen, and the news, hopes, and fears of civil war were whipping across the American states.

"So where are you from?" the bald man demanded, seizing the young man's sleeve as though to force an answer.

"Take your hands off me!" The tall young man had a temper.

"I asked you civil," the bald man said, but nevertheless let go of the younger man's sleeve.

The young man tried to turn away, but the crowd pressed around him too thickly and he was forced back across the street toward the

Columbian Hotel where an older man dressed in respectable though disheveled clothes had been tied to the cast-iron palings that protected the hotel's lower windows. The young man was still not the crowd's prisoner, but neither was he free unless he could somehow satisfy their curiosity.

"You got papers?" another man shouted in his ear.

"Lost your voice, son?" The breath of his questioners was fetid with whiskey and tobacco. The young man made another effort to push against his persecutors, but there were too many of them and he was unable to prevent them from trapping him against a hitching post on the hotel's sidewalk. It was midmorning on a warm spring day. The sky was cloudless, though the dark smoke from the Tredegar Iron Works and the Gallegoe Mills and the Asa Snyder Stove Factory and the tobacco factories and Talbott's Foundry and the City Gas Works all combined to make a rank veil that haloed the sun. A Negro teamster, driving an empty wagon up from the wharves of Samson and Pae's Foundry, watched expressionless from atop his wagon's box. The crowd had stopped the carter from turning his horses out of Shockoe Slip, but the man was too wise to make any protest.

"Where are you from, boy?" The bald tanner thrust his face close to the young man's. "What's your name?"

"None of your business." The tone was defiant.

"So we'll find out!" The bald man seized the bundle of books and tried to pull them away. For a moment there was a fruitless tug of war, then the frayed rope holding the books parted and the volumes spilt across the cobbles. The bald man laughed at the accident and the young man hit him. It was a good hard blow and it caught the bald man off his balance so that he rocked backward and almost fell.

Someone cheered the young man, admiring his spirit. There were about two hundred people in the crowd with some fifty more onlookers who half hung back from the proceedings and half encouraged them. The crowd itself was mischievous rather than ugly, like children given an unexpected vacation from school. Most of them were in working clothes, betraying that they had used the news of Fort Sumter's fall as an excuse to leave their benches and lathes and presses. They wanted some excitement, and errant northerners caught in the city's streets would be this day's best providers of that excitement.

The bald man rubbed his face. He had lost dignity in front of his friends and wanted revenge. "I asked you a question, boy."

"And I said it was not your business." The young man was trying to pick up his books, though two or three had already been snatched away. The prisoner already tied to the hotel's window bars watched in silence.

"So where are you from, boy?" a tall man asked, but in a conciliatory voice, as though he was offering the young man a chance to make a dignified escape.

"Faulconer Court House." The young man heard and accepted the note of conciliation. He guessed that other strangers had been accosted by this mob, then questioned and released, and that if he kept his head then he too might be spared whatever fate awaited the middle-aged man already secured to the railings.

"Faulconer Court House?" the tall man asked.

"Yes."

"Your name?"

"Baskerville." He had just read the name on a fascia board of a shop across the street; "Bacon and Baskerville," the board read, and the young man snatched the name in relief. "Nathaniel Baskerville." He embellished the lie with his real Christian name.

"You don't sound like a Virginian, Baskerville," the tall man said.

"Only by adoption." His vocabulary, like the books he had been carrying, betrayed that the young man was educated.

"So what do you do in Faulconer County, boy?" another man asked.

"I work for Washington Faulconer." Again the young man spoke defiantly, hoping the name would serve as a talisman for his protection.

"Best let him go, Don!" a man called.

"Let him be!" a woman intervened. She did not care that the boy was claiming the protection of one of Virginia's wealthiest landowners; rather she was touched by the misery in his eyes as well as by the unmistakable fact that the crowd's captive was very good-looking. Women had always been quick to notice Nathaniel, though he himself was too inexperienced to realize their interest.

"You're a Yankee, boy, aren't you?" the taller man challenged.

"Not any longer."

"So how long have you been in Faulconer County?" That was the tanner again.

"Long enough." The lie was already losing its cohesion. Nathaniel had never visited Faulconer County, though he had met the county's richest inhabitant, Washington Faulconer, whose son was his closest friend.

"So what town lies halfway between here and Faulconer Court House?" the tanner, still wanting revenge, demanded of him.

"Answer him!" the tall man snapped.

Nathaniel was silent, betraying his ignorance.

"He's a spy!" a woman whooped.

"Bastard!" The tanner moved in fast, trying to kick Nathaniel, but the young man saw the kick coming and stepped to one side. He slapped a fist at the bald man, clipping an ear, then drove his other hand at the man's ribs. It was like hitting a hog carcass for all the good it did. Then a dozen hands were mauling and hitting Nathaniel; a fist smacked into his eye and another bloodied his nose to hurl him back hard against the hotel's wall. His carpetbag was stolen, his books were finally gone, and now a man tore open his coat and ripped his pocket book free. Nathaniel tried to stop that theft, but he was overwhelmed and helpless. His nose was bleeding and his eye swelling. The Negro teamster watched expressionless and did not even betray any reaction when a dozen men commandeered his wagon and insisted he jump down from the box. The men clambered aboard the vehicle and shouted they were going to Franklin Street where a gang was mending the road. The crowd parted to let the wagon turn while the carter, unregarded, edged his way to the crowd's fringe before running free.

Nathaniel had been thrust against the window bars. His hands were jerked down hard across the bar's spiked tops and tied with rope to the iron cage. He watched as one of his books was kicked into the gutter, its spine broken and its pages fluttering free. The crowd tore apart his carpetbag, but found little of value except a razor and two more books.

"Where are you from?" The middle-aged man who was Nathaniel's fellow prisoner must have been a very dignified figure before the jeering crowd had dragged him to the railings. He was a portly man, balding, and wearing an expensive broadcloth coat.

"I come from Boston." Nathaniel tried to ignore a drunken woman who pranced mockingly in front of him, brandishing her bottle. "And you, sir?"

"Philadelphia. I only planned to be here for a few hours. I left my traps at the railroad depot and thought I'd look around the city. I have an interest in church architecture, you see, and wanted to see St. Paul's Episcopal." The man shook his head sorrowfully, then flinched as he looked at Nathaniel again. "Is your nose broken?"

"I don't think so." The blood from his nostrils was salty on Nathaniel's lips.

"You'll have a rare black eye, son. But I enjoyed seeing you fight. Might I ask your profession?"

"I'm a student, sir. At Yale College. Or I was."

"My name is Doctor Morley Burroughs. I'm a dentist."

"Starbuck, Nathaniel Starbuck." Nathaniel Starbuck saw no need to hide his name from his fellow captive.

"Starbuck!" The dentist repeated the name in a tone that implied recognition. "Are you related?"

"Yes."

"Then I pray they don't discover it," the dentist said grimly.

"What are they going to do to us?" Starbuck could not believe he was in real danger. He was in the plumb center of an American town in broad daylight! There were constables nearby, magistrates, churches, schools! This was America, not Mexico or Cathay.

The dentist pulled at his bonds, relaxed, pulled again. "From what they're saying about road menders, son, my guess is tar and feathers, but if they find out you're a Starbuck?" The dentist sounded half-hopeful, as though the crowd's animosity might be entirely diverted onto Starbuck, thus leaving him unscathed.

The drunken woman's bottle smashed on the roadway. Two other women were dividing Starbuck's grimy shirts between them while a small bespectacled man was leafing through the papers in Starbuck's pocket book. There had been little money there, just four dollars, but Starbuck did not fear the loss of his money. Instead he feared the discovery of his name, which was written on a dozen letters in the pocket book. The small man had found one of the letters, which he now opened, read, turned over, then read again. There was nothing private in the letter, it merely confirmed the time of a train on the Penn Central Road, but Starbuck's name was written in block letters on the letter's cover and the small man had spotted it. He looked up at Starbuck, then back to the letter, then up at Starbuck yet again. "Is your name Starbuck?" he asked loudly.

Starbuck said nothing.

The crowd smelled excitement and turned back to the prisoners. A bearded man, red-faced, burly and even taller than Starbuck, took up the interrogation. "Is your name Starbuck?"

Starbuck looked around, but there was no help in sight. The constables were leaving this mob well alone, and though some respectable-looking people were watching from the high windows of the houses on the far side of Cary Street, none was moving to stop the persecution. A few women looked sympathetically at Starbuck, but they were powerless to help. There was a minister in a frock coat and Geneva bands hovering at the crowd's edge, but the street was too fired with whiskey and political passion for a man of God to achieve any good, and so the minister was contenting himself with making small ineffective cries of protest that were easily drowned by the raucous celebrants.

"You're being asked a question, boy!" The red-faced man had taken hold of Starbuck's tie and was twisting it so that the double loop around Starbuck's throat tightened horribly. "Is your name Starbuck?" He shouted the question, spraying Starbuck's face with spittle laced with drink and tobacco.

"Yes." There was no point in denying it. The letter was addressed to him, and a score of other pieces of paper in his luggage bore the name, just as his shirts had the fatal name sewn into their neckbands.

"And are you any relation?" The man's face was broken veined. He had milky eyes and no front teeth. A dribble of tobacco juice ran down his chin and into his brown beard. He tightened the grip on Starbuck's neck. "Any relation, cuffee?"

Again it could not be denied. There was a letter from Starbuck's father in the pocket book and the letter must be found soon, and so Starbuck did not wait for the revelation, but just nodded assent. "I'm his son."

The man let go of Starbuck's tie and yelped like a stage red Indian. "It's Starbuck's son!" He screamed his victory to the mob. "We got ourselves Starbuck's son!"

"Oh, Christ in his holy heaven," the dentist muttered, "but you are in trouble."

And Starbuck was in trouble, for there were few names more calculated to incense a southern mob. Abraham Lincoln's name would have done it well enough, and John Brown's and Harriet Beecher Stowe's would have sufficed to inflame a crowd, but lacking those luminaries the name of the Reverend Elial Joseph Starbuck was next best calculated to ignite a blaze of southern rage.

For the Reverend Elial Starbuck was a famous enemy of southern aspirations. He had devoted his life to the extirpation of slavery, and his sermons, like his editorials, ruthlessly savaged the South's slavocracy: mocking its pretensions, flaying its morals, and scorning its arguments. The Reverend Elial's eloquence in the cause of Negro liberty had made his name famous, not just in America, but wherever Christian men read their journals and prayed to their God, and now, on a day when the news of Fort Sumter's capture had so inspired the South, a mob in Richmond, Virginia, had taken hold of one of the Reverend Elial Starbuck's sons.

In truth Nathaniel Starbuck detested his father. He wanted nothing more to do with his father ever again, but the crowd could not know that, nor would they have believed Starbuck if he had told them. This crowd's mood had turned dark as they demanded revenge on the Reverend Elial Starbuck. They were screaming for that revenge, baying for it. The crowd was also growing as people in the city heard the news about Fort Sumter's fall and came to join the commotion that celebrated southern liberty and triumph.

"String him up!" a man called.

"He's a spy!"

"Nigger lover!" A hunk of horse dung sailed toward the prisoners, missing Starbuck, but hitting the dentist on the shoulder.

"Why couldn't you have stayed in Boston?" the dentist complained.

The crowd surged toward the prisoners, then checked, uncertain exactly what they wanted of their captives. A handful of ringleaders had emerged from the crowd's anonymity, and those ringleaders now shouted for the crowd to be patient. The commandeered wagon had gone to fetch the road mender's tar, the crowd was assured, and in the meantime a sack of feathers had been fetched from a mattress factory in nearby Virginia Street. "We're going to teach you gennelmen a lesson!" the big bearded man crowed to the two prisoners. "You Yankees think you're better than us southrons, isn't that what you think?" He took a handful of the feathers and scattered them in the dentist's face. "All high and mighty, are you?"

"I am a mere dentist, sir, who has been practicing my trade in Petersburg." Burroughs tried to plead his case with dignity.

"He's a dentist!" the big man shouted delightedly.

"Pull his teeth out!"

Another cheer announced the return of the borrowed wagon, which now bore on its bed a great black steaming vat of tar. The wagon clattered to a halt close to the two prisoners, and the stench of its tar even overwhelmed the smell of tob acco, which permeated the whole city.

"Starbuck's whelp first!" someone shouted, but it seemed the ceremonies were to be conducted in the order of capture, or else the ringleaders wanted to save the best till last, for Morley Burroughs, the Philadelphia dentist, was the first to be cut free of the bars and dragged toward the wagon. He struggled, but he was no match for the sinewy men who pulled him onto the wagon bed that would now serve as a makeshift stage.

"Your turn next, Yankee." The small bespectacled man who had first discovered Starbuck's identity had come to stand beside the Bostoner. "So what are you doing here?"

The man's tone had almost been friendly, so Starbuck, thinking he might have found an ally, answered him with the truth. "I escorted a lady here."

"A lady now! What kind of lady?" the small man asked. A whore, Starbuck thought bitterly, a cheat, a liar and a bitch, but God, how he had fallen in love with her, and how he had worshiped her, and how he had let her twist him about her little finger and thus ruin his life so that now he was bereft, impoverished and homeless in Richmond. "I asked you a question," the man insisted.

"A lady from Louisiana," Starbuck answered mildly, "who wanted to be escorted from the North."

"You'd better pray she comes and saves you quick!" the bespectacled man laughed, "before Sam Pearce gets his hands on you."

Sam Pearce was evidently the red-faced bearded man who had become the master of ceremonies and who now supervised the stripping away of the dentist's coat, vest, trousers, shoes, shirt and undershirt, leaving Morley Burroughs humiliated in the sunlight and wearing only his socks and a pair of long drawers, which had been left to him in deference to the modesty of the watching ladies. Sam Pearce now dipped a long-handled ladle into the vat and brought it up dripping with hot treacly tar. The crowd cheered. "Give it him, Sam!"

"Give it him good!"

"Teach the Yankee a lesson, Sam!"

Pearce plunged the ladle back in the vat and gave the tar a slow stir before lifting the ladle out with its deep bowl heaped high with the smoking, black, treacly substance. The dentist tried to pull away, but two men dragged him toward the vat and bent him over its steaming mouth so that his plump, white, naked back was exposed to the grinning Pearce, who moved the glistening, hot mass of tar over his victim.

The expectant crowd fell silent. The tar hesitated, then flowed off the ladle to strike the back of the dentist's balding head. The dentist screamed as the hot thick tar scalded him. He jerked away, but was pulled back, and the crowd, its tension released by his scream, cheered.

Starbuck watched, smelling the thick rank stench of the viscous tar that oozed past the dentist's ears onto his fat white shoulders. It steamed in the warm spring air. The dentist was crying, whether at the ignominy or for the pain it was impossible to tell, but the crowd didn't care; all they knew was that a northerner was suffering, and that gave them pleasure.

Pearce scooped another heavy lump of tar from the vat. The crowd screamed for it to be poured on, the dentist's knees buckled and Starbuck shivered.

"You next, boy." The tanner had moved to stand beside Starbuck. "You next." He suddenly swung his fist, burying it in Starbuck's belly to drive the air explosively out of his lungs and making the young man jerk forward against his bonds. The tanner laughed. "You'll suffer, cuffee, you'll suffer."

The dentist screamed again. A second man had leaped onto the wagon to help Pearce apply the tar. The new man used a short-handled spade to heave a mass of thick black tar out of the vat. "Save some for Starbuck!" the tanner shouted.

"There's plenty more here, boys!" The new tormentor slathered his spadeful of tar onto the dentist's back. The dentist twitched and howled, then was dragged up from his knees as yet more tar was poured down his chest so that it dripped off his belly onto his clean white drawers. Trickles of the viscous substance were dribbling down the sides of his head, down his face and down his back and thighs. His mouth was open and distorted, as though he was crying, but no sound came from him now. The crowd was ribald at the sight of him. One woman was doubled over, helpless with mirth.

"Where are the feathers?" another woman called.

"Make him a chicken, Sam!"

More tar was poured on till the whole of the dentist's upper body was smothered in the gleaming black substance. His captors had released him, but he was too stricken to try and escape now. Besides, his stockinged feet were stuck in puddles of tar, and all he could do for himself was to try and paw the filthy mess away from his eyes and mouth while his tormentors finished their work. A woman filled her apron with feathers and climbed up to the wagon's bed where, to huge cheers, the feathers were sprinkled over the humiliated dentist. He stood there, black draped, feathered, steaming, mouth agape, pathetic, and around him the mob howled and jeered and hooted. Some Negroes on the far sidewalk were convulsed in laughter, while even the minister who had been so pathetically protesting the scene was finding it hard not to smile at the ridiculous spectacle. Sam Pearce, the chief ringleader, released one last handful of feathers to stick in the congealing, cooling tar then stepped back and flourished a proud hand toward the dentist. The crowd cheered again.

"Make him cluck, Sam! Make him cluck like a hen!"

The dentist was prodded with the short-handled spade until he produced a pathetic imitation of a chicken's cluck.

"Louder! Louder!"

Doctor Burroughs was prodded again, and this time he managed to make the miserable noise loud enough for the crowd's satisfaction. Laughter echoed from the houses and sounded clear down to the river where the barges jostled at the quays.

"Bring on the spy, Sam!"

"Give it him good!"

"Show us Starbuck's bastard!"

Men seized Starbuck, released his bonds and hurried him toward the wagon. The tanner helped them, still striking and kicking at the helpless Starbuck, spitting his hatred and taunting him, anticipating the humiliation of Elial Starbuck's whelp. Pearce had crammed the dentist's top hat onto its owner's grotesque, tar-thick, feathered head. The dentist was shaking, sobbing silently.

Starbuck was pushed hard against the wagon's wheel. Hands reached down from above, grabbed his collar and heaved up. Men pushed at him, his knee cracked hard against the wagon side, then he was sprawling on the wagon bed, where his hand was smeared by a warm patch of spilt tar. Sam Pearce hauled Starbuck upright and displayed his bloody face to the crowd. "Here he is! Starbuck's bastard!"

"Fillet him, Sam!"

"Push him in, Sam!"

Pearce rammed Starbuck's head over the vat, holding his face just inches from the stinking liquid. The vat had been stolen from its coals, but it was big enough and full enough to have retained almost all its heat.

Starbuck tried to flinch away as a bubble slowly erupted just beneath his bleeding nose. The tar plopped tiredly back, then Pearce jerked him back upright. "Let's have your clothes off, cuffee."

Hands pulled at Starbuck's coat, tearing off its sleeves and ripping it clean off his back. "Strip him naked, Sam!" a woman screamed excitedly.

"Give his pa something to preach about!" A man was jumping up and down beside the wagon. A child stood by the man, hand at her mouth, eyes bright, staring. The dentist, unremarked now, had sat on the wagon's box, where he pathetically and uselessly tried to scrape the hot tar off his scorched skin.

Sam Pearce gave the vat a stir. The tanner was spitting again and again at Starbuck while a gray-haired man fumbled at Starbuck's waist, loosing the buttons of his pants. "Don't you dare piss on me, boy, or I'll leave you nothing to piss with." He pulled the trousers down to Starbuck's knees, provoking a shrill scream of approval from the crowd.

And a gunshot sounded too.

The gunshot cracked the still air of the street junction to startle a score of flapping birds up from the roofs of the warehouses that edged the Shockoe Slip. The crowd turned. Pearce moved to tear at Starbuck's shirt, but a second gunshot sounded hugely loud, echoing off the far houses and causing the crowd to go very still. "Touch the boy again," a confident, lazy voice spoke, "and you're a dead man."

"He's a spy!" Pearce tried to brazen out the moment.

"He's my guest." The speaker was mounted on a tall black horse and was wearing a slouch hat, a long gray coat and high boots. He was carrying a long-barreled revolver, which he now pushed into a holster on his saddle. It was a marvelously insouciant gesture, suggesting he had nothing to fear from this mob. The man's face was shadowed by the hat's brim, but clearly he had been recognized, and as he spurred the horse forward the crowd silently parted to give him passage. A second horseman followed, leading a riderless horse.

The first horseman reined in beside the wagon. He tilted his hat upward with the tip of a riding crop then stared with incredulity at Star-buck. "It's Nate Starbuck! Yes?"

"Yes, sir." Starbuck was shivering.

"You remember me, Nate? We met in New Haven last year?"

"Of course I remember you, sir." Starbuck was shaking, but with relief rather than fear. His rescuer was Washington Faulconer, father of Star-buck's best friend and the man whose name Starbuck had earlier invoked to save himself from this mob's wrath.

"You seem to be getting a wrong impression of Virginian hospitality," Washington Faulconer said softly. "Shame on you!" These last words were spoken to the crowd. "We're not at war with strangers in our city! What are you? Savages?"

"He's a spy!" The tanner tried to restore the crowd's supremacy.

Washington Faulconer turned scornfully on the man. "And you're a black-assed fool! You're behaving like Yankees, all of you! Northerners might want a mobocracy for a government, but not us! Who is this man?" He pointed with his riding crop at the dentist.

The dentist could not speak, so Starbuck, released from the grip of his enemies and with his trousers safely restored to his waist, answered for his fellow victim. "His name is Burroughs, sir. He's a dentist passing through town."

Washington Faulconer glanced about until he saw two men he recognized. "Bring Mister Burroughs to my house. We shall do our best to make reparations to him." Then, that remonstrance delivered to the shamed crowd, he looked back to Starbuck and introduced his companion, who was a dark-haired man a few years older than Starbuck. "This is Ethan Ridley." Ridley was leading the riderless horse, which he now urged alongside the wagon bed. "Mount up, Nate!" Washington Faulconer urged Starbuck.

"Yes, sir." Starbuck stooped for his coat, realized that it was torn beyond repair, so straightened up empty-handed. He glanced at Sam Pearce, who gave a tiny shrug as though to suggest there were no hard feelings, but there were, and Starbuck, who had never known how to control his temper, stepped fast toward the big man and hit him. Sam Pearce twisted away, but not soon enough, and Starbuck's blow landed on his ear. Pearce stumbled, put a hand out to save himself but only succeeded in plunging the hand deep into the tar vat. He screamed, jerked himself free, but his balance was gone, and he flailed hopelessly as he tripped off the wagon's outer end to fall with skull-cracking force onto the road. Starbuck's hand was hurting, stung by the wild and clumsy blow, but the crowd, with the unpredictability of an impassioned mob, suddenly started laughing and cheering him.

"Come on, Nate!" Washington Faulconer was grinning at Pearce's downfall.

Starbuck stepped off the wagon directly onto the horse's back. He fumbled with his feet for the stirrups, took the reins, and kicked back with his tar-stained shoes. He guessed he had lost his books and clothes, but the loss was hardly important. The books were exegetical texts left over from his studies at the Yale Theological Seminary and at best he might have sold them for a dollar fifty. The clothes were of even less value, and so he abandoned his belongings, instead following his rescuers out of the crowd and up Pearl Street. Starbuck was still shaking, and still hardly daring to believe he had escaped the crowd's torment. "How did you know I was there, sir?" he asked Washington Faulconer.

"I didn't realize it was you, Nate, I just heard that some young fellow claiming to know me was about to be strung up for the crime of being a Yankee, so I thought we should take a look. It was a teamster who told me, a Negro fellow. He heard you say my name and he knew my house, so he came and told my steward. Who told me, of course."

"I owe you an extraordinary debt, sir."

"You certainly owe the Negro fellow a debt. Or rather you don't, because I thanked him for you with a silver dollar." Washington Faulconer turned and looked at his bedraggled companion. "Does that nose hurt?"

"No more than a usual bloody nose, sir."

"Might I ask just what you're doing here, Nate? Virginia doesn't seem the healthiest place for a Massachusetts man to be running loose."

"I was looking for you, sir. I was planning to walk to Faulconer Court House."

"All seventy miles, Nate!" Washington Faulconer laughed. "Didn't Adam tell you we keep a town house? My father was a state senator, so he liked to keep a place in Richmond to hang his hat. But why on earth were you looking for me? Or was it Adam you wanted? He's up north, I'm afraid. He's trying to avert war, but I think it's a little late for that. Lincoln doesn't want peace, so I fear we'll have to oblige him with war." Faulconer offered this mix of questions and answers in a cheerful voice. He was an impressive-looking man of middle years and medium height, with a straight back and wide square shoulders. He had short fair hair, a thick square-cut beard, a face that seemed to radiate frankness and kindness, and blue eyes that were crinkled in an expression of amused benignity. To Starbuck he seemed just like his son, Adam, whom Starbuck had met at Yale and whom Starbuck always thought of as the decentest man he had ever met. "But why are you here, Nate?" Faulconer asked his original question again.

"It's a long story, sir." Starbuck rarely rode a horse and did it badly. He slouched in the saddle and jolted from side to side, making a horrid contrast to his two elegant companions, who rode their horses with careless mastery.

"I like long stories," Washington Faulconer said happily, "but save it for when you're cleaned up. Here we are." He gestured with his riding crop at a lavish four-storied stone-faced house, evidently the place where his father had hung his hat. "No ladies staying here this week, so we can be free and easy. Ethan will get you some clothes. Show him to Adam's room, will you, Ethan?"

Negro servants ran from the house's stable yard to take the horses and suddenly, after weeks of uncertainty and danger and humiliation, Starbuck felt himself being surrounded by security and comfort and safety. He could almost have wept for the relief of it. America was collapsing in chaos, riot was loose on its streets, but Starbuck was safe.

* * *

"You're looking a deal more human, Nate!" Washington Faulconer greeted Starbuck in his study, "and those clothes more or less fit. Are you feeling better?"

"Much better. Thank you, sir."

"Bath hot enough?"

"Perfect, sir."

"That eye looks sore. Maybe a poultice before you sleep? We had to call a doctor for your Philadelphia friend. They're trying to unpeel the poor fellow in the stable yard. While my problem is whether to buy one thousand rifles at twelve bucks each."

"Why shouldn't we?" Ethan Ridley, who had settled Starbuck into Adam's room then arranged for his bath and a change of clothes, was now perched on a sofa at the window of Washington Faulconer's study, where he was toying with a long-barreled revolver that he occasionally sighted at pedestrians in the street below.

"Because I don't want to take the first available guns, Ethan," Washington Faulconer said. "Something better may come along in a month or two."

"There's not much better than the Mississippi rifle." Ridley silently picked off the driver of a scarlet barouche. "And the price won't go down, sir. With respect, it won't go down. Prices never do."

"I guess that's true." Faulconer paused, but still seemed reluctant to make a decision.

A clock ticked heavily in a corner of the room. A wagon axle squealed in the street. Ridley lit a long thin cigar and sucked hungrily on its smoke. A brass tray beside him was littered with ash and cigar butts. He drew on the cigar again, making its tip glow fierce, then glanced at Starbuck. "Will the North fight?" he demanded, evidently expecting that a Yankee like Starbuck must have the answer pat.

But Starbuck had no idea what the North intended to do in the aftermath of Fort Sumter's fall. In these last weeks Nathaniel Starbuck had been much too distracted to think about politics, and now, faced with the question that was energizing the whole south country, he did not know what to respond.

"In one sense it doesn't matter if they fight or not," Washington Faulconer spoke before Starbuck could offer any answer. "If we don't seem prepared to fight, Ethan, then the North will certainly invade. But if we stand firm, why, then they may back down."

"Then buy the guns, sir," Ridley urged, reinforcing his encouragement by pulling the trigger of his empty revolver. He was a lean tall man, elegant in black riding boots, black breeches and a black coat that was smeared with traces of cigar ash. He had long dark hair oiled sleek against his skull and a beard trimmed to a rakish point. In Adam's bedroom, while Starbuck had tidied and cleaned himself, Ridley had paced up and down the room, telling Starbuck how he was planning to marry Washington Faulconer's daughter, Anna, and how the prospect of war had delayed their wedding plans. Ridley had talked of the possible war as an irritation rather than a calamity, and his slow, attractive southern accent had only made the confidence in his voice all the more convincing.

"There goes twelve thousand dollars!" Washington Faulconer now said, evidently putting his signature to a money draft as he spoke. "Buy the guns for me, Ethan, and well done." Starbuck wondered why Washington Faulconer was buying so many rifles, but he did not need to wonder that Faulconer could afford the weapons, for he knew his friend's father to be one of the richest men in Virginia, indeed in all the precariously United States. Faulconer could boast that the most recent survey done of his family's land in Faulconer County had been accomplished by a raw young surveyor named George Washington, and since that day not one acre had been lost to the family and a good many had been added. Among the new acres was the land on which Faulconer's Richmond town house stood—one of the grandest houses on Clay Street that had, at its rear, a wide stable yard with a carriage house and quarters for a dozen grooms and stalls for thirty horses. The house boasted a ballroom, a music room, and what was commonly regarded as Richmond's finest staircase, a magnificent circling stair that swept around and up a gilded well hung with family portraits, the oldest of which had been brought from England in the seventeenth century. The books in Washington Faulconer's study had the family's coat of arms tooled in gold into their leather covers, while the desks, chairs and tables had all been made by Europe's finest craftsmen because, for a man as wealthy as Washington Faulconer, only the very best would do. Flowers stood on every table, not just for decoration, but in an attempt to overwhelm the smell of the city's tobacco factories.

"Now, Nate," Washington Faulconer said heartily when he had decided to buy the twelve-dollar guns, "you promised us a story. There's coffee there, or something stronger? Do you drink? You do? But not with your father's blessing, I'm sure. Your father can hardly approve of ardent spirits, or does he? Is the Reverend Elial a prohibitionist as well as an abolitionist? He is! What a ferocious man he must be, to be sure. Sit down." Washington Faulconer was full of energy and happy to conduct a conversation with himself as he stood up, pulled a chair for Starbuck away from the wall, poured Starbuck coffee, then sat back at his desk. "So come! Tell me! Aren't you supposed to be at the seminary?"

"Yes, sir, I am." Starbuck felt inhibited suddenly, ashamed of his story and of his pathetic condition. "It's a very long tale," he protested to Washington Faulconer.

"The longer the better. So come along, tell!"

So Starbuck had no choice but to tell his pathetic story of obsession, love and crime; a shameful tale of how Mademoiselle Dominique Demarest of New Orleans had persuaded Nathaniel Starbuck of Yale that life had more to offer than lectures in didactic theology, sacred literature or the sermonizing arts.

"A bad woman!" Washington Faulconer said with happy relish when Starbuck first mentioned her. "Every tale should have a bad woman."

Starbuck had first glimpsed Mademoiselle Dominique Demarest in the Lyceum Hall at New Haven where Major Ferdinand Trabell's touring company was presenting the *Only True and Authorized Stage Version of Uncle Tom's Cabin, Complete with Real Bloodhounds*. Trabell's had been the third such traveling *Tom* company to visit New Haven that winter, and each had claimed to be presenting the only true and authorized dramatic version of the great work, but Major Trabell's production had been the first that Starbuck dared attend. There had been impassioned debate in the seminary about the propriety of attending a thespian performance, even one dedicated to moral instruction and the abolition of slavery, but Starbuck had wanted to go because of the bloodhounds mentioned on the playbill. There had been no bloodhounds in Mrs. Beecher Stowe's fine work, but Starbuck suspected the animals might make a dramatic addition to the story, and so he had visited the Lyceum where, awestruck, he had watched as a veritable angel who was playing the part of the fugitive slave Eliza had tripped lightly across the make-believe ice floes pursued by a pair of lethargic and dribbling dogs that might or might not have been bloodhounds.

Not that Starbuck cared about the dogs' pedigree, but only about the angel, who had a long face, sad eyes, shadowed cheeks, a wide mouth, hair black as night, and a gentle voice. He had fallen in love instantly, furiously and, so far as he could tell, eternally. He had gone to the Lyceum the next night, and the next, and the next, which was also New Haven's final performance of the great epic, and on the following day he had offered to help Major Trabell strike and crate the scenery, and the major, who had recently been abandoned by his only son and was therefore in need of a replacement to play the parts of Augustine St. Clair and Simon Legree, and recognizing Starbuck's good looks and commanding presence, had offered him four dollars a week, full board, and Major Trabell's own tutelage in the thespian arts. Not even those enticements could have persuaded Starbuck to abandon his seminary education, except that Mademoiselle Dominique Demarest had added her entreaties to those of her

employer, and so, on a whim, and for his adoration of Dominique, Starbuck had become a traveling player.

"You upped stakes and went? Just like that?" Washington Faulconer
asked with obvious amusement, even admiration.

"Yes, sir." Though Starbuck had not confessed the full extent of his
humiliating surrender to Dominique. He had admitted attending the theater night after night, but he had not described how he had lingered in
the streets wanting a glimpse of his angel, or how he had written her
name again and again in his notebooks, nor how he had tried to capture
in pencil the delicacy of her long, misleadingly ethereal face, nor how he
had yearned to repair the spiritual damage done to Dominique by her
appalling history.

That history had been published in the New Haven newspaper that
had noticed the *Tom* company's performance, which notice revealed that
although Mademoiselle Demarest appeared to be as white as any other
respectable lady, she was in truth a nineteen-year-old octoroon who had
been the slave of a savage New Orleans gentleman whose behavior
rivaled that of Simon Legree. Delicacy forbade the newspaper from pub-
lishing any details of his behavior, except to say that Dominique's owner
had threatened the virtue of his fair property and thus forced Dominique,
in an escape that rivaled the drama of Eliza's fictional flight, to flee northward for liberty and the safeguard of her virtue. Starbuck tried to imagine
his lovely Dominique running desperately through the Louisiana night
pursued by yelping fiends, howling dogs, and a slavering owner.

"Like hell I escaped! I was never a slave, never!" Dominique told
Starbuck next day when they were riding the cars for Hartford, where the
show would play for six nights in the Touro Hall. "I ain't got nigger blood,
not one drop. But the notion sells tickets, so it does, and tickets is money,
and that's why Trabell tells the newspapers I'm part nigger."

"You mean it's a lie?" Starbuck was horrified.

"Of course it's a lie!" Dominique was indignant. "I told you, it just
sells tickets, and tickets is money." She said the only truths in the fable
were that she was nineteen and had been raised in New Orleans, but in a
white family that she claimed was of irreproachable French ancestry. Her
father possessed money, though she was vague about the exact process
whereby the daughter of a wealthy Louisiana merchant came to be per-
forming the part of Eliza in Major Ferdinand Trabell's touring *Tom* company. "Not that Trabell's a real major," Dominique confided to Starbuck,
"but he pretends to have fought in Mexico. He says he got his limp there
off a bayonet, but I reckon he more likely got stabbed by a whore in
Philadelphia." She laughed. She was two years younger than Starbuck but
seemed immeasurably older and far more experienced. She also seemed to
like Starbuck, who returned her liking with a blind adoration and did not

care that she was not an escaped slave. "How much is he paying you?" Dominique asked Starbuck.

"Four dollars a week."

She laughed scornfully. "Robbing you!"

For the next two months Starbuck happily learned the acting trade as he worshiped at the shrine of Miss Demarest's virtue. He enjoyed being on stage, and the fact that he was the son of the Reverend Elial Starbuck, the famous abolitionist, served to swell both Trabell's audiences and receipts. It also brought Nathaniel's new profession to the attention of his father who, in a terrifying fury, sent Starbuck's elder brother, James, to bring the sinner to repentance.

James's mission had failed miserably, and two weeks later Dominique, who had so far not permitted Starbuck any liberty beyond the holding of her hand, at last promised him the reward of his heart's whole desire if he would just help her steal that week's takings from Major Trabell. "He owes me money," Dominique said, and she explained that her father had written to say he was waiting for her in Richmond, Virginia, and she knew Major Trabell would not pay her any of the six months' wages he owed and so she needed Starbuck's help in purloining what was, by rights, already hers. For the reward she was offering, Starbuck would have helped Dominique steal the moon, but he settled for the eight hundred and sixty-four dollars he found in Major Trabell's portmanteau, which he stole while, in the next-door room, the major took a hip bath with a young lady who was hoping for a career upon the stage and had therefore offered herself to the major's professional inspection and judgment.

Starbuck and Dominique fled that same night, reaching Richmond just two days later. Dominique's father was supposed to have been waiting at the Spotswood House Hotel on Main Street, but instead it was a tall young man, scarce a year older than Starbuck himself, who waited in the hotel's parlor and who laughed with joy when Dominique appeared. The young man was Major Trabell's son, Jefferson, who was estranged from his father, and who now dismissed Starbuck with a patronizing ten dollars. "Make yourself scarce, boy," he had said, "before you're strung up for crow bait. Northerners ain't popular in these parts right now." Jefferson Trabell wore buckskin breeches, top boots, a satin vest and a scarlet coat. He had dark knowing eyes and narrow side-whiskers which, like his long black hair, were oiled smooth as jet. His tie was secured with a large pearl pin and his holstered revolver had a polished silver handgrip. It was that revolver rather than the tall young man's dandyish air that persuaded Starbuck there was little point in trying to claim his promised reward from Mademoiselle Dominique Demarest.

"You mean she just dropped you?" Washington Faulconer asked in disbelief.

"Yes, sir." The shameful memory convulsed Starbuck with misery.

"Without even giving you a ride?" Ethan Ridley laid down the empty revolver as he asked the question and, though the query earned him a reproving glance from Washington Faulconer, it was also clear the older man wanted to know the answer. Starbuck offered no reply, but he had no need to. Dominique had made him into a fool, and his foolishness was obvious.

"Poor Nate!" Washington Faulconer was amused. "What are you going to do now? Go home? Your father won't be too happy! And what of Major Trabell? He'll be wanting to nail your gizzards to his barn door, won't he? That and get his money back! Is he a southerner?"

"A Pennsylvanian, sir. But his son pretends to be a southerner."

"So where is the son? Still at the Spotswood?"

"No, sir." Starbuck had spent the night in a boarding house in Canal Street and, in the morning, still seething with indignation, he had gone to the Spotswood House Hotel to confront Dominique and her lover, but instead a clerk had told him that Mr. and Mrs. Jefferson Trabell had just left for the Richmond and Danville Railroad Depot. Starbuck had followed them, only to discover that the birds were flown and that their train was already steaming south out of the depot, its locomotive pumping a bitter smoke into the spring air that was so briskly filled with the news of Fort Sumter's capitulation.

"Oh, it's a rare tale, Nate! A rare tale!" Washington Faulconer laughed. "But you shouldn't feel so bad. You ain't the first young fellow to be fooled by a petticoat, and you won't be the last, and I've no doubt Major Trabell's a scoundrel as deep as they come." He lit a cigar, then tossed the spent match into a spittoon. "So what are we going to do with you?" The lightness with which he asked the question seemed to imply that whatever answer Starbuck desired could be easily supplied. "Do you want to go back to Yale?"

"No, sir." Starbuck spoke miserably.

"No?"

Starbuck spread his hands. "I'm not sure I should be at the seminary, sir. I'm not even sure I should have been there in the first place." He stared down at his scarred, grazed knuckles, and bit his lip as he considered his answer. "I can't become a minister now, sir, not now that I'm a thief." And worse than a thief, Starbuck thought. He was remembering the fourth chapter of first Timothy where St. Paul had prophesied how in the latter times some men would depart from the faith, giving heed to seducing spirits and doctrines of devils, and Starbuck knew he had fulfilled that prophecy, and the realization imbued his voice with a terrible anguish. "I'm simply not worthy of the ministry, sir."

"Worthy?" Washington Faulconer exclaimed. "Worthy! My God,

Nate, if you could see the plug-uglies who shove themselves into our pul-
pits you wouldn't say that! My God, we've got a fellow in Rosskill Church
who preaches blind drunk most Sunday mornings. Ain't that so, Ethan?"

"Poor old fool toppled into a grave last year," Ridley added with
amusement. "He was supposed to be burying someone and damn near
buried himself instead."

"So I wouldn't worry about being worthy," Faulconer said scornfully.
"But I suppose Yale won't be too happy to have you back, Nate, not if you
walked out on them for some chickabiddy trollop? And I suppose you're a
wanted man too, eh? A thief no less!" Faulconer evidently found this notion
hugely entertaining. "Go back north and they'll clap you in jail, is that it?"

"I fear so, sir."

Washington Faulconer hooted with amusement. "By God, Nate, but
you are stuck in the tar patch. Both feet, both hands, ass, crop and pri-
vates! And what will your sacred father do if you go home? Give you a
whipping before he turns you over to the constables?"

"Like as not, sir, yes."

"So the Reverend Elial's a whipper, is he? Likes to thrash?"

"Yes, sir, he does."

"I can't allow that." Washington Faulconer stood and walked to a
window overlooking the street. A magnolia was in bloom in his narrow
front garden, filling the window bay with its sweet scent. "I never was a
believer in a thrashing. My father didn't beat me and I've never beaten
my children. Fact is, Nate, I've never laid a hand on any child or servant,
only on my enemies." He spoke sententiously, as though he was accustomed to defending his strange behavior, as in truth he was, for, not ten
years before, Washington Faulconer had made himself famous for freeing
all his slaves. For a brief time the northern newspapers had hailed
Faulconer as a precursor of southern enlightenment, a reputation that had
made him bitterly unpopular in his native Virginia, but his neighbors'
animosity had died away when Faulconer had refused to encourage other
southerners to follow his example. He claimed the decision had been
purely personal. Now, the furor long in his past, Faulconer smiled at Starbuck. "Just what are we going to do with you, Nate?"

"You've done enough, sir," Starbuck said, though in reality he was
hoping that far more might yet be done. "What I must do, sir, is find
work. I have to repay Major Trabell."

Faulconer smiled at Starbuck's earnestness. "The only work around
here, Nate, is common soldiering, and I don't think that's a trade to pay
off debts in a hurry. No, I think you'd better raise your sights a little
higher." Faulconer was taking an obvious enjoyment in solving Starbuck's
problem. He smiled, then gestured about the lavishly appointed room.
"Maybe you'd consider staying here, Nate? With me? I'm in need of

someone who can be my private secretary and do some purchasing as well."

"Sir!" Ethan Ridley sat bolt upright on the sofa, his irate tone betraying that the job being offered to Starbuck was one Ridley considered his own.

"Oh come, Ethan! You detest clerking for me! You can't even spell!" Faulconer chided his future son-in-law gently. "Besides, with the guns purchased, your main job's done. At least for the moment." He sat thinking for a few seconds, then clicked his fingers. "I know, Ethan, go back to Faulconer County and start some proper recruiting. Beat the drum for me. If we don't raise the county, someone else will, and I don't want Faulconer County men fighting for other Virginia regiments. Besides, don't you want to be with Anna?"

"Of course I do, sir." Though Ridley, offered this chance to be close to his betrothed, seemed somewhat less than enthusiastic.

Washington Faulconer turned back to Starbuck. "I'm raising a regiment, Nate, a legion. The Faulconer Legion. I'd hoped it wouldn't be necessary, I'd hoped common sense would prevail, but it seems the North wants a fight and, by God, we'll have to give them one if they insist. Would it offend your loyalties to help me?"

"No, sir." That seemed an entirely inadequate response, so Starbuck imbued his voice with more enthusiasm. "I'd be proud to help you, sir."

"We've made a beginning," Faulconer said modestly. "Ethan has been buying equipment and we've found our guns now, as you heard, but the paperwork is already overwhelming. Do you think you can handle some correspondence for me?"

Could Starbuck handle correspondence? Nathaniel Starbuck would have done all Washington Faulconer's correspondence from that moment until the seas ran dry. Nathaniel Starbuck would do whatever this marvelous, kind, decent and carelessly generous man wanted him to do. "Of course I can help, sir. It would be a privilege."

"But, sir!" Ethan Ridley tried one last patriotic protest. "You can't trust military affairs to a northerner."

"Nonsense, Ethan! Nate's stateless! He's an outlaw! He can't go home, not unless he goes to jail, so he'll just have to stay here. I'm making him an honorary Virginian." Faulconer bestowed a bow on Starbuck in recognition of this elevated status. "So welcome to the southland, Nate."

Ethan Ridley looked astonished at his future father-in-law's quixotic kindness, but Nathaniel Starbuck did not care. He had fallen on his feet, his luck had turned clean round, and he was safe in the land of his father's enemies. Starbuck had come south.

2

Starbuck's first days in Richmond were spent accompanying Ethan Ridley to warehouses that held the stores and supplies that would equip the Faulconer Legion. Ridley had arranged for the purchase of the equipment and now, before he left to begin the major recruiting effort in Faulconer County, he made certain Starbuck was able to take over his responsibilities. "Not that you need bother with the finances, Reverend," Ridley told Starbuck, using the half-mocking and half-teasing nickname he had adopted for the northerner, "I'll just let you arrange the transport." Starbuck would then be left to kick his heels in big echoing warehouses or in dusty counting houses while Ridley talked business in the private inner office before emerging to toss another instruction Starbuck's way. "Mister Williams will have six crates ready for collection next week. By Thursday, Johnny!"

"Ready by Thursday, Mister Ridley." The Williams warehouse was selling the Faulconer Legion a thousand pairs of boots, while other merchants were selling the regiment rifles, uniforms, percussion caps, buttons, bayonets, powder, cartridges, revolvers, tents, skillets, haversacks, canteens, tin mugs, hemp line, webbing belts: all the mundane necessities of military paraphernalia, and all of it coming from private warehouses because Washington Faulconer refused to deal with the Virginian government. "You have to understand, Reverend," Ridley told Starbuck, "that Faulconer ain't fond of the new governor, and the new governor ain't fond of Faulconer. Faulconer thinks the governor will let him pay for the Legion, then steal it away from him, so we ain't allowed to have anything to do with the state government. We're not to encourage them, see? So we can't buy goods out of the state armories, which makes life kind of difficult." Though plainly Ethan Ridley had overcome many of the difficulties, for Starbuck's notebook was filling impressively with lists of crates, boxes, barrels and sacks that needed to be collected and delivered to the town of Faulconer Court House. "Money," Ridley told him, "that's the key, Reverend. There's a thousand fellows trying to buy equipment, and there's a shortage of everything, so you need deep pockets. Let's go get a drink."

Ethan Ridley took a perverse delight in introducing Starbuck to the city's taverns, especially the dark, rancid drinking houses that were hidden among the mills and lodging houses on the northern bank of the James River. "This ain't like your father's church, is it, Reverend?" Ridley would ask of some rat-infested, rotting hovel, and Starbuck would agree that the liquor den was indeed a far cry from his ordered, Boston upbringing where cleanliness had been a mark of God's favor and abstinence a surety of his salvation.

Ridley evidently wanted to savor the pleasure of shocking the Reverend Elial Starbuck's son, yet even the filthiest of Richmond's taverns held a romance for Starbuck solely because it was such a long way from his father's Calvinist joylessness. It was not that Boston lacked drinking houses as poverty stricken and hopeless as any in Richmond, but Starbuck had never been inside Boston's drinking dens and thus he took a strange satisfaction out of Ridley's midday excursions into Richmond's malodorous alleyways. The adventures seemed proof that he really had escaped his family's cold, disapproving grasp, but Starbuck's evident enjoyment of the expeditions only made Ridley try yet harder to shock him. "If I abandoned you in this place, Reverend," Ridley threatened Starbuck in one seamen's tavern that stank from the sewage dripping into the river from a rusting pipe not ten feet from the stillroom, "you'd have your throat cut inside five minutes."

"Because I'm a northerner?"

"Because you're wearing shoes."

"I'd be all right," Starbuck boasted. He had no weapons, and the dozen men in the tavern looked capable of slitting a congregation of respectable throats with scarce a twinge of conscience, but Starbuck would not let himself show any fear in front of Ethan Ridley. "Leave me here if you want."

"You wouldn't dare stay here on your own," Ridley said.

"Go on. See if I mind." Starbuck turned to the serving hatch and snapped his fingers. "One more glass here. Just one!" That was pure bravado, for Starbuck hardly drank any alcohol. He would sip at a whiskey, but Ridley always finished the glass. The terror of sin haunted Starbuck, indeed it was that terror which gave the tavern excursions their piquancy, and liquor was one of the greater sins whose temptations Starbuck half-flirted with and half-resisted.

Ridley laughed at Starbuck's defiance. "You've got balls, Starbuck, I'll say that."

"So leave me here."

"Faulconer won't forgive me if I get you killed. You're his new pet puppy, Reverend."

"Pet puppy?" Starbuck bridled at the words.

"Don't take offense, Reverend." Ridley stamped on the butt of a smoked cigar and immediately lit another. He was a man of impatient appetites. "Faulconer's a lonely man, and lonely men like having pet puppies. That's why he's so keen on secession."

"Because he's lonely?" Starbuck did not understand.

Ridley shook his head. He was lounging with his back against the counter, staring through a cracked dirty window to where a two-masted ship creaked against a crumbling river quay. "Faulconer supports the rebellion because he thinks it'll make him popular with his father's old friends. He'll prove himself a more fervent southerner than any of them, because in a way he ain't a southerner at all, you know what I mean?"

"No."

Ridley grimaced, as though unwilling to explain himself, but then tried anyway. "He owns land, Reverend, but he don't use it. He doesn't farm it, he doesn't plant it, he doesn't even graze it. He just owns it and stares at it. He doesn't have niggers, at least not as slaves. His money comes out of railroads and paper, and the paper comes out of New York or London. He's probably more at home in Europe than here in Richmond, but that don't stop wanting him to belong here. He wants to be a southerner, but he ain't." Ridley blew a plume of cigar smoke across the room, then turned his dark, sardonic gaze on Starbuck. "I'll give you a piece of advice."

"Please."

"Keep agreeing with him," Ridley said very seriously. "Family can disagree with Washington, which is why he don't spend too much time with family, but private secretaries like you and me ain't allowed any disagreements. Our job is to admire him. You understand me?"

"He's admirable anyway," Starbuck said loyally.

"I guess we're all admirable," Ridley said with amusement, "so long as we can find a pedestal high enough to stand on. Washington's pedestal is his money, Reverend."

"And yours too?" Starbuck asked belligerently.

"Not mine, Reverend. My father lost all the family money. My pedestal, Reverend, is horses. I'm the best damned horseman you'll find this side of the Atlantic. Or any side for that matter." Ridley grinned at his own lack of modesty, then tossed back his glass of whiskey. "Let's go and see if those bastards at Boyle and Gamble have found the field glasses they promised me last week."

In the evenings Ridley would disappear to his half-brother's rooms in Grace Street, leaving Starbuck to walk back to Washington Faulconer's house through streets that were swarming with strange-looking creatures come from the deeper, farther reaches of the South. There were thin-shanked, gaunt-faced men from Alabama, long-haired leather-skinned horse riders from Texas and bearded homespun volunteers from Mississippi, all of them armed like buccaneers and ready to drink themselves into fits of instant fury. Whores and liquor salesmen made small fortunes, city rents doubled and doubled again, and still the railroads brought fresh volunteers to Richmond. They had come, one and all, to protect the new Confederacy from the Yankees, though at first it looked as if the new Confederacy would be better advised to protect itself from its own defenders, but then, obedient to the insistent commands of the state's newly appointed military commander, all the ragtag volunteers were swept away to the city's Central Fair Grounds where cadets from the Virginia Military Institute were brought to teach them basic drill.

That new commander of the Virginian militia, Major-General Robert Lee, also insisted on paying a courtesy call on Washington Faulconer. Faulconer suspected that the proposed visit was a ploy by Virginia's new governor to take control of the Legion, yet, despite his misgivings, Faulconer could scarcely refuse to receive a man who came from a Virginia family as old and prominent as his own. Ethan Ridley had left Richmond the day before Lee's visit, and so Starbuck was ordered to be present at the meeting. "I want you to make notes of what's said," Faulconer warned him darkly. "Letcher's not the kind of man to let a patriot raise a regiment. You mark my words, Nate, he'll have sent Lee to take the Legion away from me."

Starbuck sat at one side of the study, a notebook open on his knees, though in the event nothing of any great importance was discussed. The middle-aged Lee, who was dressed in civilian clothes and attended by one young captain in the uniform of the state militia, first exchanged civilities with Faulconer, then formally, almost apologetically, explained that Governor Letcher had appointed him to command the state's military forces and his first duty was to recruit, equip and train those forces, in which connection he understood that Mister Faulconer was raising a regiment in Faulconer County?

"A legion," Faulconer corrected him.

"Ah yes, indeed, a legion." Lee seemed quite flummoxed by the word.

"And not one stand of its arms, not one cannon, not one cavalry saddle, not one buttonhook or one canteen, indeed not one item of its equipment, Lee, will be a charge upon the state," Faulconer said proudly. "I am paying for it, down to the last bootlace."

"An expensive undertaking, Faulconer, I'm sure." Lee frowned, as though puzzled by Faulconer's generosity. The general had a great reputation, and folk in Richmond had taken immense comfort from the fact that he had returned to his native state rather than accept the command of Abraham Lincoln's northern armies, but Starbuck, watching the quiet, neat, gray-bearded man, could see little evidence of the general's supposed genius. Lee seemed reticent to the point of timidity and was entirely dwarfed by Washington Faulconer's energy and enthusiasm. "You mention cannon and cavalry," Lee said, speaking very diffidently, "does that mean your regiment, your Legion I should say, will consist of all arms?"

"All arms?" Washington Faulconer was unfamiliar with the phrase.

"The Legion will not consist of infantry alone?" Lee explained courteously.

"Indeed. Indeed. I wish to bring the Confederacy a fully trained, fully equipped, wholly useful unit." Faulconer paused to consider the wisdom of his next words, but then decided a little bombast would not be misplaced. "I fancy the Legion will be akin to Bonaparte's elite troops. An imperial guard for the Confederacy."

"Ah, indeed." It was hard to tell whether Lee was impressed or aghast at the vision. He paused for a few seconds, then calmly remarked that he looked forward to the day when such a Legion would be fully assimilated into the state's forces. That was precisely what Faulconer feared most—a naked grab by Governor John Letcher to take command of his Legion and thus reduce it to yet another mediocre component in the state militia. Faulconer's vision was much grander than the governor's lukewarm ambitions, and, in defense of that vision, he made no response to Lee's words. The general frowned. "You do understand, Mister Faulconer, that we must have order and arrangement?"

"Discipline, you mean?"

"The very word. We must use discipline."

Washington Faulconer ceded the point graciously, then enquired of Lee whether the state would like to assume the cost of outfitting and equipping the Faulconer Legion? He let that dangerous question dangle for a few seconds, then smiled. "As I made clear to you, Lee, my ambition is to provide the Confederacy with a finished article, a trained Legion, but if the state is to intervene"—he meant *interfere*, but was too tactful to use the word—"then I think it only right that the state should take over the necessary funding and, indeed, reimburse me for the monies already expressed. My secretary, Mister Starbuck, can give you a full accounting."

Lee received the threat without changing his placid, somewhat anxious expression. He glanced at Starbuck, seemed curious about the young man's fading black eye, but made no comment. Instead he looked back to Washington Faulconer. "But you do intend to place the Legion under the proper authority?"

"When it is trained, indeed." Faulconer chuckled. "I am hardly proposing to wage a private war on the United States."

Lee did not smile at the small jest, instead he seemed rather downcast, but it seemed triumphantly clear to Starbuck that Washington Faulconer had won his victory over Governor Letcher's representative and that the Faulconer Legion would not be assimilated into the new regiments being hurriedly raised across the state. "Your recruitment goes well?" Lee asked.

"I have one of my best officers supervising the process. We're only levying recruits in the county, not outside." That was not wholly true, but Faulconer felt the state would respect his proprietorial rights inside Faulconer County, whereas if he too openly recruited outside the county the state might complain that he was poaching.

Lee seemed happy enough with the reassurance. "And the training?" he asked. "It will be in competent hands?"

"Extremely competent," Faulconer said enthusiastically, but without adding any of the detail Lee clearly wanted to hear. In Faulconer's absence the Legion's training would be supervised by the Legion's second in command, Major Alexander Pelham, who was a neighbor of Faulconer's and a veteran of the War of 1812. Pelham was now in his seventies, but Faulconer claimed he was as able and vigorous as a man half his age. Pelham was also the only officer connected to the Legion who had ever experienced warfare, though as Ethan Ridley had cattily remarked to Starbuck, that experience had been confined to a single day's action, and that single action had been the defeat at Bladensburg.

Lee's visit ended with an inconsequential exchange of views on how the war should be prosecuted. Faulconer vigorously pressed the necessity of capturing the city of Washington, while Lee talked of the urgent need to secure Virginia's defenses, and afterward, with mutual assurances of goodwill, the two men parted. Washington Faulconer waited until the general had gone down the famous curved staircase, then exploded at Starbuck. "What chance do we have when fools like that are put in command? Dear God, Nate, but we need younger men, energetic men, hard-driving men, not washed-out, cautious buffoons!" He paced the room vigorously, impotent to express the full measure of his frustration. "I knew the governor would try to kidnap the Legion! But he'll need to send someone with sharper claws than that!" He gestured scornfully toward the door through which Lee had left.

"The newspapers say he's the most admired soldier in America." Starbuck could not resist the observation.

"Admired for what? Keeping his pants clean in Mexico? If there's going to be war, Nate, it will not be a romp against an ill-armed pack of Mexicans! You heard him, Nate! 'The paramount importance of keeping the northern forces from attacking Richmond.'" Faulconer gave a rather good imitation of the softspoken Lee, then savaged him with criticism. "Defending Richmond isn't paramount! What's paramount is winning the war. It means hitting them hard and soon. It means attack, attack, attack!" He glanced at a side table where maps of the western part of Virginia lay beside a timetable of the Baltimore and Ohio Railroad. Despite his denial of planning to wage a private war on the North, Washington Faulconer was plotting an attack on the rail line that fed supplies and recruits from the western states to the city of Washington. His ideas for the raid were still forming, but he was imagining a small, fast force of mounted soldiers who would burn down trestles, derail locomotives and tear up track. "I hope the fool didn't see those maps," he said in sudden worry.

"I covered them with maps of Europe before General Lee arrived, sir," Starbuck said.

"You're a brisk one, Nate! Well done! Thank God I've got young men like you, and none of Lee's dullards from West Point. Is that why we're supposed to admire him? Because he was a good superintendent of West Point? And what does that make him? It makes him a schoolmaster!" Faulconer's scorn was palpable. "I know schoolmasters, Nate. My brother-in-law's a schoolmaster and the man isn't fit to be a cookhouse corporal, but he still insists I should make him an officer in the Legion. Never! Pecker is a fool! A cretin! A lunkhead! A heathen! A he-biddy. That's what my brother-in-law is, Nate, a he-biddy!"

Something in Washington Faulconer's energetic tirade triggered Starbuck's memory of the amusing stories Adam liked to tell about his eccentric schoolmaster uncle. "He was Adam's tutor, sir, yes?"

"He tutored both Adam and Anna. Now he runs the county school, and Miriam wants me to make him a major." Miriam was Washington Faulconer's wife, a woman who remained secluded in the country and suffered from a debilitating variety of mysterious maladies. "Make Pecker a major!" Faulconer hooted with derisive laughter at the very idea. "My God, you wouldn't put the pathetic fool in charge of a henhouse, let alone a regiment of fighting men! He's a poor relation, Nate. That's what Pecker is. A poor relation. Ah well, to work!"

There was plenty of work. The house was besieged by callers, some wanting monetary help to develop a secret weapon they swore would bring instant victory to the South, others seeking an officer's appointment with the Legion. A good number of the latter were professional European soldiers on half pay from their own armies, but all such petitioners were told that the Faulconer Legion would elect only local men to be its company officers and that Faulconer's appointed aides would all be Virginians too. "Except for you, Nate," Washington Faulconer told Starbuck, "that's if you'd like to serve me?"

"I'd be honored, sir." And Starbuck felt a warm rush of gratitude for the kindness and trust that Faulconer was showing him.

"You won't find it hard to fight against your own kind, Nate?" Faulconer asked solicitously.

"I feel more at home here, sir."

"And so you should. The South is the real America, Nate, not the North."

Not ten minutes later Starbuck had to refuse an appointment to a scarred Austrian cavalry officer who claimed to have fought in a half-dozen hard battles in northern Italy. The man, hearing that only Virginians would be allowed to command in the Legion, sarcastically enquired how he could reach Washington. "Because if no one will have me here, then by Gott I shall fight for the North!"

The beginning of May brought the news that northern warships had begun a blockade of the Confederate coast. Jefferson Davis, the new president of the Provisional Government of the Confederate States of America, retaliated by signing a declaration of war against the United States, though the State of Virginia seemed in two minds about waging that war. State troops were withdrawn from Alexandria, a town just across the Potomac River from Washington, an act that Washington Faulconer scathingly condemned as typical of Letcher's caviling timidity. "You know what the governor wants?" he asked Nate.

"To take the Legion from you, sir?"

"He wants the North to invade Virginia, because that'll ease him off the political fence without tearing his britches. He's never been fervent for secession. He's a trimmer, Nate, that's his trouble, a trimmer." Yet the very next day brought news that Letcher, far from waiting supine while the North restored the Union, had ordered Virginian troops to occupy the town of Harper's Ferry fifty miles upstream of Washington. The North had abandoned the town without a fight, leaving behind tons of gun-making equipment in the federal arsenal. Richmond celebrated the news, though Washington Faulconer seemed rueful. He had cherished his idea of an attack on the Baltimore and Ohio Railroad whose track crossed the Potomac at Harper's Ferry, but now, with the town and its bridge safe in southern hands, there no longer seemed any need to raid the line farther west. The news of the river town's occupation also promoted a flurry of speculation that the Confederacy was about to make a preemptive attack across the Potomac, and Faulconer, fearing that his rapidly growing Legion might be denied its proper place in such a victorious invasion, decided his place was at Faulconer Court House, where he could hasten the Legion's training. "I'll bring you out to Faulconer County as soon as I can," Faulconer promised Starbuck as he mounted his horse for the seventy-mile ride to his country estate. "Write to Adam for me, will you?"

"I will, sir, of course."

"Tell him to come home." Faulconer raised a gloved hand in farewell, then released his tall black horse to the road. "Tell him to come home!" he shouted as he went.

Starbuck dutifully wrote, addressing his letter to the church in Chicago that forwarded Adam's mail. Adam, just like Starbuck, had abandoned his studies at Yale, but where Starbuck had done it for an obsession with a girl, Adam had gone to Chicago to join the Christian Peace Commission which, by prayer, tracts and witness had been trying to bring the two parts of America back into peaceful amity.

No answer came from Chicago, yet every post brought Starbuck new and urgent demands from Washington Faulconer. "How long will it take Shaffers to make officers' uniforms?" "Do we have a determination of officers' insignia? This is important, Nate! Enquire at Mitchell and Tylers," "Visit Boyle and Gambles and ask about saber patterns," "In my bureau, third drawer down, is a revolver made by Le Mat, send it back with Nelson." Nelson was one of the two Negro servants who carried the letters between Richmond and Faulconer Court House. "The Colonel's mighty anxious to collect his uniforms," Nelson confided to Starbuck. "The Colonel" was Washington Faulconer, who had begun signing his letters "Colonel Faulconer," and Starbuck took good care to address Faulconer with the self-bestowed rank. The Colonel had ordered notepaper printed with the legend "The Faulconer Legion, Campaign Headquarters, Colonel Washington Faulconer, State of Virginia, Commanding," and Starbuck used the proof sheet to write the Colonel the happy news that his new uniforms were expected to be ready by Friday and promising he would have them sent out to Faulconer County immediately.

On that Friday morning Starbuck was sitting down to bring his account books up-to-date when the door to the music room banged open and a tall stranger glowered angrily from the threshold. He was a tall thin man, all bony elbows, long shanks and protruding knees. He looked to be in early middle age, had a black beard streaked with gray, a sharp nose, slanted cheekbones and tousled black hair, and was wearing a threadbare black suit over scuffed brown work boots; altogether a scarecrow figure whose sudden appearance had made Starbuck jump.

"You must be Starbuck, ah-ha?"

"I am, sir."

"I heard your father preach once." The curious man bustled into the room, looking for somewhere to drop his bag and umbrella and walking stick and coat and hat and book bag, and, finding no place suitable, clung to them. "He was impassioned, yes, but he tortured his logic. Does he always?"

"I'm not sure what you mean. You, sir, are?"

"It was in Cincinatti. At the old Presbyterian Hall, the one on Fourth Avenue, or was it Fifth? It was in '56, anyway, or maybe it was '55? The hall has since burned down, but is no loss to the architecture of what is left of the Republic. Not a fine building in my opinion. Of course none of the fools in the audience noted your father's logic. They just wanted to cheer his every word. Down with the slavocracy! Up with our sable brethren! Hallelujah! Evil in our midst! Slur on a great nation! Bah!"

Starbuck, even though he disliked his father, felt pressed to defend him. "You made your opposition known to my father, sir? Or do you just start quarrels with his son?"

"Quarrels? Opposition? I hold no opposition to your father's views! I agree with them, each and every one. Slavery, Starbuck, is a menace to our society. I simply disagree with your father's contemptible logic! It is not enough to pray for an end to the peculiar institution, we have to propose practical arrangements for its abolition. Are the slaveholders to be recompensed for their pecuniary loss? And if so, by whom? By the federal government? By a sale of bonds? And what of the Negroes themselves? Are we to repatriate them to Africa? Settle them in South America? Or are we to breed the darkness out of them by forcible miscegenation, a process, I might say, which has been well begun by our slave owners. Your father made no mention of these matters, but merely had recourse to indignation and prayer, as if prayer has ever settled anything!"

"You do not believe in prayer, sir?"

"Believe in prayer!" The thin man was scandalized by the very thought of such a belief. "If prayer solved anything there'd be no unhappiness in this world, would there? All the moaning women would be smiling! There would be no more disease, no more hunger, no more appalling children picking their snot-filled nostrils in our schoolrooms, no more sniveling infants brought for my admiration. Why should I admire their mewling, puking, whimpering, filthy-faced offspring? I do not like children! I have been telling Washington Faulconer that simple fact for fourteen years now! Fourteen years! Yet my brother-in-law seems incapable of understanding the simplest sentence of plain-spoken English and insists I run his schoolroom. Yet I do not like children, I have never liked children and I hope that I never shall like children. Is that so very hard to understand?" The man still clung to his awkward burdens, even as he waited for Starbuck's response.

Starbuck suddenly understood who this bad-tempered disorganized man was. This was the he-biddy, the poor relation, Faulconer's brother-in-law. "You're Mister Thaddeus Bird," he said.

"Of course I'm Thaddeus Bird!" Bird seemed angry that his identity needed confirmation. He glared bright-eyed and bristling at Starbuck. "Have you heard a word I said?"

"You were telling me you do not like children."

"Filthy little beasts. In the North, mark you, you raise children differently. There you are not afraid to discipline them. Or beat them, indeed! But here, in the South, we need differentiate our children from our slaves and so we beat the latter and destroy the former with kindness."

"Mister Faulconer beats neither, I believe?"

Bird froze, staring at Starbuck as though the younger man had just uttered an extraordinary profanity. "My brother-in-law, I perceive, has been advertising his good qualities to you. His good qualities, Starbuck, are dollars. He buys affection, adulation and admiration. Without money he would be as empty as a Tuesday night pulpit. Besides he does not need to beat his servants or children because my sister can beat enough for twenty."

Starbuck was offended by this ungrateful attack on his patron. "Mister Faulconer freed his slaves, did he not?"

"He freed twenty house slaves, six garden boys and his stable people. He never had field hands because he never needed them. The Faulconer fortune is not based on cotton or tobacco, but upon inheritance, railroads and investment, so it was a painless gesture, Starbuck, and principally done, I suspect, to spite my sister. It is, perhaps, the one good deed Faulconer ever did, and I refer to the exercise of spitefulness rather than to the act of manumission." Bird, failing to find anywhere to put down his belongings, simply opened his arms and let them all drop untidily onto the music room's parquet floor. "Faulconer wants you to deliver the uniforms."

Starbuck was taken aback, but then realized the subject had abruptly been changed to the Colonel's new finery. "He wants me to take them to Faulconer Court House?"

"Of course he does!" Bird almost screamed at Starbuck. "Must I state the obvious? If I say that Faulconer wishes you to deliver his uniforms, must I first define uniforms? And afterward identify Washington Faulconer? Or the Colonel, as we must all now learn to call him? Good God, Starbuck, and you were at Yale?"

"At the seminary."

"Ah! That explains all. A mind that can credit the bleatings of theology professors can hardly be expected to understand plain English." Thaddeus Bird evidently found this insult amusing, for he began to laugh and, at the same time, to jerk his head backward and forward in a motion so like a woodpecker that it was instantly obvious how his nickname had arisen. Yet if Starbuck himself had been asked to christen this thin, angular and unpleasant man with a nickname it would not have been Pecker, but Spider, for there was something about Thaddeus Bird that irresistibly reminded Starbuck of a long-legged, hairy, unpredictable and malevolent spider. "The Colonel has sent me to run some errands in Richmond, while you are to go to Faulconer Court House," Pecker Bird went on, but in a plump, mocking voice such as he might use to a small and not very clever child. "Stop me if your Yale-educated mind finds any of these instructions difficult to understand. You will go to Faulconer Court House where the Colonel"—Bird paused to make a mocking salute—"wishes for your company, but only if the tailors have finished making his uniforms. You are to be the official conveyor of those uniforms, and of his daughter's manifold petticoats. Your responsibilities are profound."

"Petticoats?" Starbuck asked.

"Women's undergarments," Bird said maliciously, then sat at Washington Faulconer's grand piano where he played a swift and remarkably impressive arpeggio before settling into the tune of "John Brown's Body" to which, without regard to either scansion or tune, he chanted conversationally. "Why does Anna want so many petticoats? Especially as my niece already possesses more petticoats than a reasonable man might have thought necessary for a woman's comfort, but reason and young ladies have never kept close company. But why does she want Ridley? I cannot answer that question either." He stopped playing, frowning. "Though he is a remarkably talented artist."

"Ethan Ridley?" Starbuck, trying to follow the tortuous changes in Bird's conversation, asked in surprise.

"Remarkably talented," Bird confirmed rather wistfully, as though he envied Ridley's skill, "but lazy, of course. Natural talent going to waste, Starbuck. Just wasted! He won't work at his talent. He prefers to marry money rather than make it." He accentuated this judgment by playing a gloomy minor chord, then frowned. "He is a slave of nature," he said, looking expectantly at Starbuck.

"And a son of hell?" The second half of the Shakespearean insult slipped gratifyingly into Starbuck's mind.

"So you have read something other than your sacred texts." Bird seemed disappointed, but then recovered his malevolence as he lowered his voice into a confiding hiss, saying, "But I shall tell you, Starbuck, that the slave of nature will marry the Colonel's daughter! Why does that family contract such marriages? God knows, and he is not saying, though at present, mark my words, young Ridley is in bad odor with the Colonel. He has failed to recruit Truslow! Ah-ha!" Bird crashed a demonic and celebratory discord on the piano. "No Truslow! Ridley had better look to his laurels, had he not? The Colonel is not best pleased."

"Who is Truslow?" Starbuck asked somewhat despairingly.

"Truslow!" Bird said portentously, then paused to play a foreboding couplet of bass notes. "Truslow, Starbuck, is our county's murderer! Our outlaw! Our hardscrabble demon from the hills! Our beast, our creature of darkness, our fiend!" Bird cackled at this fine catalog of mischief, then twisted on the piano bench to face Starbuck. "Thomas Truslow is a rogue, and my brother-in-law the Colonel, who lacks common sense, wishes to recruit Truslow into the Legion because, he says, Truslow served as a soldier in Mexico. And so Truslow did, but the real reason, mark my words well, Starbuck, is that my brother-in-law believes that by recruiting him he can harness Truslow's reputation to the greater glory of his ridiculous Legion. In brief, Starbuck, the great Washington Faulconer desires the murderer's approval. The world is a strange place indeed. Shall we now go and buy petticoats?"

"You say Truslow's a murderer?"

"I did indeed. He stole another man's wife, and killed the man thus to obtain her. He then volunteered for the Mexican War to escape the constables, but after the war he took up where he left off. Truslow's not a man to ignore his talents, you understand? He killed a man who insulted his wife, and cut the throat of another who tried to steal his horse, which is a rare jest, believe me, because Truslow must be the biggest horse thief this side of the Mississippi." Bird took a thin and very dark cigar from one of his shabby pockets. He paused to bite the tip off the cigar, then spat the shred of tobacco across the room in the vague direction of a porcelain spittoon. "And he hates Yankees. Detests them! If he meets you in the Legion, Starbuck, he'll probably hone his murdering talents still further!" Bird lit the cigar, puffed smoke and cackled amusement, his head nodding back and forth. "Have I satisfied your curiosity, Starbuck? Have we gossiped sufficiently? Good, then we shall go and see if the Colonel's uniforms are truly ready and then we shall buy Anna her petticoats. To war, Starbuck, to war!"

Thaddeus Bird first strode across town to Boyle and Gambles's huge warehouse where he placed an order for ammunition. "Minié bullets. The nascent Legion is firing them faster than the factories can make them. We need more, and still more. You can provide minié bullets?"

"Indeed we can, Mister Bird."

"I am not Mister Bird!" Bird announced grandly, "but Major Bird of the Faulconer Legion." He clicked his heels together and offered the elderly salesman a bow.

Starbuck gaped at Bird. Major Bird? This ludicrous man whom Washington Faulconer had declared would never be commissioned? A man, Faulconer claimed, not fit to be a cookhouse corporal? A man, if Starbuck remembered rightly, who would be commissioned only over Faulconer's dead body? And Bird was to be made a major while professional European soldiers, veterans of real wars, were being turned down for mere lieutenancies?

"And we need still more percussion caps"—Bird was oblivious of Starbuck's astonishment—"thousands of the little devils. Send them to the Faulconer Legion Encampment at Faulconer Court House in Faulconer County." He signed the order with a flourish, Major Thaddeus Caractacus Evillard Bird. "Grandparents," he curtly explained the grandiose names to Starbuck, "two Welsh, two French, all dead, let us go." He led the way out of the warehouse and downhill toward Exchange Alley.

Starbuck matched strides with the long-pacing Bird and broached the difficult subject. "Allow me to congratulate you on your commission, Major Bird?"

"So your ears work, do they? That's good news, Starbuck. A young man should possess all his faculties before age, liquor and stupidity erase them. Yes, indeed. My sister bestirred herself from her sickbed to prevail upon the Colonel to commission me a major in his Legion. I do not know upon what precise authority Colonel Brigadier General Captain Lieutenant Admiral the Lord High Executioner Faulconer makes such an appointment, but perhaps we do not need authority in these rebellious days. We are, after all, Robinson Crusoes marooned upon an authority-less island, and we must therefore fashion what we can out of what we find there, and my brother-in-law has discovered within himself the power to make me a major, so that is what I am."

"You desired such an appointment?" Starbuck asked very politely, because he could not really imagine this extraordinary man wanting to be a soldier.

"Desired?" Pecker Bird came to an abrupt stop on the pavement, thus forcing a lady to make an exaggerated swerve about the obstacle he had so suddenly created. "Desired? That is a pertinent question, Starbuck, such as one might have expected from a Boston youth. Desired?" Bird tangled his beard in his fingers as he thought of his answer. "My sister desired it, that is certain, for she is stupid enough to believe that military rank is an automatic conferrer of respectability, which quality she feels I lack, but did I desire the appointment? Yes I did. I must confess I did, and why, you ask? Because firstly, Starbuck, wars are customarily conducted by fools and it thus behooves me to offer myself as an antidote to that sad reality." The schoolmaster offered this appalling immodesty in all apparent sincerity and in a voice that had attracted the amused attention of several pedestrians. "And secondly it will take me away from the school-room. Do you know how I despise children? How I dislike them? How their very voices make me wish to scream in protest! Their mischief is cruel, their presence demeaning and their conversation tedious. Those are my chief reasons." Suddenly, and as abruptly as he had stopped his forward progress, Major Thaddeus Caractacus Evillard Bird began striding downhill again with his long ragged pace.

"There were arguments against accepting the appointment," Bird continued when Starbuck had caught up with him. "First, the necessary close association with my brother-in-law, but upon balance that is preferable to the company of children, and second, the expressed wish of my dear intended, who fears that I might fall upon the field of battle. That would be tragic, Starbuck, tragic!" Bird stressed the enormity of the tragedy by gesturing violently with his right hand, almost sending a passing gentleman's hat flying. "But my darling Priscilla understands that at this time a man must not be seen laggard in his patriotic duty and so she has consented, albeit with sweet reservations, to my going for a soldier."

"You're engaged to be married, sir?"

"You find that circumstance extraordinary, perhaps?" Bird demanded vehemently.

"I find it cause to offer you still further congratulations, sir."

"Your tact exceeds your truthfulness," Bird cackled, then swerved into the doorway of Shaffer's, the tailors, where Colonel Faulconer's three identical bespoke uniforms were indeed ready as promised, as was the much cheaper outfit that Faulconer had ordered for Starbuck. Pecker Bird insisted on examining the Colonel's uniform, then ordered one exactly like it for himself, except, he allowed, his coat's collar should only have a major's single star and not the three gold stars that decorated the Colonel's collar wings. "Put the uniform upon my brother-in-law's account," Bird said grandly as two tailors measured his awkward, bony frame. He insisted upon every possible accoutrement for the uniform, every tassel and plume and braided decoration imaginable. "I shall go into battle gaudy," Bird said, then turned as the spring-mounted bell on the shop's door rang to announce the entrance of a new customer. "Delaney!" Bird delightedly greeted a short, portly man who, with an owlish face, peered about myopically to discover the source of the enthusiastic greeting.

"Bird? Is that you? They have uncaged you? Bird! It is you!" The two men, one so lanky and unkempt, the other so smooth and round and neat, greeted each other with unfeigned delight. It was immediately clear that though they had not met for many months, they were resuming a conversation full of rich insults aimed at their mutual acquaintances, the best of whom were dismissed as mere nincompoops while the worst were utter fools. Starbuck, forgotten, stood fingering the parcels containing the Colonel's three uniforms until Thaddeus Bird, suddenly remembering him, beckoned him forward.

"You must meet Belvedere Delaney, Starbuck. Mister Delaney is Ethan's half-brother, but you should not allow that unhappy circumstance to prejudice your judgment."

"Starbuck," Delaney said, offering a half bow. He was at least twelve inches shorter than the tall Starbuck and a good deal more elegant. Delaney's black coat, breeches and top hat were of silk, his top boots gleamed, while his puff-bosomed shirt was a dazzling white and his tie pinned with a gold-mounted pearl. He had a round myopic face that was sly and humorous. "You are thinking," he accused Starbuck, "that I do not resemble dear Ethan. You were wondering, were you not, how a swan and a buzzard could be hatched from the same egg?"

"I was wondering no such thing, sir," Starbuck lied.

"Call me Delaney. We must be friends. Ethan tells me you were at Yale?"

Starbuck wondered what else Ethan had divulged. "I was at the seminary, yes."

"I shall not hold that against you, so long as you do not mind that I am a lawyer. Not, I hasten to say, a successful one, because I like to think of the law as my amusement rather than as my profession, by which I mean that I do a little probate work when it is plainly unavoidable." Delaney was being deliberately modest, for his flourishing practice was being nurtured by an acute political sensibility and an almost Jesuitical discretion. Belvedere Delaney did not believe in airing his clients' dirty linen in open court and thus did his subtle work in the quiet back rooms of the Capitol Building, or in the city's dining clubs or in the elegant drawing rooms of the big houses on Grace Street and Clay Street. He was privy to the secrets of half Virginia's lawmakers and was reckoned to be a rising power in the Virginian capital. He told Starbuck that he had met Thaddeus Bird at the University of Virginia and that the two men had been friends ever since. "You shall both come and have dinner with me," Delaney insisted.

"On the contrary," Bird said, "you shall have dinner with me."

"My dear Bird!" Delaney pretended horror. "I cannot afford to eat on a country schoolmaster's salary! The horrors of secession have stirred my appetites, and my delicate constitution requires only the richest of foods and the finest of wines. No, no! You shall eat with me, as will you, Mister Starbuck, for I am determined to hear all your father's secret faults. Does he drink? Does he consort with evil women in the vestry? Reassure me on these matters, I beg you."

"You shall dine with me," Bird insisted, "and you will have the finest wine in the Spotswood's cellars because, my dear Bird, it is not I who shall pay, but Washington Faulconer."

"We are to eat on Faulconer's account?" Delaney asked in delight.

"We are indeed," Bird answered with relish.

"Then my business with Shaffer's will wait for the morrow. Lead me to the trough! Lead on, dear Bird, lead on! Let us make gluttons of ourselves, let us redefine greed, let us consume comestibles as they have never been consumed before, let us wallow in the wines of France, and let us gossip. Above all, let us have gossip."

"I'm supposed to be buying petticoats," Starbuck demurred.

"I suspect you look better in trousers," Delaney said sternly, "and besides, petticoats, like duty, can wait till the morrow. Pleasure summons us, Starbuck, pleasure summons us, let us surrender to its call."

3

Seven Springs, Washington Faulconer's house in Faulconer County, was everything Starbuck dreamed it would be, everything Adam had ever told him it would be, and everything Starbuck thought he might ever want a house to be. It was, he decided from the very first moment he saw it on that Sunday morning in late May, just perfect.

Seven Springs was a sprawling white building just two stories high except where a white clock tower surmounted a stable gate and where a rickety cupola, steepled with a weathervane, graced the main roof. Starbuck had expected something altogether more pretentious, something with high pillars and elegant pilasters, with arching porticoes and frowning pediments, but instead the big house seemed more like a lavish farmhouse that over the years had absent-mindedly spread and multiplied and reproduced itself until it was a tangle of steep roofs, shadowed reentrants and creeper-hung walls. The heart of the house was made of thick fieldstone, the outer wings were timber, while the black-shuttered and iron-balconied windows were shaded by tall trees under which were set white painted benches, long-roped swings, and broad tables. Smaller trees were brilliant with red and white blossom that fell to make drifts of color on the well-scythed lawn. The house and its garden cradled a marvelous promise of warm domesticity and unassuming comforts.

Starbuck, greeted by a Negro servant in the front hall, had first been relieved of the paper-wrapped bundles containing Washington Faulconer's new uniforms, then a second servant took the carpetbag containing Starbuck's own uniform, and afterward a turbanned maid came for the two heavy bundles of petticoats that had hung so awkwardly from Starbuck's saddle bow.

He waited. A longcase clock, its painted face orbiting with moons, stars and comets, ticked heavily in a corner of the tiled hallway. The walls were papered in a floral pattern on which hung gold-framed portraits of George Washington, Thomas Jefferson, James Madison and Washington Faulconer. The portrait of Faulconer depicted him mounted on his mag-

nificent black horse, Saratoga, and gesturing toward what Starbuck took
to be the estate surrounding Seven Springs. The hallway grate held the
ashes of a fire, suggesting that the nights were still cold in this upland
county. Fresh flowers stood in a crystal vase on the table where two newspapers lay folded, their headlines celebrating North Carolina's formal
secession to the Confederate cause. The house smelt of starch, lye soap
and apples. Starbuck fidgeted as he waited. He did not quite know what
was expected of him. Colonel Faulconer had insisted that Starbuck bring
the three newly made uniforms directly to Faulconer Court House, but
whether he was to be a guest in the house or was expected to find a berth
with the encamped Legion, Starbuck still did not know, and the uncertainty made him nervous.

A flurry of feet on the stairs made him turn. A young woman, fair-
haired, dressed in white, and excited, came running down the final flight,
then checked on the bottom stair with her hand resting on the white-
painted newel post. She solemnly inspected Starbuck. "You're Nate Starbuck?" she finally asked.

"Indeed, ma'am." He offered her a small, awkward bow.

"Don't 'ma'am' me, I'm Anna." She stepped down onto the hall floor.
She was small, scarce more than five feet tall, with a pale, waiflike face
that was so anxiously wan that Starbuck, if he had not known her to be
one of Virginia's wealthiest daughters, might have thought her an orphan.

Anna's face was familiar to Starbuck from the portrait that hung in the
Richmond town house, but however accurately the picture had caught her
narrow head and diffident smile, the painter had somehow missed the
essence of the girl, and that essence, Starbuck decided, was oddly pitiable.
Anna, despite her prettiness, looked childishly nervous, almost terrified, as
if she expected the world to mock her and cuff her and discard her as
worthless. That look of extraordinary timidity was not helped by the hint
of a strabismus in her left eye, though the squint, if it existed at all, was
very slight. "I'm so glad you've come," she said, "because I was looking for
an excuse not to attend church, and now I can talk to you."

"You received the petticoats?" Starbuck asked.

"Petticoats?" Anna paused, frowning, as if the word were unfamiliar
to her.

"I brought you the petticoats you wanted," Starbuck explained, feeling as though he was speaking to a rather stupid child.

Anna shook her head. "The petticoats were for father, Mister Starbuck, not me, though why he should want them, I don't know. Maybe he
thinks the supply will be constricted by war? Mother says we must stock
up on medicines because of the war. She's ordered a hundredweight of
camphor, and the Lord knows how much niter paper and hartshorn too.
Is the sun very hot?"

"No."

"I cannot go into too fierce a sunlight, you see, in case I burn. But you say it isn't fierce?" She asked the question very earnestly.

"It isn't, no."

"Then shall we go for a walk? Would you like that?" She crossed the hall and slipped a hand under Starbuck's arm and tugged him toward the wide front door. The impetuous gesture was strangely intimate for such a timid girl, yet Starbuck suspected it was a pathetic appeal for companionship. "I've been so wanting to meet you," Anna said. "Weren't you supposed to come here yesterday?"

"The uniforms were a day late," Starbuck lied. In truth his dinner with Thaddeus Bird and the beguiling Belvedere Delaney had stretched from the early afternoon to late suppertime, and so the petticoats had not been bought till late Saturday morning, but it hardly seemed politic to admit to such dalliance.

"Well, you're here now," Anna said as she drew Starbuck into the sunlight, "and I'm so glad. Adam has talked so much about you."

"He often spoke of you," Starbuck said gallantly and untruthfully, for in fact Adam had rarely spoken of his sister, and never with great fondness.

"You surprise me. Adam usually spends so much time examining his own conscience that he scarcely notices the existence of other people." Anna, thus revealing a more astringent mind than Starbuck had expected, nevertheless blushed, as if apologizing for her apparently harsh judgment. "My brother is a Faulconer to the core," she explained. "He is not very practical."

"Your father is practical, surely?"

"He's a dreamer," Anna said, "a romantic. He believes that all fine things will come true if we just have enough hope."

"And surely this house was not built by mere hopes?" Starbuck waved toward the generous facade of Seven Springs.

"You like the house?" Anna sounded surprised. "Mother and I are trying to persuade Father to pull it down and build something altogether grander. Something Italian, perhaps, with columns and a dome? I would like to have a pillared temple on a hill in the garden. Something surrounded by flowers, and very grand."

"I think the house is lovely as it is," Starbuck said.

Anna made a face to show her disapproval of Starbuck's taste. "Our great-great-grandfather Adam built it, or most of it. He was very practical, but then his son married a French lady and the family blood became ethereal. That's what mother says. And she's not strong either, so her blood didn't help."

"Adam doesn't seem ethereal."

"Oh, he is," Anna said, then she smiled up at Starbuck. "I do so like northern voices. They sound so much cleverer than our country accents. Would you permit me to paint you? I'm not so good a painter as Ethan, but I work harder at it. You can sit beside the Faulconer River and look melancholy, like an exile beside the waters of Babylon."

"You'd like me to hang my harp upon the willows?" Starbuck jested clumsily.

Anna withdrew her arm and clapped her hands with delight. "You will be marvelous company. Everyone else is so dull. Adam is being pious in the North, father is besotted with soldiering, and mother spends all day wrapped in ice."

"In ice?"

"Wenham ice, from your home state of Massachusetts. I suppose, if there's war, there'll be no more Wenham ice and we shall have to suffer the local product. But Doctor Danson says the ice might cure mother's neuralgia. The ice cure comes from Europe, so it must be good." Starbuck had never heard of neuralgia, and did not want to enquire into its nature in case it should prove to be one of the vague and indescribable feminine diseases that so often prostrated his mother and elder sister, but Anna volunteered that the affliction was a very modern one and was consti-tuted by what she described as "facial headaches." Starbuck murmured his sympathy. "But father thinks she makes it up to annoy him," Anna con-tinued in her timid and attenuated voice.

"I'm sure that can't be true," Starbuck said.

"I think it might," Anna said in a very sad voice. "I sometimes won-der if men and women always irritate each other?"

"I don't know."

"This isn't a very cheerful conversation, is it?" Anna asked rather despairingly and in a tone that suggested all her conversations became similarly bogged down in melancholy. She seemed to sink further into despair with every second, and Starbuck was remembering Belvedere Delaney's malicious tales of how intensely his half-brother disliked this girl, but how badly Ridley needed her dowry. Starbuck hoped those tales were nothing more than malicious gossip, for it would be a cruel world, he thought, that could victimize a girl as fey and tremulous as Anna Faulconer. "Did Father really say the petticoats were for me?" she sud-denly asked.

"Your uncle said as much."

"Oh, Pecker," Anna said, as if that explained everything.

"It seemed a very strange request," Starbuck said gallantly.

"So much is strange these days," Anna said hopelessly, "and I daren't ask Father for an explanation. He isn't happy, you see."

"No?"

"It's poor Ethan's fault. He couldn't find Truslow, you see, and Father has set his heart on recruiting Truslow. Have you heard about Truslow?"

"Your uncle told me about him, yes. He made Truslow sound rather fearful."

"But he is fearful. He's frightful!" Anna stopped to look up into Starbuck's face. "Shall I confide in you?"

Starbuck wondered what new horror story he was about to hear of the dreaded Truslow. "I should be honored by your confidence, Miss Faulconer," he said very formally.

"Call me Anna, please. I want to be friends. And I tell you, secretly, of course, that I don't believe poor Ethan went anywhere near Truslow's lair. I think Ethan is much too frightened of Truslow. Everyone's frightened of Truslow, even Father, though he says he isn't." Anna's soft voice was very portentous. "Ethan says he went up there, but I don't know if that's true."

"I'm sure it is."

"I'm not." She put her arm back into Starbuck's elbow and walked on. "Maybe you should ride up to find Truslow, Mister Starbuck?"

"Me?" Starbuck asked in horror.

A sudden animation came into Anna's voice. "Think of it as a quest. All my father's young knights must ride into the mountains and dare to challenge the monster, and whoever brings him back will prove himself the best, the noblest and the most gallant knight of all. What do you think of that idea, Mister Starbuck? Would you like to ride on a quest?"

"I think it sounds terrifying."

"Father would appreciate it if you went, I'm sure," Anna said, but when Starbuck made no reply she just sighed and pulled him toward the side of the house. "I want to show you my three dogs. You're to say that they're the prettiest pets in all the world, and after that we shall fetch the painting basket and we'll go to the river and you can hang that shabby hat on the willows. Except we don't have willows, at least I don't think we have. I'm not good at trees."

But there was to be no meeting with the three dogs, nor any painting expedition, for the front door of Seven Springs suddenly opened and Colonel Faulconer stepped into the sunlight.

Anna gasped with admiration. Her father was dressed in one of his new uniforms and looked simply grand. He looked, indeed, as though he had been born to wear this uniform and to lead free men across green fields to victory. His gray frock coat was thickly brocaded with gilt and yellow lace that had been folded and woven to make a broad hem to the coat's edges, while the sleeves were richly embroidered with intricately looped braid that climbed from the broad cuffs to above the elbows. A pair of yellow kidskin gloves was tucked into his shiny black belt, beneath

which a tasseled red silk sash shimmered. His top boots gleamed, his
saber's scabbard was polished to mirror brightness and the yellow plume
on his cocked hat stirred in the small warm wind. Washington Faulconer
was quite plainly delighted with himself as he moved to watch his reflection in one of the tall windows. "Well, Anna?" he asked.

"It's wonderful, Father!" Anna said with as much animation as Starbuck suspected her capable. Two black servants had come from the house
and nodded their agreement.

"I expected the uniforms yesterday, Nate." Faulconer half-asked and
half-accused Starbuck with the statement.

"Shaffer's was a day late, sir"—the lie came smoothly—"but they were
most apologetic."

"I forgive them, considering the excellency of their tailoring." Washington Faulconer could hardly take his eyes from his reflection in the
window glass. The gray uniform was set off with golden spurs, gilded spur
chains and golden scabbard links. He had a revolver in a soft leather
pouch, the weapon's butt looped to the belt with another golden chain.
Braids of white and yellow ribbons decorated the outer seams of his
breeches while his jacket's epaulettes were cushioned in yellow and hung
with gold links. He drew the ivory-hilted saber, startling the morning
with the harsh scrape of the steel on the scabbard's throat. The sun's light
slashed back from the curved and brilliantly polished blade. "It's French,"
he told Starbuck, "a gift from Lafayette to my grandfather. Now it will be
carried in a new crusade for liberty."

"It's truly impressive, sir," Starbuck said.

"So long as a man needs to dress in uniform to fight, then these rags
are surely as good as any," the Colonel said with mock modesty, then
slashed the saber in the empty air. "You're not feeling exhausted after
your journey, Nate?"

"No, sir."

"Then unhand my daughter and we'll find you some work."

But Anna would not let Starbuck go. "Work, Father? But it's Sunday."

"And you should have gone to church, my dear."

"It's too hot. Besides, Nate has agreed to be painted and surely you
won't deny me that small pleasure?"

"I shall indeed, my dear. Nate is a whole day late in arriving and
there's work to be done. Now why don't you go and read to your mother?"

"Because she's sitting in the dark enduring Doctor Danson's ice cure."

"Danson's an idiot."

"But he's the only medically qualified idiot we possess," Anna said,
once more showing a glimpse of vivacity that her demeanor otherwise
hid. "Are you really taking Nate away, Father?"

"I truly am, my dear."

Anna let go of Starbuck's elbow and gave him a shy smile of farewell. "She's bored," the Colonel said when he and Starbuck were back in the house. "She can chatter all day, mostly about nothing." He shook his head disapprovingly as he led Starbuck down a corridor hung with bridles and reins, snaffles and bits, cruppers and martingales. "No trouble finding a bed last night?"

"No, sir." Starbuck had put up at a tavern in Scottsville where no one had been curious about his northern accent or had demanded to see the pass that Colonel Faulconer had provided him.

"No news of Adam, I suppose?" the Colonel asked wistfully.

"I'm afraid not, sir. I did write, though."

"Ah well. The northern mails must be delayed. It's a miracle they're still coming at all. Come"—he pushed open the door of his study—"I need to find a gun for you."

The study was a wonderfully wide room built at the house's western extremity. It had creeper-framed windows on three of its four walls and a deep fireplace on the fourth. The heavy ceiling beams were hung with ancient flintlocks, bayonets and muskets, the walls with battle prints, and the mantel stacked with brass-hilted pistols and swords with snake-skin handles. A black labrador thumped its tail in welcome as Faulconer entered, but was evidently too old and infirm to climb to its feet. Faulconer stooped and ruffled the dog's ears. "Good boy. This is Joshua, Nate. Used to be the best gun dog this side of the Atlantic. Ethan's father bred him. Poor old fellow." Starbuck was not sure whether it was the dog or Ethan's father who had earned the comment, but the Colonel's next words suggested it was not Joshua being pitied. "Bad thing, drink," the Colonel said as he pulled open a bureau's wide drawer that proved to be filled with handguns. "Ethan's father drank away the family land. His mother died of the milksick when he was born, and there's a half-brother who scooped up all the mother's money. He's a lawyer in Richmond now."

"I met him," Starbuck said.

Washington Faulconer turned and frowned at Starbuck. "You met Delaney?"

"Mister Bird introduced me to him in Shaffer's." Starbuck had no intention of revealing how the introduction had led to ten hours of the Spotswood House Hotel's finest food and drink, all of it placed on the Faulconer account, or how he had woken on Saturday morning with a searing headache, a dry mouth, a churning belly and a dim memory of swearing eternal friendship with the entertaining and mischievous Belvedere Delaney.

"A bad fellow, Delaney." The Colonel seemed disappointed in Starbuck. "Too clever for his own good."

"It was a very brief meeting, sir."

"Much too clever. I know lawyers who'd like to have a rope, a tall tree and Mister Delaney all attached to each other. He got all the mother's money and poor Ethan didn't get a thin dime out of the estate. Not fair, Nate, not fair at all. If Delaney had an ounce of decency he'd look after Ethan."

"He mentioned that Ethan is a very fine artist?" Starbuck said, hoping the compliment about his future son-in-law might restore the Colonel's good humor.

"So Ethan is, but that won't bring home the bacon, will it? A fellow might as well play the piano prettily, like Pecker does. I'll tell you what Ethan is, Nate. He's one of the finest hunters I've ever seen and probably the best horseman in the county. And he's a damned fine farmer. He's managed what's left of his father's land these last five years, and I doubt anyone else could have done half as well." The Colonel paid Ridley this generous compliment, then drew out a long-barreled revolver and tentatively spun its chambers before deciding it was not the right gun. "Ethan's got solid worth, Nate, and he'll make a good soldier, a fine soldier, though I confess he didn't make the best recruiting officer." Faulconer turned to offer Starbuck a shrewd look. "Did you hear about Truslow?"

"Anna mentioned him, sir. And Mister Bird did, too."

"I want Truslow, Nate. I need him. If Truslow comes he'll bring fifty hard men out of the hills. Good men, natural fighters. Rogues, of course, every last one of them, but if Truslow tells them to knuckle under, they will. And if he doesn't join up? Half the men in the county will fear to leave their livestock unguarded, so you see why I need him."

Starbuck sensed what was coming and felt his confidence plummet. Truslow was the Yankee hater, the murderer, the demon of the hardscrabble hills.

The Colonel spun the cylinder of another revolver. "Ethan says Truslow's away thieving horses and won't be home for days, maybe weeks, but I have a feeling Truslow just avoided Ethan. He saw him coming and knew what he wanted, so ducked out of sight. I need someone Truslow doesn't know. Someone who can talk to the fellow and discover his price. Every man has his price, Nate, especially a blackguard like Truslow." He put the revolver back and picked out another still more lethal-looking gun. "So how would you feel about going, Nate? I'm not pretending it's an easy task because Truslow isn't the easiest of men, and if you tell me you don't want to do it, then I'll say no more. But otherwise?" The Colonel left the invitation dangling.

And Starbuck, presented with the choice, suddenly found that he did want to go. He wanted to prove that he could bring the monster down from his lair. "I'd be happy to go, sir."

"Truly?" The Colonel sounded mildly surprised.

"Yes, truly."

"Good for you, Nate." Faulconer snapped back the cock of the lethal-looking revolver, pulled the trigger, then decided that gun was not right either. "You'll need a gun, of course. Most of the rogues in the mountains don't like Yankees. You've got your pass, of course, but it's a rare creature who can read up there. I'd tell you to wear the uniform, except folk like Truslow associate uniforms with excise men or tax collectors, so you're much safer in ordinary clothes. You'll just have to bluff your way if you're challenged, and if that doesn't work, shoot one of them." He chuckled, and Starbuck shuddered at the errand that now faced him. Not six months before he had been a student at Yale Theological College, immersed in an intricate study of the Pauline doctrine of atonement, and now he was supposed to shoot his way through a countryside of illiterate Yankee haters in search of the district's most feared horse thief and murderer? Faulconer must have sensed his premonition, for he grinned. "Don't worry, he won't kill you, not unless you try and take his daughter or, worse, his horse."

"I'm glad to hear that, sir," Starbuck said drily.

"I'll write you a letter for the brute, though God only knows if he can read. I'll explain you're an honorary southron, and I'll make him an offer. Say fifty dollars as a signing bounty? Don't offer him anything more, and for God's sake don't encourage him into thinking I want him to be an officer. Truslow will make a good sergeant, but you'd hardly want him at your supper table. His wife's dead, so she won't be a problem, but he's got a daughter who might be a nuisance. Tell him I'll find her a position in Richmond if he wants her placed. She's probably a filthy piece of work, but no doubt she can sew or tend store." Faulconer had laid a walnut box on his desk, which he now turned round so that the lid's catch faced Starbuck. "I don't think this is for you, Nate, but take a look at her. She's very pretty."

Starbuck raised the walnut lid to reveal a beautiful ivory-handled revolver that lay in a specially shaped compartment lined with blue velvet. Other velvet-lined compartments held the gun's silver-rimmed powder horn, bullet mold and crimper. The gold-lettered label inside the lid read "R. Adams, Patentee of the Revolver, 79 King William Street, London EC." "I bought her in England two years ago." The Colonel lifted the gun and caressed its barrel. "She's a lovely thing, isn't she?"

"Yes, sir, she is." And the gun did indeed seem beautiful in the soft morning light that filtered past the long white drapes. The shape of the weapon was marvelously matched to function, a marriage of engineering and design so perfectly achieved that for a few seconds Starbuck even forgot exactly what the gun's function was.

"Very beautiful," Washington Faulconer said reverently. "I'll take her to the Baltimore and Ohio in a couple of weeks."

"The Baltimore …" Starbuck began, then stopped as he realized he had not misheard. So the Colonel still wanted to lead his raid on the railroad? "But I thought our troops at Harper's Ferry had blocked the line, sir."

"So they have, Nate, but I've discovered the cars are still running as far as Cumberland, then they move their supplies on by road and canal." Faulconer put the beautiful Adams revolver away. "And it still seems to me that the Confederacy is being too quiescent, too fearful. We need to attack, Nate, not sit around waiting for the North to strike at us. We need to set the South alight with a victory! We need to show the North that we're men, not craven mudsills. We need a quick, absolute victory that will be written across every newspaper in America! Something to put our name in the history books! A victory to begin the Legion's history." He smiled. "How does that sound?"

"It sounds marvelous, sir."

"And you'll come with us, Nate, I promise. Bring me Truslow, then you and I will ride to the rails and break a few heads. But you need a gun first, so how about this beast?" The Colonel offered Nate a clumsy, long-barreled, ugly revolver with an old-fashioned hook-curved hilt, an awkward swan-necked hammer and two triggers. The Colonel explained that the lower ring trigger revolved the cylinder and cocked the hammer, while the upper lever fired the charge. "She's a brute to fire," Faulconer admitted, "until you learn the knack of releasing the lower trigger before you pull the upper one. But she's a robust thing. She can take a knock or two and still go on killing. She's heavy and that makes her difficult to aim, but you'll get used to her. And she'll scare the wits out of anyone you point her at." The pistol was an American-made Savage, three and a half pounds in weight and over a foot in length. The lovely Adams, with its blue sheened barrel and soft white handle, was smaller and lighter, and fired the same size bullet, yet it was not nearly as frightening as the Savage.

The Colonel put the Adams back into his drawer, then turned and pocketed the key. "Now, let's see, it's midday. I'll find you a fresh horse, give you that letter and some food, then you can be on your way. It isn't a long ride. You should be there by six o'clock, maybe earlier. I'll write you that letter, then send you Truslow hunting. Let's be to work, Nate!"

The Colonel accompanied Starbuck for the first part of his journey, ever encouraging him to sit his horse better. "Heels down, Nate! Heels down! Back straight!" The Colonel took amusement from Starbuck's riding, which was admittedly atrocious, while the Colonel himself was a superb horseman. He was riding his favorite stallion and, in his new uniform and mounted on the glossy horse, he looked marvelously impressive as he led Starbuck through the town of Faulconer Court House, past the water mill

and the livery stable, the inn and the courthouse, the Baptist and the
Episcopal churches, past Greeley's Tavern and the smithy, the bank and
the town gaol. A girl in a faded bonnet smiled at the Colonel from the
schoolhouse porch. The Colonel waved to her, but did not stop to talk.
"Priscilla Bowen," he told Nate, who had no idea how he was supposed to
remember the flood of names that was being unleashed on him. "She's a
pretty enough thing if you like them plump, but only nineteen, and the
silly girl intends to marry Pecker. My God, but she could do better than
him! I told her so too. I didn't mince my words either, but it hasn't done a
blind bit of good. Pecker's double her age, double! I mean it's one thing to
bed them, Nate, but you don't have to marry them! Have I offended
you?"

"No, sir."

"I keep forgetting your strict beliefs." The Colonel laughed happily.
They had passed through the town, which had struck Starbuck as a con-
tented, comfortable community and much larger than he had expected.
The Legion itself was encamped to the west of the town, while
Faulconer's house was to the north. "Doctor Danson reckoned that the
sound of military activity would be bad for Miriam," Faulconer explained.
"She's delicate, you understand."

"So Anna was telling me, sir."

"I was thinking of sending her to Germany once Anna's safely married. They say the doctors there are marvelous."

"So I've heard, sir."

"Anna could accompany her. She's delicate too, you know. Danson
says she needs iron. God knows what he means. But they can both go if
the war's done by fall. Here we are, Nate!" The Colonel gestured toward a
meadow where four rows of tents sloped down toward a stream. This was
the Legion's encampment, crowned by the three-banded, seven-starred
flag of the new Confederacy. Thick woods rose on the stream's far bank,
the town lay behind, and the whole encampment somehow had the
jaunty appearance of a traveling circus. A baseball diamond had already
been worn into the flattest part of the meadow, while the officers had
made a steeplechase course along the bank of the stream. Girls from the
town were perched along a steep bank that formed the meadow's eastern
boundary, while the presence of carriages parked alongside the road
showed how the gentry from the nearby countryside were making the
encampment into the object of an excursion. There was no great air of
purpose about the men who lounged or played or strolled around the
campground, which indolence, as Starbuck well knew, resulted from
Colonel Faulconer's military philosophy, which declared that too much
drill simply dulled a good man's appetite for battle. Now, in sight of his
good southerners, the Colonel became markedly more cheerful. "We just

need two or three hundred more men, Nate, and the Legion will be unbeatable. Bringing me Truslow will be a good beginning."

"I'll do my best, sir," Starbuck said, and wondered why he had ever agreed to face the demon Truslow. His apprehensions were sharpened because Ethan Ridley, mounted on a spirited chestnut horse, had suddenly appeared at the encampment's main entrance. Starbuck remembered Anna Faulconer's confident assertion that Ridley had not even dared face Truslow, and that only made him all the more nervous. Ridley was in uniform, though his gray woolen tunic looked very drab beside the Colonel's brand-new finery.

"So what do you think of Shaffer's tailoring, Ethan?" the Colonel demanded of his future son-in-law.

"You look superb, sir," Ridley responded dutifully, then nodded a greeting to Starbuck, whose mare edged to the side of the road and lowered her head to crop at the grass while Washington Faulconer and Ridley talked. The Colonel was saying how he had discovered two cannon that might be bought, and was wondering if Ridley would mind going to Richmond to make the purchase and to ferret out some ammunition. The Richmond visit would mean that Ridley could not ride on the raid against the Baltimore and Ohio Railroad, and the Colonel was apologizing for denying his future son-in-law the enjoyment of that expedition, but Ridley seemed not to mind. In fact his dark, neatly bearded face even looked cheerful at the thought of returning to Richmond.

"In the meantime Nate's off to look for Truslow." The Colonel brought Starbuck back into the conversation.

Ridley's expression changed instantly to wariness. "You're wasting your time, Reverend. The man's off stealing horses."

"Maybe he just avoided you, Ethan?" Faulconer suggested.

"Maybe," Ridley sounded grudging, "but I'll still wager that Starbuck's wasting his time. Truslow can't stand Yankees. He blames a Yankee for his wife's death. He'll tear you limb from limb, Starbuck."

Faulconer, evidently affected by Ridley's pessimism, frowned at Starbuck. "It's your choice, Nate."

"Of course I'll go, sir."

Ridley scowled. "You're wasting your time, Reverend," he said again, with just a hint of too much force.

"Twenty bucks says I'm not," Starbuck heard himself saying, and immediately regretted the challenge as a stupid display of bravado. It was worse than stupid, he thought, but a sin too. Starbuck had been taught that all wagering was sinful in the sight of God, yet he did not know how to withdraw the impulsive offer.

Nor was he sure that he wanted to withdraw because Ridley had hesitated, and that hesitation seemed to confirm Anna's suspicion that her fiancé might indeed have evaded looking for the fearful Truslow.

"Sounds a fair offer to me," the Colonel intervened happily.

Ridley stared at Starbuck, and the younger man thought he detected a hint of fear in Ridley's gaze. Was he frightened that Starbuck would reveal his lie? Or just frightened of losing twenty dollars? "He'll kill you, Reverend."

"Twenty dollars says I'll have him here before the month's end," Starbuck said.

"By the week's end," Ridley challenged, seeing a way out of the wager.

"Fifty bucks?" Starbuck recklessly raised the wager.

Washington Faulconer laughed. Fifty dollars was nothing to him, but it was a fortune to penniless young men like Ridley and Starbuck. Fifty dollars was a month's wages to a good man, the price of a decent carriage horse, the cost of a fine revolver. Fifty dollars turned Anna's quixotic quest into a harsh ordeal. Ethan Ridley hesitated, then seemed to feel he demeaned himself by that hesitation and so held out a gloved hand. "You've got till Saturday, Reverend, not a moment more."

"Done," Starbuck said, and shook Ridley's hand.

"Fifty bucks!" Faulconer exclaimed with delight when Ridley had ridden away. "I do hope you're feeling lucky, Nate."

"I'll do my best, sir."

"Don't let Truslow bully you. Stand up to him, you hear me?"

"I will, sir."

"Good luck, Nate. And heels down! Heels down!"

Starbuck rode west toward the blue-shadowed mountains. It was a lovely day under an almost cloudless sky. Starbuck's fresh horse, a strong mare named Pocahontas, trotted tirelessly along the grass verge of the dirt road, which climbed steadily away from the small town, past orchards and fenced meadows, going into a hilly country of small farms, lush grass and quick streams. These Virginia foothills were not good for tobacco, less good still for the famous southern staples of indigo, rice and cotton, but they grew good walnuts and fine apples, and sustained fat cattle and plentiful corn. The farms, though small, looked finely kept. There were big barns and plump meadows and fat herds of cows whose bells sounded pleasantly languorous in the midday warmth. As the road climbed higher the farms became smaller until some were little more than corn patches hacked out of the encroaching woods. Farm dogs slept beside the road, waking to snap at the horse's heels as Starbuck rode by.

Starbuck became more apprehensive as he rode higher into the hills. He had the insouciance and cockiness of youth, believing himself capable of any deed he set his mind to achieve, but as the sun declined he began to perceive Thomas Truslow as a great barrier that defined his whole future. Cross the barrier and life would be simple again, fail it and he would never again look in a mirror and feel respect for himself. He tried to steel himself against whatever hard reception Truslow might have for him, if indeed Truslow was in the hills at all, then he tried to imagine the triumph of success if the grim Truslow came meekly down to join the Legion's ranks. He thought of Faulconer's pleasure and of Ridley's chagrin, and then he wondered how he was ever to pay the wager if he lost. Starbuck had no money and, though the Colonel had offered to pay him wages of twenty-six dollars a month, Starbuck had yet to see a cent of it.

By midafternoon the dirt road had narrowed to a rough track that ran alongside a tumbling, white whipped river that foamed at rocks, coursed between boulders and worried at fallen trees. The woods were full of bright red blossom, the hills steep, the views spectacular. Starbuck passed two deserted cabins, and once he was startled by the crash of hooves and turned, fumbling for the loaded revolver, only to see a white-tailed deer galloping away through the trees. He had begun to enjoy the landscape, and that enjoyment made him wonder whether his destiny belonged in the wild new western lands where Americans struggled to claw a new country from the grip of heathen savages. My God, he thought, but he should never have agreed to study for the ministry! At night the guilt of that abandoned career often assailed him, but here, in the daylight, with a gun at his side and an adventure ahead, Starbuck felt ready to meet the devil himself, and suddenly the words *rebel* and *treason* did not seem so bad to him after all. He told himself he wanted to be a rebel. He wanted to taste the forbidden fruits against which his father preached. He wanted to be an intimate of sin, he wanted to saunter through the valley of the shadow of death because that was the way of a young man's dreams.

He reached a ruined sawmill where a track led south. The track was steep, forcing Starbuck off Pocahontas's back. Faulconer had told him there was another, easier road, but this steep path was the more direct and would bring him onto Truslow's land. The day had become hot, and sweat was prickling at Starbuck's skin. Birds screamed from among the new pale leaves.

By late afternoon he reached the ridge line, where he remounted to stare down into the red-blossomed valley where Truslow lived. It was a place, the Colonel said, where fugitives and scoundrels had taken refuge over the years, a lawless place where sinewy men and their tough wives hacked a living from a thin soil, but a soil happily free of government. It was a high, hanging valley famous for horse thieves, where animals stolen from the rich Virginia lowlands were corralled before being taken north and west for resale. This was a nameless place where Starbuck had to confront the demon of the hardscrabble hills whose approval was so important to the lofty Washington Faulconer. He turned and looked behind, seeing the great spread of green country stretching toward the hazed horizon, then he looked back to the west, where a few trickles of smoke showed where homesteads were concealed among the secretive trees.

He urged Pocahontas down the vague path that led between the trees. Starbuck wondered what kind of trees they were. He was a city boy and did not know a redbud from an elm or a live oak from a dogwood. He could not slaughter a pig or hunt a deer or even milk a cow. In this countryside of competent people he felt like a fool, a man of no talent and too much education. He wondered whether a city childhood unfitted a man for warfare, and whether the country people with their familiarity with death and their knowledge of landscape made natural soldiers. Then, as so often, Starbuck swung from his romantic ideals of war to a sudden feeling of horror at the impending conflict. How could there be a war in this good land? These were the United States of America, the culmination of man's striving for a perfect government and a Godly society, and the only enemies ever seen in this happy land had been the British and the Indians, and both of those enemies, thanks to God's providence and American fortitude, had been defeated.

No, he thought, but these threats of war could not be real. They were mere excitements, politics turned sour, a spring fever that would be cooled by fall. Americans might fight against the Godless savages of the untamed wilderness, and were happy to slaughter the hirelings of some treacherous foreign king, but they would surely never turn on one another! Sense would prevail, a compromise would be reached, God would surely reach out his hand to protect his chosen country and its good people. Though maybe, Starbuck guiltily hoped, there would be time for one adventure first—one sunlit raid of bright flags and shining sabers and drumming hoofbeats and broken trains and burning trestles.

"Go one pace more, boy, and I'll blow your goddamned brains to kingdom come," the hidden voice spoke suddenly.

"Oh, Christ!" Starbuck was so astonished that he could not check the blasphemous imprecation, but he did retain just enough sense to haul in the reins, and the mare, well schooled, stopped.

"Or maybe I'll blow your brains out anyhows." The voice was as deep and harsh as a rat-tailed file scraping on rusted iron, and Starbuck, even though he had still not seen the speaker, suspected he has found his murderer. He had discovered Truslow.

4

The Reverend Elial Starbuck leaned forward in his pulpit and gripped his lectern so hard that his knuckles whitened. Some of his congregation, sitting close to the great man, thought the lectern must surely break. The reverend's eyes were closed and his long, bony, white-bearded face contorted with passion as he sought the exact word that would inflame his listeners and fill the church with a vengeful righteousness.

The tall building was silent. Every pew was taken and every bench in the gallery full. The church was foursquare, undecorated, plain, as simple and functional a building as the gospel that was preached from its white-painted pulpit. There was a black-robed choir, a new-fangled harmonium, and high clear-glass windows. Gas lamps provided lighting, and a big black pot-bellied stove offered a grudging warmth in winter, though that small comfort would not be needed for many months now. It was hot inside the church; not so hot as it would be in high summer when the atmosphere would be stifling, but this spring Sunday was warm enough for the worshipers to be fanning their faces, but as the Reverend Elial's dramatic silence stretched so, one by one, the paper fans were stilled until it seemed as if every person inside the church's high bare interior was as motionless as a statue.

They waited, hardly daring to breathe. The Reverend Elial, white haired, white bearded, fierce eyed, gaunt, held his silence as he savored the word in his mind. He had found the right word, he decided, a good word, a word in due season, a word from his text, and so he drew in a long breath and raised a slow hand until it seemed as though every heart in the whole high building had paused in its beating.

"Vomit!" the Reverend Elial screamed, and a child in the gallery cried aloud with fear of the word's explosive power. Some women gasped.

The Reverend Elial Starbuck smashed his right fist onto the pulpit's rail, struck it so hard that the sound echoed through the church like a gunshot. At the end of a sermon the edges of his hands were often dark

with bruises, while the power of his preaching broke the spines of at least
a half-dozen Bibles each year. "The slavocracy has no more right to call
itself Christian than a dog can call itself a horse! Or an ape a man! Or a
man an angel! Sin and perdition! Sin and perdition! The slavocracy is
diseased with sin, polluted with perdition!" The sermon had reached the
point where it no longer needed to make sense, because now the logic of
its exposition could give way to a series of emotional reminders that
would hammer the message deep into the listeners' hearts and fortify
them against one more week of worldly temptations. The Reverend Elial
had been preaching for one and a quarter hours, and he would preach for
at least another half hour more, but for the next ten minutes he wanted
to lash the congregation into a frenzy of indignation.

The slavocracy, he told them, was doomed for the deepest pits of hell,
to be cast down into the lake of burning sulfur where they would suffer
the torments of indescribable pain for the length of all eternity. The Reverend Elial Starbuck had cut his preaching teeth on descriptions of hell
and he offered a five-minute reprise of that place's horrors, so filling his
church with revulsion that some of the weaker brethren in the congregation seemed near to fainting. There was a section in the gallery where
freed southern slaves sat, all of them sponsored in some way by the
church, and the freedmen echoed the reverend's words, counterpointing
and embroidering them so that the church seemed charged and filled
with the Spirit.

And still the Reverend Elial racked the emotion higher and yet
higher. He told his listeners how the slavocracy had been offered the
hand of northern friendship, and he flung out his own bruised hand as if
to illustrate the sheer goodness of the offer. "It was offered freely! It was
offered justly! It was offered righteously! It was offered lovingly!" His
hand stretched farther and farther out toward the congregation as he
detailed the generosity of the northern states. "And what did they do
with our offer? What did they do? What did they do?" The last repetition
of the question had come in a high scream that locked the congregation
into immobility. The Reverend Elial glared round the church, from the
rich pews at the front to the poor benches at the back of the galleries,
then down to his own family's pew, where his eldest son, James, sat in his
new stiff blue uniform. "What did they do?" The Reverend Elial sawed
the air as he answered his question. "They returned to their folly! 'For as a
dog returneth to his vomit, so a fool returneth to his folly.'" That had
been the Reverend Elial Starbuck's text, taken from the eleventh verse of
the twenty-sixth chapter of the Book of Proverbs. He shook his head
sadly, drew his hand back, and repeated the awful word in a tone of resig-
nation and puzzlement. "Vomit, vomit, vomit."

The slavocracy, he said, was mired in its own vomit. They wallowed in it. They reveled in it. A Christian, the Reverend Elial Starbuck declared, had only one choice in these sad days. A Christian must armor himself with the shield of faith, weapon himself with the weapons of righteousness, and then march south to scour the land free of the southern dogs that supped of their own vomit. And the members of the slavocracy are dogs, he emphasized to his listeners, and they must be whipped like dogs, scourged like dogs and made to whimper like dogs.

"Hallelujah!" a voice called from the gallery, while in the Starbuck pew, hard beneath the pulpit, James Starbuck felt a pulse of pious satisfaction that he would be going forth to do the Lord's work in his country's army, then he felt a balancing spurt of fear that perhaps the slavocracy would not take its whipping quite as meekly as a frightened dog. James Elial MacPhail Starbuck was twenty-five, yet his thinning black hair and perpetual expression of pained worry made him look ten years older. He was able to console himself for his balding scalp by the bushy thickness of his fine deep beard that well matched his corpulent, tall frame. In looks he took more after his mother's side of the family than his father's, though in his assiduity to business he was every bit Elial's son for, even though he was only four years out of Harvard's Dane Law School, James was already spoken of as a coming man in the Commonwealth of Massachusetts, and that fine reputation, added to his famous father's entreaties, had earned him a place on the staff of General Irvin McDowell. This sermon would thus be the last James would hear from his father for many a week for, in the morning, he would take the cars for Washington to assume those new duties.

"The South must be made to whimper like dogs supping their own vomit!" The Reverend Elial began the summation which, in turn, would lead to the sermon's fiery and emotive conclusion, but one worshiper did not wait for those closing pyrotechnics. Beneath the gallery at the very back of the church a box pew door clicked open and a young man slipped out. He tiptoed the few paces to the rear door, then edged through into the vestibule. The few people who noticed his going assumed he was feeling unwell, though in truth Adam Faulconer was not feeling physically sick, but heartsick. He paused on the street steps of the church and took a deep breath while behind him the voice of the preacher rose and fell, muffled now by the granite walls of the tall church.

Adam looked astonishingly like his father. He had the same broad shoulders, stocky build and resolute face, with the same fair hair, blue eyes, and square-cut beard. It was a dependable, trustworthy face, though at this moment it was also a very troubled face.

Adam had come to Boston after receiving a letter from his father that had described Starbuck's arrival in Richmond. Washington Faulconer had sketched an outline of Nate's troubles, then continued: "For your sake I shall offer him shelter and every kindness, and I assume he will stay here as long as he needs to, and I further assume that need might be for ever, but I surmise it is only the fear of his family that keeps him in Virginia. Perhaps, if you can spare the time from your endeavors," and Adam had smelt the rancor in his father's choice of that word, "you might inform Nate's family that their son is penitent, humiliated and dependent on charity, and so gain for him a token of their forgiveness?"

Adam had wanted to visit Boston. He knew the city was the most influential in the North, a place of learning and piety where he hoped to find men who could offer some hope of peace, but he had also hoped to discover some peace for Nate Starbuck to which end he had gone to the Reverend Elial Starbuck's house, but the reverend, apprised of Adam's business, had refused to receive him. Now Adam had listened to his friend's father preach and he suspected there was as little hope for America as there was for Nate. As the venom had poured from the pulpit Adam had understood that so long as such hatred went unassuaged there could be no compromise. The Christian Peace Commission had become irrelevant, for the churches of America could no more bring peace than a candle flame could melt the Wenham Lake in midwinter. America, Adam's blessed land, must go to war. It made no sense to Adam, for he did not understand how decent men could ever think that war could adjudicate matters better than reason and goodwill, but dimly and reluctantly, Adam was beginning to understand that goodwill and reason were not the mainsprings of mankind, but instead that passion, love and hate were the squalid fuels that drove history blindly onward.

Adam walked the plump ordered streets of residential Boston, beneath the new-leafed trees and beside the tall clean houses that were so gaily decorated with patriotic flags and bunting. Even the carriages waiting to take the worshipers back to their comfortable homes sported American flags. Adam loved that flag, and could be made misty eyed by all it stood for, yet now he recognized in its bright stars and broad stripes a tribal emblem being flaunted in hate, and he knew that everything he had worked for was about to be melted in the crucible. There was going to be war.

Thomas Truslow was a short, dark-haired stump of a man; a flint-faced, bitter-eyed creature whose skin was grimy with dirt and whose clothes were shiny with grease. His black hair was long and tangled like the thick beard that jutted pugnaciously from his dark-tanned face. His boots were thick-soled cowhide brogans, he wore a wide-brimmed hat, filthy Kentucky jeans and a homespun shirt with sleeves torn short enough to show the corded muscles of his upper arms. There was a heart tattooed on his right forearm with the odd word *Emly* written beneath it, and it took

Starbuck a few seconds to realize that it was probably a misspelling of *Emily*.

"Lost your way, boy?" This unprepossessing creature now challenged Starbuck. Truslow was carrying an antique flintlock musket that had a depressingly blackened muzzle pointing unwaveringly at Starbuck's head.

"I'm looking for Mister Thomas Truslow," Starbuck said.

"I'm Truslow." The gun muzzle did not waver, nor did the oddly light eyes. When all was said and done, Starbuck decided, it was those eyes that scared him most. You could clean up this brute, trim his beard, scrub his face and dress him in a churchgoing suit, and still those wild eyes would radiate the chilling message that Thomas Truslow had nothing to lose.

"I've brought you a letter from Washington Faulconer."

"Faulconer!" The name was expressed as a joyless burst of laughter. "Wants me for a soldier, is that it?"

"He does, Mister Truslow, yes." Starbuck was making an effort to keep his voice neutral and not betray the fear engendered by those eyes and by the threat of violence that came off Truslow as thick as the smoke from a green bonfire. It seemed that at any second a trembling mechanism could give way in the dark brain behind those pale eyes to unleash a pulverizing bout of destructiveness. It was a menace that seemed horribly close to madness, and very far from the reasoned world of Yale and Boston and Washington Faulconer's gracious house.

"Took his time in sending for me, didn't he?" Truslow asked suspiciously.

"He's been in Richmond. But he did send someone called Ethan Ridley to see you last week."

The mention of Ridley's name made Truslow strike like a starving snake. He reached up with his left hand, grabbed Starbuck's coat, and pulled down so that Starbuck was leaning precariously out of his saddle. He could smell the rank tobacco on Truslow's breath, and see the scraps of food caught in the wiry black bristles of his beard. The mad eyes glared into Starbuck's face. "Ridley was here?"

"I understand he visited you, yes." Starbuck was struggling to be courteous and even dignified, though he was remembering how his father had once tried to preach to some half-drunken immigrant longshoremen working on the quays of Boston Harbor and how even the impressive Reverend Elial had struggled to maintain his composure in the face of their maniacal coarseness. Breeding and education, Starbuck reflected, were poor things with which to confront raw nature. "He says you were not here."

Truslow abruptly let go of Starbuck's coat, at the same time making a growling noise that was half-threat and half-puzzlement. "I wasn't here," he said, but distantly, as if trying to make sense of some new and important information, "but no one told me how he was here either. Come on, boy."

Starbuck pulled his coat straight and surreptitiously loosened the big Savage revolver in its holster. "As I said, Mister Truslow, I have a letter for you from Colonel Faulconer ..."

"Colonel is he, now?" Truslow laughed. He had stumped ahead of Starbuck, forcing the northerner to follow him into a wide clearing that was evidently the Truslow homestead. Bedraggled vegetables grew in long rows, there was a small orchard, its trees a glory of white blossom, while the house itself was a one-story log cabin surmounted by a stout stone chimney from which a wisp of smoke trickled. The cabin was ramshackle and surrounded by untidy stacks of timber, broken carts, sawhorses and barrels. A brindled dog, seeing Starbuck, lunged furiously at the end of its chain, scattering a flock of terrified chickens that had been scratching in the dirt. "Get off your horse, boy," Truslow snapped at Starbuck.

"I don't want to detain you, Mister Truslow. I have Mister Faulconer's letter here." Starbuck reached inside his coat.

"I said get off that damned horse!" Truslow snapped the command so fiercely that even the dog, which had seemed wilder than its own master, suddenly whimpered itself into silence and skulked back to the shade of the broken porch. "I've got work for you, boy," Truslow added.

"Work?" Starbuck slid out of the saddle, wondering just what kind of hell he had come to.

Truslow snatched the horse's reins and tied them to a post. "I was expecting Roper," he said in impenetrable explanation, "but till he comes, you'll have to do. Over there, boy." He pointed at a deep pit which lay just beyond one of the piles of broken carts. It was a saw pit, maybe eight feet deep and straddled by a tree trunk in which a massive great double-handed ripsaw was embedded.

"Jump down, boy! You'll be bottom man," Truslow snapped.

"Mister Truslow!" Starbuck tried to stem the madness with an appeal to reason.

"Jump, boy!" That tone of voice would have made the devil snap to attention, and Starbuck did take an involuntary step toward the pit's edge, but then his innate stubbornness took command.

"I'm not here to work."

Truslow grinned. "You've got a gun, boy, you'd better be prepared to use it."

"I'm here to give you this letter." Starbuck took the envelope from an inside pocket.

"You could kill a buffalo with that pistol, boy. You want to use it on me? Or you want to work for me?"

"I want you to read this letter ..."

"Work or fight, boy." Truslow stepped closer to Starbuck. "I don't give a sack of shit which one you want, but I ain't waiting all day for you to make up your mind on it either."

There was a time for fighting, Starbuck thought, and a time for deciding he would be bottom man in a saw pit. He jumped, landing in a slurry of mud, sawdust and woodchips.

"Take your coat off, boy, and that hog pistol with it."

"Mister Truslow!" Starbuck made one last effort to retain a shred of control over this encounter. "Would you just read this letter?"

"Listen, boy, your letter's just words, and words never filled a belly yet. Your fancy Colonel is asking me for a favor, and you'll have to work to earn him his answer. You understand me? If Washington Faulconer himself had come I'd have him down that pit, so leave off your whining, get off your coat, take hold of that handle, and give me some work."

So Starbuck left off his whining, took off his coat, took hold of the handle and gave him some work.

It seemed to Starbuck that he was mired in a pit beneath a cackling and vengeful demon. The great pit saw, singing through the trunk, was repeatedly rammed down at him in a shower of sawdust and chips that stung Starbuck's eyes and clogged his mouth and nostrils, yet each time he took a hand off the saw to try and cuff his face, Truslow would bellow a reproof. "What's the matter, boy? Gone soft on me? Work!"

The pit was straddled by a pinewood trunk that, judging by its size, had to be older than the Republic. Truslow had grudgingly informed Starbuck that he was cutting the trunk into planks which he had promised to deliver for a new floor being laid at the general store at Hankey's Ford. "This and two other trunks should manage it," Truslow announced before they were even halfway through the first cut, by which time Starbuck's muscles were already aching like fire and his hands were smarting.

"Pull, boy, pull!" Truslow shouted. "I can't keep the cut straight if you're lollygagging!" The saw blade was nine feet long and supposed to be powered equally by the top and bottom men, though Thomas Truslow, perched on top of the trunk in his nailed boots, was doing by far the greater amount of work. Starbuck tried to keep up. He gathered that his role was to pull down hard, for it was the downstroke that provided most of the cutting force, and if he tried to push up too hard he risked buckling the saw, so it was better to let Truslow yank the great steel blade up from the pit, but though that upward motion gave Starbuck a half second of blessed relief, it immediately led to the crucial, brutal downstroke. Sweat was pouring off Starbuck.

He could have stopped. He could have refused to work one more moment and instead have just let go of the great wooden handle and shouted up at this foul man that Colonel Faulconer was unaccountably offering him a fifty-dollar bonus to sign up as a soldier, but he sensed that Truslow was testing him, and suddenly he resented the southern attitude that assumed he was a feeble New Englander, too educated to be of any real use and too soft to be trusted with real men's work. He had been fooled by Dominique, condemned as pious by Ethan Ridley and now he was being ridiculed by this filthy, tobacco-stained, bearded fiend, and Starbuck's anger made him whip the saw down again and again and again so that the great blade rang through the slashing wood grain like a church bell.

"Now you're getting it!" Truslow grunted.

"And damn you, damn you too," Starbuck said, though under his panting breath. It felt extraordinarily daring to use the swear words, even under his breath for, though the devil above him could not hear the cursing, heaven's recording angel could, and Starbuck knew he had just added another sin to the great list of sins marked to his account. And swearing was among the bad sins, almost as bad as thieving. Starbuck had been brought up to hate blaspheming and to despise the givers of oaths, and even the profane weeks he had spent with Major Trabell's foul-mouthed *Tom* company had not quelled his unhappy conscience about cursing, but somehow he needed to defy God as well as Truslow at this moment, and so he went on spitting the word out to give himself strength.

"Hold it!" Truslow suddenly shouted, and Starbuck had an instant fear that his muttered imprecations had been heard, but instead the halt had merely been called so that the work could be adjusted. The saw had cut to within a few inches of the pit's side, so now the trunk had to be moved. "Catch hold, boy!" Truslow tossed down a stout branch that ended in a crutch. "Ram that under the far end and heave when I tell you."

Starbuck heaved, moving the great trunk inch by painful inch until it was in its new position. Then there was a further respite as Truslow hammered wedges into the sawn cut.

"So what's Faulconer offering me?" Truslow asked.

"Fifty dollars." Starbuck spoke from the pit and wondered how Truslow had guessed that anything was being offered. "You'd like me to read you the letter?"

"You suggesting I can't read, boy?"

"Let me give you the letter."

"Fifty, eh? He thinks he can buy me, does he? Faulconer thinks he can buy whatever he wants, whether it's a horse, a man or a whore. But in the end he tires of whatever he buys, and you and me'll be no different."

"He isn't buying me," Starbuck said, and had that lie treated with a silent derision by Truslow. "Colonel Faulconer's a good man," Starbuck insisted.

"You know why he freed his niggers?" Truslow asked.

Pecker Bird had told Starbuck that the manumission had been intended to spite Faulconer's wife, but Starbuck neither believed the story nor would he repeat it. "Because it was the right thing to do," he said defiantly.

"So it might have been," Truslow allowed, "but it was for another woman he did it. Roper will tell you the tale. She was some dollygob church girl from Philadelphia come to tell us southrons how to run our lives, and Faulconer let her stroll all over him. He reckoned he had to free his niggers before she'd ever lie with him, so he did but she didn't anyway." Truslow laughed at this evidence of a fool befuddled. "She made a mock of him in front of all Virginia, and that's why he's making this Legion of his, to get his pride back. He thinks he'll be a warrior hero for Virginia. Now, take hold, boy."

Starbuck felt he had to protect his hero. "He's a good man!"

"He can afford to be good. His wealth's bigger than his wits, now take hold, boy. Or are you afraid of hard work, is that it? I tell you boy, work should be hard. No bread tastes good that comes easy. So take hold. Roper will be here soon enough. He gave his word, and Roper don't break his word. But you'll have to do till he comes." Starbuck took hold, tensed, pulled, and the hellish rhythm began again. He dared not think of the blisters being raised on his hands, nor of the burning muscles of his back, arms and legs. He just concentrated blindly on the downstroke, dragging the pit saw's teeth through the yellow wood and closing his eyes against the constant sifting of sawdust. In Boston, he thought, they had great steam-driven circular saws that could rip a dozen trunks into planks in the same time it took to make just one cut with this ripping saw, so why in God's name were men still using saw pits?

They paused again as Truslow hammered more wedges into the cut trunk. "So what's this war about, boy?"

"States' rights" was all Starbuck could say.

"What in hell's name does that mean?"

"It means, Mister Truslow, that America disagrees on how America should be governed."

"You could fill a bushel the way you talk, boy, but it don't add up to a pot of turnips. I thought we had a Constitution to tell us how to govern ourselves?"

"The Constitution has evidently failed us, Mister Truslow."

"You mean we ain't fighting to keep our niggers?"

"Oh, dear God," Starbuck sighed gently. He had once solemnly promised his father that he would never allow that word to be spoken in his presence, yet ever since he had met Dominique Demarest he had ignored the promise. Starbuck felt all his goodness, all his honor in the sight of God, slipping away like sand trickling through fingers.

"Well, boy? Are we fighting for our niggers or aren't we?"

Starbuck was leaning weakly on the dirt wall of the pit. He stirred himself to answer. "A faction of the North would dearly like to abolish slavery, yes. Others merely wish to stop it spreading westward, but the majority simply believe that the slave states should not dictate policy to the rest of America."

"What do the Yankees care about niggers? They ain't got none."

"It is a matter of morality, Mister Truslow," Starbuck said, trying to wipe the sweat-matted sawdust out of his eyes with his sawdust-matted sleeve.

"Does the Constitution say anything worth a piece of beaver shit about morality?" Truslow asked in a tone of genuine enquiry.

"No, sir. No, sir, it does not."

"I always reckon when a man speaks about morals he don't know nothing about what he's saying. Unless he's a preacher. So what do you think we should do with the niggers, boy?" Truslow asked.

"I think, sir"—Starbuck wished to hell he was anywhere but in this mud and sawdust pit answering this foulmouth's questions—"I think, sir," he said again as he tried desperately to think of anything that might make sense, "I think that every man, of whatever color, has an equal right before God and before man to an equal measure of dignity and happiness." Starbuck decided he sounded just like his elder brother, James, who could make any proposition sound pompous and lifeless. His father would have trumpeted the rights of the Negroes in a voice fit to rouse echoes from the angels, but Starbuck could not raise the energy for that kind of defiance.

"You like the niggers, is that the size of it?"

"I think they are fellow creatures, Mister Truslow."

"Hogs are fellow creatures, but it don't stop me killing 'em come berry time. Do you approve of slavery, boy?"

"No, Mister Truslow."

"Why not, boy?" The grating, mocking voice sounded from the brilliant sky above.

Starbuck tried to remember his father's arguments, not just the easy one that no man had the right to own another, but the more complex ones, such as how slavery enslaved the owner as much as it enslaved the possessed, and how it demeaned the slaveholder, and how it denied God's dignity to men who were the ebony image of God, and how it stultified the slavocracy's economy by driving white artisans north and west, but somehow none of the complex, persuasive answers would come and he settled for a simple condemnation instead. "Because it's wrong."

"You sound like a woman, boy." Truslow laughed. "So Faulconer thinks I should fight for his slave-holding friends, but no one in these hills can afford to feed and water a nigger, so why should I fight for them that can?"

"I don't know, sir, I really don't know." Starbuck was too tired to argue.

"So I'm supposed to fight for fifty bucks, is that it?" Truslow's voice was scathing. "Take hold, boy."

"Oh, God." The blisters on Starbuck's hands had broken into raw patches of torn skin that were oozing blood and pus, but he had no choice but to seize the pit saw's handle and drag it down. The pain of the first stroke made him whimper aloud, but the shame of the sound made him grip hard through the agony and to tear the steel teeth angrily through the wood.

"That's it, boy! You're learning!"

Starbuck felt as if he were dying, as if his whole body had become a shank of pain that bent and pulled, bent and pulled, and he shamelessly allowed his weight to sag onto the handles during each upstroke so that Truslow caught and helped his tiredness for a brief instant before he let his weight drag the saw down once again. The saw handle was soggy with blood, the breath was rasping in his throat, his legs could barely hold him upright and still the toothed steel plunged up and down, up and down, up and mercilessly down.

"You ain't gettin' tired now, boy, are you?"

"No."

"Hardly started, we are. You go and look at Pastor Mitchell's church in Nellysford, boy, and you'll see a wide heart-pine floor that me and my pa whipsawed in a single day. Pull on, boy, pull on!"

Starbuck had never known work like it. Sometimes, in the winter, he went to his Uncle Matthew's home in Lowell and they would saw ice from the frozen lake to fill the family ice house, but those excursions had been playful occasions, interspersed with snowball fights or bouts of wild skating along the lake banks beneath the icicle-hung trees. This plank sawing was relentless, cruel, remorseless, yet he dared not give up for he felt that his whole being, his future, his character, indeed his very soul were being weighed in the furious balance of Thomas Truslow's scorn.

"Hold there, boy, time for another wedge."

Starbuck let go of the pit saw's handle, staggered, tripped and half fell against the pit's wall. His hands were too painful to uncurl. His breath hurt. He had been half aware that a second man had come to the saw pit and had been chatting to Truslow these last few painful minutes, but he did not want to look up and see whoever else was witnessing this humiliation.

"You ever see anything to match it, Roper?" Truslow's voice was mocking.

Starbuck still did not look up.

"This is Roper, boy," Truslow said. "Say your greeting."

"Good day, Mister Roper," Starbuck managed to say.

"He calls you mister!" Truslow found that amusing. "He thinks you niggers are his fellow creatures, Roper. Says you've got the same equal rights before God as he has. You reckon that's how God sees it, Roper?"

Roper paused to inspect the exhausted Starbuck. "I reckon God would want me in his bosom long before he ever took that," Roper finally answered, and Starbuck looked unwillingly upward to see that Roper was a tall black man who was clearly amused by Starbuck's predicament. "He don't look good for nothing, does he now?" Roper said.

"He ain't a bad worker," Truslow, astonishingly, came to Starbuck's defense, and Starbuck, hearing it, felt as though he had never in all his life received a compliment half so valuable. Truslow, the compliment delivered, jumped down into the pit. "Now I'll show you how it's done, boy." Truslow took hold of the pit saw's handle, nodded up at Roper, and suddenly the great blade of steel blurred as the two men went into an instant and much practiced rhythm. "This is how you do it!" Truslow shouted over the saw's ringing noise to the dazed Starbuck. "Let the steel do the work! You don't fight it, you let it slice the wood for you. Roper and me could cut half the forests in America without catching breath." Truslow was using one hand only, and standing to one side of the work so that the flood of dust and chips did not stream onto his face. "So what brings you here, boy?"

"I told you, a letter from—"

"I mean what's a Yankee doing in Virginia. You are a Yankee, aren't you?"

Starbuck, remembering Washington Faulconer's assertion of how much this man hated Yankees, decided to brazen it out. "And proud of it, yes."

Truslow jetted a stream of tobacco juice into a corner of the pit. "So what are you doing here?"

Starbuck decided this was not the time to talk of Mademoiselle Demarest, nor of the *Tom* company, so offered an abbreviated and less-anguished version of his story. "I've fallen out with my family and taken shelter with Mister Faulconer."

"Why him?"

"I am a close friend of Adam Faulconer."

"Are you now?" Truslow actually seemed to approve. "Where is Adam?"

"The last we heard he was in Chicago."

"Doing what?"

"He works with the Christian Peace Commission. They hold prayer meetings and distribute tracts."

Truslow laughed. "Tracts and prayers won't help, because America don't want peace, boy. You Yankees want to tell us how to live our lives, just like the British did last century, but we ain't any better listeners now than we were then. Nor is it their business. Who owns the house uses the best broom, boy. I'll tell you what the North wants, boy." Truslow, while talking, was whipping the saw up and down in his slicing, tireless rhythm. "The North wants to give us more government, that's what they want. It's these Prussians, that's what I reckon. They keep telling the Yankees how to make better government, and you Yankees is fool enough to listen, but I tell you it's too late now."

"Too late?"

"You can't mend a broken egg, boy. America's in two pieces, and the North will sell herself to the Prussians and we'll mess through as we are."

Starbuck was far too tired to care about the extraordinary theories that Truslow had about Prussia. "And the war?"

"We just have to win it. See the Yankees off. I don't want to tell them how to live, so long as they don't tell me."

"So you'll fight?" Starbuck asked, sensing some hope for the success of his errand.

"Of course I'll fight. But not for fifty dollars." Truslow paused as Roper hammered a wedge into the new cut.

Starbuck, whose breath was slowly coming back, frowned. "I'm not empowered to offer more, Mister Truslow."

"I don't want more. I'll fight because I want to fight, and if I weren't wanting to fight then fifty times fifty dollars wouldn't buy me, though Faulconer would never understood that." Truslow paused to spit a stream of viscous tobacco juice. "His father now, he knew that a fed hound never hunts, but Washington? He's a milksop, and he always pays to get what he wants, but I ain't for sale. I'll fight to keep America the way she is, boy, because the way she is makes her the best goddamned country in the whole goddamned world, and if that means killing a passel of you chicken-shit northerners to keep her that way, then so be it. Are you ready, Roper?"

The saw slashed down again, leaving Starbuck to wonder why Washington Faulconer had been willing to pay so dearly for Truslow's enlistment. Was it just because this man could bring other hard men from the mountains? In which case, Starbuck thought, it would be money well spent, for a regiment of hardscrabble demons like Truslow would surely be invincible.

"So what are you trained to be, boy?" Truslow kept sawing as he asked the question.

Starbuck was tempted to lie, but he had neither the energy nor the will to sustain a fiction. "A preacher," he answered wearily.

The sawing abruptly stopped, causing Roper to protest as his rhythm was broken. Truslow ignored the protest. "You're a preacher?"

"I was training to be a minister." Starbuck offered a more exact definition.

"A man of God?"

"I hope so, yes. Indeed I do." Except he knew he was not worthy and the knowledge of his backsliding was bitter.

Truslow stared incredulously at Starbuck and then, astonishingly, he wiped his hands down his filthy clothes as though trying to smarten himself up for his visitor. "I've got work for you," he announced grimly.

Starbuck glanced at the wicked-toothed saw. "But ..."

"Preacher's work," Truslow said curtly. "Roper! Ladder."

Roper dropped a homemade ladder into the pit and Starbuck, flinching from the pain in his hands, let himself be chivied up its crude rungs.

"Did you bring your book?" Truslow demanded as he followed Starbuck up the ladder.

"Book?"

"All preachers have books. Never mind, there's one in the house. Roper! You want to ride down to the Decker house? Tell Sally and Robert to come here fast. Take the man's horse. What's your name, mister?"

"Starbuck. Nathaniel Starbuck."

The name evidently meant nothing to Truslow. "Take Mister Starbuck's mare," he called to Roper, "and tell Sally I won't take no for an answer!" All these instructions had been hurled over Truslow's shoulders as he hurried to his log house. The dog scurried aside as its master stalked past, then lay staring malevolently at Starbuck, growling deep in its throat.

"You don't mind if I take the horse?" Roper asked. "Not to worry. I know her. I used to work for Mister Faulconer. I know this mare, Pocahontas, isn't she?"

Starbuck waved a feeble hand in assent. "Who is Sally?"

"Truslow's daughter." Roper chuckled as he untied the mare's bridle and adjusted the saddle. "She's a wild one, but you know what they say of women. They're the devil's nets, and young Sally will snare a few souls before she's through. She don't live here now. When her mother was dying she took herself off to Missus Decker, who can't abide Truslow." Roper seemed amused by the human tangle. He swung himself into Pocahontas's saddle. "I'll be off, Mister Truslow!" he called toward the cabin.

"Go on, Roper! Go!" Truslow emerged from the house carrying an enormous Bible that had lost its back cover and had a broken spine. "Hold it, mister." He thrust the delapidated Bible at Starbuck, then bent over a water butt and scooped handfuls of rainwater over his scalp. He tried to pat the matted filthy hair into some semblance of order, then crammed his greasy hat back into place before beckoning to Starbuck. "Come on, mister."

Starbuck followed Truslow across the clearing. Flies buzzed in the warm evening air. Starbuck, cradling the Bible in his forearms to spare his skinned palms, tried to explain the misunderstanding to Thomas Truslow. "I'm not an ordained minister, Mister Truslow."

"What's ordained mean?" Truslow had stopped at the edge of the clearing and was unbuttoning his filthy jeans. He stared at Starbuck, evidently expecting an answer, then began to urinate. "It keeps the deer off the crop," he explained. "So what's ordained mean?"

"It means that I have not been called by a congregation to be their pastor."

"But you've got the book learning?"

"Yes, most of it."

"And you could be ordained?"

Starbuck was immediately assailed with guilt about Mademoiselle Dominique Demarest. "I'm not sure I want to be, anymore."

"But you could be?" Truslow insisted.

"I suppose so, yes."

"Then you're good enough for me. Come on." He buttoned his trousers and beckoned Starbuck under the trees to where, in a tended patch of grass and beneath a tree that was brilliant with red blossom, a single grave lay. The grave marker was a broad piece of wood, rammed into the earth and marked with the one word *Emly*. The grave did not look old, for its blossom-littered earth ridge was still sparse with grass. "She was my wife," Truslow said in a surprisingly meek and almost shy voice.

"I'm sorry."

"Died Christmas Day." Truslow blinked, and suddenly Starbuck felt a wave of sorrow come from the small, urgent man, a wave every bit as forceful and overwhelming as Truslow's more habitual emanation of violence. Truslow seemed unable to speak, as though there were not words to express what he felt. "Emily was a good wife," he finally said, "and I was a good husband to her. She made me that. A good woman can do that to a man. She can make a man good."

"Was she sick?" Starbuck asked uneasily.

Truslow nodded. He had taken off his greasy hat, which he now held awkwardly in his strong hands. "Congestion of the brain. It weren't an easy death."

"I'm sorry," Starbuck said inadequately.

"There was a man might have saved her. A Yankee." Truslow spoke the last word with a sour hatred that made Starbuck shiver. "He was a fancy doctor from up north. He was visiting relatives in the valley last Thanksgiving." He jerked his head westward, indicating the Shenandoah Valley beyond the intervening mountains. "Doctor Danson told me of him, said he could work miracles, so I rode over and begged him to come up and see my Emily. She couldn't be moved, see. I went on bended knee." Truslow fell silent, remembering the humiliation, then shook his head. "The man refused to move. Said there was nothing he could do, but the truth was he didn't want to stir off his fat ass and mount a horse in that rain. They ran me off the property."

Starbuck had never heard of anyone being cured of congestion of the brain and suspected the Yankee doctor had known all along that anything he tried would be a waste of time, but how was anyone to persuade a man like Thomas Truslow of that truth?

"She died on Christmas Day," Truslow went on softly. "The snow was thick up here then, like a blanket. Just me and her, the girl had run off, damn her skin."

"Sally?"

"Hell, yes." Truslow was standing to attention now with his hands crossed awkwardly over his breast, almost as if he was imitating the death stance of his beloved Emily. "Emily and me weren't married proper," he confessed to Starbuck. "She ran off with me the year before I went to be a soldier. I was just sixteen, she weren't a day older, but she was already married. We were wrong, and we both knew it, but it was like we couldn't help ourselves." There were tears in his eyes, and Starbuck suddenly felt glad to know that this tough man had once behaved as stupidly and foolishly as Starbuck had himself just behaved. "I loved her," Truslow went on, "and that's the truth of it, though Pastor Mitchell wouldn't wed us because he said we were sinners."

"I'm sure he should have made no such judgment," Starbuck said gravely.

"I reckon he should. It was his job to judge us. What else is a preacher for except to teach us conduct? I ain't complaining, but God gave us his punishment, Mister Starbuck. Only one of our children lived, and she broke our hearts, and now Emily's dead and I'm left alone. God is not mocked, Mister Starbuck."

Suddenly, unexpectedly, Starbuck felt an immense surge of sympathy for this awkward, hard, difficult man who stood so clumsily beside the grave he must have dug himself. Or perhaps Roper had helped him, or one of the other fugitive men who lived in this high valley out of sight of the magistrates and the taxmen who infested the plains. At Christmastime, too, and Starbuck imagined them carrying the limp body out into the snow and hacking down into the cold ground.

"We weren't married proper, and she were never buried proper, not with a man of God to see her home, and that's what I want you to do for her. You're to say the right words, Mister Starbuck. Say them for Emily, because if you say the right words then God will take her in."

"I'm sure he will." Starbuck felt entirely inadequate to the moment.

"So say them." There was no violence in Thomas Truslow now, just a terrible vulnerability.

There was silence in the small glade. The evening shadows stretched long. Oh dear God, Starbuck thought, but I am not worthy, not nearly worthy. God will not listen to me, a sinner, yet are we not all sinners? And the truth, surely, was that God had already heard Thomas Truslow's prayer, for Truslow's anguish was more eloquent than any litany that Starbuck's education could provide. Yet Thomas Truslow needed the comfort of ritual, of old words lovingly said, and Starbuck gripped the book tight, closed his eyes and raised his face toward the dusk-shadowed blossoms, but suddenly he felt a fool and an imposter and no words would come. He opened his mouth, but he could not speak.

"That's right," Truslow said, "take your time."

Starbuck tried to think of a passage of scripture that would give him a start. His throat was dry. He opened his eyes and suddenly a verse came to him. "Man that is born of a woman," he began, but his voice was scratchy and uncertain so he began again, "man that is born of a woman is of few days, and full of trouble."

"Amen," Thomas Truslow said, "amen to that."

"He cometh forth like a flower …"

"She was, she was, praise God, she was."

"And is cut down."

"The Lord took her, the Lord took her." Truslow, his eyes closed, rocked back and forth as he tried to summon all his intensity.

"He fleeth also as a shadow, and continueth not."

"God help us sinners," Truslow said, "God help us."

Starbuck was suddenly dumb. He had quoted the first two verses of the fourteenth chapter of Job, and suddenly he was remembering the fourth verse, which asked who can bring a clean thing from an unclean? Then gave its hard answer, no one. And surely Truslow's unsanctified household had been unclean?

"Pray, Mister, pray," Truslow pleaded.

"Oh Lord God"—Starbuck clenched his eyes against the sun's dying light—"remember Emily who was thy servant, thy handmaid, and who was snatched from this world into thy greater glory."

"She was, she was!" Truslow almost wailed the confirmation.

"Remember Emily Truslow—" Starbuck went on lamely.

"Mallory," Truslow interrupted, "that was her proper name, Emily Marjory Mallory. And shouldn't we kneel?" He snatched off his hat and dropped onto the soft loamy soil.

Starbuck also dropped to his knees. "Oh, Lord," he began again, and for a moment he was speechless, but then, from nowhere it seemed, the words began to flow. He felt Truslow's grief fill him, and in turn he tried to lay that grief upon the Lord. Truslow moaned as he listened to the prayer, while Starbuck raised his face to the green leaves as though he could project his words on strong hard wings out beyond the trees, out beyond the darkening sky, out beyond the first pale stars, out to where God reigned in all his terrible brooding majesty. The prayer was good, and Starbuck felt its power and wondered why he could not pray for himself as he prayed for this unknown woman. "Oh God," he finished, and there were tears on his face as his prayer came to an end, "oh dear God, hear our prayer, hear us, hear us."

And then there was silence again, except for the wind in the leaves and the sound of the birds and from somewhere in the valley a lone dog's barking. Starbuck opened his eyes to see that Truslow's dirty face was streaked with tears, yet the small man looked oddly happy. He was leaning forward to hold his stubby, strong fingers into the dirt of the grave as if, by thus holding the earth above his Emily's corpse, he could talk with her.

"I'll be going to war, Emily," he said, without any embarrassment at so addressing his dead woman in Starbuck's presence. "Faulconer's a fool, and I won't be going for his sake, but we've got kin in his ranks, and I'll go for them. Your brother's joined this so-called Legion, and cousin Tom is there, and you'd want me to look after them both, girl, so I will. And Sally's going to be just dandy. She's got her man now and she's going to be looked after, and you can just wait for me, my darling, and I'll be with you in God's time. This is Mister Starbuck who prayed for you. He did it well, didn't he?" Truslow was weeping, but now he pulled his fingers free of the soil and wiped them against his jeans before cuffing at his cheeks. "You pray well," he said to Starbuck.

"I think perhaps your prayer was heard without me," Starbuck said modestly.

"A man can never be sure enough, though, can he? And God will soon be deafened with prayers. War does that, so I'm glad we put our word in before the battles start drowning his ears with words. Emily will have enjoyed hearing you pray. She always did like a good prayer. Now I want you to pray over Sally."

Oh God, Starbuck thought, but this was going too far! "You want me to do what, Mister Truslow?"

"Pray over Sally. She's been a disappointment to us." Truslow climbed to his feet and pulled his wide-brimmed hat over his hair. He stared at the grave as he went on with his tale. "She's not like her mother, nor like me. I don't know what bad wind brought her to us, but she came and I promised Emily as how I'd look after her, and I will. She's bare fifteen now and going to have a child, you see."

"Oh." Starbuck did not know what else to say. Fifteen! That was the same age as his younger sister, Martha, and Starbuck still thought of Martha as a child. At fifteen, Starbuck thought, he had not even known where babies came from, assuming they were issued by the authorities in some secret, fuss-laden ceremony involving women, the church and doctors.

"She says it's young Decker's babe, and maybe it is. And maybe it isn't. You tell me Ridley was here last week? That worries me. He's been sniffing round my Sally like she was on heat and him a dog. I was down the valley last week on business, so who knows where she was?"

Starbuck's first impulse was to declare that Ridley was engaged to Anna Faulconer, so could not be responsible for Sally Truslow's pregnancy, but some impulse told him that such a naive protest would be met with a bitter scorn and so, not knowing what else to say, he sensibly said nothing.

"She's not like her mother," Truslow spoke on, more to himself than to Starbuck. "There's a wildness in her, see? Maybe it's mine, but it weren't Emily's. But she says it's Robert Decker's babe, so let it be so. And he believes her and says he'll marry her, so let that be so too." Truslow stooped and plucked a weed from the grave. "That's where Sally is now," he explained to Starbuck, "with the Deckers. She said she couldn't abide me, but it was her mother's pain and dying she couldn't abide. Now she's pregnant, so she needs to be married with a home of her own, not living on charity. I promised Emily I'd look after Sally, so that's what I'm doing. I'll give Sally and her boy this homestead, and they can raise the child here. They won't want me. Sally and me have never seen eye to eye, so she and young Decker can take this place and be proper together. And that's what I want you to do, Mister Starbuck. I want you to marry them proper. They're on their way here now."

"But I can't marry them!" Starbuck protested.

"If you can send my Emily's soul to heaven, you can marry my daughter to Robert Decker."

Starbuck wondered how in God's name he was to correct Thomas Truslow's egregious misunderstanding of both theology and the civil powers. "If she is to be married," he insisted, "then she must go before a magistrate and—"

"God bears a bigger clout than a magistrate." Truslow turned and walked away from the grave. "Sally will be married by a man of God, and that's more important than being wed by some buzzard of a lawyer who just wants his fee."

"But I'm not ordained!"

"Don't start that excuse again. You'll do for me. I've heard you, Mister Starbuck, and if God don't listen to your words then he won't listen to any man's. And if my Sally is to be married, then I want her to be properly married by God's law. I don't want her roaming again. She's been wild, but it's time she was settled down. So you pray over her."

Starbuck was not at all sure that prayer could stop a girl roaming, but he did not like to say as much to Thomas Truslow. "Why don't you take her down to the valley? There must be proper ministers there who'll marry them?"

"The ministers in the valley, mister"—Truslow had turned to stab a finger hard into Starbuck's chest to emphasize his words—"were too high and goddamned mighty to bury my Emily, so believe me, mister, they are too high and goddamned mighty to wed my daughter to her boy. And are you now trying to tell me that you're also too good for the likes of us?" His finger rammed one last time into Starbuck's chest, then stayed there.

"I think it would be a privilege to perform the service for your daughter, sir," Starbuck said hurriedly.

Sally Truslow and her boy came just after dark. Roper brought them, leading Sally on the horse. She dismounted in front of her father's porch where a lantern-shielded candle burned. She kept her face low, not daring to look up into her father's face. She wore a black bonnet and a blue dress. She was slim waisted, not yet showing her pregnancy.

Beside her was a young man with a round and innocent face. He was clean-shaven, indeed he looked as if he could not grow a beard if he tried. He might have been sixteen, but Starbuck guessed he was younger. Robert Decker had sandy coarse hair, trusting blue eyes, and a quick smile, which he struggled to subdue as he nodded a cautious greeting to his future father-in-law. "Mister Truslow," he said warily.

"Robert Decker," Truslow said, "you're to meet Nathaniel Starbuck. He's a man of God and he's agreed to marry you and Sally."

Robert Decker, fidgeting with his round hat that he held in front of him with both hands, nodded cheerfully at Starbuck. "Right pleased to make your acquaintance, mister."

"Look up, Sally!" Truslow growled.

"I ain't sure I want to be married." She whined the protest.

"You'll do as you're told to do," her father growled.

"I want to be church married!" the girl insisted. "Like Laura Taylor was, by a proper preacherman!" Starbuck hardly heard what she said, or even cared what she said, because instead he was gazing at Sally Truslow and wondering why God ordained these mysteries. Why was some country girl, whelped off an adulteress to a hard-bitten man, born to make the very sun seem dim? For Sally Truslow was beautiful. Her eyes were blue as the sky over the Nantucket sea, her face sweet as honey, her lips as full and inviting as a man's dreams could want. Her hair was a dark brown, streaked with lighter veins and rich in the lantern's light. "A marriage should be proper," she complained, "not like jumping over a broomstick." Leaping a broomstick was the deep country way of wedlock, or the slave's way of signifying a marriage.

"You planning on raising the child on your own, Sally," Truslow demanded, "without marrying?"

"You can't do that, Sally," Robert Decker said with a pathetic anxiety. "You need a man to work for you, to look after you."

"Maybe there won't be any child," she said petulantly.

Truslow's hand moved like lightning, slashing hard and open across his daughter's cheek. The sound of the blow was like a whip cracking. "You kill that baby," he threatened, "and I'll take a leather to your skin that will leave your bones like bed slats. You hear me?"

"I won't do nothing." She was crying, cringing from the vicious blow. Her face had reddened from the slap, but there was still a cunning belligerence in her eyes.

"You know what I do to a cow that won't carry its young?" Truslow shouted at her. "I slaughter 'em. You think anyone would care if I put another aborting bitch under the dirt?"

"I ain't going to do nothing! I told you! I'll be a good girl!"

"She will, Mister Truslow," Robert Decker said. "She won't do anything."

Roper, impassive, stood behind the couple as Truslow stared hard into Robert Decker's eyes. "Why do you want to marry her, Robert?"

"I'm real fond of her, Mister Truslow." He was embarrassed to make the admission, but grinned and looked sideways at Sally. "And it's my baby. I just know it is."

"I'm going to have you married proper," Truslow looked back to his daughter, "by Mister Starbuck, who knows how to talk to God, and if you break your vows, Sally, then God will whip your hide till it bleeds dry. God won't be mocked, girl. You offend him and you'll end up like your mother, dead before your time and food to worms."

"I'll be a good girl," Sally whined, and she looked straight at Starbuck for the first time, and Starbuck's breath checked in his throat as he stared back. Once, when Starbuck had been a small child, his Uncle Matthew had taken him to Faneuil Hall to see a demonstration of the electrical force, and Starbuck had held hands in a ring of onlookers as the lecturer fed a current through their linked bodies. He felt then something of what

he experienced now, a tingling thrill that momentarily made the rest of
the world seem unimportant. Then, as soon as he recognized the excitement, he felt a kind of desperation. This feeling was sin. It was the devil's
work. Surely he must be soul sick? For surely no ordinary, decent man
would be so entranced by every girl who had a pretty face? Then, jeal-
ously, he wondered whether Thomas Truslow's suspicions were right and
that Ethan Ridley had been this girl's sweetheart, and Starbuck felt a stab
of corrosive jealousy as sharp as a blade, then a fierce anger that Ridley
could deceive Washington and Anna Faulconer. "Are you a proper
preacherman?" Sally cuffed her nose and asked Starbuck.

"I wouldn't ask him to wed you otherwise," her father insisted.

"I was asking him myself," she said defiantly, keeping her eyes on
Starbuck, and he knew she had seen clean into his soul. She was seeing
his lust and his weakness, his sinfulness and his fear. Starbuck's father had
often warned him against the powers of women, and Starbuck had
thought he had met those powers at their most devilish in Mademoiselle
Dominique Demarest, but Dominique had possessed nothing to compare
with this girl's intensity. "And if a girl can't ask a preacherman who's marrying her just what kind of a preacherman he is," Sally insisted, "then
what can she ask?" Her voice was low, like her father's, but where his gen-
erated fear, hers suggested something infinitely more dangerous. "So are
you a proper preacherman, mister?" she demanded of Starbuck again.

"Yes." Starbuck told the lie for the sake of Thomas Truslow, and
because he dared not let the truth enslave him to this girl.

"I guess we're all ready, then," Sally said defiantly. She did not want
to be married, but neither did she want to appear browbeaten. "You got a
ring for us, pa?"

The question appeared casual, but Starbuck was immediately aware
that it carried a heavy freight of emotion. Truslow stared defiantly at his
daughter, the mark of his hand still across her cheek, but she matched his
defiance. Robert Decker looked from daughter to father, then back to the
daughter, and had the sense to keep his mouth shut.

"The ring's special," Truslow said.

"You holding it for another woman, is that it?" Sally sneered the
question, and for a second Starbuck thought Truslow would hit her again,
but instead he pushed a hand into a pocket of his coat and brought out a
small leather bag. He untied the drawstrings and took out a scrap of blue
cloth, which he unwrapped to reveal a ring. It glinted in the darkness, a
ring of silver, etched with some design that Starbuck could not decipher.

"This was your mother's ring," Truslow said.

"And Ma always said it should be mine," Sally insisted.

"I should have buried it with her." Truslow gazed down at the ring,
which was clearly a relic of great power for him, but then, impulsively, as

though he knew he would regret the decision, he shoved the ring toward Starbuck. "Say the words," Truslow snapped.

Roper snatched off his hat while young Decker composed his face into a serious expression. Sally licked her lips and smiled at Starbuck, who looked down at the silver ring laying on the ragged Bible. He saw the ring was engraved with words, but, in the dim light, he could not make them out. My God, he thought, but just what words was he to find for this travesty of a marriage act? This was a worse ordeal than the saw pit.

"Speak up, mister," Truslow growled.

"God has ordained marriage," Starbuck heard himself saying as he desperately tried to remember the marriage services he had attended in Boston, "to be an instrument of his love, and an institution in which we can bring our children into this world to be his servants. The commandments of marriage are simple, that you love one another." He had been looking at Robert Decker as he spoke, and the young man nodded eagerly, as though Starbuck needed the reassurance, and Starbuck felt a terrible sob of pity for this honest fool who was being yoked to a temptress, then he glanced at Sally. "And that you are faithful to each other until death do you part."

She smiled at Starbuck, and whatever words he had been about to say vanished like mist under a midday sun. He opened his mouth to speak, found nothing to say, so closed it.

"You hear the man, Sally Truslow?" her father demanded.

"Hell, yes, I ain't deaf."

"Take the ring, Robert," Starbuck ordered, and was amazed at his temerity. He had been taught in seminary that the sacraments were solemn rituals offered to God by special men, the most Godly of men, yet here he was, a sinner, inventing this tawdry service in the flickering light of a moth-haunted lantern under a nascent Virginia moon. "Put your right hand on the Bible," he told Robert, who lay his work-stained hand on the broken-spined family Bible that Starbuck was still holding. "Say after me," Starbuck said, and somehow he invented a marriage oath that he administered to each in turn, and afterward he told Robert to put the ring on Sally's finger, and then he declared them man and wife, and closed his eyes and raised his shut eyelids to the starry heaven. "May the blessing of Almighty God," Starbuck said, "and his love, and his protection, be with you each, and keep you both from harm from this time on until the world's ending. We ask it in the name of him who loved us so much that he gave his only son for our redemption. Amen."

"Amen to that," Thomas Truslow said, "and amen."

"Praise be, amen." Roper spoke from behind the couple.

"Amen and amen." Robert Decker's face was suffused with happiness.

"Is that all there is?" Sally Decker asked.

"The rest of your life is all there is," her father snapped, "and you've made a promise to be faithful, and you keep that promise, girl, or you'll suffer." He snatched at her left hand and, though Sally tried to shrink back, he dragged her hard toward him. He looked down at the silver ring on her finger. "And you look after that ring, girl."

Sally said nothing and Starbuck got the impression that by gaining the ring from her father she had won a victory over him, and the victory was far more important to her than the fact of the wedding.

Truslow let her hand go. "You'll write their names in the Bible?" he asked Starbuck. "To make it proper?"

"Of course," Starbuck said.

"There's a table in the house," Truslow said, "and a pencil in the jar on the mantel. Kick the dog if he troubles you."

Starbuck carried the lantern and the Bible into the house that comprised one simply furnished room. There was a box bed, a table, a chair, two trunks, a fireplace with a pothook, a bench, a spinning wheel, a meal sifter, a rack of guns, a scythe and a framed portrait of Andrew Jackson. Starbuck sat at the table, opened the Bible and found the family register. He wished he had ink to write the entry, but Thomas Truslow's pencil would have to suffice. He looked at the names in the register, which stretched back to when the first Truslows had come to the New World in 1710, and saw that someone had written the fact of Emily Truslow's death on the last filled line of the register, writing her name in ill-formed block capitals and adding Mallory afterward in square brackets in case God did not know who Emily Truslow really was. Above that was the simple record of Sally Emily Truslow's birth in May 1846, and Starbuck realized the girl was just two days over her fifteenth birthday.

"Sunday, May 26, 1861" he wrote with difficulty, hampered by the pain in his blistered hands. "Sally Truslow to Robert Decker, united in holy matrimony." There was a column where the officiating minister was supposed to write his name. Starbuck hesitated, then put his name there: Nathaniel Joseph Starbuck.

"You ain't a real preacherman, are you?" Sally had come into the house and challenged him with her stare.

"God makes us what we are, and what God has made me is not for you to question," Starbuck said as sternly as he could, and felt horribly pompous, but he feared this girl's effect on him and so retreated into pomposity.

She laughed, knowing he had lied. "You got a real nice voice, I will say that." She came to the table and looked down at the open Bible. "I can't read. A man promised to teach me, but he ain't had time yet."

Starbuck feared he knew who the man was, and though one part of him did not want confirmation, another part wanted the suspicion given solidity. "Did Ethan Ridley promise you that?" he asked her.

"You know Ethan?" Sally sounded surprised, then she nodded. "Ethan promised he'd teach me to read," she said, "he promised me a lot, but he hasn't kept a one of the promises. Not yet, anyways, but there's still time, isn't there?"

"Is there?" Starbuck asked. He told himself he was shocked by Ridley's betrayal of the gentle Anna Faulconer, but he also knew that he was horribly jealous of Ethan Ridley.

"I like Ethan." Sally was provoking Starbuck now. "He drew my picture. It was real good."

"He's a good artist," Starbuck said, trying to keep his voice toneless.

Sally was standing over him. "Ethan says he's going to take me away one day. Make me a real lady. He said he'd give me pearls, and a ring for my finger. A gold one. A proper ring, not like this one." She reached out her newly beringed finger and stroked Starbuck's hand, sending a jolt like lightning straight to his heart. She lowered her voice into something scarce above a conspiratorial whisper. "Would you do that for me, preacherman?"

"I'd be happy to teach you to read, Mrs. Decker." Starbuck felt lightheaded. He knew he should move his hand from beneath that stroking finger, but he did not want to, he could not. He was captured by her. He stared at the ring. The letters cut into the silver were worn, but just legible. *Je t'aime*, they said. It was a cheap French ring for lovers, of no great value except to the man whose love had worn it.

"You know what the ring says, preacherman?" Sally asked him.

"Yes."

"Tell me."

He looked up into her eyes and immediately had to look down again. The lust was like a pain in him.

"What does it say, mister?"

"It's French."

"But what does it say?" Her finger was still on his hand, pressing lightly.

"It says 'I love you.'" He could not look at her.

She laughed very softly and drew her touch down his hand, tracing the line of his longest finger. "Would you give me pearls? Like Ethan says he will?" She was mocking him.

"I would try." He should not have said it, he was not even sure he had meant to say it, he just heard himself speaking, and there was such a sadness in his voice.

"You know something, preacherman?"

"What?" He looked up at her.

"You've got eyes just like my pa."

"I do?"

Her finger still rested on his hand. "I ain't real married, am I?" She was no longer teasing, but was suddenly wistful. Starbuck said nothing and she looked hurt. "Would you really help me?" she asked, and there was a genuine note of despair in her voice. She had abandoned her flirtation and had spoken like an unhappy child.

"Yes," Starbuck said, even though he knew he should not have promised such help.

"I can't stay up here," Sally said. "I just want to be away from here."

"If I can help you, I will," Starbuck said, and knew he was promising more than he could deliver, and that the promise came from foolishness, yet even so he wanted her to trust him. "I promise you I will help," he said, and he moved his hand to take hold of hers, but then she jerked her fingers away as the cabin door opened.

"As you're here, girl," Truslow said, "then make us some supper. There's a fowl in the pot."

"I ain't your cook any longer," Sally complained, then dodged aside as her father raised his hand. Starbuck closed the Bible and wondered if his betrayal was obvious to Truslow. The girl cooked, and Starbuck gazed into the fire, dreaming.

Next morning Thomas Truslow gave his house and his land and his best leather belt to Robert Decker. He charged the boy only to look after Emily's grave. "Roper will help you with the land. He knows what grows best and how, and he knows the beasts I'm leaving you. He's your tenant now, but he's a good neighbor and he'll help you, boy, but you help him too. Good neighbors make for a good living."

"Yes, sir."

"And Roper will be using the saw pit these next days. Let him."

"Yes, sir."

"And the belt's for Sally. Don't let her be your master. One taste of pain and she'll learn her place."

"Yes, sir," Robert Decker said again, but without conviction.

"I'm going to war, boy," Truslow said, "and the Lord alone knows when I'll be back. Or even if."

"I ought to be fighting, sir. It ain't right that I can't fight."

"You can't." Truslow was brusque. "You've a woman and a child to look after. I've none. I've had my life, so I might as well spend what's left of it teaching the Yankees to keep their thieving hands to themselves." He shifted the tobacco wad in his cheek, spat, then looked back at Decker. "Make sure she looks after that ring, boy. It belonged to my Emily, and I ain't even sure I should have given it to her, except that's what Emily herself wanted."

Sally stayed in the cabin. Starbuck wanted her to come out. He wanted to have a few moments with her. He wanted to speak to her, to say that he understood her unhappiness and that he shared it, but Sally stayed hidden and Truslow did not demand to see her. So far as Starbuck could tell Truslow did not even bid farewell to his daughter. Instead he selected a bowie knife, a long rifle and a pistol, and left the rest of his weapons for his son-in-law. Then he saddled a sullen-looking horse, spent a few private moments at the grave of his Emily, and afterward led Starbuck toward the ridge.

The sun was shining, making the leaves seem luminous. Truslow paused at the ridge's crest, not to gaze back at the home he was leaving, but rather to stare east to where the land lay bright and clean, mile after mile of America, stretching toward the sea and waiting for the butchers to begin its dismembering.

PART TWO

5

Dust sifted the air above Richmond's Central Fair Grounds. The dust was being kicked up by the eleven regiments that were marching and countermarching on the massive field that had been abraded free of every last blade of grass, then pounded into a fine powder by the endless exercises of drill that Major General Robert Lee insisted on inflicting upon the recruits who came to defend the Confederacy. The reddish-brown dust had been carried by the wind to settle on every wall, roof and hedge within a half mile of the Fair Grounds so that even the blossoms of the magnolias that edged the site seemed to have been dulled into a curious pale brick color. Ethan Ridley's uniform was powdered with the dust, giving the gray cloth a fleshlike tinge. Ridley had come to the Fair Grounds to find his plump and myopic half-brother, Belvedere Delaney, who was mounted on a sway-backed piebald horse, which he sat with all the elegance of a collapsing sack as he watched the regiments march smartly past. Delaney, though in civilian clothes, saluted the passing troops with all the aplomb of a full general. "I'm practicing for when I join the army, Ethan," he greeted his half-brother, showing no surprise at Ridley's sudden appearance in the city.

"You'll not join the army, Bev, you're too soft."

"On the contrary, Ethan, I am to be a legal officer. I invented the post myself and suggested it to the governor, who was kind enough to have me commissioned. I shall be a captain for the moment, but I shall promote myself if I find that rank too lowly for a man of my tastes and distinction. Well done, men! Well done! Very smart!" Delaney called these encouragements to a bemused company of Alabamian infantry that was marching past the applauding spectators. A visit to these Fair Grounds was a popular excursion for the citizens of Richmond, who now found themselves living in the new capital of the Confederate States of America, a fact that gave especial pleasure to Belvedere Delaney. "The more politicians there are in Richmond then the greater will be the corruption," he explained to Ridley, "and the greater the corruption, the greater the profit. I doubt we shall ever compete with Washington in these matters, but we must do our best in the short time God grants us." Delaney bestowed a beatific smile on his scowling half-brother. "So how long shall you be in Richmond this time? I presume you will be using Grace Street? Did George tell you I was here?" George was Delaney's manservant, a slave, but with the manners and demeanor of an aristocrat. Ridley did not really like the supercilious George, but he had to put up with the slave if he was to use his brother's rooms on Grace Street. "So just what brings you to our fair city?" Delaney enquired. "Beyond the charms of my company, of course."

"Cannon. Two six pounders that Faulconer discovered in Bowers Foundry. The guns were supposed to be melted down, but Faulconer's bought them."

"No profit for us there, then," Delaney said.

"He needs ammunition"—Ridley paused to light a cigar—"and limbers. And caissons."

"Ah! I hear the soft chink of dollars changing hands," Belvedere Delaney said with delight, then turned to watch a regiment of Virginian militia march past with the fine precision of shuttles on a mechanical loom. "If all the troops were as good as that," he told his half-brother, "then the war would be as good as won, but my Lord, you should see some of the rabble that turns up wanting to fight. Yesterday I saw a company that called itself McGarritty's Mounted Lincoln Killers, McGarritty being their self-proclaimed colonel, you understand, and the fourteen mudsills shared ten horses, two swords, four shotguns and a hanging rope between them. The rope was twenty feet long, with a noose, and more than adequate for Abe, they told me."

Ethan Ridley was not interested in the rarer breeds of southern soldier, but only in the profits he might make with his half-brother's help. "You've got six-pounder ammunition?"

"In lavish quantities, I'm afraid," Delaney confessed. "We're virtually giving the round shot away. But we can certainly make an indecent profit on the canister and shell." He paused to touch his hat to a state senator who had been avid for war before the first guns fired, but who had since discovered a lame leg, a crooked back and a troublesome liver. The invalid politician, propped up with lavish cushions in his carriage, feebly raised his gold-headed cane in response to Delaney's salute. "And I can certainly find some limbers and caissons at a wicked profit," Delaney went on happily.

His happiness was occasioned by the profits that stemmed from Washington Faulconer's insistence that not one boot or button be bought for his Legion from the state, which obstinacy Delaney had seen as his opportunity. Delaney had used his extensive friendships within the state government to buy goods from the state armories himself, which goods he sold on to his half-brother, who acted as Washington Faulconer's purchasing agent. The price of the goods invariably doubled or even quadrupled during the transaction, and the brothers shared the profits equally. It was a happy scheme that had, among other things, brought Washington Faulconer twelve thousand dollars' worth of Mississippi rifles that had cost Belvedere Delaney just six thousand dollars, forty-dollar tents that had cost sixteen dollars, and a thousand pairs of two-dollar boots that the brothers had purchased for eighty cents a pair. "I imagine a gun limber must cost at least four hundred dollars," Delaney now mused aloud. "Say eight hundred to Faulconer?"

"At least." Ridley needed the profits far more than his older brother, which was why he had been so happy to return to Richmond, where he could not only make money, but also be free of Anna's cloying affections. He told himself that marriage would surely make things easier between himself and Faulconer's daughter, and that once he had the security of the family's wealth behind him he would not so resent Anna's petulant demands. In affluence, Ridley believed, lay the solution to all life's griefs.

Belvedere Delaney also liked affluence, but only if it brought power in its wake. He checked his horse to watch a company of Mississippians march by; fine-looking bearded men, thin and tanned, but all armed with old-fashioned flintlocks like the ones their grandfathers had carried against the redcoats. The coming war, Delaney hoped, must be brief, because the North would surely wipe away these enthusiastic amateurs with their homely weapons and gangling gait, and when that happened Delaney intended to realize an even larger profit than the paltry dollars he now made from equipping Washington Faulconer's Legion. For Belvedere Delaney, though a southerner by birth and breeding, was a northerner by calculation, and though he had not yet become a spy he had quietly permitted his friends in the northern states to understand that he intended to serve their cause from within the Virginian capital. And when that northern victory came, as it surely must, then Delaney reckoned that the southern supporters of the legitimate federal government could expect a rich reward. That, Delaney knew, was a long view, but holding the long view while all around him fools gambled their lives and property on the short gave Belvedere Delaney an immense amount of satisfaction. "Tell me about Starbuck," he suddenly asked his brother as they walked their horses about the Fair Grounds perimeter.

"Why?" Ridley was surprised by the abrupt question.

"Because I am interested in Elial Starbuck's son." In truth it had been thoughts of southerners supporting the North and northerners fighting for the South that had made Delaney think of Starbuck. "I met him, did you know?"

"He didn't say anything." Ridley sounded resentful.

"I rather liked him. He has a quick mind. Much too mercurial to be successful, I suspect, but he's not a dull young man."

Ethan Ridley sneered at that generous assessment. "He's a goddamn preacher's son. A pious son of a Boston bitch."

Delaney, who fancied he knew more of the world than his half-brother, suspected that any man who was willing to risk his whole future for some strumpet off the stage was probably much less virtuous and a deal more interesting that Ridley was suggesting, and Delaney, in his long drunken meal with Starbuck, had sensed something complicated and interesting in the younger man. Starbuck, Delaney reflected, had immured himself in a dark maze where creatures like Dominique Demarest fought against the virtues instilled by a Calvinist upbringing, and that battle would be a rare and vicious affair. Delaney instinctively hoped that the Calvinism would be defeated, but he also understood that the virtuous aspect of Starbuck's character had somehow got under his half-brother's skin. "Why do we find virtue so annoying?" Delaney wondered aloud.

"Because it is the highest aspiration of the stupid," Ridley said nastily.

"Or is it because we admire virtue in others, knowing we cannot attain it ourselves?" Delaney was still curious.

"You might want to attain it, I don't."

"Don't be absurd, Ethan. And tell me why you dislike Starbuck so much."

"Because the bastard took fifty bucks off me."

"Ah! Then he did touch you to the quick." Delaney, who knew the extent of his half-brother's greed, laughed. "And how did the preacher's son achieve this appropriation?"

"I wagered him that he couldn't fetch a man called Truslow out of the hills, and goddamn it, he did."

"Pecker told me about Truslow," Delaney said. "But why didn't you recruit him?"

"Because if Truslow sees me near his daughter, he'll murder me."

"Ah!" Delaney smiled, and reflected how everyone created their own tangled snares. Starbuck was enmeshed between sin and pleasure, he himself was caught between North and South, and his half-brother was snagged on lust. "Does the murderer have cause to kill you?" Delaney asked, then took a cigarette from a box and borrowed his half-brother's cigar to light it. The cigarette was wrapped in yellow paper and filled with lemon-scented tobacco. "Well?" Delaney prompted Ridley.

"He has cause," Ridley admitted, then could not resist a boastful laugh. "He's going to have a bastard grandchild soon."

"Yours?"

Ridley nodded. "Truslow doesn't know the baby's mine, and the girl's been married off anyway, so all in all I came out smelling like rosewater. Except that I had to pay for the bitch's silence."

"A lot?"

"Enough." Ridley inhaled his cigar's bitter smoke, then shook his head. "She's a greedy bitch, but my God, Bev, you should see the girl."

"The murderer's daughter is beautiful?" Delaney was amused at the thought.

"She's extraordinary," Ridley said with a genuine tone of awe in his voice. "Here, look." He took a leather case from his top uniform pocket and handed it to Delaney.

Delaney opened the case to find a drawing, five inches by four inches, which showed a naked girl sitting in a woodland glade beside a small stream. Delaney was constantly astonished at his half-brother's talent which, though untrained and lazily applied, was still startlingly good. God, he thought, poured his talents into the strangest vessels. "Have you exaggerated her looks?"

"No. Truly no."

"Then she is indeed lovely. A nymph."

"But a nymph with a tongue like a nigger driver and a temper to match."

"And you're done with her, yes?" Delaney enquired.

"Finished. Done." Ridley, as he took back the portrait, hoped that was true. He had paid Sally a hundred silver dollars to keep silent, yet he had remained frightened that she would not keep her side of the bargain. Sally was an unpredictable girl with more than a touch of her father's savagery, and Ethan Ridley had been terrified that she might appear in Faulconer Court House and brandish her pregnancy in front of Anna. Not that Washington Faulconer probably minded a man fathering bastards, but whelping them on slaves was one thing and having a girl as wild as Truslow's daughter screaming her outrage up and down the main street of Faulconer Court House was something entirely different.

But now, thank God, Ridley had heard how Sally had been married off to her straw-haired puppy-boy. Ridley had heard no details of the wedding, nothing about the where or the how or the when, only that Truslow had sloughed his daughter off onto Decker and given the couple his patch of stony land, his beasts and his blessing, and by so doing he had left Ridley feeling much safer. "It's all turned out well," he grunted to Delaney, yet not without some regret, for Ethan Ridley suspected that he would never again in his life know a girl as beautiful as Sally Truslow. Yet to lie with her had been to play with fire and he had been lucky to have emerged unscorched.

Belvedere Delaney watched a pack of recruits trying to march in step.

A cadet from the Virginia Military Institute who looked about half the age of the men he was drilling screamed at them to straighten their backs, to keep their heads up and to stop looking around like mill girls on an outing. "Does Colonel Faulconer drill his men like this?" Delaney asked.

"He believes drill will only blunt the men's enthusiasm."

"How interesting! Perhaps your Faulconer is cleverer than I thought. These poor devils begin their drill at six in the morning and don't cease till the moon rises." Delaney touched his hat in salute of a judge he frequently met at the brothel on Marshall Street that was always known as Mrs. Richardson's house, though in fact the major shareholder in the house was Belvedere Delaney himself. In times of war, Delaney believed, a man could do a lot worse than invest in weapons and women, and so far Delaney's investments were all showing a fine profit.

"Faulconer believes war should be enjoyed," Ridley said caustically, "which is why he's going on a cavalry raid."

"A cavalry raid?" Delaney said in a surprised tone. "Tell me."

"There's nothing to tell."

"Describe me the nothing, then." Delaney sounded unnaturally petulant.

"Why?"

"For God's sake, Ethan, I am a friend to half the lawmakers in the state, and if Virginia's citizens are waging a private war on the North then the government is supposed to know about it. Or Robert Lee is. In fact Lee's supposed to sanction military movements, even by your incipient father-in-law. So tell me."

"Faulconer's leaving on a raid, or maybe he's already left, I'm not sure. Does it matter?"

"Where? What?"

"He's upset because we let the Yankees occupy Alexandria. He thinks Richmond doesn't care about the war. He says Letcher has always been soft on the North and is probably a secret Union man. He thinks Lee is too cautious, and so is everyone else, and if someone doesn't go and kick the Yankees where it hurts then the Confederacy will collapse."

"You mean the idiot is going to attack Alexandria?" Delaney asked in astonishment. Alexandria was the Virginian town across the Potomac from Washington that, since its abandonment by southern troops, had been heavily fortified.

"He knows he can't attack Alexandria," Ridley said, "so he's planning to cut the Baltimore and Ohio Railroad."

"Where?"

"He didn't tell me," Ridley sounded sour, "but it can't be east of Cumberland, because the trains aren't running between there and Harper's Ferry." Ridley suddenly became alarmed. "For God's sake, Bev, you're not going to stop him, are you? He'll kill me if you do!"

"No," Delaney said soothingly, "no, I'll let him have his fun. So how many men has he taken? The whole Legion?"

"Just thirty men. But you promise me you'll say nothing?" Ridley was terrified that he had been indiscreet.

Delaney could see Robert Lee inspecting recruits on the far side of the Fair Grounds. Delaney had deliberately made himself useful to Lee's office and had found himself being unwillingly impressed by the general's combination of intelligence and honesty. Delaney tried to imagine Lee's fury if he were to discover that Faulconer was free-lancing a raid on the Baltimore and Ohio Railroad, but tempting though it was, Delaney decided he would say nothing to his friends in Virginia's government. Instead he would let the North do the stopping.

For there was still time to write one last letter to a friend in Washington who, Delaney knew, was intimate with the northern government's secretary of war. Delaney reckoned that if the North discovered that he could be a source of useful military information, then their full trust would surely follow.

"Of course I'll say nothing to the governor," he now reassured his terrified younger brother, then sawed on his reins to stop his horse. "Do you mind if we turn back? The dust is irritating my throat."

"I was hoping ..." Ridley began.

"You were hoping to visit Mrs. Richardson's house." That enticement, Delaney knew, was Richmond's main attraction for his half-brother. "And so you shall, my dear Ethan, so you shall." Delaney spurred back toward the city, his good day's work well done.

The raiding party reached the Baltimore and Ohio Railroad two hours before dawn on the sixth day of a journey that Washington Faulconer had confidently predicted would last no more than three. The ride would have taken a full week if Faulconer had not stubbornly insisted on riding throughout the final night. Starbuck, reeling from tiredness and in whimpering agony from his saddle sores, was not at first aware that their journey was almost done. He was slumped in the saddle, half-sleeping, half-scared of falling, when he was suddenly startled by a brilliant glare of light that flared far beneath him in a deep, moon-shadowed valley. For a moment he thought he was dreaming, then he feared he was not dreaming at all but had instead reached the trembling edge of the Valley of Gehenna, the Bible's hell, and that at any moment he would be cast down into the flaming pit where the devils cackled as they tormented the sinners. He even cried out in terror.

Then he came fully awake and realized that Faulconer's bedraggled band of raiders had stopped on the crest of a high ridge and were looking

down into a dark valley where a train ran westward. The door of the locomotive's firebox was open, and the furnace's brilliant glow was reflecting
on the underside of the boiling smoke plume which looked, Starbuck
thought, like the lurid breath of a great dragon. The boiling smoke moved
steadily westward, preceded by the feeble glow of the locomotive's oil-
fired lantern. No other lights showed, suggesting that the locomotive was
hauling freight wagons. The noise of the train changed to a hollow rumble as it crossed trestles spanning a river that lay to Starbuck's left, and he
felt a sudden pulse of excitement as he suddenly understood how close
they had come to their target.

For the great spume of fiery smoke that ripped through the night
marked where the Baltimore and Ohio Railroad ran along the bank of the
North Branch of the Potomac River. Until Thomas Jackson had occupied
Harper's Ferry, and so cut the rail passage to Washington and Baltimore,
this line had been the major link between the western states and the
American capital, and even since Jackson's occupation the rails had
stayed busy as they fetched supplies, recruits, weapons and food from Mis-
souri, Illinois, Indiana and Ohio, all of them carried to Cumberland
where they were reloaded onto canal boats or else onto wagons that were
hauled by teams of horses to the Hagerstown depot of the Cumberland
Valley Railroad. Colonel Faulconer claimed that if the Baltimore and
Ohio could be cut in the Alleghenies west of Cumberland then it might
take months before that busy supply line was restored.

That, at least, was the military justification for the raid, though Starbuck knew the Colonel expected to gain much more from this foray.
Faulconer believed a successful attack would bolster southern belligerence
and hurt northern pride. Better still it would begin the history of the
Faulconer Legion with a victory, which was the real reason why the
Colonel had led a group of thirty picked horsemen who escorted four
packhorses loaded with four barrels of black powder, six axes, four crow-
bars, two sledgehammers, and two coils of quick-fuse—the materials necessary to destroy the tall trestles of the bridges that carried the Baltimore
and Ohio Railroad across the streams and rivers that flowed fast through
the Alleghenies.

Three of the Legion's officers accompanied their Colonel on the raid.
Captain Paul Hinton was an easygoing man who farmed eight hundred
acres in the eastern part of Faulconer County and was a hunting friend of
Faulconer's. Then there was Captain Anthony Murphy, who was a tall,
black-haired Irishman who had emigrated to America ten years before,
planted one spread of cotton in Louisiana, sold the spread before harvest,
taken a riverboat north and played twenty-card poker for three days and
nights, and stepped off the boat with a pretty Italian girl and enough
money to last the rest of his days. He had brought his Italian bride to Vir-

ginia, put his money in the Faulconer County Bank and purchased himself four farms to the north of Seven Springs. He kept three slaves on the largest farm, rented out the others, got drunk with his tenants every quarter day and could rarely find anyone rash enough to deal him into a game of bluff. The last officer was Second Lieutenant Starbuck, who had never played poker in his life.

Among the twenty-six men accompanying the four officers was Sergeant Thomas Truslow and a half dozen of the rogues who had followed him down from the hills. Truslow's group rode together, ate together, and treated the three most senior officers with a tolerant disdain, though, to the surprise of all those who knew just how much Truslow hated Yankees, the dour sergeant clearly liked Starbuck, and that acceptance made Starbuck a welcome member of Truslow's group. No one understood the unlikely association, but then no one, not even Colonel Faulconer, had heard about either the prayer Starbuck had offered by Emily's grave or how Starbuck had extemporized a wedding ceremony in the Virginian night.

Not that Faulconer would have been in any mood to have listened to such stories for, as the raiders had moved north and west into the Alleghenies, his dreams of a swift, slashing victory had become mired in rain and fog. The journey had begun well enough. They had crossed the Blue Ridge Mountains into the wide, rich Shenandoah Valley, then climbed into the Alleghenies, and that was when the rains had struck, not gentle rains to swell the growing grain in the valleys, but a succession of sky-lacerating storms that had cracked and ripped the sky as the raiders struggled through the inhospitable mountains. Faulconer had insisted they avoid all settlements, for these regions west of the Shenandoah were hostile to the Confederacy, indeed, there was even talk of this part of Virginia seceding to form a new state altogether, and so Faulconer's men had slunk through the rain-drenched mountains like thieves, not even wearing uniforms. There was no point, the Colonel said, in taking unnecessary risks with the traitorous mudsills of the Alleghenies.

Yet the weather proved far more hostile than the inhabitants. Faulconer became lost in the steep cloud-wrapped mountains, spending one whole day groping west into a blind valley, and it was only Thomas Truslow's canny sense that had brought them back to the right route, and from that moment it had seemed to many of the raiding party that Thomas Truslow had become the real leader of the expedition. He gave no orders, but the horsemen all looked to him rather than the Colonel for a lead. It was Washington Faulconer's resentment of that usurpation of his authority that had made him insist that the raiders keep traveling through the fifth night. It had been an unpopular order, but by enforcing it the Colonel had at least demonstrated who was in command.

Now, perched at last above the railroad, the horsemen waited for the dawn. The clouds of the last few days had torn ragged and a few stars showed around a mist-shrouded moon. Far to the north a tiny spot of light flickered in the far hills that Starbuck realized could be in Pennsylvania. The view from this high crest looked over the misted river, across a strip of Maryland and deep into the hostile north. It seemed incredible to Starbuck that he was poised above a frontier between two warring states; indeed, that America could be at war at all seemed unreal, a denial of all childhood's certainties. Other lesser countries went to war, but men had come to America to avoid war, yet now Starbuck shivered on a mountaintop with the Savage revolver at his side and armed men all around him. No more trains passed. Most of the men slept while a few, like Truslow, squatted at the crest's edge and stared north.

The light seeped slowly from the east to reveal that the horsemen had chanced upon an almost perfect place to cut the railroad. To their left a swift river churned across rocks to join the North Branch of the Potomac, and a high trestle bridge spanned the tributary on a latticework of stilts sixty feet high. There were no guards on the bridge and no blockhouse. Nor were there any farms or settlements within sight; indeed if it had not been for the dull sheen of the steel rails and the spindly lattice of the trellis this could have been unexplored wilderness.

Faulconer gave his final orders as the sky lightened. The raiders would divide into three parties. Captain Murphy would take a dozen men to block the rails leading east, Captain Hinton would take another dozen men west, while the six remaining men, led by the Colonel, would clamber down into the tributary's gorge and there destroy the tall contraption of trestles and rails. "Nothing can go wrong now," Faulconer said, trying to cheer his damp and somewhat dispirited troops. "We've planned it properly." In fact even the most optimistic of the raiders must have realized that the Colonel's planning had been slipshod. Faulconer had not foreseen the possibility of drenching rain and so the powder barrels and quick-fuses had been bereft of tarpaulins. There had been no proper maps provided so that even Truslow, who had crossed these hills a score of times, was not entirely sure what bridge they now threatened. Yet despite all the doubts and difficulties they had succeeded in reaching the railroad, which had proved unguarded, and so, in the first weak light of the new day, they slid and slithered down the steep slope toward the North Branch.

They picketed the horses beside the railroad close to the bridge. Starbuck, shivering in the gray dawn, walked to the gorge's edge to see that the trestles, which had looked so flimsy from the hilltop, were in truth massive timbers that had been stripped of their bark, coated with tar, then sunk into the earth or else braced against the huge boulders that protruded from the chasm's slopes. The trestles were fastened to one another with metal collars, thus linked into a dense trellis structure that rose sixty feet from the stream and spanned two hundred feet across the gorge. The timbers, despite their tar coating, felt clammy, just as the wind that gusted cold from the river felt damp. The clouds were once more building, promising rain.

Captain Hinton's men crossed the bridge, Murphy's went eastward while the Colonel's party, which included Starbuck, struggled down to the bed of the gorge. The slope was slippery and the brush still soaked from the previous day's rain so that by the time the six men reached the bank of the fast-flowing stream their already damp clothes were drenched through. Starbuck helped Sergeant Daniel Medlicott, a morose and uncommunicative man who was a miller by trade, maneuver a barrel of black powder down the steep slope. Washington Faulconer, watching them struggle with the cask, shouted a warning for Nate to beware of a patch of poison ivy, a warning that seemed to disappoint Medlicott. The other three barrels of powder were already at the bottom of the chasm. The Colonel had considered saving two of the gunpowder casks but had decided it was better to make certain that this one substantial bridge was utterly destroyed than to look for a second trestle later in the day. Medlicott stacked the fourth barrel with the others, then knocked its bung out so as to insert a length of quick-fuse. "Powder feels mighty damp to me, Colonel."

"Sir." Faulconer snapped the word. He was trying to persuade his erstwhile neighbors to use the military honorific.

"Still feels damp," Medlicott insisted, obstinately refusing to humor Faulconer.

"We'll try the fuse, and we'll light a fire as well," Faulconer said, "and if the one doesn't work, the other will. So get on with it!" He walked a few paces upstream with Starbuck. "They're good fellows," he said morosely, "but with no idea of military discipline."

"It's a difficult transition, sir," Starbuck said tactfully. He was feeling somewhat sorry for Faulconer, whose hopes for a jaunty and defiant raid had turned into this damp nightmare of delay and difficulty.

"Your fellow Truslow's the worst," the Colonel grumbled. "No respect there at all." He sounded disappointed. He had so wanted Truslow in the Legion, thinking that the man's character would give the regiment a fearsome reputation, yet now he found himself resenting Truslow's truculent and independent manner. Washington Faulconer had corralled himself a tiger and did not know how to handle the beast. "And you're not helping me, Nate," the Colonel suddenly said.

"Me, sir?" Starbuck, who had been feeling sympathy for the Colonel, was taken aback by the accusation.

The Colonel did not respond immediately. He was standing beside the stream and watching Medlicott's men use bowie knives to cut the timber that would be used as firewood around the barrels of gunpowder. "You don't want to be too familiar with these fellows," the Colonel finally said. "One day you'll have to command them in battle and they won't respect you if you don't keep a distance." Washington Faulconer did not look at Starbuck as he spoke, but instead gazed through the trestle at the sliding gray river down which a twisted black tree branch was being carried. Faulconer appeared very miserable. His beard was untrimmed, his clothes damp and dirty, and his normally brisk manner subdued. Bad weather soldiering, Starbuck reflected with surprise, did not seem to suit the Colonel. "Officers should keep company with other officers." The Colonel embroidered his criticism petulantly. "If you're forever with Truslow, how will you command him?"

That was unfair, Starbuck thought, for he had spent far more time on the journey with Washington Faulconer than with Truslow, yet Starbuck dimly understood that the Colonel was jealous that Starbuck, and not he, had so earned Truslow's regard. Truslow was a man whose good opinion other men wanted, and the Colonel clearly thought he deserved it more than some stray student from Massachusetts, so Starbuck said nothing and the Colonel, his complaints against his aide delivered, turned back toward Medlicott. "How much longer, Sergeant?"

Medlicott stepped back from his work. He had stacked the powder kegs around one of the bridge's tallest legs, then surrounded the gunpowder with a thick stack of brush and logs. "There's a terrible lot of wet in everything," he observed gloomily.

"You've got kindling in there?"

"Plenty of that, Colonel."

"Paper? Cartridges?"

"There's enough to make a fire," Medlicott allowed.

"So when will we be ready?"

"We're as good as ready now, I'd say." Medlicott scratched his head as he considered the answer he had just given, then nodded. "It should do, Colonel."

"You'll go to Hinton." Faulconer turned to Starbuck. "Tell him to pull back over the bridge. Warn Captain Murphy to ready the horses! Tell everyone to look lively now, Nate!"

Starbuck wondered why no signal had been readied to tell everyone to withdraw. A series of gunshots would have served much faster than a damp scramble up the gorge's side to deliver the messages, but he knew this was no time to ask the Colonel a question that would doubtless be construed as critical, and so he simply climbed the gorge's eastern flank, then crossed the trestle bridge to find that Sergeant Truslow had made a huge barricade of felled pine trees to block the line's western approach. Captain Hinton, a short and cheerful man, had been content to let Truslow manage affairs. "I suspect he's stopped trains before," he explained to Starbuck, then proudly showed how, beyond the barricade, the rails had been ripped up and hurled down toward the North Branch. "So the Colonel's ready?"

"Yes, sir."

"Pity. I would rather have liked to have robbed a train. It would have been a new line of work for me, but horribly complicated." Hinton explained that the Truslow method of train robbery demanded that the thieves wait some distance from the barricade, then leap aboard the passing locomotive and its cars. "If you wait for the train to stop before climbing aboard then you're likely to have pesky passengers jumping off with guns and then everything gets rather untidy. You also have to have men on each car to wind the brakes if the train is to stop properly. It seems there's quite an art to these things. Ah well, will you go and fetch the rogue, Nate?" Truslow, with the remainder of Hinton's squad, was a quarter mile down the track, evidently prepared for the complicated business of stopping a train. "Off you go, Nate," Hinton said, encouraging Starbuck.

But Starbuck did not move. Instead he stared down the line to where, beyond the shoulder of the hill, a sudden plume of white smoke was showing. "A train," he said dully, as though he did not really believe his own eyes.

Hinton wheeled round. "Good God, so there is." He cupped his hands. "Truslow! Come back!" But Truslow either did not hear or chose to ignore the summons because he began running west, away from the barricade and toward the train. "The Colonel will just have to wait," Hinton grinned.

Starbuck could hear the train now. It was coming very slowly, its bell clanging and pistons laboring as it climbed the slight gradient toward the curve and the waiting ambush. Behind Starbuck a voice shouted from the gorge, urging him to hurry the withdrawal, but it was all too late for haste to be of any help. Thomas Truslow wanted to rob a train.

Thaddeus Bird and Priscilla Bowen were married at eleven o'clock in the morning in the Episcopal Church opposite the Faulconer County Bank in the main street of Faulconer Court House. It had been threatening rain since dawn, but the weather stayed dry through most of the morning and Priscilla had dared to hope that the rain would hold off altogether, but a half hour before the ceremony the heavens opened. Rain seethed on the church roof, splashed on the graveyard, flooded the main street and drenched the schoolchildren who, in honor of their teachers' wedding, had been given a morning off to attend the service.

Priscilla Bowen, nineteen years old and an orphan, was given away by her uncle who was the postmaster in the neighboring town of Rosskill. Priscilla had a round face, a quick smile and a patient disposition. No one would have called her beautiful, yet after a few moments in her company no one would have dismissed her as plain either. She had light brown hair, which she wore in a tight bun, hazel eyes, which were half hidden by steel-rimmed spectacles, and work-roughened hands. For her wedding she carried a spray of redbud blossoms and wore her best Sunday gown of blue-dyed cambric on which, in celebration of the day, she had pinned a garland of white handkerchiefs. Thaddeus Bird, who was twenty years older than his bride, wore his best black suit, which he had carefully mended himself, and a smile of deep content. His niece, Anna Faulconer, was present, but his sister stayed in her bedroom in Seven Springs. Miriam Faulconer had fully intended to be at the wedding, but the threat of rain and the onslaught of a cold wind had brought on a sudden attack of neuralgia complicated by asthma, and so she had remained in the big house where the servants banked the fires and burned niter papers to relieve her labored breath. Her husband was somewhere beyond the Shenandoah Valley, leading his cavalry raid, and that absence, if the truth were to be told, was why Pecker Bird had chosen this day for his wedding.

The Reverend Ernest Moss conducted the affair, pronouncing Thaddeus and Priscilla man and wife just as a clap of thunder rattled the church shingles and caused some of the children to call out in fright. Afterward the wedding guests all splashed down Main Street to the schoolroom where two tables had been set with corn cake, apple butter, jars of honey, hung beef, apple pie, smoked hams, pickled cucumber, pickled oysters and buckwheat bread. Miriam Faulconer had sent six bottles of wine to her brother's wedding feast and there were also two barrels of lemonade, a jug of beer and a vat of water. Blanche Sparrow, whose husband owned the dry goods store, made a vast pot of coffee on the church stove and ordered two of the Legion's soldiers to carry it to the schoolroom where Major Pelham, dressed in his old United States uniform, made a fine speech. Doctor Danson then gave a humorous speech during which Thaddeus Bird smiled benignly on all the guests and even managed to smile when six of the schoolchildren, coached by Caleb Tennant, who was the Episcopal choirmaster, sang "Flora's Holiday" in thin, rather unconvincing voices.

Afternoon school was necessarily less demanding than usual, yet somehow Thaddeus and Priscilla Bird managed to subdue the excited schoolroom and even persuade themselves that some decent work had been achieved. Priscilla had been appointed as Bird's assistant, which appointment had been intended to release Pecker Bird to his duties in the

Faulconer Legion, but in fact Bird still ran the school, for his military duties had proved happily light. Major Thaddeus Bird kept the regiment's books. He compiled the pay lists, noted the punishments, and kept the guard rosters and commissary invoices. The work, he claimed, could have been adequately discharged by a bright six-year-old, but Bird was happy to perform it because, as an integral part of his duties, he was expected to pay himself a major's salary out of his brother-in-law's bank account. Most of the officers were receiving no pay, having private means, while the men were being paid their eleven dollars a month in newly printed Faulconer County Bank dollar bills, which depicted the town's courthouse on the one side and had a portrait of George Washington and an engraved bale of cotton on the other. A legend printed across the bale of cotton read "States' Rights and Southern Liberty. The Faith of the Bank is Pledged to Pay One Dollar on Demand." The bills were not very well printed and Bird suspected they might easily be forged, which was why he took good care to have his own Legion salary of thirty-eight dollars a month paid in good old-fashioned silver coins.

On the evening of his wedding, when the schoolhouse had been swept and the water pumped for the next morning and the firewood stacked beside the newly blacked stove, Bird could at last close his front door, edge past the piled books in the hallway, and offer his new wife a shy smile. On the kitchen table was one bottle of wine left from the wedding feast. "I think we shall have that!" Bird rubbed his hands in anticipatory glee. In truth he was feeling extraordinarily timid, so much so that he had deliberately dallied over his evening chores.

"I thought perhaps we might eat what was left from the wedding?" Priscilla, equally timid, suggested.

"Capital idea! Capital!" Thaddeus Bird was hunting for a corkscrew. He did not often get to drink a bottle of wine in his own house, indeed he could hardly remember the last time he had enjoyed such a luxury, but he was sure there was a corkscrew somewhere.

"And I thought perhaps I might rearrange the shelves." Priscilla watched her husband's frantic attempts to find the corkscrew amidst the jumble of handle-less skillets, holed pans and chipped plates that Bird had inherited from the previous schoolmaster. "If you have no objection," she added.

"You must do whatever you wish! This is your home, my dear one."

Priscilla had already tried to cheer up the dingy kitchen. She had put her wedding spray of redbud blossoms in a vase and pinned strips of cloth to either side of the window to suggest curtains, but somehow the touches did little to alleviate the gloom of the dark, low-beamed, smoke-stained room, which contained a stove, a table, an open hearth with an iron bread oven, two chairs and two old dressers, which were stacked with

chipped plates, mugs, bowls, pitchers and the inevitable books and broken musical instruments that Thaddeus Bird accumulated. The illumina-
tion in the kitchen, as in the rest of the small house, came from candles,
and Priscilla, who was ever mindful of the cost of good wax candles, lit
only two as night fell. It was still raining hard.

The corkscrew was at last discovered and the wine opened, but Bird
immediately declared himself dissatisfied with the glasses. "Somewhere
there are a pair of proper glasses. Ones with stems. The kind they use in
Richmond."

Priscilla had never been to Richmond and was about to say that she
doubted Richmond glasses could make the wine taste any better, but
before she could open her mouth to speak there was a sudden hammering
on the front door.

"Oh, no! This is too bad! I expressly said I was not to be disturbed
today!" Bird clumsily extricated himself from the cupboard in which he
had been searching for wineglasses. "Davies cannot find the muster roll.
Or he's lost the pay books! Or he cannot add twenty cents eight times
over! I shall ignore it." Davies was a young lieutenant who was supposed
to assist Bird with the Legion's paperwork.

"It's raining hard," Priscilla pleaded for the unknown caller.

"I don't care if it's raining fit to drown the planet. I do not care if the
animals are lining up two by two to get aboard. If a man cannot be left in
peace on his wedding day, when can he hope for rest? Am I so indispens-
able that I must be dragged from your company whenever Lieutenant
Davies discovers that his education is entirely insufficient for the
demands of modern life? He was at Centre College in Kentucky. Have
you ever heard of such a place? Is it possible that there could be anyone
capable of teaching anything worth knowing in Kentucky? Yet Davies
boasts of having been educated there! Boasts of it! Why I entrust the regiment's books to him, I don't know. I might as well hand them over to a
baboon. Let the fool get wet. Maybe his Kentucky brains will improve
after a drenching."

The knocking redoubled in intensity. "I really do think, my dear,"
Priscilla murmured in the gentlest of all possible reproofs.

"If you insist. You're too kind, Priscilla, altogether too kind. It's a
womanly fault, so I won't dwell on it, but there it is. Too kind altogether."
Thaddeus Bird took a candle into the hallway and, still grumbling, made
his way to the front door. "Davies!" He snapped as he pulled the door
open, then checked, for the caller was not Lieutenant Davies at all.

Instead a young couple stood at Thaddeus Bird's street door. Bird
noticed the girl first for, even in the wet windy darkness that threatened
to overwhelm his candle's flame, her face was striking. More than striking

for she was, Bird realized, truly beautiful. Behind her was a sturdy young man holding the reins of a tired horse. The young man, scarce more than a boy and still with a child's innocence on his face, looked familiar. "You remember me, Mister Bird?" he asked hopefully, then supplied the answer anyway. "I'm Robert Decker."

"So you are, so you are." Bird was shielding the candle flame with his right hand, peering at his callers.

"We'd like a talk with you, Mister Bird," Robert said courteously.

"Ah," Bird said, to give himself time to devise a reason to send them packing, but no reason occurred to him so he stepped grudgingly aside. "You'd better come in."

"The horse, Mister Bird?" Robert Decker asked.

"You can't bring that in! Don't be a fool. Oh, I see! Tie it to the hitching ring. There's a ring somewhere. There, by the step."

Eventually the two young people were ushered into Bird's front parlor. His house had two rooms downstairs, the kitchen and parlor, and a bedroom upstairs, which was reached by a flight of stairs in the next-door schoolroom. The parlor contained a fireplace, a broken armchair, a wooden bench discarded by the church and a table piled high with schoolbooks and sheet music. "It's been a long time since I last saw you," Bird remarked to Robert Decker.

"Six years, Mister Bird."

"That long?" Bird remembered that the Decker family had fled Faulconer Court House after their father had been involved in an abortive robbery on the Rosskill Road. They had taken refuge in the hills where, judging by Robert Decker's clothes, they had not prospered. "How is your father?" Bird now demanded of Robert.

Decker said his father had been killed by a fall from a bolting horse. "And I'm married now." Decker, who was standing dripping in front of the empty fireplace, gestured at Sally, who was perched warily among the tufts of horsehair that protruded from Bird's sorry armchair. "This is Sally," Decker said proudly, "my wife."

"Indeed, indeed." Bird felt oddly embarrassed, maybe because Sally Decker was a girl of such extraordinary looks. Her clothes were rags and her face and hair were filthy and her shoes were held together with twine, but she was nevertheless as breathtaking a beauty as any of the girls who paraded in their carriages around Richmond's Capitol Square.

"I ain't his real wife," Sally said cattily, trying to hide a ring on her wedding finger.

"Yes, you are," Decker insisted. "We were minister married, Mister Bird."

"Good, good. Whatever." Bird, mindful of his own new minister-married wife in the kitchen, wondered what on earth these two wanted of him. An education? Sometimes a grown pupil came back to Bird and asked the schoolmaster to repair the years of inattention or truancy.

"I came to see you, Mister Bird, because they said you could enlist me in the Legion," Decker explained.

"Ah!" Bird, relieved at the commonplace explanation, glanced from the honest-faced boy to the sullen beauty. They were, he thought, an ill-assorted couple, then he wondered if folks thought the same of Priscilla and himself. "You want to enlist in the Faulconer Legion, is that it?"

"I reckon I do," Decker said, and glanced at Sally, which suggested that she, rather than he, had engendered the wish.

"Is it a petticoat?" Bird asked, struck by a sudden and unsavory thought.

Decker looked puzzled. "Petticoat, Mister Bird?"

"You haven't received a petticoat?" Bird asked intensely, clawing his left hand through his ragged beard. "Left on your doorstep?"

"No, Mister Bird." Decker clearly thought his old schoolmaster was at best eccentric, at worst crazy.

"Good, good." Bird did not offer an explanation. In the last two weeks a number of men had discovered petticoats left on their porches or in their wagons. All were men who had failed to volunteer for the Legion. Some were men with ailments, some were the only supporters of large families, others were boys with glowing futures promised at colleges, and only a few, a very few, might have been considered timid, yet the mocking gift of petticoats had lumped them all together in the category of cowardice. The incident had led to bad feeling in the community, dividing those who were enthusiastic for the threatened war against those who believed the war fever must pass. Bird, who knew full well where the petticoats had come from, had kept a politic silence.

"Sally says I ought to join," Decker explained.

"If he wants to be a proper husband," Sally explained, "then he has to prove himself. Every other man's gone to war. Or all the proper men have."

"I wanted to go anyway," Robert Decker went on, "like Sally's father did. Only he'd be real angry if he knew I was here, so I want to be enlisted proper before I go to the camp. Then he can't have me put out, can he? Not if I've been properly signed on. And I want it arranged so that Sally can draw my pay. I'm told they can do that, is that right, Mister Bird?"

"Many wives draw their husbands' pay, yes." Bird glanced at the girl, and was again astonished that such beauty could have been bred in the ragged hills. "Your father's in the Legion?" he asked.

"Thomas Truslow." She said the name bitterly.

"Good God." Bird could not hide his surprise that Truslow had whelped this girl. "And your mother," he asked tentatively, "I'm not sure I know your mother, do I?"

"She's dead," Sally said defiantly, intimating that it was none of Bird's business anyway.

Nor was it, Bird allowed, so busied himself by explaining to Decker that he should go to the Legion's encampment and there seek out Lieutenant Davies. He almost added that he doubted anything could be achieved before morning, but he checked himself in case such an observation might suggest he should offer the couple a night's shelter. "Davies, he's your man," he said, then stood up to signify that their business was finished.

Decker hesitated. "But if Sally's father sees me, Mister Bird, before I'm all signed in, he'll kill me!"

"He's not here. He's gone away with the Colonel." Bird gestured his visitors toward the door. "You're quite safe, Decker."

Sally stood up. "Go and look after the horse, Robert."

"But—"

"I said go and look after the horse!" She snapped the order, thus sending the hapless Decker scuttling back into the rain. Once he was safe out of earshot Sally closed the parlor door and turned back to Thaddeus Bird. "Is Ethan Ridley here?" she demanded.

Thaddeus Bird's hand clawed nervously in his tangled beard. "No."

"So where is he?" There was no politeness in her voice, just a bald demand and a hint that she might unleash a violent temper if her demands were frustrated.

Bird felt overwhelmed by the girl. She had a force of character not unlike her father's, but where Truslow's presence suggested a threat of violence coupled with a dour muscular competence, the daughter seemed to possess a more sinuous strength that could bend and twist and manipulate other folk to her wishes. "Ethan is in Richmond," Bird finally answered.

"But where?" she insisted.

Bird was taken aback by the intensity of the question and appalled by its implications. He had no doubts what business this girl had with Ethan and he disapproved of it mightily, yet he felt powerless to resist her demands. "He stays in his brother's rooms. His half-brother, that is, in Grace Street. Shall I write the address down? You can read, yes?"

"No, but others can if I ask them to."

Bird, sensing that he did something wrong, or at least something horribly tactless, wrote his friend Belvedere Delaney's address on a piece of paper and then tried to salve his conscience with a sternly asked question. "Might I ask what your business with Ethan is?"

"You can ask, but you'll get no answer," Sally said, sounding more like her father than she might have cared to know, then she plucked the scrap of paper from Bird's hand and tucked it deep inside her rain-soaked clothes. She was wearing two threadbare homespun dresses dyed in butternut, two frayed aprons, a faded shawl, a moth-eaten black bonnet and an oilcloth sheet as an inadequate cape. She was also carrying a heavy canvas bag, suggesting to Bird that she stood in his parlor with all her worldly goods. Her only adornment was the silver ring on her left hand, a ring that struck Bird as old and rather fine. Sally, returning Bird's appraisal with her scornful blue eyes, had clearly dismissed the schoolmaster as a nonentity. She turned to follow Decker out to the street, but then paused to look back. "Is there a Mister Starbuck here?"

"Nate? Yes. Well, not exactly here. He went with the Colonel. And your father."

"Gone far?"

"Indeed." Bird tried to indulge his curiosity as tactfully as possible. "You've met Mister Starbuck, then?"

"Hell, yes." She laughed briefly, though at what she did not explain. "He's kind of nice," she added in lame explanation, and Thaddeus Bird, even though he was as newly married as a man could be, felt a sudden surge of jealousy against Starbuck. He immediately chided himself for having had such an unworthy envy, then marveled that a daughter of Truslow's could have provoked it. "Is Mister Starbuck a proper preacherman?" Sally frowned at Bird as she asked the odd question.

"A preacherman!" Bird exclaimed. "He's a theologian, certainly. I've not heard him preach, but he isn't ordained, if that's what you mean."

"What's ordained?"

"It is a superstitious ceremony entitling a man to administer the Christian sacraments." Bird paused, wondering if he had confused her with his impiety. "Is it important?"

"To me it is, yes. So he ain't a minister? Is that what you're saying?"

"No, he is not."

Sally smiled, not at Bird, but at some inner amusement, then she ducked into the hall and so out into the wet street. Bird watched the girl climb into the saddle and felt as though he had been scorched by a sudden fierce flame.

"Who was that?" Priscilla called from the kitchen as she heard the front door close.

"Trouble." Thaddeus Bird bolted the door. "Double toil and trouble, but not for us, not for us, not for us." He carried the candle back into the small kitchen where Priscilla was arranging the leftovers from the wedding feast onto a plate. Thaddeus Bird stopped her work, gathered her into his thin arms, and held her close and wondered why he would ever want to leave this small house with this good woman. "I don't know that I should go to war," he said softly.

"You must do what you want," Priscilla said, and felt her heart leap at the prospect that perhaps her man would not march to the guns. She loved and admired this awkward, difficult, clever man, but she could not see him as a soldier. She could imagine the handsome Washington Faulconer as a soldier, or even the unimaginative Major Pelham, or almost any of the sturdy young men who carried a rifle with the same assurance with which they had once wielded a spade or a pitchfork, but she could not envisage her irascible Thaddeus on a battlefield. "I can't think why you should ever have wanted to go for a soldier," she said, but very mildly so that he would not construe her words as criticism.

"Do you know why?" Thaddeus asked, then answered his own question. "Because I have a fancy that I might be good at soldiering."

Priscilla almost laughed, then saw her new husband was serious. "Truly?"

"Soldiering is merely the application of force by intelligence, and I am, for all my faults, intelligent. I also believe that every man needs to discover an activity at which he can excel and it is a constant regret that I have never found mine. I can write a fair prose, it is true, and I am no mean flautist, but those are common enough accomplishments. No, I need to discover an endeavor in which I can demonstrate mastery. Till now I have been too cautious."

"I dearly hope that you will go on being cautious," Priscilla said sternly.

"I have no wish to make you a widow." Bird smiled. He could see his wife was unhappy, so he sat her down and poured her some wine into an inadequate unstemmed glass. "But you should not worry," he told her, "as I daresay it will all prove to be a dreadful fuss about nothing. I can't imagine there'll be any serious fighting. There'll just be a deal of posturing and boasting and much ado about not very much and at summer's end we'll all march home and brag about our bravery, and things won't be a whole lot different than they are now, but, my darling, for those of us who don't join the farce the future will be very bleak."

"How so?"

"Because our neighbors will judge us cowards if we refuse to join. We're like men bidden to a dance who cannot abide dancing and who don't even much like music, but who must caper nimbly if we are to sit down to supper afterward."

"You're frightened of Washington sending you a petticoat?" Priscilla asked the pertinent question in a humble voice.

"I'm frightened," Bird said honestly, "of not being good enough for you."

"I don't need a war to show me your goodness."

"But it seems you have one anyway, and your ancient husband shall astonish you with his capabilities. I shall prove to be a Galahad, a Roland, a George Washington! No, why be so modest? I shall be an Alexander!" Bird had made his new wife laugh with his bravado, and then he kissed her and afterward he placed the glass of wine into her hand and made her drink. "I shall be your hero," he said.

"I'm frightened," Priscilla Bird said, and her husband did not know whether she spoke of what this night promised or what the whole summer held in store, so he just held her hand, and kissed it, and promised that all would be well. While in the dark the rain beat on.

6

It began to rain as the train clanked and hissed to a full halt with the locomotive's great skirtlike cowcatcher just twenty paces from the gap that Truslow had torn in the rails. The smoke from the high and bulbous funnel was whipped in the rainy wind toward the river. Steam hissed momentarily from a valve, then the locomotive's two engineers were chivied out of their cab by one of Truslow's men.

Starbuck had already returned to the bridge to shout down the news of the train to the Colonel who, standing beside the stream sixty feet below, demanded to know why the appearance of a train should delay the bridge's destruction. Starbuck had no good answer. "Tell Hinton to come back across the bridge now!" Faulconer cupped his hands to shout the order up to Starbuck. He sounded angry. "You hear me, Nate? I want everyone back now!"

Starbuck edged past the barricade to see the engineers standing with their backs against the locomotive's huge driving wheels. Captain Hinton was talking to them, but turned as Starbuck approached. "Why don't you go and help Truslow, Nate? He's working his way forward from the caboose."

"The Colonel wants everyone back across the bridge, sir. He sounds kind of urgent."

"You go and tell Truslow that," Hinton suggested. "And I'll wait for you here." The hissing locomotive smelt of woodsmoke, soot and oil. It had a brass-edged nameplate above the forward driving wheel with the name "Swiftsure" cast into the metal. Behind the locomotive was a tender stacked high with cordwood, and beyond the tender four passenger cars, a boxcar and the caboose. Truslow had men inside each car to keep the passengers docile while he went to deal with the guards in the caboose. Those guards had locked themselves in and, as Starbuck started down beside the stalled train, Truslow put his first shots through the caboose's side.

Some women passengers screamed at the sound of the gunshots. "Use your gun if anyone gives you trouble!" Hinton shouted after Starbuck.

Starbuck had almost forgotten the big twin-triggered Savage revolver that he had carried ever since the day he had ridden to fetch Truslow from the hills. Now he tugged the long barrel free. The cars towered above him, their small furnace chimneys wisping dribbles of smoke into the cold wet wind. Some of the car's axle boxes were so hot that the rain falling on their metal cases was boiled into instant steam. Passengers watched Starbuck from behind panes of window glass that were streaked with rain and dirt, and their gaze made Nathaniel Starbuck feel oddly heroic. He was dirty, disheveled, unshaven and with long, uncut hair, but under the passengers' fearful scrutiny he was transformed into a dashing rogue like one of the raiders who galloped the marcher fells in Sir Walter Scott's books. Behind the train's dirty window glass lay the respectable, mundane world which, not six months before, Starbuck had inhabited, while out here was discomfort and danger, risk and devilment and so, with a young man's pride, he strutted before the frightened passengers. A woman put a hand over her mouth, as though shocked to see his face, while a child rubbed a window free of mist just to see Starbuck better. Starbuck waved to the child, who shrank away in fear. "You'll hang for this!" a man with muttonchop whiskers shouted from an open window, and the angry threat made Starbuck realize that the passengers had mistaken Faulconer's raiders for common thieves. He found the idea absurdly flattering and laughed aloud. "You'll hang!" the man shouted, then was told to sit down and shut the hell up by one of the raiders inside the car.

Starbuck reached the caboose just as one of the men inside shouted for Truslow to stop shooting. Truslow, armed with a revolver, had been working his way calmly down the caboose's side, putting a bullet into every third plank and thus driving the inmates to the very back of the wagon, but now, knowing that the next bullet must surely hit one of them, the men inside shouted their surrender. The rear door opened very cautiously and two middle-aged men, one thin and the other fat, appeared on the caboose's platform. "I ain't even supposed to be here," the fat man wailed at Truslow, "I was just taking a ride with Jim here. Don't shoot me, mister. I got a wife and children!"

"Key to the boxcar?" Truslow enquired of the thin man in a very bored voice.

"Here, mister." The thin man, who was uniformed as a guard, held up a heavy ring of keys, then, when Truslow nodded, he tossed it down. The guard, like Truslow, gave the impression of having been through the whole performance before.

"What's in the housecar?" Truslow demanded.

"Nothing much. Mostly hardware. Some white lead." The guard shrugged.

"I'll have a look anyways," Truslow said, "so both you boys come on down." Truslow was very calm. He even thrust his empty revolver into his belt as the two men climbed down to the stones of the railbed. "Hold your hands up. High," Truslow ordered, then nodded at Starbuck. "Search them. You're looking for guns."

"I left mine inside!" the guard said.

"Search 'em, boy," Truslow insisted.

Starbuck found it embarrassing to stand so close that he could smell the fat man's terror. The fat man had a cheap gilt watch chain thick with seals stretched across his belly. "Take the watch, sir," he said when Starbuck's hand brushed against the seals, "go on, sir, take it, sir, please." Starbuck left the watch alone. A pulse in the man's neck fluttered wildly as Starbuck emptied his pockets. There was a flask, a cigar case, two handkerchiefs, a tinder box, a handful of coins and a pocket book.

"No guns," Starbuck said when he was finished with both men.

Truslow nodded. "Any soldiers where you boys come from?"

The two men paused, almost as if they were preparing to lie, then the guard nodded. "There's a whole bunch of 'em 'bout ten mile back. Maybe a hundred horse soldiers from Ohio? They said how they was expecting rebels." He paused, frowning. "Are you rebels?"

"Just plain rail thieves," Truslow said, then paused to jet a stream of tobacco juice onto the ties. "Now you walk back to those soldiers, boys."

"Walk?" the fat man said, aghast.

"Walk," Truslow insisted, "and don't look back or we'll start shooting. Walk between the rails, walk real slow, and just keep going. I'm watching you real good. Start now!"

The two men began walking. Truslow waited till they were out of earshot, then spat again. "Sounds like someone knew we were coming."

"I told no one," Starbuck said defensively.

"I never said you did, never thought you did. Hell, the Colonel's been talking about this raid for days! It's just amazing there ain't half the U.S. Army waiting for us." Truslow climbed up into the caboose and disappeared into its dark interior. "Mind you," he went on, speaking from inside the wagon, "there are men who think you're a spy. Just 'cos you're a Yankee."

"Who says that?"

"Just men. And it ain't anything to worry you. They've got nothing else to talk about and so they wonder what in hell's name a Yankee's doing in a Virginia regiment. You want some coffee off the stove here? It's warm. Ain't hot, just warm."

"No." Starbuck was offended that his loyalty had been so impugned.

Truslow reappeared on the back platform with the guard's discarded pistol and a tin mug of coffee. He checked that the gun was loaded then drained the coffee before jumping down to the track. "Right. Now we go and search the passenger cars."

"Shouldn't we leave?" Starbuck suggested.

"Leave?" Truslow frowned. "Why the hell would we want to leave? We just got the son of a bitch train stopped."

"The Colonel wants us to go. He's ready to blow the bridge."

"The Colonel can wait," Truslow said, then gestured Starbuck toward the passenger cars. "We'll start with the last car. If any bastard gives us trouble, shoot him. If any women or kids start screaming, slap them down fast. Passengers are like hens. Once you get 'em flustered they're noisy as hell, but treat 'em tough and they'll stay nice and quiet. And don't take any big stuff, because we've got to ride fast. Money, jewelry and watches, that's what we're after."

Starbuck stood stock still. "You're not robbing the passengers!" He was genuinely shocked at the thought. It was one thing to stride down the train like a freebooter under the gaze of awestruck passengers, but quite another to break the Sixth Commandment. The worst beatings Starbuck had ever taken had been as punishments for theft. When he was four he had helped himself to some almonds from a jar in the kitchen, and two years later he had taken a toy wooden boat from his elder brother's toy chest, and both times the Reverend Elial had drawn blood for a recompense. From that day until Dominique had persuaded him to take Major Trabell's money, Starbuck had been terrified of theft, and the consequences of helping Dominique had only reinforced his childhood lessons that thieving was a terrible crime which God would surely punish. "You can't steal," he told Truslow. "You can't."

"You expect me to buy their belongings off them?" Truslow asked mockingly. "Now come on, don't lag."

"I'm not helping you steal!" Starbuck stood his ground. He had sinned so much in these last weeks. He had committed the sin of lust, he had drunk ardent spirits, he had made a wager, he had failed to honor his father and mother and he had failed to keep the Sabbath Day holy, but he would not become a thief. He had only helped Dominique steal because she had persuaded him that the money was owed to her, but he would not help Truslow steal from innocent train passengers. So much of sin seemed nebulous and hard to avoid, but theft was an absolute and undeniable sin, and Starbuck would not risk the slippery path to hell by adding that transgression to his woefully long list of wrongdoings.

Truslow suddenly laughed. "I keep forgetting you're a preacherman. Or half a preacherman." He tossed Starbuck the ring of keys. "One of those will open the boxcar. Get inside, search it. You don't have to steal anything"—the sarcasm was heavy—"but you can look for military supplies and if you see anything else worth stealing, you can tell me about it.

And take this." Truslow whipped his enormous bowie knife from its scabbard and tossed it to Starbuck.

Starbuck missed the catch, but retrieved the clumsy blade from the
railbed. "What's it for?"

"It's for cutting throats, boy, but you can use it for opening boxes.
Unless you were planning on using your teeth to get into the crates?"

The heavy brass padlock on the boxcar's sliding door was a good ten
feet above the railbed, but a rusted iron stirrup suggested how Starbuck
could reach the lock. He pulled himself up and clung precariously to the
hasp as he fiddled with the keys. He eventually found the right one,
unlocked and slid the heavy door aside, then stepped inside.

The wagon was filled with boxes and sacks. The sacks were more easily opened than the crates and proved to hold seed, though Starbuck had
no idea what kind of seed. He trickled the grains through his fingers, then
gaped up at the stacked boxes and wondered how he was ever to search
them all. The easiest way would have been to hurl the boxes out onto the
ground, but the boxes were probably private property and he did not want
to risk breaking anything. Most of the crates were marked for collection
at either the Baltimore or Washington depot, proof that the occupation
of Harper's Ferry had not entirely closed federal traffic through the mountains. One of the crates marked for Washington was a dark-painted box
that bore a stenciled and misspelled legend on its side: "1000 Rifle Musket 69IN Cartridgs."

That at least had to be war material, and thus fair plunder. He used
the clumsy bowie knife to cut the ropes that had tethered the stacks in
place, then began shifting the obstructing crates onto the sacks of seed. It
took him the best part of five minutes to reach the dark-painted crate and
still more time to lever the well-nailed lid off the heavy box to discover
that it was indeed packed with paper cartridges, each one containing a
bullet and a measure of powder. Starbuck did his best to hammer the lid
back into place, then manhandled the box down to the ground. It was
still raining, so he thumped the lid with the heel of his right boot, trying
to bang the top down tight and thus keep out the rain.

There was another dark painted box under a second stack and so he
climbed back into the boxcar and moved still more crates until he had
excavated the second box which, like the first, bore a stenciled legend
denoting that its contents were also cartridges. He added that box to the
first, then climbed back inside to continue his laborious search.

"What in hell's name are you doing, boy?" Truslow appeared at the
boxcar door. He was carrying a heavy leather bag in his right hand and
the guard's pistol in his left.

"Those are cartridges"—Starbuck gestured at the two boxes beside
Truslow—"and I think there might be more in here."

Truslow kicked the lid off the nearest box, looked down, then spat tobacco juice over the cartridges. "No more use than tits on a bull."

"What?"

"They're point six nines like I used in Mexico. The rifles the Colonel bought in Richmond are five eights."

"Oh." Starbuck felt himself coloring with embarrassment.

"You could light a fire with these?" Truslow suggested.

"So they're no use?"

"Not to us, boy." Truslow shoved the revolver into his belt then picked up one of the cartridges and bit off its bullet. "Big son of a bitch, ain't she?" He showed Starbuck the bullet. "Anything valuable in there?"

"I've only found the bullets so far."

"Jesus wept, boy." Truslow dropped the heavy leather bag which chinked ominously as it fell, then clambered into the boxcar and seized the bowie knife from Starbuck. "I've got to get our boys out of the cars before the passengers get ideas. I took as many guns as I could, but some of those sons of bitches will have kept them well hid. There's always some bastard who wants to be a hero. I remember a young fellow on the Orange and Alexandria couple of years ago. Thought he would capture me." He spat in derision.

"What happened?"

"He finished his journey in the caboose, boy. Flat on his back and covered with a tarpaulin." As Truslow spoke he wrenched lids off crates, gave the contents a cursory glance, then hurled them out into the rain. A box of china plates decorated with painted lilies smashed itself on the railbed. A clothes mangle followed, then a crate of tin saucepans and a consignment of delicate gas mantles. It had begun to rain more heavily, the drops pattering loud on the boxcar's wooden roof.

"Shouldn't we be leaving?" Starbuck asked nervously.

"Why?"

"I told you. Colonel Faulconer's ready to blow the bridge up."

"Who cares about the bridge? How long do you think it will take to rebuild it?"

"The Colonel says months."

"Months!" Truslow was raking through a box of clothes, seeing if anything took his fancy. He decided nothing did and hurled the box out into the weather. "I could rebuild that trestle in a week. Give me ten men and I'll have it up and working in two days. Faulconer don't know goose shit from gold dust, boy." He jettisoned a barrel of soda and another of clearing starch. "There's nothing here," he sniffed, then clambered back to the ground. He glanced west, but the landscape was empty. "Go to the caboose, boy," he ordered Starbuck, "and bring me some hot coals."

"What are you doing?"

"Thinking that if you ask me another goddamned question I'll shoot you. Now go and get me some damned coals." Truslow upended both boxes of .69 cartridges into the boxcar while Starbuck climbed into the caboose where a small pot-bellied stove still burned. There was a zinc bucket of coal beside the stove. He tipped the coal out, used a poker to open the stove's door, then raked a handful of the glowing lumps into the empty bucket.

"Right," Truslow said when Starbuck got back. "Throw the coals onto the cartridges."

"You're going to burn the wagon?" The rain hissed as it fell into the bucket.

"For the Lord's sake!" Truslow grabbed the bucket and chucked the coals onto the spilt cartridges. For a second the coals just glowed among the paper tubes, then the first cartridge exploded with a soft cough and suddenly the whole pile of ammunition was a blazing, exploding, twisting mass of fire.

Truslow picked up his leather bag of loot, then beckoned Starbuck away. "Come on!" Truslow shouted up to the two men he had left in the rear passenger car.

As the guards left each car they warned the passengers that anyone following the raiders would be shot. Most of those raiders were burdened with bags or sacks, and all had the looks of men well satisfied with their work. Some walked backward with drawn pistols to make certain that none of the passengers tried to be heroic. "The trouble's going to come when we're past the barricade," Truslow warned. "Tom? Micky? You hang back with me. Captain Hinton! Get the engineers aboard!"

Hinton chivied the two engineers back into their locomotive's cabin, then followed with his drawn revolver. A second later the great machine gave an enormous hiss of steam, a gigantic clank, and suddenly the whole train jerked forward. A woman in one of the passenger cars screamed. The boxcar was well ablaze now, spewing black smoke into the driving sheets of rain.

"Go on!" Truslow shouted encouragement to Captain Hinton.

The locomotive clanked forward, its funnel giving off small and urgent puffs of gray-white smoke. A black soot smut, hot and sudden, landed on Starbuck's cheek. Hinton was grinning, shouting at the engineer who must have suddenly opened his throttle because the train jerked forward off the rail ends and shoved its cowcatcher deep into the bed. Stones and timber shattered apart. The four drive wheels, each one nearly six foot in diameter, began spinning and shrieking, but they found just enough traction so that, inch by agonizing inch, the monstrous machine shuddered forward as its small front wheels tore up the broken ties. The cowcatcher crumpled in a screech of tearing metal.

Hinton gestured with his revolver and the engineer opened the throttle full and the thirty-ton locomotive lurched forward like a great wounded beast as it toppled a few degrees sideways. Starbuck feared it was about to plunge down the river's bank, dragging its full cars behind, but then, mercifully, the huge machine stuck fast. Steam began to jet from its farther side. One of its small front wheels spun free above the churned dirt while the drive wheels on the farther side of the engine churned a foot-deep trench into the railbed before the engineer disconnected the pistons and more steam slashed out into the rain.

"Set the tender ablaze!" Truslow yelled and Hinton ordered one of the engineers to take a shovel load of red hot timbers from the firebox and thrust it deep into the tender's cordwood. "More!" Truslow urged, "more!" Truslow had found the venting faucet for the tender's water storage tank and turned it on. Water poured out of one end of the tender while the other began to blaze as fiercely as the burning boxcar.

"Go!" Truslow shouted, "go!"

The raiders pushed past the barricade and ran toward the bridge. Truslow stayed with two men to guard against any pursuit as Captain Hinton led the others across the narrow planks laid beside the rails on the trestles. Colonel Faulconer was waiting on the farther bank and shouting at Hinton's men to hurry. "Light the fires! Medlicott!" Faulconer called down into the gorge. "Hurry!" Faulconer shouted at Hinton. "For God's sake! What held you up?"

"Had to make sure the train didn't go back for help," Captain Hinton said.

"No one obeys orders here!" The Colonel had given the order to withdraw at least a quarter hour before and every second of the delay had been an insult to his already fragile authority. "Starbuck!" he shouted. "Didn't I order you to bring the men back?"

"Yes, sir."

"Then why didn't you?"

"My fault! Faulconer," Hinton intervened.

"I gave you an order, Nate!" the Colonel shouted. His other men were already mounted, all but for Medlicott, who had struck a light to the mass of combustibles about the trestle leg. "Now the fuse!" the Colonel shouted.

"Truslow!" Captain Hinton bellowed at the three men left on the far side of the gorge.

Truslow, the leather bag in his hand, was the last man away from the barricade. As he crossed the bridge he kicked the planks aside, making pursuit difficult. A gun was fired from the far barricade, the smoke of its powder snatched instantly away by the breeze. The bullet struck a rail on the bridge and whined off across the river. Two dense plumes of smoke from the burning boxcar and tender were drifting low and acrid above the North Branch.

"Fuse is lit!" Medlicott shouted and began clawing his way up the gorge's side. Behind him a dribble of smoke spat and writhed from the lit fuse as it snaked down the slope toward the great heap of timber and brush stacked about the gunpowder.

"Hurry!" the Colonel shouted. A horse whinnied and reared. More men fired from the barricade, but Truslow was across the bridge now and well out of effective revolver range. "Come on, man!" Washington Faulconer shouted. Truslow still had his leather bag, just as all Hinton's men had similar bags. Faulconer must have known from the heavy bags why his order to withdraw had been so long ignored, but he chose to say nothing. Sergeant Medlicott, muddy and damp, scrambled out of the gorge and fumbled for his stirrup just as the smoking fuse darted into the pile of brush. Sergeant Truslow hauled himself into his saddle, and Faulconer turned away. "Let's go!" He led his men off the railroad's embankment. The fire in the gorge had to be quickening, for thick smoke was writhing about the trestle's lattice, though the gunpowder had still not exploded. "Come on!" Faulconer urged, and behind him the horses scrambled and slipped on the muddy slope until, at last, they were concealed from the train by foliage and, though a few random bullets ripped through the leaves and twigs, none of the Legion's men was hit.

Faulconer stopped at the crest and turned to look back at the stricken train. The fires in the boxcar and tender had spread to the cars and the erstwhile passengers, wet and miserable, now clambered up the wet slope to escape the danger. The long passenger cars served like funnels in which the heat roared fierce until the windows cracked open and released billowing gusts of flame that licked into the driving rain.

The train was a blazing wreck, its engine derailed and cars destroyed, but the bridge, which had been the object of the raid, still stood. The fuse had failed to detonate the gunpowder, probably because the powder was damp, while the fire, which had been supposed to dry the powder and then explode it if the fuse failed, now seemed to be succumbing to wet fuel and wind-driven rain. "If you had obeyed my orders," the Colonel charged Starbuck bitterly, "there would have been time to reset the charges."

"Me, sir?" Starbuck was astonished at the unfairness of the accusation.

Captain Hinton was equally surprised by the Colonel's words. "I told you, Faulconer, it was my fault."

"I didn't give you the order, Hinton. I gave it to Starbuck, and the order was disobeyed." Faulconer spoke in a cold, clipped fury, then twisted his horse away and raked back with his spurs. The horse whinnied and started abruptly forward.

"Goddamn Yankee," Sergeant Medlicott said softly, then followed Faulconer.

"Forget them, Nate," Hinton said. "It wasn't your fault. I'll square the Colonel for you."

Starbuck still could not believe that he was being blamed for the failure of the attack. He sat dumbstruck, appalled at the Colonel's unfairness. Down on the rail line, unaware that a handful of the raiders still lingered above them, some of the train's passengers were edging out onto the undamaged trestle while others had begun to pull the barricade clear of the broken tracks. The fire in the gorge seemed to have gone out completely.

"He's used to getting his own way." Truslow pulled his horse alongside Starbuck. "He thinks he can buy what he wants and have it perfect, right from the start."

"But I didn't do anything wrong!"

"You didn't have to. He wants someone to blame. And he reckons that if he pisses all over you, then you won't piss back at him. That's why he chose you. He wasn't going to piss on me, was he?" Truslow spurred on.

Starbuck looked back to the gorge. The bridge was undamaged and the cavalry raid, which had been intended as a glorious victory to launch the Legion's triumphant crusade, had turned into a muddled, rain-soaked farce. And Starbuck was being blamed.

"Goddamn it," he swore aloud, defying his God, then turned and followed Truslow south.

"Can this really be it?" Belvedere Delaney had a four-day-old copy of the *Wheeling Intelligencer* that had been brought to Richmond from Harper's Ferry. The *Intelligencer*, though a Virginian paper, was soundly pro-Union.

"What?" Ethan Ridley was distracted and utterly uninterested in whatever the newspaper might have reported.

"Thieves stopped an eastbound passenger train on Wednesday last, one man hurt, locomotive temporarily unrailed." Delaney was condensing the story as he scanned the column. "Four cars badly burned, a boxcar and the passengers looted, rails torn up, replaced very next day." He peered at Ridley through gold-rimmed half-moon reading glasses. "You don't really think this can be the first great triumph of your Faulconer Legion, do you?"

"It doesn't sound like Faulconer. Now listen, Bev."

"No, you listen to me." The half-brothers were in Delaney's rooms in Grace Street. The parlor windows looked through velvet curtains at the graceful spire of St. Paul's and, beyond it, toward the elegant white Capitol Building that was now the seat of the Provisional Confederate government. "You listen, because I am going to read the best part to you,"

Delaney said with exaggerated relish. "'It might be thought, from their despicable behavior, that the plug-uglies who intercepted the cars on Wednesday were mere vagabond thieves, but thieves do not attempt to destroy railway trestles, and it is that feeble effort of destruction which has convinced authorities that the villains were southern agents and not common criminals, though how it is possible to differentiate, we cannot tell.' Isn't this delicious, Ethan? 'The world is well instructed now in southern manners, for the bravery of the rebels encompassed the robbing of women, the frightening of children, and an abject failure to destroy the Anakansett Bridge which, though lightly toasted, was carrying freight the very next day.' Lightly toasted! Isn't that amusing, Ethan?"

"No, goddamn it, no!"

"I think it's highly amusing. Let's see now, bold pursuit by Ohio cavalry, held up by rains, swollen streams. Rogues got clear away, so clearly the pursuit wasn't near bold enough. Raiders are thought to have retired east toward the Shenandoah Valley. 'Our brethren of eastern Virginia who so like to boast of their greater civilization, seem to have sent these men as emissaries of that vaunted superiority. If this be the best we can hope to see of their belligerent skills then we can rest assured that the nation's crisis will be short-lived and that the glorious Union will be reknit within weeks.' Oh, splendid!" Delaney took off his reading glasses and smiled at Ridley. "Not a very impressive display if it was your future father-in-law. One toasted bridge? He'll have to do better than that!"

"For God's sake, Bev!" Ridley pleaded.

Delaney made a great play of folding the newspaper, then of slipping it into the rosewood rack of other newspapers and journals that stood beside his armchair. His parlor was wonderfully comfortable with leather chairs, a big round polished table, books on every wall, plaster busts of great Virginians and, over the mantel, a massive mirror with a gilded frame of linked cherubs and aspiring angels. Some of Delaney's precious porcelain collection was displayed on the mantel, while other pieces stood among the leather-bound books. Delaney now made his brother wait even longer as he polished the half-moon glasses and carefully folded them into a velvet-lined case. "What on earth," he finally asked, "do you expect me to do about the damned girl?"

"I want you to help me," Ridley said pathetically.

"Why should I? The girl is one of your whores, not one of mine. She sought you out, not me. She's carrying your child, not mine, and her father's revenge threatens your life, certainly not mine, and do I really need to continue?" Delaney stood, crossed to the mantel, and took one of his yellow paper-wrapped cigarettes, which he used to import from France, but which now, he supposed, would become rarer than gold dust. He lit the cigarette with a spill ignited from the coal fire. It was astonishing that he should need a fire this late in the year, but the rains that had come thundering out of the east had brought unseasonably cold winds. "Besides, what can I do?" He went on airily. "You've already tried to buy her off and it didn't work. So clearly you'll just have to pay her more."

"She'll just come back," Ridley said. "And back again."

"So what exactly does she want?" Delaney knew he would have to help his half-brother, at least if he was to go on profiting from the Faulconer Legion purchases, but he wanted to stretch Ethan on the rack a little before he agreed to find a solution to the problem posed by Sally Truslow's unexpected arrival in the city.

"She wants me to find her somewhere to live. She expects me to pay for that, then to give her still more money every month. Naturally I've got to keep her bastard too. Jesus Christ!" Ridley swore viciously as he considered Sally's outrageous demands.

"Not just her bastard, but yours, too," Delaney pointed out unhelpfully. "Indeed, my own nephew! Or niece. I think I'd prefer a niece, Ethan. Would she be a half-niece, do you think? Maybe I could be her half-godfather."

"Don't be so damned unhelpful," Ridley said, then scowled through the window at a city being pounded by rain. Grace Street was almost empty. There was just one carriage clattering toward Capitol Square and two Negroes sheltering in the doorway of the Methodist Church. "Does Mrs. Richardson have anyone who can get rid of babies?" Ridley turned to ask. Mrs. Richardson presided over the brothel in which his half-brother had such a significant investment.

Delaney gave a delicate shrug that might have signified almost anything.

"Mind you," Ridley went on, "Sally wants to keep the bastard, and she says if I won't help her then she'll tell Washington Faulconer about me. And she says she'll tell her father. You know what he'll do to me?"

"I don't suppose he'll choose to have a prayer meeting with you," Delaney chuckled. "Why don't you take the inconvenient bitch down to the Tredegar works and leave her on a spoil heap?" The Tredegar Iron Works by the James River was Richmond's filthiest, darkest and grimmest place, and not many enquiries were made about the tragedies that occurred around its satanic edges. Men died in fights, whores were knifed in its alleys, and dead or dying babies were abandoned in its filthy canals. It was a corner of hell in downtown Richmond.

"I'm not a murderer," Ridley said sullenly, though in truth he had considered some such extraordinary and saving act of violence, but he was much too frightened of Sally Truslow who, he suspected, was hiding a gun somewhere among her property. She had come to him three nights before, arriving at Belvedere Delaney's rooms in the early evening.

Delaney had been in Williamsburg, swearing a will, so Ridley had been alone in the apartment when Sally had rung the front bell. He had heard a commotion at the front door and gone downstairs to find George, his brother's house slave, confronting a bedraggled, wet and angry Sally. She had pushed past George who, with his customary and dignified politeness, had been trying to keep her from entering the house. "Tell this nigger to keep his hands off me," she screamed at Ridley.

"It's all right, George. She's my cousin," Ridley had said, then had arranged for Sally's bedraggled horse to be stabled and for Sally herself to be shown upstairs to his brother's parlor. "What the hell are you doing here?" he had asked her in horror.

"I came to you," she announced, "like you said I could." Her ragged clothes dripped water onto Belvedere Delaney's fine Persian rug that lay in front of his red marble fireplace. Wind and rain howled at the casements, but in this warm and comfortable room, insulated by the thick velvet curtains under their deep-tasseled valances, the fire burned softly and the candle flames scarcely flickered. Sally turned about on the rug, admiring the books, the furniture and the leather chairs. She was dazzled by the reflection of candlelight from decanters, from the glint of gilded frames, and from the precious European porcelain on the mantel. "This is nice, Ethan. I never knew you had a brother?"

Ridley had crossed to the credenza where he opened a silver humidor and took out one of the cigars his brother kept for visitors. He needed a cigar to help recover his poise. "I thought you were married?"

"I'll take one of those cigars," Sally said.

He lit the cigar, gave it to her, then took another for himself. "You're wearing a wedding ring," he said, "so you are married. Why don't you go back to your husband?"

She deliberately ignored his question, instead holding her ring finger up to the candlelight. "The ring belonged to my ma and she had it from her ma. My pa wanted to keep it, but I made him give it me. Ma always wanted me to have it."

"Let me see it." Ridley took her finger and felt the thrill he always felt when he touched Sally and he wondered just what accident of bone and skin and lip and eye had made such a terrible beauty out of this foul-mouthed, sour-minded child of the hills. "It's pretty." He turned the ring on her finger, feeling the dry lightness of her touch. "It's quite old, too." He suspected it was very old, and perhaps quite special and so he tried to pull it off her finger, but Sally jerked her hand away.

"My pa wanted to keep it," she looked at the ring, "so I took it away from him." She laughed and drew on the cigar. "Besides, I ain't married proper. No more proper than if I jumped a broomstick."

That was precisely what Ridley feared, but he tried not to show any apprehension. "Your husband will still come looking for you, won't he?"

"Robert?" She laughed. "He won't do anything. A gelded hog's got more balls than Robert. But what about your lady friend? What will your Anna do when she knows I'm here?"

"Will she know?"

"She will, honey, 'cos I'll tell her. Unless you keep your word to me. Which means looking after me proper. I want to live in a place like this." She turned around the room, admiring its comfort, then looked back at Ridley. "Do you know a man called Starbuck?"

"I know a boy called Starbuck," Ridley said.

"A good-looking boy," Sally said coquettishly. A length of ash dropped off her cigar onto a rug. "He was the one that married me off to Robert. My pa made him do it. He made it sound all proper, with a book and all, and he even wrote it down to make it legal, but I know it wasn't proper."

"Starbuck married you?" Ridley was amused.

"He was nice about it. Real nice." Sally cocked her head at Ridley, wanting him to be jealous. "So then I told Robert he should go for a soldier, and I came here. To be with you."

"But I won't be staying here," Ridley said. Sally watched him, her eyes catlike. "I'm going to the Legion," Ridley explained. "I shall just finish my business here, then I shall go back."

"Then I tell you what other business you've got to finish, honey." Sally walked toward him, unconsciously graceful as she crossed the rich rugs and wax-polished boards. "You're going to find me a place to live, Ethan. Somewhere nice, with carpets like this and real chairs and a proper bed. And you can visit me there, like you said you would. Ain't that what you said? That you'd find a place where I could live? Where you'd keep me? And love me?" The last three words were said very softly and so close that Ridley could smell the cigar smoke on her breath.

"I said that, yes." And he knew he could not resist her, but he also knew that as soon as they had made love he would hate Sally for her vulgarity and commonness. She was a child, scarce fifteen, yet she knew her power and Ridley knew it too. He knew she would fight to have her way and she would not care what destruction she caused in the fighting, and so, the very next day, Ridley moved her out of his brother's Grace Street rooms. If Delaney had returned to find any of his precious porcelain broken he would never have agreed to help Ethan, and so Ridley had taken a front room at a boardinghouse on Monroe Street where he registered himself and Sally as a married couple. Now he pleaded for his brother's help. "For God's sake, Bev! She's a witch! She'll destroy everything!"

"A succuba, is she? I'd like to meet her. Is she really as beautiful as your sketch?"

"She is extraordinary. So for God's sake take her from me! You want her? She's yours." Ridley had already tried introducing her to his friends who met to drink in the Spotswood House Saloon, but Sally, even though dressed in newly purchased finery and hugely admired by every officer in the hotel, had refused to leave Ridley's side. She had her claws deep into her man and would not let go for the unknown opportunities of another. "Please, Bev!" Ridley pleaded.

Belvedere Delaney thought how much he hated being called "Bev" as he warmed himself by his small, glowing fire. "You're not willing to kill her?" he asked in a dangerous voice.

Ridley paused, then shook his head. "No."

"And you won't give her what she wants?"

"I can't."

"And you can't give her away?"

"Damn it, no."

"And she won't leave you of her own accord?"

"Never."

Delaney drew on his cigarette, then puffed a reflective smoke ring at his ceiling. "A toasted bridge! I do find that amusing."

"Please, Bev, please!"

"I showed the newspaper to Lee this afternoon," Delaney said, "but he dismissed the account. None of our men, he assured me. He reckons the bridge toasters must have been mere brigands. I think you should find a way of letting Faulconer hear that verdict. Brigands! The word will annoy Faulconer considerably."

"Please, Bev! For God's sake."

"Oh, not for God's sake, Ethan. God wouldn't like what I intend to do with your Sally. He wouldn't like it one little bit. But yes, I can help you."

Ridley gazed at his brother with palpable relief. "What will you do?"

"Bring her to me tomorrow. Bring her to the corner of, say, Cary and Twenty-fourth, that'll be out of the way. At four o'clock. There'll be a carriage there. I may be there or I may not. Find some story that'll get her into the carriage, then forget her. Forget her altogether."

Ridley gaped at his brother. "You're going to kill her?"

Delaney winced at the question. "Please do not imagine I am so crude. I am going to remove her from your life and you are going to be grateful to me forever."

"I will. I promise!" Ridley's gratitude was pathetic.

"Tomorrow then, at four o'clock, at Cary and Twenty-fourth. Now go and be nice to her, Ethan, be very nice, so she suspects nothing."

Colonel Washington Faulconer ignored Starbuck for almost the entire journey home. Faulconer rode with Captain Hinton, sometimes with

Murphy, and at other times alone, but always setting a fast pace, as though he wanted to distance himself from the scene of his raid's failure. When he did speak to Starbuck he was curt and unfriendly, though he was hardly any more forthcoming with anyone else. Even so, Starbuck felt hurt, while Truslow was merely amused by the Colonel's sulking. "You have to learn to walk away from stupidity," Truslow said.

"Is that what you do?"

"No, but who ever said I was a good example?" He laughed. "You should have taken my advice and helped yourself to the money." Truslow had made a fair sum from the raid, as had the men who had gone with him into the train.

"I'd rather be a fool than a thief," Starbuck said sententiously.

"No you wouldn't. No sensible man would. Besides, war's coming, and the only way you'll get through a war is by thieving. All soldiers are thieves. You thieve everything you want, not from your friends, but from everyone else. The army won't look after you. The army shouts at you, shits on you and does its best to starve you, so you get by as best you can, and the best getters-by are the ones who thieve best." Truslow rode in silence for a few paces. "I reckon you should be glad you came to say a prayer for my Emily, 'cos it means you've got me to look after you."

Starbuck said nothing. He felt ashamed of that prayer he had uttered beside the grave. He should never have said it, for he was not worthy.

"And I never thanked you for not telling anyone about my Sally, either. How she married, I mean, and why." Truslow cut a slice of tobacco off the plait he kept in a belt pouch and shoved it into a cheek. He and Starbuck were riding alone, separated by a few paces from the men before and those behind. "You always hope your children will do you proud," Truslow went on softly, "but I reckon Sally's a bad one. But she's wed now, and that's the end of it."

Is it? Starbuck wondered, but was not so foolish as to ask the question aloud. Marriage had not been the end for Sally's mother, who had subsequently run off with the small, fierce Truslow. Starbuck tried to picture Sally's face in his mind, but he could not piece it together. He just remembered someone who was very beautiful, and someone he had promised to help if she ever asked. What would he do if she came? Would he run away with her as he had with Dominique? Would he dare defy her father? At night, lying sleepless, Starbuck wove fantasies about Sally Truslow. He knew the dreams were as stupid as they were impractical, but he was a young man and he so wanted to be in love and thus he dreamed the stupid and impractical dreams.

"I'm real grateful you said nothing about Sally." Truslow seemed to want a response, perhaps an affirmation that Starbuck had indeed kept the night wedding a secret instead of making fun of the family's misfortune.

"I never thought to tell anyone," Starbuck said. "It's no one else's business." It was pleasant to sound so virtuous again, though Starbuck suspected his silence about the marriage had been prompted more by an instinctive fear of Truslow's enmity than by any principle of reticence.

"So what did you make of Sally?" Truslow asked in all seriousness.

"She is a very pretty girl." Starbuck gave the response equally seriously, as though he had not imagined riding away with her to the new western lands or sometimes sailing east to Europe where, in his daydreams, he dazzled her with his sophistication in palatial hotels and brilliant ballrooms.

Truslow nodded acceptance of Starbuck's compliment. "She looks like her mother. Young Decker's a lucky boy, I suppose, though maybe he ain't. Prettiness ain't always a gift in a woman, especially if they own a mirror. Emily now, she never thought twice on it, but Sally." He said the name sadly, then rode in silence for a long time, evidently reflecting on his family. Starbuck, because he had shared a moment's intimacy with that family, had unwittingly become a confidant of Truslow who, after his silence, shook his head, spat out his tobacco spittle and declared his verdict. "Some men ain't intended to be family men, but young Decker is. He'd like to join his cousin in the Legion, but he's not the fighting type. Not like you."

"Me?" Starbuck was surprised.

"You're a fighter, boy. I can tell. You won't wet your pants when you see the elephant."

"See the elephant?" Starbuck asked, amused.

Truslow made a face as if to suggest that he was tired of single-handedly correcting Starbuck's education, but then deigned to explain anyway. "If you grow up in the country you're always being told about the circus. All the wonders of it. The freak shows and the animals acts, and the elephant, and all the children keep asking what the elephant is, and you can't explain, so one day you take the children and they see for themselves. That's what a man's first battle is like. Like seeing the elephant. Some men piss their pants, some run like hell, some make the enemy run. You'll be all right, but Faulconer won't." Truslow jerked a scornful head at the Colonel, who was riding alone at the head of the small column. "You mark me well, boy, but I tell you Faulconer won't last one battle."

The thought of battle made Starbuck shiver suddenly. Sometimes the anticipation was exciting, other times it was terrifying, and this time the thought of seeing the elephant was scaring him, perhaps because the raid's failure had shown just how much could go wrong. He did not want to think about the consequences of things going wrong in battle, so changed the subject by blurting out the first question that came to his tongue. "Did you really murder three men?"

Truslow gave him a strange look, as though he did not understand why such a question would ever be asked. "At least," Truslow said scornfully. "Why?"

"So how does it feel to murder someone?" Starbuck asked. He had really wanted to ask why the murders had been committed, and how, and whether anyone had tried to bring Truslow to justice, but instead he asked the stupid question about sensation.

Truslow mocked the query. "How does it feel? Jesus, boy, there are times when you make more noise than a cracked pot. How does it feel? You find out for yourself, boy. You go and murder someone, then you tell me the answer." Truslow spurred ahead, evidently disgusted with Starbuck's prurient question.

They camped that night on a wet ridge above a small settlement where a smelting furnace blazed like the maw of hell and seeped the foul stench of coal smoke up to the ridge where Starbuck could not sleep. Instead he sat with the guards, shivering and wishing the rain would stop. He had eaten his supper of cold dried beef and damp bread with the other three officers, and Faulconer had been livelier than on the previous nights and had even sought some consolation for the raid's failure. "Our powder might have let us down," he said, "but we showed we could be a threat."

"That's true, Colonel," Hinton said loyally.

"They'll have to post guards on every bridge," the Colonel claimed, "and a man guarding a bridge can't be invading the South."

"That's the truth, too," Hinton said cheerfully. "And it could take them days to clear that locomotive off the track. It was dug in brutally deep."

"So it wasn't a failure," the Colonel said.

"Far from it!" Captain Hinton was resolutely optimistic.

"And it was a good piece of training for our cavalry scouts," the Colonel said.

"Indeed it was." Hinton grinned at Starbuck, trying to include him in the friendlier atmosphere, but the Colonel just frowned.

Now, as the night inched by, Starbuck was plunged deep down into a young man's despair. It was not just his alienation from Washington Faulconer that oppressed him, but the knowledge that his life had gone so utterly wrong. There were excuses, good excuses maybe, but at heart he knew he was the one who had gone astray. He had left his family and his church, even his own country, to live among strangers, and the ties of their affection did not run deeply enough or strongly enough to offer him any hope. Washington Faulconer was a man whose bitter disappointment was as sour as the reek of the smelter's furnace. Truslow was an ally, but for how long? And what did Starbuck have in common with Truslow?

Truslow and his followers would thieve and kill, but Starbuck could not see himself behaving so, and as for the others, like Medlicott, they hated Starbuck for being an intrusive Yankee, an outsider, a stranger, a favorite of the Colonel's who had become the Colonel's scapegoat.

Starbuck shivered in the rain, his knees drawn up to his chest. He felt utterly alone. So what should he do? The rain dripped monotonously, while behind him a picketed horse stamped the wet ground. The wind was cold, coming up from the settlement with its grim furnace house and rows of dull houses. The furnace illuminated the buildings with a sullen glow against which the tangled trees of the intervening slope were intricately and smokily silhouetted to form an impenetrable tangle of twisted black limbs and splintered trunks. It was a wilderness, Starbuck thought, and at its far side lay nothing but hellfire, and the dark horror of the intervening downward slope seemed a prophecy of all his future life.

So go home, he told himself. It was time to admit that he had been wrong. The adventure was over and he had to go home. He had been made a fool, first by Dominique and now by these Virginians who disliked him because he was a northerner. So he should go home. He might still be a soldier, indeed he should be a soldier, but he would fight for the North. He would fight for Old Glory, for the continuation of a glorious century of American progress and decency. He would give up the specious arguments that pretended slavery was not the issue, and instead join the crusade of righteousness and he suddenly imagined himself as a crusader with a red cross on his white surcoat galloping across the sunny uplands of history to defeat a huge wickedness.

He would go home. He had to go home for his soul's sake, because otherwise he would stay enmeshed in the tangled dark of the wilderness. He was not yet sure just how he would manage to reach home and, for a few wild moments, he toyed with the idea of seizing his horse and just galloping free of this hilltop, except that the horses were all tethered and Colonel Faulconer, fearing a pursuit by northern cavalry, had insisted on setting sentries who would be sure to stop Starbuck. No, he decided, he would wait till he reached Faulconer Court House and there he would seek an honest interview with Washington Faulconer and confess his failure and his disappointment. He would then ask for help to go back home. He had an idea there were truce boats sailing up the James River and Faulconer would surely help him find a berth aboard one of those ships.

He felt the decision settle in his mind, and also the contentment of a choice well made. He even slept a little, waking with a clearer eye and a happier heart. He felt like Christian in *Pilgrim's Progress,* as if he had escaped from both Vanity Fair and the Slough of Despond and were once again heading toward the Celestial City.

Next day the raiding party reached and crossed the Shenandoah Valley, and the following morning they rode out of the Blue Ridge Mountains under a clearing sky and a warming wind. Scraps of white cloud blew northward, their shadows flying across the green good land. The disappointment of the raid seemed forgotten as the horses scented home and quickened into a trot. The town of Faulconer Court House was spread before them, the copper-coated cupola of its courthouse bright in the sun and the steeples of its churches rising sharp above the blossom-rich trees. Nearer, beside the quick river, the tents of the Legion lay white in the meadow.

Tomorrow, Starbuck thought, he would seek a long talk with Washington Faulconer. Tomorrow he would confront his mistake and put it right. Tomorrow he would begin to straighten himself with man and God. Tomorrow he would be born again, and that idea cheered him and even made him smile, and then he forgot the thought entirely, indeed he let the whole plan of going back to the North slide free of his mind altogether, for there, coming from the Legion's encampment and mounted on a pale horse, was a young stocky man with a square beard and a welcoming smile, and Starbuck, who had been feeling so lonely and so mistreated, galloped madly ahead to greet his friend.

For Adam had come home.

7

The friends met, reined in, both spoke at once, checked, laughed, spoke again, but were each too full of news and the pleasure of reunion to make much sense of the other. "You look weary." Adam at last managed to edge in an intelligible remark.

"I am."

"I must meet Father. Then we'll talk." Adam spurred on toward Washington Faulconer who, the failure of his raid apparently forgotten, was beaming with happiness at his son's return.

"How did you get back?" Faulconer called as his son galloped toward him.

"They wouldn't let me over the Long Bridge at Washington, so I went upriver and paid a ferryman near Leesburg."

"When did you get home?"

"Just yesterday." Adam reined in to receive his father's greeting. It was plain to everyone that Washington Faulconer's happiness was entirely restored. His son had come home, and the uncertainties of Adam's loyalty were thus resolved. The Colonel's pleasure expanded to include and even to seek forgiveness from Starbuck. "I've been distracted, Nate. You must forgive me," he said quietly to Nate when Adam had gone on to greet Murphy, Hinton and Truslow.

Starbuck, too embarrassed by the older man's apology, said nothing.

"You'll join us for dinner at Seven Springs, Nate?" Faulconer had mistaken Starbuck's silence for pique. "I'd take it hard if you refused."

"Of course, sir." Starbuck paused, then bit an unfair bullet. "And I'm sorry if I let you down, sir."

"You didn't, you didn't, you didn't." Faulconer thus hurriedly brushed away Starbuck's apology. "I've been distracted, Nate. Nothing else. I put too many hopes in that raid, and didn't foresee the weather. That was all it was, Nate, the weather. Adam, come!" Adam had spent much of his morning meeting his old friends in the Legion, but his father now insisted on showing his son around the whole encampment one more time, and

Adam good-humoredly expressed his admiration of the tent lines and the horse lines, and of the cook house, the wagon park and the meeting tent.

There were now six hundred and seventy-eight volunteers in the camp, almost all of them from within a half day's ride of Faulconer Court House. They had been divided into ten companies, which had then elected their own officers though, as Faulconer cheerfully admitted, a deal of bribery had been needed to make sure that the best men won. "I think I used four barrels of best mountain whiskey," Faulconer confided in his son, "to make sure that Miller and Patterson weren't elected." Each company had selected a captain and two lieutenants, while some had a second lieutenant as well. Washington Faulconer had appointed his own headquarters staff with the elderly Major Pelham as his second in command and the egregious Major Bird as his over-promoted clerk. "I tried to rid us of Pecker, but your mother absolutely insisted," the Colonel confided in Adam. "Have you seen your mother?"

"This morning, sir, yes."

"And is she well?"

"She says not."

"She usually improves when I go away," the Colonel said in a dryly amused voice. "And these are the headquarter tents." Unlike the bell-shaped tents of the infantry companies the four headquarter tents were large wall-sided ridge tents, each equipped with a groundsheet, camp beds, folding stools, washing bowl, jug and a collapsible camp table which folded into a canvas bag. "That's mine." Faulconer gestured at the cleanest tent. "Major Pelham's is next to me. I'll put Ethan and Pecker over there, and you and Nate can share the fourth tent. I guess that will please you?" Adam and Ridley had both been appointed as captains, while Starbuck was the lowest of the low, a second lieutenant, and together the three young men formed what the Colonel called his corps of aides. Their job, he told Adam, was to be his messengers, as well as to serve as his eyes and ears on the battlefield. He made it all sound very ominous.

The Legion consisted of more than just the headquarters staff and ten companies of infantry. There was a band, a medical unit, a color party, a force of fifty cavalrymen who would be led by a captain and serve as the Legion's scouts, and the battery of two bronze six-pounder cannon, both twenty years old and with smoothbore barrels that Faulconer had purchased from Bowers Foundry in Richmond where the guns had gone to be melted down and so made into newer weapons. He proudly showed the pair of guns to his son. "Aren't they marvelous?"

The guns were certainly smart. Their bronze barrels had been buffed to a sun-reflecting dazzle, the wheel spokes and rims were newly varnished, while the guns' accoutrements, the chains and buckets and rammers and wormscrews, had all been variously polished or painted, yet there was something oddly unsettling about the two weapons. They looked too grim for this summer morning, too full of the menace of death.

"They're not the last word in guns." Faulconer took his son's silence for an unspoken criticism. "They're hardly Parrotts, and not even rifled, but I fancy we can strew a few Yankee corpses across the field with these beauties. Ain't that so, Pelham?"

"If we can find some ammunition for them, Colonel." Major Pelham, who was accompanying the Colonel on this inspection tour, sounded very dubious.

"We'll find ammunition!" Now that his son had returned from the North, the Colonel's ebullient optimism was wholly restored. "Ethan will find us ammunition."

"He's sent none yet," Pelham answered gloomily. Major Alexander Pelham was a tall, thin, white-haired man whom Starbuck, in the days before the raiding party had ridden north and west, had discovered to be almost perpetually morose. Pelham now waited till the Colonel and his son had ridden out of earshot then cocked a rheumy eye at Starbuck. "The best thing that can happen, Lieutenant Starbuck, is that we never find the ammunition for these cannon. The barrels will probably crack apart if we do. Artillery isn't for amateurs." He sniffed. "So the raid went badly?"

"It was disappointing, sir."

"Aye, so I heard from Murphy." Major Pelham shook his head, as though he had known all along that such adventurousness would be doomed. He was dressed in his old United States uniform that he had last worn in the War of 1812—a faded blue tunic with washed-out braid, buttons bereft of their gilt and crossbelts made of leather as cracked as sundried mud. His saber was a huge, black-scabbarded hook of a blade. He winced as the band, which had been practicing in the shade of the Legion's meeting tent, started playing "My Mary-Anne." "They've been playing that all week," he grumbled. "Mary-Anne, Mary-Anne, Mary-Anne. Maybe we can drive the Yankees off with bad music?"

"I like the tune."

"Not when you've heard it fifty times, you won't. They should be playing marching tunes. Good solid marches, that's what we need. But how much drill are we doing now? Four hours a day? It should be twelve, but the Colonel won't permit it. You can rest on it that the Yankees won't be playing baseball like us." Pelham paused to spit tobacco juice. He had an almost mystical belief in the necessity of endless drill and was supported in that creed by all the old soldiers in the Legion, and opposed by the Colonel, who still feared that too much close-order drill would dull his volunteers' enthusiasm. "Wait till you've seen the elephant," Pelham said, "then you'll know why you should be drilling."

Starbuck felt his customary response to the idea of seeing the elephant. First there was a pulse of pure fear, as palpable as a chill of liquid pumped from the heart, then there was a surge of excitement that seemed to come from the head rather than the heart, as though sheer resolution could overcome the terror and thus create a vigorous ecstasy from battle. Then came the unnerving knowledge that nothing could be understood, neither the terror nor the ecstasy, until the mystery of battle had been experienced. Starbuck's impatience to understand that mystery was mixed with a desire to delay the confrontation, and his eagerness with a fervent wish that battle would never happen. It was all very confusing.

Adam, released from his father's company, turned his horse back toward Starbuck. "We'll go down the river and have a swim."

"A swim?" Starbuck feared this activity might be a new enthusiasm in Adam's life.

"Swimming is good for you!" Adam's eagerness confirmed Starbuck's fear. "I've been talking with a doctor who claims that soaking in water prolongs life!"

"Nonsense!"

"I'll race you!" Adam kicked back his heels and galloped away.

Starbuck followed more slowly on his already tired mare as Adam led him around the town on paths he had known since childhood and that led eventually to a stretch of parkland which Starbuck assumed was part of the Seven Springs estate. By the time Starbuck reached the river Adam was already undressing. The water was limpid, tree edged and bright in the spring sunshine. "What doctor?" Starbuck challenged his friend.

"He's called Wesselhoeft. I went to see him in Vermont, on mother's behalf, of course. He recommends a diet of brown bread and milk, and frequent immersions in what he calls a *sitz-bad*."

"A sitting bath?"

"*Sitz-bad* please, my dear Nate. It works better in German, all cures do. I told Mother about Doctor Wesselhoeft and she promises me she'll try each of his specifics. Are you coming in?" Adam did not wait for an answer, but instead leaped naked into the river. He came up shouting, evidently in reaction to the water's temperature. "It doesn't really warm up until July!" he explained.

"Maybe I'll just watch you."

"Don't be absurd, Nate. I thought you New Englanders were hardy?"

"Not foolhardy," Starbuck quipped, and thought how good it was to be back with Adam. They had been apart for months, yet the very first moment they were back together it seemed as if no time had passed at all.

"Come on in, you coward," Adam called.

"Dear God." Starbuck leaped into the cleansing coldness, and came up shouting just as Adam had done. "It's freezing!"

"But good for you! Wesselhoeft recommends a cold bath every morning."

"Does Vermont not provide asylums for the insane?"

"Probably," Adam laughed, "but Wesselhoeft is very sane and very successful."

"I'd rather die young than be this cold every day." Starbuck scrambled up the bank and lay on the grass under the warm sun.

Adam joined him. "So what happened on the raid?"

Starbuck told him, though leaving out the details of Washington Faulconer's moroseness on the return ride. Instead he made the foray into something comical, a chapter of errors in which no one was hurt and no one offended. He finished by saying he did not think the war would get any more serious than the raid had been. "No one wants a real war, Adam. This is America!"

Adam shrugged. "The North isn't going to release us, Nate. The Union's too important to them." He paused. "And to me."

Starbuck did not reply. Across the river a herd of cows grazed, and in the silence the sound of their teeth tearing at the grass was surprisingly loud. Their cowbells were plangent, matching Adam's suddenly ominous mood. "Lincoln called for seventy-five thousand volunteers," he said.

"I heard."

"And the northern papers say that three times that many will be ready by June."

"You're frightened of numbers?" Starbuck asked unfairly.

"No. I'm frightened of what the numbers mean, Nate. I'm frightened of seeing America struck down into barbarism. I'm frightened of seeing fools ride yelling into battle just for the joy of it. I'm frightened of seeing our classmen become the Gadarene swine of the nineteenth century." Adam squinted across the river to where the distant hills were bright with blossoms and new leaf. "Life is so good!" he said after a while, though with a sad intensity.

"People fight to make it better," Starbuck said.

Adam laughed. "Don't be absurd, Nate."

"Why else do they fight?" Starbuck bridled.

Adam spread his hands, as if to suggest there could be a thousand answers, and none of them significant. "Men fight because they're too proud and too stupid to admit they're wrong," he finally said. "I don't care what it takes, Nate, but we've got to sit down, call a convention, talk the whole thing out! It doesn't matter if it takes a year, two years, five years! Talk must be better than war. And what's Europe going to think of us? For years we've been saying that America is the noblest, best experiment of history, and now we're going to tear it apart! For what? For states' rights? To keep slavery?"

"Your father doesn't see it as you do," Starbuck said.

"You know Father," Adam said fondly. "He's always seen life as a game. Mother says he's never really grown up."

"And you grew up before your time?" Starbuck suggested.

Adam shrugged. "I can't take matters lightly. I wish I could, but I can't. And I can't take tragedy easily, at least not this tragedy." He waved toward the cows, evidently intending those innocent and motionless beasts to stand for the spectacle of America rushing headlong into warfare. "But what about you?" He turned to Starbuck. "I hear you've been in trouble."

"Who told you?" Starbuck was instantly embarrassed. He stared up at the clouds, unable to meet his friend's gaze.

"My father wrote to me, of course. He wanted me to go to Boston and plead with your father."

"I'm glad you didn't."

"But I did. Except your father wouldn't receive me. I heard him preach though. He was formidable."

"He usually is," Starbuck said, though inwardly he was wondering why Washington Faulconer could possibly want Adam to plead with the Reverend Elial. Was Faulconer wanting to be rid of him?

Adam plucked a blade of grass and shredded it between his square, capable fingers. "Why did you do it?"

Starbuck, who had been lying on his back, suddenly felt ashamed of his nakedness and so rolled onto his belly and stared down at the clover and grass. "Dominique? Lust, I suppose."

Adam frowned, as if the concept was unknown to him. "Lust?"

"I wish I could describe it. Except that it's overwhelming. One moment everything is normal, like a ship in a calm sea, then suddenly this enormous wind comes from nowhere, this enormous, exciting, howling wind and you can't help it, but just sail madly off with it." He stopped, dissatisfied with his imagery. "It's the sirens' song, Adam. I know it's wrong, but you can't help it." Starbuck suddenly thought of Sally Truslow and the memory of her beauty hurt so much that he flinched.

Adam took the flinch as evidence of remorse. "You have to pay back the man Trabell, don't you?"

"Oh, yes. Of course I do." That necessity weighed heavily on Starbuck's conscience, at least when he allowed himself to remember the theft of Major Trabell's money. Until a few hours ago, when he had still been planning his return north, he had convinced himself that he wanted nothing more than to repay Trabell, but now, with Adam home, Starbuck wanted nothing more than to stay in Virginia. "I wish I knew how," he said vaguely.

"I think you should go home," Adam suggested firmly, "and put things straight with your family."

Starbuck had spent the last two days thinking precisely the same thing, though now he demurred from that sensible plan. "You don't know my father."

"How can a man be scared of his own father, yet contemplate going into battle without fear?"

Starbuck smiled quickly to acknowledge the point, then shook his head. "I don't want to go home."

"Must we always do what we want? There is duty and obligation."

"Maybe things didn't go wrong when I met Dominique," Starbuck said, striking obliquely away from his friend's stern words. "Maybe they went wrong when I first went to Yale. Or when I agreed to be baptized. I've never felt like a Christian, Adam. I should never have let Father baptize me. I should never have let him send me to seminary. I've been living a lie." He thought of his prayers at a dead woman's grave, and blushed. "I don't think I've even been converted. I'm not a true Christian at all."

"Of course you are!" Adam was shocked at his friend's apostasy.

"No," Starbuck insisted. "I wish I was. I've seen other men converted. I've seen the happiness in them, and the power of the Holy Spirit in them, but I've never really experienced the same thing. I've wanted to, I've always wanted to." He paused. He could think of no one else to whom he could speak like this, only Adam. Good honest Adam who was like Faithful to John Bunyan's Christian. "My God, Adam," Starbuck went on, "but I've prayed for conversion! I've begged for it! But I've never known it. I think, maybe, that if I was saved, if I was born again, I'd have the strength to resist lust, but I don't and I don't know how to find that strength." It was an honest, pathetic admission. He had been raised to believe that nothing in his whole life, not even his life itself, was as important as the necessity for conversion. Conversion, Starbuck had been taught, was the moment of being born again into Christ, that miraculous instant in which a man allowed Jesus Christ into his heart as his Lord and Savior, and if a man did allow that marvelous ingress to happen, then nothing would ever be the same again because all of life and all of subsequent eternity would be transmuted into a golden existence. Without salvation life was nothing but sin and hell and disappointment; with it there was joy, love and heaven everlasting.

Except Starbuck had never found that moment of mystical conversion. He had never experienced the joy. He had pretended to, because such a pretense was the only way to satisfy his father's insistence on salvation, yet all his life had been a lie since that moment of pretense. "There's something worse," he confessed to Adam now. "I'm beginning to suspect that real salvation, real happiness, doesn't lie in the experience of conversion at all, but in abandoning the whole concept. Maybe I'll only be happy if I can reject the whole paraphernalia?"

"My God," Adam said, horrified at the very idea of such Godlessness. He thought for a few seconds. "I don't think," he went on slowly, "that conversion depends on an outside influence. You can't expect a magical change, Nate. True conversion comes from an inner determination."

"You mean Christ has nothing to do with it?"

"Of course he does, yes, but he's powerless unless you invite him in. You have to unleash his power."

"I can't!" The protest was almost a wail, the cry of a young man desperate to be released from the travails of religious struggle, a struggle that pitted Christ and his salvation against the temptation of Sally Truslow and Dominique and of all the other forbidden and wonderful delights that seemed to tear Starbuck's soul in two.

"You should begin by going home," Adam said. "It's your duty."

"I'm not going home," Starbuck said, utterly ignoring his recent decision to do just that. "I won't find God at home, Adam. I need to be on my own." That was not true. Starbuck, now that his friend had returned to Faulconer Court House, wanted to stay in Virginia because the summer which had looked so threatening under Washington Faulconer's disapproval was suddenly promising to be golden again. "And why are you here?" Starbuck turned the questioning on his friend. "For duty?"

"I suppose so." Adam was uncomfortable with the question. "I suppose we all look for home when things seem bad. And they are bad, Nate. The North is going to invade."

Starbuck grinned. "So we fight them off, Adam, and that will be the end of it. One battle! One short, sweet battle. One victory, and then peace. You'll get your convention then, you'll get everything you want probably, but you have to fight one battle first."

Adam smiled. It seemed to him that his friend Nate existed only for sensation. Not for thought, which Adam liked to think was his own touchstone. Adam believed that the truth of everything, from slavery to salvation, could be adduced by reason, while Starbuck, he realized, was swayed solely by emotion. In some ways, Adam thought with a surprise, Starbuck resembled his father, the Colonel. "I'm not going to fight," Adam said after a long pause. "I won't fight."

It was Starbuck's turn to be shocked. "Does your father know that?"

Adam shook his head, but said nothing. It seemed that he too was wary of a father's disapproval.

"So why did you come home?" Starbuck asked.

Adam was quiet for a long while. "I think," he said at last, "because I knew that nothing I could say would help any longer. No one was listening to reason, only to passion. The people I thought wanted peace turned out to want victory more. Fort Sumter changed them, you see. It didn't matter that no one had died there, the bombardment proved to them that the slave states would never yield to reason, and then they demanded that I add my voice to their demands, and those demands weren't for moderation anymore, but for the destruction of all this." He gestured at the Faulconer domain, at the sweet fields and heavy trees. "They wanted me to attack Father and his friends, and I refused to do it. So I came home instead."

"But you won't fight?"

"I don't think so."

Starbuck frowned. "You're braver than me, Adam, my God you are."

"Am I? I wouldn't have dared run away with a, with a"—Adam paused, unable to find a word delicate enough to describe the very indelicate Dominique—"I wouldn't have dared risk my whole life for a whim!" He made it sound admirable instead of shameful.

"It was nothing but stupidity," Starbuck confessed.

"And you'd never do it again?" Adam asked with a smile, and Starbuck thought of Sally Truslow, and said nothing. Adam plucked a blade of grass and twisted it about his finger. "So what do you think I should do?"

So Adam's mind was not made up after all? Starbuck smiled. "I'll tell you exactly what to do. Just go along with your father. Play at soldiers, enjoy the encampment, have a marvelous summer. Peace will come, Adam, maybe after one battle, but peace will come, and it will be soon. Why ruin your father's happiness? What do you gain by doing that?"

"Honesty?" Adam suggested. "I have to live with myself, Nate."

Adam found living with himself difficult, as Nate well knew. Adam was a stern and demanding young man, especially of himself. He might forgive weakness in others, but not in his own character. "So why did you come back?" Starbuck went on the attack. "Just to raise your father's hopes before disappointing him? My God, Adam, you talk about my duty to my father, what's yours? To preach to him? To break his heart? Why are you here? Because you expect your tenants and neighbors to fight, but think you can sit the battle out because you've got scruples? My God, Adam, you'd have done better to stay in the North."

Adam paused a long time before responding. "I'm here because I'm weak."

"Weak!" That was the last quality Starbuck would have ascribed to his friend.

"Because you're right; I can't disappoint Father. Because I know what he wants, and it doesn't seem such a great deal to give him." Adam shook his head. "He's such a generous man, and he's so often disappointed in people. I really would like to make him happy."

"Then for God's sake put on the uniform, play soldiers and pray for peace. Besides," Starbuck said, deliberately lightening the mood, "I can't bear the thought of a summer without your company. Can you imagine just me and Ethan as your father's aides?"

"You don't like Ethan?" Adam had detected the distaste in Starbuck's voice and seemed surprised by it.

"He seems not to like me. I took fifty bucks off him in a bet and he hasn't forgiven me for it."

"He's touchy about money," Adam agreed. "In fact I sometimes wonder if that's why he wants to marry Anna, but that's a very unworthy suspicion, isn't it?"

"Is it?"

"Of course it is."

Starbuck remembered Belvedere Delaney voicing the same suspicion, but did not mention it. "Why does Anna want to marry Ethan?" he asked instead.

"She just wants to escape," Adam said. "Can you imagine life in Seven Springs? She sees marriage as her ticket to freedom." Adam suddenly leaped to his feet and scrambled to pull on his trousers, his haste occasioned by the approach of a small dog cart that was being driven by Anna herself. "She's here!" Adam warned Starbuck who, like his friend, hurriedly tugged on his pants and shirt and was just pulling on his stockings as Anna reined in. Her cart was escorted by three yapping spaniels that now leaped excitedly at Adam and Starbuck.

Anna, sheltered from the sun by a wide, lace-fringed parasol, stared reproachfully at her brother. "You're late for dinner, Adam."

"My Lord, is that the time?" Adam fumbled for his watch among his rumpled clothes. One of the spaniels leaped up and down at him while the other two lapped noisily from the river.

"It doesn't really matter that you're late," Anna said, "because there's been some trouble at the camp."

"What trouble?" Starbuck asked.

"Truslow discovered his son-in-law had joined the Legion while he was away. So he hit him!" Anna seemed very shocked at the violence.

"He hit Decker?"

"Is that his name?" Anna asked.

"What happened to Decker's wife?" Starbuck asked a little too urgently.

"I'll tell you at dinner," Anna said. "Now why don't you finish dressing, Mister Starbuck, then tie your tired horse to the back of the cart and ride home with me. You can hold the parasol and tell me all about the raid. I want to hear everything."

Ethan Ridley took Sally Truslow to Muggeridge's Drapery and Millinery in Exchange Alley where he bought her a parasol in printed calico to match her pale green linen cambric dress. She was also wearing a fringed paisley shawl, yarn stockings, a wide-brimmed hat trimmed with silk lilies, white ankle-length boots and white lace gloves. She carried a small beaded handbag and, in rude contrast, her old canvas bag.

"Let me hold the bag for you," Ridley said. Sally wanted to try on a linen hat with a stiffened brim and a muslin veil.

"Take care of it." Sally gave him the bag reluctantly.

"Of course." The canvas bag was heavy, and Ridley wondered if she did have a gun in there. Ridley himself had a gun at his hip as part of his uniform. He was in the yellow trimmed gray of the Faulconer Legion, with a saber at his left hip and the revolver on his right side.

Sally turned around in front of the cheval mirror, admiring the hat. "It's real nice," she said.

"You look lovely," Ridley said, though in truth he had found her company ever more grating in these last few days. She had no education, no subtlety and no wit. What she had was the face of an angel, the body of a whore, and his bastard in her belly. She also had a desperation to escape the narrow world of her father's cramped homestead, but Ridley was too concerned for his own future to comprehend Sally's plight. He did not see her as attempting to escape from an unbearable past, but as an extortioner trying to gouge a parasitical future. He did not see the fear in her, only the determination to take what she wanted. He despised her. At night, impassioned, he wanted nothing more than to be with her, but by day, exposed to her crude ideas and lacerating voice, he wanted only to be rid of her. And today he would be rid of her, but first it was necessary to lull her into complacency.

He took her to Lascelles Jewelry store on Eighth Street where he listened to the owner's splenetic complaints about the proposal to lay a railroad line directly outside his shop window. The line, which would run down the center of the steep street, was intended to connect the Richmond, Fredericksburg and Potomac rails with the Richmond and Petersburg line so that military supplies could be carried across the city without the need to unload one set of rail wagons into horse-drawn carts. "But have they considered the effect upon trade, Captain Ridley? Have they? No! And who will buy fine jewelry with locomotives smoking outside? It's preposterous!"

Ridley bought Sally a filigree necklace that was flashy enough to please her and cheap enough not to offend his parsimony. He also bought a narrow gold ring, scarce more than a curtain band, which he pushed into his uniform pocket. The purchases, with the parasol and linen hat, cost him fourteen dollars, and the brisket of beef that he bought as dinner in the Spotswood House cost another dollar thirty. He was lulling Sally's apprehensions, and the price was worth it if she went quietly to whatever fate awaited her. He gave her wine to drink with the meal, and brandy afterward. She wanted a cigar and was quite unworried that no other lady in the dining room chose to smoke. "I've always liked a cigar. My ma used a pipe, but I like a cigar." She smoked contentedly, oblivious of the amused stare of the other diners. "This is real nice." She had taken to luxury like a starved cat to a creamery.

"You should get used to this sort of place," Ridley said. He lolled in his chair, an elegantly booted leg propped on the cold radiator that stood beneath the window and looked onto the hotel's courtyard. His scabbarded saber hung from its slings on the radiator's purge valve. "I am going to make you a lady," he lied to her. "I am going to teach you how a lady speaks, how a lady behaves, how a lady eats, how a lady dances, how a lady reads, how a lady dresses. I am going to make you into a great lady."

She smiled. To be a great lady was Sally's dream. She imagined herself in silks and lace, ruling a parlor like the one in Belvedere Delaney's house, no, an even bigger parlor, a vast parlor, a parlor with cliffs for walls and a vaulted heaven for a ceiling and golden furniture and hot water all day long. "Are we really looking for a house this afternoon?" she asked wistfully. "I'm real tired of Mrs. Cobbold." Mrs. Cobbold owned the boardinghouse in Monroe Street and was suspicious of Ridley's relationship with Sally.

"We're not looking for a house," Ridley corrected her, "but a set of rooms. My brother knows some that are for rent."

"Rooms." She was suspicious.

"Large rooms. Tall ceilings, carpets." Ridley waved his hands to suggest opulence. "A place you can keep your own niggers."

"I can have a nigger?" she asked excitedly.

"Two." Ridley embroidered his promise. "You can have a maid and a cook. Then, of course, when the baby comes, you can have a nurse."

"I want a carriage, too. A carriage like that." She gestured through the window at a four-wheeled carriage that had an elegant shell body slung on leather springs and a black canvas hood folded back to reveal an interior of scarlet buttoned leather. The carriage was drawn by four matching bays. A Negro coachman sat on the box while another black, either slave or servant, handed a woman up into the open coach.

"That's a barouche," Ridley told her.

"Barouche." Sally tried the word and liked it.

A tall, rather cadaverous man followed the woman into the barouche. "And that," Ridley told Sally, "is our president."

"The skinny one!" She leaned forward to stare at Jefferson Davis who, his top hat in his hand, was standing in the carriage to finish a conversation with two men who stood on the hotel steps. His business finished, President Davis sat opposite his wife and crammed the glossy hat on his head. "Is that really Jeff Davis?" Sally asked.

"It is. He's staying in the hotel while they find him a house."

"I never thought I'd see a president," Sally said, and watched wide-eyed as the barouche turned in the courtyard before clattering under the arch into Main Street. Sally smiled at Ridley. "You're trying real hard to be nice, aren't you?" she said, as though Ridley had personally arranged for the president of the Provisional Government of the Confederate States of America to parade for Sally's benefit.

"I'm trying real hard," he said, and reached across the table to take hold of her left hand. He drew it toward him and kissed her fingers. "I'm going to go on trying real hard," he said, "so that you'll always be happy."

"And the baby." Sally was beginning to feel motherly.

"And our baby," Ridley said, though the words very nearly stuck in his craw, but he managed to smile, then took the new gold ring out of his pocket, shook it free of its small wash-leather bag and placed it on her ring finger. "You should have a wedding ring," he explained. Sally had started to wear the antique silver ring on her right hand, and her left was consequently bare.

Sally examined the effect of the small gold ring on her finger, then laughed. "Does this mean we're married?"

"It means you should look respectable for a landlord," he said, then took her right hand in his and tugged the silver ring over her knuckle.

"Careful!" Sally tried to pull her hand away, but Ridley kept firm hold.

"I'm going to have it cleaned," he said. He placed the silver ring in the wash-leather bag. "I'll take good care of it," he promised, though in truth he had decided that the antique ring would make a good keepsake to remember Sally by. "Now come!" He glanced at the big clock above the carving table. "We have to meet my brother."

They walked through the spring sunshine and folks thought what a fine couple they made; a handsome southern officer and his beautiful, graceful girl who, flushed with wine, laughed beside her man. Sally even danced a few steps as she imagined what happiness these next months would bring. She would be a respectable lady, with her own slaves and living in luxury. When Sally had been small her mother would sometimes talk about the fine houses of the wealthy and how they had candles in every room and feather mattresses on every bed and ate off golden plates and never knew what the cold was. Their water did not come from a stream that froze in winter, their beds had no lice and their hands were never chipped and sore like Sally's. Now Sally would live just like that. "Robert said I'd be happy if I just stopped dreaming," she confided in her lover, "and if he could see me now!"

"Did you tell him you were coming here?" Ridley asked.

"Of course not! I'm not wanting to see him ever again. Not till I'm a great lady and then I'll let him open my carriage door and he won't even know who I am." She laughed at that fine revenge on her previous poverty. "Is that your brother's coach?"

They had come to the corner of Cary Street and Twenty-fourth. It was a grim quarter of town, close to the York River Railroad that lay between the cobbled street and the rocky riverbank. Ridley had explained to Sally that his brother did business in this part of town, which is why they needed to walk through its streets. Now, on the point of ridding himself of the girl, he felt a pang of remorse. Her company this afternoon had been light and easy, her laughter unforced, and the glances of other men in the streets had been flatteringly jealous. Then Ridley thought of her ambition that was so unrealistic and of the threat she represented, and so he hardened his heart to the inevitable. "That's the carriage," he said, guessing that the big, ugly, close-curtained coach was indeed Delaney's vehicle, though there was no sign of Delaney himself. Instead there was a massive Negro on the box and two gaunt sway-backed horses in the delapidated harness.

The Negro looked down at Ridley. "You Mister Ridley, Massa?"

"Yes." Ridley felt Sally's hands clutch fearfully at his arm.

The Negro knocked twice on the coach roof and the curtained door opened to reveal a thin, middle-aged white man with a gap-toothed grin, dirty hair and a walleye. "Mister Ridley. And you must be Miss Truslow?"

"Yes." Sally was nervous.

"Welcome, ma'am. Welcome." The ugly creature leaped down from the carriage to offer Sally a deep bow. "My name is Tillotson, ma'am, Joseph Tillotson, and I am your servant, ma'am, your most obedient servant." He looked up at her from his bowed position, blinked in astonishment at her beauty and seemed to leer in anticipation as he swept his hand in an elaborate gesture inviting her into the coach's interior. "Be so pleased, dear lady, as to step inside the coach and I shall wave my wand and turn it into a golden carriage fit for a princess as lovely as you." He snuffled with laughter at his own wit.

"This ain't your brother, Ethan." Sally was suspicious and apprehensive.

"We're going to meet him, ma'am, indeed we are," Tillotson said and offered her his grotesque welcoming bow again.

"You're coming, Ethan?" Sally still clung to her lover's arm.

"Of course I am," Ridley reassured Sally, then persuaded her to walk toward the coach as Tillotson folded down a set of steps covered in threadbare carpet.

"Give me your parasol, ma'am, and allow me." Tillotson took Sally's parasol, then handed her up into the dark, musty interior. The coach's windows were covered by leather-blinds that had been unrolled from their spindles and nailed to the bottom sill. Ridley stepped toward the coach, uncertain what to do next, but Tillotson pushed him unceremoniously away, folded up the carriage steps then leapt nimbly into the coach's dark interior. "Got her, Tommy!" he shouted to the driver. "Go on!" He tossed the brand-new parasol into the gutter and slammed the door.

"Ethan!" Sally's voice called in pathetic protest as the big coach lurched forward. Then she called again, but louder. "Ethan!"

There was the sound of a slap, a scream, then silence. The Negro coachman cracked his whip, the carriage's iron-rimmed wheels screeched on the cobbles as the heavy vehicle slewed around the corner, and thus Ridley was rid of his succuba. He felt remorse, for her voice had been so pathetic in that last desperate cry, but he knew there had been no other alternative. Indeed, he told himself, the whole wretched business had been Sally's own fault, for she had made herself into a nuisance, good for one thing only, but now she was gone and he told himself he was well shot of her.

He still held Sally's heavy bag. He pulled it open to find there was no gun inside, just the one hundred silver dollars he had originally paid to bribe her into silence. Each coin had been separately wrapped in a torn sheet of blue sugar paper, as if each was peculiarly special, and for a moment Ridley's heart was touched by that childish tribute, but then he realized that Sally had probably wrapped the coins to stop them chinking and thus attracting predatory attention. Whatever, the coins were now his again, which only seemed right. He tucked the bag under his arm, pulled on his gloves, tipped his uniform hat over his eyes, tugged his saber to a jaunty angle, and sauntered slowly home.

"It seems"—Anna reached across the table for a bread roll that she broke into two, then dipped one half in gravy as a titbit for her noisy spaniels— "that Truslow has a daughter, and the daughter got herself pregnant, so he married her off to some poor boy and now the daughter's run away and the boy's in the Legion, and Truslow is angry."

"Damned angry," her father said in high amusement. "Hit the boy."

"Poor Truslow," Adam said.

"Poor boy." Anna dropped another morsel of bread among her yapping, scrapping dogs. "Truslow broke his cheekbone, isn't that right, Papa?"

"Broke it badly," Faulconer confirmed. The Colonel had managed to repair the ravages imposed on him by the abortive cavalry raid. He had bathed, trimmed his beard and donned uniform so that he once again looked like a dashing soldier. "The boy's called Robert Decker," the

Colonel went on, "the son of Tom Decker, you remember him, Adam? Wretched man. He's dead now, it seems, and good riddance."

"I remember Sally Truslow," Adam said idly. "A sullen thing, but real pretty."

"Did you see the girl when you were up at Truslow's place, Nate?" Faulconer asked. The Colonel was trying very hard to be pleasant toward Starbuck to show that the morose disregard of the last few days was over and forgotten.

"I don't remember noticing her, sir."

"You would have noticed her," Adam said. "She's kind of noticeable."

"Well, she's bolted," Faulconer said, "and Decker doesn't know where she's run to, and Truslow's mad at him. Seems he gave the happy couple his patch of land and they've just left it in Roper's care. You remember Roper, Adam? He's living up there now. Man's a rogue, but he knew how to manage horses."

"I don't suppose they were ever properly married." Anna found the plight of the unhappy couple far more interesting than the fate of a freed slave.

"I doubt it very much," her father agreed. "It would have been one quick jump over the broomstick, if they were even that formal."

Starbuck stared down at his plate. Dinner had been a dish of boiled bacon, dried corn pie and fried potatoes. Washington Faulconer, his two children and Adam had been the only diners, and Truslow's attack on Robert Decker the only topic of conversation. "Where can the poor girl have gone?" Adam asked.

"Richmond," his father said instantly. "All the bad girls go to Richmond. She'll find herself work," he said, glancing at Anna and making a rueful face, "of a kind."

Anna blushed, while Starbuck was thinking that Ethan Ridley was also in Richmond. "What happens to Truslow?" he asked instead.

"Nothing. He's already full of remorse. I put him in the guard tent and threatened him with ten kinds of hell." In fact Major Pelham had arrested Truslow and done all the threatening, but Faulconer did not think the distinction important. The Colonel lit a cigar. "Now Truslow's insisting that Decker join his company and I suppose I'd better let him. It seems the boy's got relatives in the company. Can't you keep those dogs quiet, Anna?"

"No, Father." She dropped another scrap of gravy-soaked bread into the noisy free-for-all. "And speaking of jumping over broomsticks," she said, "you all missed Pecker's wedding."

"That was a very proper wedding, surely?" her brother said sternly.

"Of course it was. Moss officiated very damply and Priscilla looked almost pretty." Anna smiled. "Uncle Pecker glowered at us all, it poured with rain and Mother sent six bottles of wine as a present."

"Our best wine," Washington Faulconer said stonily.

"How would Mother have known?" Anna asked innocently.

"She knew," Faulconer said.

"And the schoolchildren sang a very feeble song," Anna went on. "When I get married, Father, I do not want the Tompkinson twins singing for me. Is that very ungrateful?"

"You'll get married in St. Paul's, Richmond," her father said, "with the Reverend Peterkin officiating."

"In September," Anna insisted. "I've talked with Mama, and she agrees. But only if we have your blessing, Papa, of course."

"September?" Washington Faulconer shrugged, as though he did not much mind when the wedding took place. "Why not?"

"Why September?" Adam asked.

"Because the war will be over by then," Anna declared, "and if we leave it later then there'll be bad weather for the Atlantic crossing, and Mother says we need to be in Paris by October at the latest. We'll have a winter in Paris, then go to the German spas in the spring. Mama says you might like to come, Adam?"

"Me?" Adam seemed surprised at the invitation.

"To keep Ethan company while Mama and I take the waters. And to be Mama's escort, of course."

"You can go in uniform, Adam." Washington Faulconer clearly did not resent being left out of the family expedition. "Your mother would like that. Full-dress uniform with saber, sash and medals, eh? Show the Europeans how a southern soldier looks?"

"Me?" Adam asked again, this time of his father.

"Yes, you, Adam." Faulconer tossed his napkin onto the table. "And talking of uniforms, you'll find one in your room. Put it on, then come to the study and we'll fit you out with a saber. You too, Nate. Every officer should carry a blade."

Adam paused and for a second or two Starbuck feared that this was the moment when his friend would make his pacifist stand. Starbuck tensed for the confrontation, but then, with a decisive nod that suggested he had made his choice only after a great effort of will, Adam pushed back his chair. "To work," he said quietly, almost to himself, "to work."

The work proved to be a glorious early summer of drumbeats and drill, of exercises across pastureland and of comradeship in tented encampments. They were hot days of laughter, weariness, sore muscles, tanned skin, high hopes and powder-stained faces. The Legion practiced musketry until the men's shoulders were bruised from the impact of the guns and their faces smeared black by the explosion of the percussion caps and their lips powder stained from biting open the paper-wrapped cartridges. They learned to fix bayonets, to form a firing line and to make a square to fend off cavalry. They began to feel like soldiers.

They learned to sleep through discomfort and discovered the long loping march rhythm that would see a man through endless, sun-racked days on heat-baked roads. On Sundays they formed a hollow square for a service of prayer and hymns. Their favorite was "Fight the Good Fight," while in the evenings, when men were feeling maudlin for their families, they loved to sing "Amazing Grace" very slowly so that the sweet tune lingered in the hot evening air. On other nights of the week groups of men formed Bible classes or prayer meetings, while some played cards or drank the liquor that was sold illegally by peddlers come from Charlottesville or Richmond. Once, when Major Pelham caught such a peddler, he broke the man's entire stock of stone-bottled mountain whiskey, though the Colonel was less inclined to take the hard line. "Let them have their good time," Faulconer liked to say.

Adam feared that his father was trying too hard to be popular, yet in fairness the lenience was all a part of Washington Faulconer's theory of soldiering. "These men aren't European peasants," the Colonel explained, "and they certainly ain't northern factory drudges. These are good Americans! Good southerners! They've got fire in their bellies and liberty in their hearts and if we force them into hours of drill and yet more drill and still more drill we'll simply dull them into witless fools. I want them eager! I want them to go into battle like horses fresh off a spring pasture, not like nags coming off winter hay. I want them full of spirit, élan, the French call it, and it's going to win us this war!"

"Not without drill, it won't," Major Pelham would answer gloomily. He was allowed to give four hours of drill a day and not a minute more. "I'll warrant Robert Lee is drilling his men in Richmond," Pelham would insist, "and McDowell his in Washington!"

"I warrant they are too, and so they should, just to keep the rogues out of mischief. But our rogues are better quality. They're going to make the best soldiers in America! In the world!" And when the Colonel was in this sublime mood neither Pelham, nor all the military experts in Christendom could have changed his mind.

So Sergeant Truslow simply ignored the Colonel and made his company do the extra drill anyway. At first, when Truslow had come down from his high home in the hills, the Colonel had imagined employing him as one of the fifty cavalrymen who would be the Legion's outriders and scouts, but somehow, after the raid, the Colonel felt less willing to have Truslow so close to headquarters, and so he had let Truslow become company sergeant to Company K, one of the two skirmishing companies, but even from there, on the outer flank of the Legion, Truslow's influence was baleful. Soldiering, he said, was about winning battles, not about holding prayer meetings or hymn singing, and he immediately insisted that Company K triple the amount of time it spent in drill. He had the company out of bed two hours before dawn and, by the time the other companies were just beginning to light their breakfast fires, Company K was already tired. Captain Roswell Jennings, K Company's commanding officer who had secured his election with lavish quantities of homemade whiskey, was happy so long as Truslow did not demand his presence at the extra sessions.

The other companies, seeing the extra snap and pride in Company K, had begun to lengthen their own time on the parade ground. Major Pelham was delighted, the Colonel held his peace, while Sergeant Major Proctor, who had been Washington Faulconer's bailiff, deviled through his drill books to find new and more complicated maneuvers for the rapidly improving Legion to practice. Soon even old Benjamin Ridley, Ethan's father, who had been a militia officer in his younger days, but who was now so fat and ill that he could scarcely walk, grudgingly admitted that the Legion was at last beginning to look like real soldiers.

Ethan Ridley had returned from Richmond with caissons, limbers and ammunition for the two artillery pieces. The Legion was now fully equipped. Each man had a double-breasted gray jacket with two rows of brass buttons, a pair of ankle-high boots, gray trousers and a round cap with a crown and visor stiffened with pasteboard. He carried a knapsack for his spare clothes and personal belongings, a haversack for his food, a canteen for water, a tin cup, a cap box on his belt to hold the percussion caps that fired his rifle, and a cartridge box for the ammunition. His weapons were one walnut-stocked 1841 Model Rifle, a sword-handled bayonet and whatever personal weapons he chose to carry. Nearly all the men carried bowie knives, which they were certain would prove lethal in the hand-to-hand combat they confidently expected. Some men had revolvers, and indeed, as the June days lengthened and the rumors of impending battle intensified, more and more parents provided their soldier sons with revolvers in the belief that the weapon would be a lifesaver in battle.

"What you need," Truslow told his men, "is one rifle, one mug, one haversack, and damn all else." He carried a bowie knife, but only for scavenging and cutting brush. Everything else, he told them, was just weight.

The men ignored Truslow, trusting instead in the Colonel's largesse. Each man was issued an oilcloth groundsheet in which he rolled two gray blankets. Washington Faulconer's only economy was a refusal to buy the Legion any greatcoats. The war, he declared, could not possibly last into the cold weather, and he was not spending his money to provide the men of Faulconer County with churchgoing coats, but only to make a great name for themselves in the history of southern independence. He did provide each man with a sewing kit, towels and a clothes brush, while Doctor Billy Danson insisted that every Legionnaire also carry a roll of cotton strips for bandages.

Major Thaddeus Bird, who had always been fond of long walks and was the only one of Faulconer's officers who resolutely refused to ride a horse, contended that Truslow was right and that the men had been provided with altogether too much equipment. "A man can't march cumbered like a mule," he contended. The schoolmaster was ever ready to express such military opinions, which were just as readily ignored by the Colonel, though as the summer passed a group of younger men found themselves drawn more and more to Bird's company. They would meet in his yard of an evening, sitting on the broken church bench or on stools fetched from the school-house. Starbuck and Adam went frequently, as did Bird's deputy, Lieu-tenant Davies, and a half dozen other officers and sergeants.

The men would bring their own food and drink. Priscilla would some-times have prepared a salad or a plate of biscuits, but the real business of the evenings was either to make music or else to raid Bird's jumbled pile of books for passages to read aloud. Then they would argue into the dark-ness, setting the world to rights as Adam and Starbuck used to do when they were at Yale, though these new evenings of discussion were laced with news and rumors of the war. In western Virginia, where the Colonel's raid had been so damply disappointing, the Confederacy suf-fered new defeats. The worst was at Philippi where northern forces won a humiliatingly easy victory that the northern newspapers dubbed the "Philippi Races." Thomas Jackson, fearing to be cut off in Harper's Ferry, abandoned the river town, and that event made it seem to the young offi-cers in Faulconer Court House that the North was invincible, but then, a week later, came reports of a skirmish on the seaboard of Virginia where northern troops had sallied inland from a coastal fortress only to be bloodily repulsed in the fields around Bethel Church.

Not all the news was true. There were rumors of victories that never happened and peace talks that never occurred. One day it was announced that the European powers had recognized the Confederacy and that the North was consequently suing for peace, but that turned out to be false even though the Reverend Moss had sworn on a stack of Bibles that it was the gospel truth. Bird was amused by the summer's alarms. "It's just a game," he said, "just a game."

"War is hardly a game, Uncle," Adam chided.

"Of course it's a game, and the Legion is your father's toy and a very expensive one too. Which is why I hope we never get used in battle because then the toy will be broken and your father will be inconsolable."

"Do you really hope that, Thaddeus?" his wife asked. She liked to sit in the garden till dark, but then, because she had taken over sole responsibility for the school, she would go to bed and leave the men to argue by candlelight.

"Of course I hope that," Bird said. "No one in his right mind wants a battle."

"Nate does," Adam said teasingly.

"I said 'in his right mind,'" Bird pounced. "I am careful to be precise with my words, perhaps because I never went to Yale. Do you really want to see battle, Starbuck?"

Starbuck half-smiled. "I want to see the elephant."

"Unnecessarily large, gray, curiously wrinkled and with burdensome droppings," Bird remarked.

"Thaddeus!" Priscilla laughed.

"I hope there's peace," Starbuck amended his wish, "but I am half-curious to see a battle."

"Here!" Bird tossed a book across to Starbuck. "There's an account of Waterloo in there, I think it begins on page sixty-eight. Read that, Starbuck, and you'll be cured of your desire to see elephants."

"You're not curious, Thaddeus?" his wife charged him. She was sewing a flag together, one of the many banners that would be used to decorate the town on the Fourth of July, which was now just two days away and was to be marked by a great gala at Seven Springs. There would be a feast, a parade, fireworks and dancing, and everyone in town was expected to contribute something to the celebration.

"I'm a little curious, of course." Bird paused to light one of the thin, malodorous cigars that he favored. "I have a curiosity about all the extremes of human existence because I am tempted to believe that truth is best manifested in such extremes, whether it be in the excesses of religion, violence, affection or greed. Battle is merely a symptom of one of those excesses."

"I would much rather that you applied yourself to the study of excessive affection," Priscilla said mildly, and the young men laughed. They were all fond of Priscilla and touched by the evident tenderness that she and Bird felt for each other.

The talk drifted on. The yard, which was supposed to supply the schoolmaster with vegetables, had become overgrown with black-eyed Susans and daisies, though Priscilla had made space for some herbs that were pungent in the evening warmth. The back of the yard was bounded by two apple trees and a broken fence beyond which was a meadow and a long view across the wooded foothills of the Blue Ridge Mountains. It was a lovely peaceful place.

"Are you taking a servant, Starbuck?" Lieutenant Davies asked. "Because if so I have to put his name in the servants' book."

Starbuck had been daydreaming. "A servant?"

"The Colonel, in his wisdom," Bird explained, "has decreed that officers may provide themselves with a servant, but only, mark this, if the man is black. No white servants allowed!"

"I can't afford a servant," Starbuck said. "White or black."

"I was rather hoping to make Joe Sparrow my servant," Bird said wistfully, "though unless he blacks his face now, I can't."

"Why Sparrow?" Adam asked. "So you could whistle at each other?"

"Very amusing," Bird was entirely unamused. "I promised Blanche I would keep him safe, that is why, but the Lord only knows how I'm supposed to do that."

"Poor Runt," Adam said. Joe Sparrow, a thin and scholarly sixteen-year-old, was universally known as Runt. He had won a scholarship to the University of Virginia where he was supposed to begin his studies in the fall, but he had broken his mother's heart by joining the Legion. He had been one of the recruits shamed into volunteering by receiving a petticoat. His mother, Blanche, had pleaded with Washington Faulconer to excuse her boy, but Faulconer had been adamant that every young man had a duty to serve. Joe, like many of the men, was a three-month volunteer, and the Colonel had assured Blanche Sparrow that her son would have served his stint by the time his first semester began.

"The Colonel really should have excused him," Bird said. "This war shouldn't be fought by bookish boys, but by men like Truslow."

"Because he's expendable?" one of the sergeants asked.

"Because he understands violence," Bird said, "which we all have to learn to understand if we are to be good soldiers."

Priscilla peered at her stitches in the fading light. "I wonder what happened to Truslow's daughter?"

"Did she ever talk with you, Starbuck?" Bird asked.

"With me?" Starbuck sounded surprised.

"It was just that she asked for you," Bird explained. "On the night that she came here."

"I thought you didn't know her?" Adam said idly.

"I don't. I met her at Truslow's cabin, but not to notice." Starbuck was glad that the dusk hid his blush. "No, she didn't speak to me."

"She asked for you and for Ridley, but of course neither of you was here." Bird checked suddenly, as though aware that he had been indiscreet. "Not that it matters. Did you bring your flute, Sergeant Howes? I was thinking we might attempt the Mozart?"

Starbuck listened to the music, but he could find no joy in it. In these last weeks he felt he had come to an understanding of himself, or at least he had found an equilibrium as his moods had ceased to oscillate between black despair and dizzy hope. Instead he had taken pleasure in the long days of work and exercise, yet now the reminder of Sally Truslow had utterly destroyed his peace. And she had asked for him! And that revelation, so casually made, added new and bone-dry fuel to Starbuck's dreams. She wanted his help, and he had not been here, so had she gone to Ridley? To that goddamned son of a supercilious bitch Ridley?

Next morning Starbuck confronted Ridley. They had hardly spoken in the last few weeks, not out of distaste, but simply because they kept separate friends. Ridley was leader of a small group of hard-riding, hard-drinking young officers who thought of themselves as rakes and daredevils and who despised the men who gathered in Pecker Bird's garden to talk away the long evenings. Ridley, when Starbuck found him, was stretched full-length in his tent, recovering, he said, from a night in Greeley's Tavern. One of his cronies, a lieutenant called Moxey, was sitting on the other bed with his head in his hands, groaning. Ridley similarly groaned when he saw Starbuck. "It's the Reverend! Have you come to convert me? I'm beyond conversion."

"I'd like a word with you."

"Go ahead." Under the sunlit canvas Ridley's face looked a sickly yellow.

"A word alone."

Ridley turned to look at Moxey. "Go away, Mox."

"Don't mind me, Starbuck, I am oblivious," Moxey said.

"He said to go away," Starbuck insisted.

Moxey looked up at Starbuck, saw something hostile in the tall northerner's face, so shrugged. "I am gone. I am vanishing. Goodbye. Oh, my God!" This last was in greeting to the brightness of the morning sun.

Ridley sat up and swung round so that his stockinged feet were on the groundsheet. "Oh, God." He groaned, then groped inside one of his boots where he evidently kept his cigars and matches at night. "You're looking awful grim, Reverend. Does goddamn Pelham want us to march to Rosskill and back? Tell him I'm sick." He lit the cigar, inhaled deeply, then looked up at Starbuck with bloodshot eyes. "Lay your word on me, Starbuck. Do your worst."

"Where's Sally?" Starbuck blurted out the question. He had meant to be altogether more circumspect, but when the moment of confrontation came he could find no words other than the simple, bald question.

"Sally?" Ridley asked, then feigned disbelief. "Sally! Who in the name of God is Sally?"

"Sally Truslow." Starbuck was already feeling foolish, wondering just what obscure yet undeniable passion was driving him to this humiliating enquiry.

Ridley shook his head tiredly, then sucked on the cigar. "Now why in the name of God, Reverend, would you think that I would know the first goddamned thing about Sally Truslow?"

"Because she ran away to Richmond. To you. I know that." Starbuck knew no such thing, but Pecker Bird, pressed hard, had admitted giving Sally the address of Ridley's brother in Richmond.

"She never found me, Reverend," Ridley said. "But what if she had? Would it have mattered?"

Starbuck had no answer to that question. Instead he stood foolish and uncertain between the folded back flaps of Ridley's tent.

Ridley hawked a gob of spittle that he shot past Starbuck's boots. "I'm interested, Reverend, so tell me. Just what is Sally to you?"

"Nothing."

"So why the hell are you bothering me this early in the goddamned morning?"

"Because I want to know."

"Or is it that her daddy wants to know?" Ridley asked, betraying his first uncertainty of the conversation. Starbuck shook his head and Ridley laughed. "Are you on heat for her, Reverend?"

"No!"

"But you are, Reverend, you are. I can tell, and I'll even tell you what to do about it. Go to Greeley's Tavern in Main Street and pay the tall woman in the taproom ten bucks. She's an ugly cow, but she'll cure your ailments. You got ten bucks left of that fifty you took off me?" Starbuck said nothing and Ridley shook his head, as if despairing of the northerner's common sense. "I ain't seen Sally for weeks. Not for weeks. She's married, I hear, and that was the end of her for me. Not that I ever knew her well, you understand me?" He stressed the question by jabbing the lit end of the cigar at Starbuck.

Starbuck wondered just what he had expected to achieve by this confrontation. A confession from Ridley? An address where Sally might be found? He had made a fool of himself, betraying his own vulnerability to Ridley's mockery. Now, as awkwardly as he had begun the confrontation, he tried to back out of it. "I hope you're not lying to me, Ridley."

"Oh, Reverend, there's so little you understand. Like good manners for a start. You want to accuse me of lying? Then you do it with a sword in your hand, or with a pistol. I don't mind facing you in a duel, Reverend, but I'll be damned if I have to sit here and listen to your goddamn whining and bitching without so much as a mug of coffee inside me. You mind asking my son of a bitch servant to get me some coffee on your way out? Hey, Moxey! You can come back in now. The Reverend and I have finished our morning prayers." Ridley looked up at Starbuck and jerked his head in curt dismissal. "Now go away, boy."

Starbuck went away. As he walked back down the tent lines he heard a mocking burst of laughter from Ridley and Moxey and the sound made him flinch. Oh God, he thought, but he had just made such a fool of himself. Such a goddamned fool. And for what? For a murderer's daughter who just happened to be pretty. He walked away, defeated and disconsolate.

8

Independence Day dawned clear. It promised to be hot, but there was a blessed breeze coming off the hills and the only clouds were wispy, high, and soon gone.

In the morning the Legion cleaned their uniforms. They used wire brushes, button sticks, blacking and soap until their woolen coats and trousers, leather boots and webbing belts were as spotless as honest effort could achieve. They blacked their ammunition pouches, scrubbed their canteens and haversacks, and tried to unwrinkle the pasteboard tops and visors of their forage caps. They polished their belt buckles and hat badges, then oiled the walnut stocks of their rifles until the wood shone. At eleven o'clock, anticipating the girls who would even then be gathering in the grounds of Seven Springs, the companies formed in full uniform and kit. The fifty cavalrymen made an eleventh company that formed ahead of the others, while the two cannon, which had been pulled from the ruts their wheels had made in the long grass and then attached to their limbers, paraded with the regimental band at the rear of the Legion.

The Colonel was waiting at Seven Springs, leaving Major Pelham in temporary command. At five minutes past eleven Pelham ordered the Legion to stand to attention, to order arms, to fix bayonets and then to shoulder arms. Eight hundred and seventy-two men were on parade. They were not the Legion's full strength, but those recruits who were too new to have learned their drill had been sent ahead to Seven Springs where they were employed in nailing strips of red baize to the church benches, which were being used for the communal dinner. Two massive tents had been raised on the south lawn to offer shade to the visitors, and a cook house established close to the stables where a pair of beefs and six hogs were being roasted whole by sweating cooks who had also been seconded from the Legion. The ladies of the town had donated vats of beans, bowls of salad, trays of corn cakes and barrels of dried peaches. There were pones of cornbread, and stands of sweet cured hams, smoked turkey and venison. There was hung beef with apple sauce, pickled cucumbers and, for the children, trays of doughnuts sprinkled with sugar. The teetotalers were provided with lemonade and sweet water from Seven Springs' best well, while the rest had casks of ale and barrels of hard cider brought from the cellar of Greeley's Tavern. There was wine available in the house, though past experience suggested that only a handful of gentry would bother with such a refined beverage. The provisions were generous and the decorations lavish as they always were at Seven Springs on Independence Day, but this year, in an attempt to demonstrate that the Confederacy was the true inheritor of America's revolutionary spirit, Washington Faulconer had been especially munificent.

At eight minutes past eleven Sergeant Major Proctor ordered the Legion to advance and the band, led by the Bandmaster August Little, played "Dixie" as the fifty cavalrymen led the Legion out of the field. The cavalrymen rode with drawn sabers and the companies marched with fixed bayonets. The town was deserted, because the townsfolk had all gone to Seven Springs, but the troops made a fine show as they marched past the flag-hung courthouse, and under the banners strung across the streets, and past the Sparrow's dry goods store that had a fancy window of eight large sheets of plate glass, which had been brought out from Richmond just one year before and were large enough to serve as a giant mirror in which the passing companies could admire their only slightly distorted selves. The march was noisy, not because anyone was speaking, but because the men were still not used to carrying their full kit. Their canteens banged against their bayonets, and their tin cups, hanging off the knapsacks, clanged against their cartridge boxes.

The first spectators were waiting just inside the white gates of the Seven Springs estate. They were mostly children who, equipped with paper flags of the Confederacy, ran alongside the troops as they marched beneath the avenue of live oaks that led from the Rosskill Road to Seven Springs' front door. The Legion did not march all the way to the house but instead struck off the driveway where a gap had been made in the snake fence beyond the trees and so circled the house to approach the flag-decked south lawns through two ever-thickening lines of onlookers who applauded the fine-looking troops. The cavalry, curbing in their excited horses to make them step high, made a particularly noble display as they rode past the reviewing stand on which Washington Faulconer presided with a politician who, until secession, had sat in the United States Congress. Faulconer and the erstwhile congressman were flanked by the Reverend Moss, Judge Bulstrode and Colonel Roland Penycrake, who was ninety-seven years old and had been a lieutenant in George Washington's army at Yorktown. "I don't mind him remembering Yorktown," Washington Faulconer told Captain Ethan Ridley, who was the aide accompanying the Colonel on Independence Day, "but I do wish he didn't keep reminding us at such length." But on this day, of all days, it was churlish to deny the old man his moment of glory.

Adam, dressed in his fine uniform, led the cavalrymen. Major Pelham rode a plump docile mare at the head of the ten companies, while Major Pecker Bird, whose gorgeous uniform had arrived from Richmond to the general amusement of the Legion and chagrin of his brother-in-law, marched on foot at the head of the band. Second Lieutenant Starbuck, who had no real duties this day, rode the mare Pocahontas just behind Major Bird, who made no effort to keep in step with the drumbeat but strolled long-legged and easy just as if he were taking one of his day-long country walks.

Once on the south lawns the cavalry, whose function was purely decorative this day, galloped once around the makeshift parade ground, then disappeared to place their horses in a paddock. The two guns were unharnessed from their limbers and parked on either side of the reviewing stand in front of which, and before the delighted gaze of nearly three thousand spectators, the Legion went through its maneuvers.

They marched in column of companies, each company four ranks deep, then deployed into a two-ranked line of battle. There was not quite enough space at the flanks of the parade ground for the whole line of battle, but Sergeant Truslow, K Company's sergeant, had the sense to hold his men back, which somewhat spoiled the next display, Pelham's pride, which demonstrated how the Legion would form a square to repel cavalry, though in the end the square was decently enough formed and only a true expert could have detected that one corner of the formation was slightly battered. The officers, all of them except Major Bird on horseback, were corralled in the center of the square where the band played a gloomy version of "Massa in the Cold Cold Ground." The Legion then came out of square to form two columns of companies, the band quickened into "Hail, Columbia," the crowd cheered, the Colonel beamed, and then Captain Murphy, who had appointed himself chief artillerist to the Legion, spurred forward with his gunners.

The two cannon were charged with bags of gunpowder, but without any shot or shell. The Legion possessed none of the new-fangled friction primers with which to ignite the powder, so instead Murphy used two homemade primers constructed from straw tubes filled with grade-one rifle powder. The straws were placed in the touchholes and thence down through holes pierced in the powder bags, then, on a nod from the Colonel, and just as Bandmaster Little finished playing "Hail, Columbia," the gunners applied lit matches to the primers.

There were two glorious bangs, two spears of flame, two boiling clouds of gray-white smoke and a host of startled birds sprang up from the shade trees behind the reviewing stand. The spectators gave a satisfying gasp.

The cannon shots presaged the speeches. Colonel Penycrake's speech was thankfully brief, for the old man was short of breath, then the erstwhile congressman gave a seemingly interminable peroration after which Washington Faulconer gave a fine, spirited address that first regretted the necessity of war, but then described the nest of northern vipers which, with hissing mouths, flickering tongues and noxious breath, were spreading their reeking poison across the land. "Yet we southerners know how to treat snakes!" The crowd cheered. Even the assembled black slaves, brought by their owners to the annual feast and confined to a small roped enclosure to one side of the assembly, cheered the Colonel's sentiments. The Colonel, whose voice was strong enough to reach across the whole assembly, spoke of the two races that had arisen in America, which races, though sprung from common parentage, had been separated by climate, morals and religion, and had thus grown apart until now, he declared, their ideas of honor, truth and manliness were so different that the two could no longer abide under the same government.

"The northern race must go its own way," the Colonel declared, "while we southerners, who have always been in the forefront of America's fight for Liberty, Truth, Decency and Honor, will keep alive the shining dream of the Founding Fathers. Their sword has passed to us!" And he drew the bright blade presented to his grandfather by Lafayette and the crowd cheered for the idea that they, and not the degenerate, factory-sweated, education-spoilt, Roman-Catholic infested northerners were the real heirs of those great Virginian revolutionaries, George Washington and Thomas Jefferson and James Madison.

The Colonel concluded his remarks by saying he did not think the struggle would be long. The North had blockaded southern ports and the South had responded by forbidding the export of cotton, which meant the great mills of England would inevitably fall silent, and England, he reminded the crowd, would die without the cotton to feed its mills. If the blockade was not lifted then, within weeks, the world's greatest navy would be off the coast of the Confederacy and the Yankees would flee back to their harbors like snakes to their nests. Yet the South must not look to Europe, Faulconer hurried on, nor need it look to Europe, for southern fighting men would see the Yankees off southern soil without European help. Soon, the Colonel said, the Yankees will regret their temerity, for they will be sent packing and running and screaming and hollering. The crowd liked that.

The war would be over within weeks, the Colonel promised, and every man who helped achieve victory would be honored in the new Confederacy whose flag would fly forever among the banners of the nations. That was the cue for the Legion's flags to be brought forward and presented. And, astonishingly, the Colonel's wife had stirred herself out of her sickroom to be the donor of the two colors.

Miriam Faulconer proved to be a thin, black-haired woman with a very pale face in which her eyes seemed unnaturally large. She was dressed in a purple silk so dark that it appeared almost black, and had a dark, semitransparent veil falling from her hat. She walked very slowly, so that some of the spectators thought she must surely falter before she reached the reviewing stand. She was accompanied by her daughter and by the six ladies of the town who had been chiefly responsible for sewing the two heavy banners of gorgeously fringed silk that would now be the battle flags of the Faulconer Legion.

The first flag was the new Confederate flag. It had three broad horizontal stripes, the upper and lower ones red and the center stripe white, while the upper quadrant by the staff displayed a blue field on which were sewn seven white stars to represent the first seven states to secede. The second color was an adaptation of the Faulconer coat of arms and displayed three red crescents on a white field, with the family's motto, "Forever Ardent," embroidered in letters of funereal black silk along its bottom edge.

The band, having no formal national anthem to play, kept silent, all except the drummers, who tapped a solemn beat as the colors were brought forward. Adam, appointed head of the color party, stepped forward to receive the flags accompanied by the two men chosen to be the standard bearers. One was Robert Decker, whose mended face was marvelously earnest as he advanced beside Adam, while the other was Joe "Runt" Sparrow, who took the Faulconer flag after it had first been handed by Anna to her brother. Adam shook the folds out of the silk, then gave the flag to Joe Sparrow, who seemed almost overwhelmed by the weight of the heavy banner. Then Miriam Faulconer, assisted by the ladies, handed forward the yellow-fringed Confederate flag. For a moment Adam looked reluctant to take it from his mother, then he stepped back and passed the flag to Robert Decker who proudly raised the new color high.

The spectators gave a cheer that died rather raggedly as the crowd realized that the Reverend Moss, who had been waiting patiently all day, now offered his prayer of blessing. The prayer was so long that some of the spectators thought that Joe Sparrow would surely keel over before the invocation was done. Worse, the smell of the roasting meat was ever more tantalizing, yet still Moss insisted on calling the Almighty's attention to the Legion, to its two flags, to its officers, and to the foe whom Moss prayed would be smitten mightily by the Legion. He might have gone on for even longer had he not paused for a deep breath, which gave old Colonel Penycrake a chance to intervene with a surprisingly loud amen, which was so soundly echoed by the crowd that Moss was forced to let the rest of his prayer go unspoken. The Colonel, unable to let the moment pass without a final word, shouted that the Legion would bring the colors home just as soon as the Yankees were roundly whipped. "And that won't be long! By Jiminy it won't be long!" And the crowd cheered and even the Colonel's Negro servants cheered while the band struck up Dixie.

The Colonel then paraded the colors in front of the Legion, letting each man see the two flags close up, and afterward, it already being near to two o'clock and one of the beefs already smelling more like a burnt offering than a dinner, Judge Bulstrode administered the Oath of Confederate Loyalty, which the men pronounced in loud, confident voices, and then, thus sworn to their brand-new country, they gave three cheers for the Colonel and his wife and, the hurrah given, the Legionnaires were ordered to open ranks, stack arms, unsling knapsacks and were so dismissed to their food.

Adam led Starbuck toward the open-sided tent where the guests of honor were seated. "You have to meet Mother."

"Do I really?" The pale, dark-robed Miriam Faulconer looked rather formidable.

"Of course you do." Adam stopped to greet Major Pelham's elderly sister, a tall dignified spinster whose faded clothes spoke of the hardship she endured to keep up appearances, then he and Starbuck touched their hats to the erstwhile congressman's wife, who complained how much she regretted leaving Washington's sophisticated society for the more homely surroundings of Richmond, and then at last Adam was able to draw Starbuck forward to the tent where his mother held court amidst her attendant ladies. Miriam Faulconer was enthroned in a high-backed upholstered chair brought from the house while the pale and timid-looking Anna sat at her side in a much smaller chair and cooled her mother's face with a fan made from filigreed ivory. "Mother," Adam said proudly, "this is my friend Nate Starbuck."

The big eyes, so oddly luminous under the deep shade of the dark purple hat, looked up at Starbuck. He guessed Adam's mother had to be at least forty years old, yet, to Starbuck's astonishment, she appeared hardly a day over twenty. Her skin was as smooth, white and clear as a child's, her mouth was wide and full, her eyes strangely sad, and her gloved touch, in Starbuck's nervous hand, as light as a songbird's bones. "Mister Starbuck," she said in a very soft and breathy voice. "You are welcome."

"Thank you, ma'am. This is an honor."

"To meet me? I think not. I am a most insignificant person. Am I not insignificant, Anna?"

"Of course not, Mama. You are the most significant person here."

"I can't hear you, Anna, speak up."

"I said you are significant, Mother."

"Don't shout!" Miriam Faulconer flinched from her daughter's scarcely audible voice, then looked up at Starbuck again. "I am afflicted with ill health, Mister Starbuck."

"I am sorry to hear that, ma'am."

"Not so close, Anna." Mrs. Faulconer gestured the fan away from her cheek, then pushed the veil fully back from the brim of her hat. She looked, Starbuck thought guiltily, very beautiful and very vulnerable. No wonder that a young Washington Faulconer had fallen in love with this village girl, daughter of Rosskill's postmaster, and married her despite his parents' opposition. She was a rare thing, fragile and lovely, and rarer still when Starbuck tried to imagine her as Miriam Bird, sister to the prickly Thaddeus. "Do you like it in Virginia, Mister Starbuck?" Miriam Faulconer asked in her sibilant, quiet voice.

"Yes, ma'am, very much. Your husband has been very kind to me."

"I'd forgotten how Washington can be kind," Miriam Faulconer said softly, so softly that Starbuck was forced to lean down to hear her small voice. The still air under the tent's awning smelt of newly cut grass, eau de cologne and camphor, the last, Starbuck supposed, rising from the stiff folds of Miriam Faulconer's purple dress, which must have been drenched in the liquid as a repellent for moths. Starbuck, uncomfortably close to Mrs. Faulconer, marveled that anyone's skin could be so white and smooth. Like a corpse, he thought. "Adam tells me you are a very good friend to him." The corpse spoke softly.

"I am most proud of that opinion, ma'am."

"Is friendship more important than filial duty?" There was a cat's claw of nastiness in the question.

"I am not competent to judge," Starbuck said in defensive politeness.

"Closer, Anna, closer. You wish me to die of the heat?" Miriam Faulconer licked her pale lips, her big eyes still on Starbuck. "Have you ever considered a mother's distress, Mister Starbuck?"

"My mother likes to remind me of it constantly, ma'am." Starbuck gave a swipe of his own claw back. Miriam Faulconer just gazed unblinking, weighing Starbuck and not seeming to like her judgment.

"Not so close, Anna, you will scratch me." Miriam Faulconer pushed her daughter's fan a half inch farther away. She wore a black-stoned ring on one slender finger, intriguingly worn outside the black lace glove. She had a necklace of black pearls and a brooch of carved jet was pinned to the heavy folds of dark purple silk. "I think," Miriam Faulconer said to Starbuck with an undeniable note of dislike in her voice, "that you are an adventurer."

"Is that such a bad thing to be, ma'am?"

"It is usually a selfish thing."

"Mother ..." Adam intervened.

"Be quiet, Adam, I have not asked for your opinion. Closer, Anna, bring the fan closer. Adventurers cannot be relied upon, Mister Starbuck."

"I am sure, ma'am, that there have been many great and reliable men who did not shirk from adventure. Our own Founding Fathers, indeed?"

Miriam Faulconer ignored Starbuck's words. "I shall hold you responsible for my son's safety, Mister Starbuck."

"Mother, please ..." Adam again tried to intervene.

"If I require your contribution, Adam, be assured I shall ask you for it, and until then be so good as to stay quiet." The claws were out now, bright and sharp. "I do not want you, Mister Starbuck, leading my son into adventures. I would have been happy had he pursued his pacific ventures in the north, but it seems that the belligerent party has won his soul. That party, I think, includes you, and I do not thank you for it. So be assured, Mister Starbuck, that I shall hold you and my husband jointly responsible for my son's safety."

"I am honored by your trust, ma'am." At first Starbuck had thought this woman a vulnerable, pitiful beauty, now he thought her a bitter witch.

"I am pleased to have seen you," Mrs. Faulconer said in much the same tone she might have used to express some mild satisfaction at having seen a strange beast in a traveling menagerie, then she looked away and a radiant smile came to her face as she reached both hands toward Ethan Ridley. "My dear Ethan! I just knew Washington would keep you from me, but you're here at last! I have been talking with Mister Starbuck and am consequently in need of some diversion. Come and sit here, take Anna's chair."

Adam drew Starbuck away. "Dear Lord, I am so sorry," he said. "I know she can be difficult, but I don't know why she chose today of all days."

"I'm used to it," Starbuck said. "I have a mother too." Though Starbuck's mother was nothing like the soft-spoken and thin Miriam Faulconer. Jane Abigail MacPhail Starbuck was a tall, fleshy, loud-spoken woman who was large in everything except the generosity of her spirit.

"Mother's often in pain." Adam still wanted to make excuses for his mother. "She suffers from something called neuralgia."

"So Anna told me."

Adam walked in silence, looking down at the ground, and at last shook his head. "Why do women have to be so difficult?" He asked it so wanly that Starbuck could not help bursting into laughter.

Adam's gloom did not last long for he was being reunited with old friends from all across the county, and he was soon leading a troop of young people in the various amusements that had been laid out in Washington Faulconer's park. There were archery butts with straw men targets dressed in striped clothes and top hats, supposedly representing Yankees, and any man who signed up as a recruit could fire a Model 1841 rifle at one of the Yankee dummies. If such a recruit put a bullet clean through one of the targets pinned to a straw man's chest he received a silver dollar. There were water-filled horse troughs where the children could duck for apples, a steeplechase for officers and challengers, tugs-of-war between the ten infantry companies and a ganderpull.

"Ganderpull?" Starbuck asked.

"You don't have ganderpulls in Boston?" Adam asked.

"No, we have civilization instead. We have things called libraries and churches, schools and colleges ..."

Adam hit his friend, then skipped out of retaliatory range. "You'll enjoy a ganderpull. You hang up a goose, grease its neck with butter, and the first person who manages to pull the bird's head off gets to take the body home for supper."

"A live goose?" Starbuck was horrifed.

"It would be too easy if it were dead!" Adam said. "Of course it's alive!"

But before any of these diversions could be tasted the two friends had to go to the summerhouse where a pair of photographers had set up their chairs, tripods, frames and processing wagons. The two men, specially brought out from Richmond at Washington Faulconer's expense, were charged with taking a picture of any man in the Legion who wanted his portrait made. The pictures, printed within ornate borders, would make keepsakes for the families left behind and mementoes for the men themselves in the long years ahead. The officers could have their portraits printed as *cartes de visite*, a fashionable conceit that appealed hugely to Washington Faulconer, who was first into the photographer's chair. Adam was next.

The process was long and complicated. Adam was seated in a high-backed chair that held at its rear a metal frame into which his head was pushed. The frame, hidden by his hair and cap, would keep his head perfectly still. His saber was drawn and put into his right hand and a pistol into his left. "Do I really have to look so pugnacious?" he asked his father.

"It's the fashion, Adam. Besides, one day you'll be proud of this picture."

The Legion's twin colors were arrayed behind Adam who then, stiff and awkward, stared into the photographer's machine as the sweating assistant dashed out of the wagon and into the summerhouse with the wet glass plate. The plate was put into the camera, Adam was told to take a deep breath and hold it, then the cover was whipped off.

Everyone in the room held their breath. A fly buzzed round Adam's face, but a second assistant waved a towel to drive it away.

"If you must," the photographer told Adam, "you can breathe out, but very slowly. Take care not to move your right hand."

It seemed an age, but at last Adam could relax as the glass plate was reshrouded in its wooden box and rushed off to the wagon for development. Starbuck was then positioned in the frame, his skull painfully inserted in the metal jaws and he too was caparisoned with saber and pistol, and instructed to hold his breath as the wet glass plate was exposed inside the big wooden camera.

Adam immediately began to make faces over the photographer's shoulder. He grimaced, squinted, blew out his cheeks and waggled his fingers in his ears until, to his delight, Starbuck began laughing.

"No, no, no!" The photographer was distraught and slammed a cover over the plate. "It may not have been exposed long enough," he complained, "you will look like a ghost," but Starbuck rather liked that spectral thought and had no need of a *carte de visite*, let alone a keepsake, and so he wandered off through the crowd, eating on a hunk of bread and pork while Adam went to ready his horse for the steeplechase. Ethan Ridley was expected to win the race, which carried a generous fifty-dollar purse.

Sergeant Thomas Truslow had been playing bluff with a group of his cronies, but now stirred himself to watch as the horses thumped past on their first circuit of the steeplechase course. "I've got money on the boy," he confided in Starbuck. "Billy Arkwright, on the black." He pointed toward a skinny boy riding a small black horse. The boy, who looked scarce a day over twelve, was trailing a field of officers and farmers whose horses seemed to sail over the big fences before they turned out to the country for the second time around. Ridley was comfortably in front, his chestnut jumping surely and scarcely winded after the first circuit, while Billy Arkwright's horse seemed too delicate to keep up, let alone survive the long second time around.

"You look as if you've lost your money," Starbuck said happily.

"What you know about horses, boy, I could write in the dust with one bladderful of weak piss." Truslow was amused. "So who would you put your money on?"

"Ridley?"

"He's a good horsemen, but Billy'll beat him." Truslow watched as the horsemen disappeared into the country, then shot Starbuck a suspicious look. "I hear you were asking Ridley about Sally."

"Who told you that?"

"The whole goddamn Legion knows, because Ridley's been telling them. You think he knows where she is?"

"He says not."

"Then I'd be obliged if you let sleeping bitches lie," Truslow said grimly. "The girl's gone, and that's all there is to it. I'm shot of her. I gave her a chance. I gave her land, a roof, beasts, a man, but nothing of mine was ever good enough for Sally. She'll be in Richmond now, making her living, and I daresay it'll be a good living until she crawls back here scabbed with the pox."

"I'm sorry," Starbuck said, because he could think of nothing else to say. He was just glad that Truslow had not asked why he had confronted Ridley.

"There's no harm done," Truslow said, "except that the damned girl took my Emily's ring. I should have kept it. If I don't die with that ring in my pocket, Starbuck, then I won't find my Emily again."

"I'm sure that's not true."

"I'm sure of it." Truslow stubbornly stuck to his superstition, then nodded to the left. "There, what did I tell you?" Billy Arkwright was three lengths ahead of Ethan Ridley, whose mare was now lathered with sweat. Ridley was slashing with his whip at the mare's laboring flanks, but Arkwright's small-boned black was comfortably ahead and stretching its lead. Truslow laughed. "Ridley can kick the belly out of that horse, but she won't go no faster. There ain't another step in her. Go on, Billy-boy! Go on, boy!" Truslow, his money won, turned away even before the race finished.

Arkwright won by five lengths, going away, and after him a weary stream of muddied men and horses galloped home. Billy Arkwright received his purse of fifty dollars, though what he really wanted was to be allowed to join the Legion. "I can ride and shoot. What more do you want, Colonel?"

"You'll have to wait for another war, Billy, I'm sorry."

After the steeplechase there were four ganderpulls. The birds were hung on a high beam, their necks were greased, and one by one the young people ran and leaped. Some missed entirely, others caught hold of a neck but were defeated by the butter, which made the geese necks slippery, while some were struck by a gander's sharp beak and went off sucking blood, but eventually the birds died and their heads were ripped free. The crowd cheered as the blood-drenched winners walked away with their plump prizes.

The dancing began at nightfall. Two hours later, when it was fully dark, the fireworks crackled and blazed above the Seven Springs estate. Starbuck had drunk a lot of wine and felt mildly tipsy. After the fireworks the dancing began again with an officers' cotillion. Starbuck did not dance, but instead found himself a quiet shadow under a tall tree and watched the dancers circle beneath the moth-haunted paper lanterns. The women wore white dresses garlanded with red and blue ribbons in honor of the day's festival while the men were in gray uniform and their sword scabbards swung as they turned to the music's lilt.

"You're not dancing," a quiet voice said.

Starbuck turned to see Anna Faulconer. "No," he said.

"Can I lead you into the dance?" She held out a hand. Behind her the windows of Seven Springs were lit with celebratory candles. The house looked very beautiful, almost magical. "I had to escort Mother to bed," Anna explained, "so I missed the entrance."

"No, thank you." Starbuck ignored her outstretched hand, which invited him into the cotillion.

"How very ungallant of you!" Anna said in hurt reproof.

"It is not a lack of gallantry," Starbuck explained, "but an inability to dance."

"You can't dance? People don't dance in Boston?"

"People do, yes, but not my family."

Anna nodded her comprehension. "I can't imagine your father leading a dance. Adam says he's very fierce."

"He is, yes."

"Poor Nate," Anna said. She watched Ethan Ridley put his hand into the fingers of a tall lithe beauty, and a look of puzzled sadness showed briefly on her face. "Mother was unkind to you," she said to Starbuck, though she still watched Ridley.

"I am sure she did not mean to be."

"Are you?" Anna asked pointedly, then shrugged. "She thinks you are luring Adam away," Anna explained.

"To war?"

"Yes." Anna at last looked away from Ridley and stared up into Starbuck's face. "She wants him to stay here. But he can't, can he? He can't stay safe at home while other young men go to face the North."

"No, he can't."

"But Mother doesn't see that. She just thinks that if he stays at home he can't possibly die. But I can see how a man couldn't live with that." She looked up at Starbuck, her eyes glossed by the lantern light, which oddly accentuated her small squint. "So you have never danced?" she asked. "Truly?"

"I've never danced," Starbuck admitted, "not one step."

"Perhaps I could teach you to dance?"

"That would be kind."

"We could start now?" Anna offered.

"I think not, thank you."

The cotillion ended, the officers bowed, the ladies curtseyed and then the couples scattered across the lawn. Captain Ethan Ridley offered his hand to the tall girl, then walked her to the tables where he courteously bowed her to her seat. Then, after a brief word with a man who looked like the girl's father, he turned and searched the lantern-lit lawns until he saw Anna. He crossed the lawn, ignored Starbuck, and offered his fiancée an arm. "I thought we might go for supper?" Ridley suggested. He was far from drunk, but neither was he entirely sober.

But Anna was not ready to go. "Do you know, Ethan, that Starbuck can't dance?" She asked not out of any mischief, but simply for something to say.

Ridley glanced at Starbuck. "That doesn't surprise me. Yankees aren't much good for anything. Except preaching, maybe." Ridley laughed. "And marrying. I hear he's good at marrying people."

"Marrying people?" Anna asked, and as she spoke Ridley seemed to understand that his tongue had run away with him. Not that he had any chance to retract or amend the statement, for Starbuck had lunged past Anna to seize hold of Ridley's crossbelt. Anna screamed as Starbuck yanked Ridley hard toward him.

A score of men turned toward the scream, but Starbuck was oblivious of their interest. "What did you say, you son of a bitch?" he demanded of Ridley.

Ridley's face had gone pale. "Let go of me, you ape."

"What did you say?"

"I said let go of me!" Ridley's voice was loud. He fumbled at his belt where a revolver was holstered.

Adam ran toward the two men. "Nate!" He took Starbuck's hand and gently pried it free. "Go, Ethan," Adam said and slapped Ridley's hand away from the revolver. Ridley lingered, evidently wanting to prolong the confrontation, but Adam snapped his command more sharply. The altercation had been swift, but dramatic enough to send a frisson of interest through the big crowd around the dancing lawn.

Ridley stepped back. "You want to fight that duel, Reverend?"

"Go!" Adam showed a surprising authority. "Too much drink altogether," he added in a voice loud enough to satisfy the curiosity of the spectators. "Now go!" he said again to Ridley, and watched as the tall man strode away with Anna on his arm. "Now what was that about?" Adam demanded of Starbuck.

"Nothing," Starbuck said. Washington Faulconer was frowning from the far side of the lawn, but Starbuck did not care. He had found himself an enemy and was astonished by the pure hardness of the hate he felt. "Nothing at all," he nevertheless insisted to Adam.

Adam refused to accept the denial. "Tell me!"

"Nothing. I tell you, nothing." Except that Ridley evidently knew that Starbuck had performed a travesty of a marriage service for Decker and Sally. That service had stayed a secret. No one in the Legion knew. Truslow had never talked of what had happened that night, nor had either Decker or Starbuck, yet Ridley knew of it, and only one person could have told him, and that person was Sally. Which meant that Ridley had lied when he swore he had not seen Sally since her marriage. Starbuck turned on Adam. "Will you do something for me?"

"You know I will."

"Persuade your father to send me to Richmond. I don't care how, but just find a job for me there and make him send me."

"I'll try. But tell me why, please."

Starbuck walked a few paces in silence. He remembered feeling something like this during the painful nights when he had waited outside the Lyceum Hall in New Haven, desperate for Dominique to appear. "Suppose," he finally said to Adam, "that someone had asked for your help and you had promised to give it, and then you found reason to believe that person was in trouble. What would you do?"

"I'd help, of course," Adam said.

"So find me a way of reaching Richmond." It was madness, of course, and Starbuck knew it. The girl meant nothing to him, he meant nothing to her, yet once again, just as he had in New Haven, he was ready to throw his whole life on a chance. He knew it was a sin to pursue Sally as he did, but knowing he toyed with sin made it no easier to resist. Nor did he want to resist. He would pursue Sally whatever the danger, because, so long as there was a sliver of a chance, even a chance no bigger than a firefly's glow in the eternal night, he would take the risk. He would take it even if it meant destroying himself in the pursuit of it. That much, at least, he knew about himself, and he rationalized the stupidity by thinking that if America was set on destruction then why should Starbuck not indulge in the same joyous act? Starbuck looked at his friend. "You're not going to understand this," he said.

"Try me, please?" Adam asked earnestly.

"It is the pure joy of self-destruction."

Adam frowned, then shook his head. "You're right. I don't understand. Explain, please."

But Starbuck just laughed.

In the event a trip to Richmond was easily arranged, though Starbuck was forced to wait for ten long days until Washington Faulconer found his reason to make a journey to the state capital.

The reason was glory, or rather the threat that the Legion would be denied its proper part in the glorious victory that would seal Confederate independence. Rumors, which seemed confirmed by newspaper reports, spoke of imminent battle. A Confederate army was gathering in the northern part of Virginia to face the federal army assembled in Washington. Whether the southern concentration of forces was meant as a preparation for an attack on Washington or whether it was gathering to defend against an expected Yankee invasion, no one knew, but one thing was certain: the Faulconer Legion had not been summoned to the gathering of the host.

"They want all the glory for themselves," Washington Faulconer complained, and declared that the infernal jackanapes in Richmond were doing everything possible to thwart the Legion's ambitions. Pecker Bird remarked privately that Faulconer had been so successful in keeping his regiment free of the state's intervention that he could hardly now complain if the state kept their fighting free of Washington Faulconer's interference, yet even Bird wondered whether the Legion was to be deliberately kept out of the war for, by the middle of July, there was still no summons from the army and Faulconer, knowing that the time had come to humble himself before the hated state authorities, declared he would go to Richmond himself and there offer the Legion to the Confederacy's service. He would take his son with him.

"You don't mind if Nate comes, do you?" Adam asked.

"Nate?" Faulconer had frowned. "Wouldn't Ethan be more useful to us?"

"I would be grateful if you took Nate, Father."

"Whatever." Faulconer found it hard to resist any of Adam's requests. "Of course."

Richmond seemed strangely empty to Starbuck. There were still plenty of uniformed men in the city, but they were mostly staff officers or commissary troops, for most of the fighting men had been sent northward to the rail junction at Manassas where Pierre Beauregard, a professional soldier from Louisiana and the hero of Fort Sumter's bloodless fall, was gathering the Army of Northern Virginia. Another smaller Confederate force, the Army of the Shenandoah, was assembling under General Joseph Johnston, who had taken over the command of the rebel forces in the Shenandoah Valley, but Faulconer was eager that the Legion should join Beauregard, for Beauregard's Army of Northern Virginia was closer to Washington and thus, in Faulconer's opinion, more likely to see action.

"Is that indeed what he believes?" Belvedere Delaney asked. The attorney had been delighted when a nervous Starbuck, presuming upon his one brief meeting with the attorney, called at Delaney's Grace Street rooms on the evening of his arrival in Richmond. Delaney insisted he stay for supper. "Write a note to Faulconer. Say you've met an old friend from Boston. Say he's enticed you to a Bible class at the First Baptist

Church. That's an entirely believable excuse and one that no one will ever want to explore. My man will deliver the note. Come inside, come inside." Delaney was in the uniform of a Confederate captain. "Take no notice of it. I am supposed to be a legal officer in the War Department, but truly I wear it only to stop the bloodthirsty ladies enquiring when I intend to lay down my life for Dixie. Now come inside, please."

Starbuck allowed himself to be persuaded upstairs into the comfortable parlor where Delaney apologized for the supper. "It will only be mutton, I fear, but my man does it with a delicate vinegar sauce that you will enjoy. I must confess that my greatest disappointment in New England was the cooking. Is it because you have no slaves and thus must depend on wives for your victuals? I doubt I ate one decent meal all the time I was in the North. And in Boston! Dear Lord above, but a diet of cabbage, beans and potatoes is scarcely a diet at all. You are distracted, Starbuck."

"I am, sir, yes."

"Don't 'sir' me, for God's sake. I thought we were friends. Is it the prospect of battle that distracts you? I watched some troops throw away their dice and packs of playing cards last week! They said they wanted to meet their Maker in a state of grace. An Englishman once said that the prospect of being hanged next morning concentrates a man's mind wonderfully, but I'm not sure it would make me throw away my playing cards." He brought Starbuck paper, ink and a pen. "Write your note. Will you drink some wine as we wait for supper? I hope so. Claim to be immersed in Bible study." Starbuck eschewed the wilder part of Delaney's fancy, merely explaining to Washington Faulconer that he had met an old friend and would therefore not be at Clay Street for supper.

The note was sent and Starbuck stayed to share Delaney's supper, though he proved a poor companion for the plump, sly attorney. The night was hot and very little breeze came past the gauze sheets that were stretched across the open windows to keep the insects at bay, and even Delaney seemed too listless to eat, though he did keep up a lively if one-sided conversation. He asked for news of Thaddeus Bird and was delighted to hear that the schoolmaster was a constant irritation to Washington Faulconer. "I should have dearly liked to have been at Thaddeus's wedding, but alas, duty called. Is he happy?"

"He seems very happy." Starbuck was almost too nervous to make conversation, but he tried hard. "They both seem happy."

"Pecker is an uxorious man, which makes her a lucky girl. And of course Washington Faulconer opposed the marriage, which suggests it might be a good match for Pecker. So tell me what you think of Washington Faulconer? I want to hear your most salacious opinions, Starbuck. I want you to sing for your supper with some intriguing gossip."

Starbuck eschewed the gossip, instead offering a conventional and admiring opinion of Faulconer, which left Delaney entirely unconvinced. "I don't know the man well, of course, but he always strikes me as empty. Quite hollow. And he so desperately wants to be admired. Which is why he freed his slaves."

"Which is admirable, surely?"

"Oh to be sure"—Delaney was deprecating—"except that the proximate cause of the manumission was some interfering woman from the North who was far too pious to reward Faulconer with her charms, and the poor fellow has spent the ten years since trying to persuade his fellow Virginian landowners that he isn't some dangerous radical. In truth he's just a little rich boy not quite grown up, and I'm not at all sure there's anything under that glossy exterior except a superfluity of money."

"He's been good to me."

"And he'll go on being good to you so long as you admire him. But after that?" Delaney picked up a silver fruit knife, and mimicked the action of slitting his throat. "Dear sweet God, but this night is hot," he leaned back in his chair and stretched his arms wide. "I did some business in Charleston last summer and took supper at a house where every place at table was provided with a slave whose job was to fan our brows. That sort of behavior is a bit overripe for Richmond, more's the pity." He chattered on, talking of his travels in South Carolina and Georgia while Starbuck picked at the mutton, drank too much wine, tried a little of the apple pie, and finally pushed his plate away.

"A cigarette?" Delaney suggested. "Or a cigar? Or do you still refuse to smoke? You're quite wrong in that refusal. Tobacco is a great emollient. Our Heavenly Father, I think, must have intended everything on earth to be of specific use to mankind and so he gave us wine to excite us, brandy to inflame us and tobacco to calm us. Here." Delaney had crossed to his silver humidor, cut the stem of a cigar and handed it to Starbuck. "Light it, then tell me what ails thee." Delaney knew that something extraordinary must have driven Starbuck to this desperate visit. The boy looked almost feverish.

Starbuck allowed himself to be persuaded to take the cigar, as much as anything else by the promise that tobacco was a soothing agent. His eyes stung from the smoke, he half-choked on the bitter taste, but he persisted. To have done less would have been to show himself less than a grown man and, on this night when he knew he was behaving like a half-grown youth, he needed the trappings of adulthood. "Do you think," he asked as an elliptic introduction to the delicate matter that had brought him to Delaney's door, "that the devil also put some things on earth? To snare us?"

Delaney lit a cigarette, then smiled knowingly. "So who is she?"

Starbuck said nothing. He felt such a fool, but some irresistible compulsion had driven him to this foolishness, just as it had compelled him to destroy a career for the sake of Dominique Demarest. Washington Faulconer had told him that such destructive obsessions were a disease of young men, but if so it was a disease that Starbuck could neither cure nor alleviate, and now it was driving him to make a fool of himself before this clever lawyer, who waited so patiently for his answer. Starbuck still paused, but at last, knowing that procrastination would serve no longer, he admitted his quest. "Her name is Sally Truslow."

Delaney offered the faintest, most private of smiles. "Do go on."

Starbuck was actually trembling. The rest of America was poised at the edge of battle, waiting for that terrible moment when a schism would be ripped into a gulf of blood, but all he could do was quiver for a girl he had met but for one lame evening. "I thought she might have come here. To these rooms," he said lamely.

Delaney blew a long plume of smoke that rippled the candles on the polished dining table. "I smell something of my brother here. Tell me all."

Starbuck told all, and the telling seemed pathetic to him, as pathetic as that far off day when he had confessed his foolishness to Washington Faulconer. Now he limpingly talked of a promise made in a dusky night, of an obsession he could not properly describe and could not justify and could not really account for, except to say that life would be nothing unless he could find Sally.

"And you thought she might be here?" Delaney asked with friendly mockery.

"I know she was given this address," Starbuck said pointedly.

"And so you came to me," Delaney said, "which was wise. So what do you want of me?"

Starbuck looked across the table. To his surprise he had smoked the cigar down to an inch-long stub, which he now abandoned with the mangled remains of his pie. "I want to know if you can tell me how to find her," he said, and he thought how futile this quest was, and how demeaning. Somehow, before he arrived in this elegant room, Starbuck had believed that his search for Sally was a practical dream, but now, faced with confessing his obsession to this man who was a virtual stranger, Starbuck felt utterly foolish. He also sensed the hopelessness of searching for one lost girl in a town of forty thousand people. "I'm sorry," he said, "but I should never have come here."

"I seem to remember telling you to seek my help," Delaney reminded him, "though admittedly we were both quite drunk at the time. I'm glad you came."

Starbuck stared at his benefactor. "You can help me?"

"Of course I can help you," Belvedere Delaney said very calmly. "In fact I know exactly where your Sally is."

Starbuck felt the elation of success and the terror of confronting that success to discover it was a sham. He felt as if he were at the very edge of a chasm and he did not know whether it was to heaven or to hell that he would leap. "So she's alive?" he asked.

"Come to me tomorrow evening," Delaney said in oblique answer, then held up a hand to check any further questions. "Come here at five. But—" He said the last word warningly.

"Yes?"

Delaney pointed his cigarette across the table. "You will owe me a debt for this, Starbuck."

Starbuck shivered despite the warmth. A soul was sold, he suspected, but for what coin? But nor did he really care because tomorrow night he would find Sally. Perhaps it was the wine, or the heady tobacco fumes, or else the thought of all his dreams coming to a resolution, but he did not care. "I understand," he said carefully, understanding nothing.

Delaney smiled and broke the spell. "Some brandy? And another cigar, I think." It would be amusing, Delaney thought, to corrupt the Reverend Elial Starbuck's son. Besides, if Delaney was honest, he rather liked Nathaniel Starbuck. The boy was naive, but there was steel inside him and he had quick wits even if those wits were presently obliterated by desire. Starbuck, in short, might be useful one day, and if that usefulness was ever needed Delaney would be able to call in the debt that he was forging this night out of a young man's obsession and desperation.

For Delaney was now an agent of the North. A man had come to his chambers, posing as a client, and there produced a copy of Delaney's letter offering to spy for the North. The copy had been burned, and the sight of the burning paper had sent a shiver of nerves through Delaney's soul. From now on he knew himself to be a marked man, liable to the death penalty, yet still the rewards of that loyalty to the North were worth the risk.

And the risk, he knew, could be very short-lived. Delaney did not believe the rebellion could last even to the end of July. The North's new army would roll majestically across the pathetic rebel forces gathered in northern Virginia, secession would collapse and the southern politicians would then whimper that they had never meant to preach rebellion anyway. And what would become of the little people betrayed by those politicians? Starbuck, Delaney supposed, would be sent back to his ghastly hellhound of a father and that would be the end of the boy's one adventure. So let him have a last, exotic moment to remember his whole dull life through and if, perchance, the rebellion did last a few months more, why, Starbuck would be an ally whether he wanted to be or not. "Tomorrow night, then," Delaney said mischievously, then raised his brandy glass, "at five."

Starbuck spent the next day in a torment of apprehension. He dared not tell Washington Faulconer what irked him, he dared not even tell Adam, but instead he kept a feverish silence as he accompanied father and son to the Mechanics Hall in Franklin Street where Robert Lee had his offices. Lee had now been promoted from head of Virginia's forces to be the Confederate president's chief military adviser, yet he still retained much of his state work and was, Faulconer was told, gone from the capital to inspect some fortifications that guarded the mouth of the James River. A harassed clerk, sweating in the outer office, said that the general was expected back that afternoon, or maybe next day, and no, it was not possible to make any appointment. All petitioners must wait. At least a score of men were already waiting on the landing or on the wide stairs. Washington Faulconer bristled at being lumped as a petitioner, but somehow kept his patience as the clock ticked and the clouds gathered dark over Richmond.

At a quarter to five Starbuck asked if he might leave. Faulconer turned angrily on his aide, as though about to refuse permission, but Starbuck blurted out an excuse of not feeling well. "My stomach, sir."

"Go," Faulconer said irritably, "go." He waited until Starbuck had gone down the stairs, then turned on Adam. "What the hell is the matter with him? It isn't his stomach, that's for sure."

"I don't know, sir."

"A woman? That's what it looks like. He's met an old friend? Who? And why doesn't he introduce us? It's a whore, I tell you, a whore."

"Nate doesn't have the money," Adam said stiffly.

"I wouldn't be so certain." Washington Faulconer walked to the window at the end of the landing and stared gloomily into the street where a tobacco wagon had lost a wheel and a crowd of Negroes had gathered round to offer the teamster advice.

"Why wouldn't you be certain, Father?" Adam asked.

Faulconer brooded for a moment, then turned on his son. "You remember the raid? You know why Nate disobeyed my orders? So that Truslow could steal from the passengers in the cars. Good Lord, Adam, that's not warfare! That's brigandry, pure and simple, and your friend condoned it. He risked the success of all we had achieved to become a thief."

"Nate isn't a thief!" Adam protested vigorously.

"And I trusted him with matters here in Richmond," Washington Faulconer said, "and how am I to know if his accounting was fair?"

"Father!" Adam said angrily. "Nate is not a thief."

"And what did he do to that _Tom_ company fellow?"

"That was ..." Adam began, but then did not know how to continue, for it was certain that his friend had indeed stolen Major Trabell's money. "No, Father." Adam persisted in his stubborn denial, though a lot more weakly.

"I just wish I could share your certainty." Faulconer looked gloomily down at the landing floor that was stained with dried tobacco juice that had missed the spittoons. "I'm not even sure any longer that Nate belongs here in the South," Faulconer said heavily, then looked up as a clatter of boots and a murmur of voices sounded in the downstairs hall.

Robert Lee had arrived at last, and Starbuck's character could be momentarily forgotten so that the Legion could be offered for battle.

George, Belvedere Delaney's house slave, had conducted Starbuck as far as the front door of the house in Marshall Street where he had been greeted by a middle-aged woman of stern looks and apparent respectability. "My name is Richardson," she had told Starbuck, "and Mister Delaney has given me his full instructions. This way, sir, if you would."

It was a whorehouse. That much an astonished Starbuck realized as he was escorted through the hallway and past an open parlor door beyond which a group of girls sat dressed in laced bodices and white underskirts. Some smiled at him, others did not even look up from their hands of cards, but Starbuck faltered as he understood what trade was carried on in this comfortable, even luxurious house with its dark rugs, papered walls and gilt-framed landscapes. This was one of the dens of iniquity against which his father preached the awful threat of everlasting torture, a place of hellish horrors and unbridled sins, where a varnished hall stand with brass hooks, an umbrella tray and a beveled mirror held three officers' hats, a silk top hat and a cane. "You may stay as long as you like, young man," Mrs. Richardson said, pausing beside the hall stand to pass on Delaney's instructions, "and there will be no charge. Please be careful of the loose stair rod."

Mrs. Richardson led Starbuck up a stairway that was papered in flock and lit by a fringed oil lamp that hung on a long brass chain suspended from the stairwell's high ceiling. Starbuck was in uniform and his scabbarded saber clattered awkwardly against the banisters. A curtained arch waited at the top of the stairs and beyond it the light was even dimmer, though not so dim that Starbuck could not see the framed prints on the wall. The pictures showed naked couples and at first he did not believe what he saw, then he looked again and blushed for what he did indeed see. A stern part of his conscience instructed him to turn back now. For all of his life Starbuck had struggled between sin and righteousness and he knew, better than any man, that the wages of sin were death, yet if all the choirs of heaven and all the preachers of earth had bellowed that message into his ears Starbuck could not have turned back at that moment.

He followed the black-dressed Mrs. Richardson down the long passage. A Negro maid carrying a cloth-covered bowl on a tray came the other way and stood aside to let Mrs. Richardson pass, then grinned cheekily at Starbuck. Some voices laughed in a nearby room, while from another a man's voice gasped excitedly. Starbuck felt light-headed, almost as if he was going to faint as he followed Mrs. Richardson around a corner and down a short flight of steps. They turned yet another corner, climbed a second short stair and then at last Mrs. Richardson brought out her ring of keys, selected one and pushed it into the door's lock. She paused, then turned the key to push open the door. "Go in, Mister Starbuck."

Starbuck went nervously into the room. The door closed behind him, the key turned in the lock, and there was Sally. Alive. Sitting in a chair with a book in her lap and looking even more beautiful than he had remembered her. For weeks he had tried to conjure that face in his dreams, but now, faced with the reality of her beauty again, he realized how inadequate those conjurations had been. He was overwhelmed by her.

They stared at each other. Starbuck did not know what to say. His saber scabbard scraped dully against the door. Sally was wearing a dark blue robe and her hair was gathered in heavy loops on top of her head and tied with pale blue ribbons. There was a fresh scar on her cheek, which did not make her any less beautiful, but oddly made her more fascinating. The scar was a white streak that slashed off her left cheekbone toward her ear. She stared at him, seemingly as surprised as he was nervous, then she closed the small book and put it on the table beside her. "It's the preacherman!" She sounded pleased to see him.

"Sally?" Starbuck's voice was uncertain. He was as nervous as a child.

"I'm Victoria now. Like the queen?" Sally laughed. "They gave me a new name, see? So I'm Victoria." She paused. "But you can call me Sally."

"They lock you in?"

"That's just to keep the customers out. Sometimes the men run wild, at least, the soldiers do. But I ain't a prisoner. I got a key, see?" She pulled a key out of her robe pocket. "And I mustn't say *ain't*. Mrs. Richardson doesn't like it. She says I mustn't say *ain't* and I mustn't say *nigger* neither. It ain't nice, see? And she's teaching me to read as well." She showed her book to Starbuck. It was a McGuffey's *Reading Primer*, the very first in the series and a book that Starbuck had disposed of when he was three years old. "I'm getting real good," Sally said enthusiastically.

Starbuck wanted to weep for her. He did not really know why. She looked well, she even sounded happy, yet there was something pathetic about this place that made him hate the whole world. "I was worried about you," he said lamely.

"That's nice." She gave him a half smile, then shrugged. "But I'm doing fine, real fine. Except I'll bet that piece of shit Ethan Ridley didn't worry about me?"

"I don't think he does, no."

"I'll see him in hell." Sally sounded bitter. A rumble of thunder sounded above the city, followed a moment later by the heavy sound of rain falling. The new drops twitched the tight-stretched gauze insect curtains that were pinned across the two open windows. It was dusk and summer lightning flickered pale across the western sky. "We've got wine," Sally said, reverting to cheerfulness, "and some cold chicken, see? And bread. And these are sugar fruits, see? And nuts. Mrs. Richardson said I was getting a special visitor and the girls brought all this up here. They can look after us real well, see?" She stood and crossed to one of the open windows, staring past the gauze at the ashen sheets of lightning that flickered in the gathering darkness. The summer air was heavy and sultry, suffused with Richmond's tobacco smell that filled Sally's large room which, to Starbuck's innocent eye, looked distressingly ordinary, rather like a well-furnished hotel bedroom. It had a small coal grate in a black metal fireplace, a brass fender, flowered wallpaper and framed mountain landscapes on its walls. There were two chairs, two tables and a scatter of rugs and the ubiquitous spittoons on the polished wood floor. There was also a wide bed with a carved hardwood headpiece and a heap of white pillows. Starbuck tried hard not to look at the bed while Sally still gazed through the gauze at the western horizon where the lightning stuttered. "I sometimes look over there and I think of home."

"Do you miss it?"

She laughed. "I like it here, preacherman."

"Nate, call me Nate."

She turned from the window. "I always wanted to be a fine lady, see? I wanted everything nice. My Ma used to tell me about a real nice house she once went to. She said it had candles and pictures and soft rugs and I always wanted that. I hated living up there. Up at four in the morning and hauling water and always so cold in winter. And your hands were always sore. Bleeding even." She paused and held up her hands, which now were white and soft, then she took a cigar from a jar on the table where the food had been placed. "You want a smoke, Nate?"

Starbuck crossed the room, cut the cigar, lit it, then took one for himself. "How did you find me?" Sally asked.

"I went to Ethan Ridley's brother."

"That Delaney? He's a strange one," Sally said. "I like him, I think I like him, but he's not like Ethan. I tell you, if I see Ethan again, I swear I'll kill the son of a bitch. I don't care if they hang me, Nate, I'll kill him. Mrs. Richardson swears that he won't be allowed to see me if he comes here, but I hope he does. I hope that son of a bitch comes in here and I'll stick him like a hog on a slab, so I will." She sucked on the cigar, making its tip glow a brilliant red.

"What happened?" Starbuck asked.

She shrugged, sat in a chair by the window and told how she had come to Richmond to find Ethan Ridley. For three or four days he had seemed friendly, even kind to her, but then he had told her they were going in a carriage to look at some rooms he planned to rent for her. Except there were no rooms, only two men who had carried her off to a cellar in the eastern end of the city and there they had beaten her, raped her and beaten her again until she had learned to be obedient. "I lost the baby," she said bleakly, "but they wanted that, I reckon. I mean I wasn't any good to them pregnant, not here." She waved around the room, hinting at her new trade. "And of course, he arranged it."

"Ridley?"

Sally nodded. "He had it all arranged. He wanted rid of me, see? So he had two men take me. One was a nigger, I mean a black, and the other used to be a slave trader, see, so they knew how to break people like my pa used to break horses." She shrugged and turned toward the window. "I guess I needed breaking, too."

"You can't say that!" Starbuck was appalled.

"Oh, honey!" Sally smiled at him. "How the hell am I to get what I want in this world? You give me that answer? I ain't born to money, I ain't educated for money, all I got is what men want." She drew on the cigar, then took a glass of wine from Starbuck. "A lot of the girls here started that way. I mean they have to be broken in. It ain't nice, and I don't care if I never see those two men again, but I'm here now, and I'm mended."

"They scarred you?"

"Hell, yes." She touched her left cheek. "Ain't too bad, though, is it? They did other things. Like if I wouldn't open my mouth? They had this machine they use on slaves who won't speak. It goes round your head and has a piece of iron here." She demonstrated by jabbing the cigar toward her lips, then shrugged. "That could hurt. But all I had to do was learn to be good and they stopped using it."

Starbuck was filled with inchoate indignation. "Who were the two men?"

"Just men, Nate. It don't matter." Sally made a dismissive gesture, as though she did not really blame them for what had happened. "Then after a month Mister Delaney came to the house and he said he was real shocked at what was happening to me, and he said it was all Ethan's fault, and Mrs. Richardson came as well, and they took me away and made a real fuss of me and brought me here, and Mrs. Richardson said I didn't really have much of a choice any longer. I could stay here and make money or they'd put me back on the street. So here I am."

"You could go home, surely?" Starbuck suggested.

"No!" Sally was vehement. "I don't want to be at home, Nate! Father always wanted me to be a boy. He reckons everyone should be happy with a log house, two hunting dogs, an axe and a long rifle, but that ain't my dream."

"Do you want to go away?" Starbuck asked her. "With me?"

She smiled pityingly at him. "How are we going to do that, honey?"

"I don't know. Just leave here. Walk north." He gestured toward the darkening sky that was filled with a new hard rain, and even as he made the suggestion he knew it was hopeless.

Sally laughed at the very thought of walking away from Mrs. Richardson's house. "I've got what I want here!"

"But ..."

"I've got what I want," she insisted. "Listen, people ain't no different to horses. Some are special, some are workers. Mrs. Richardson says I can be special. She don't waste me on every customer, only the special ones. And she says I can leave here if a man wants me and can pay for me proper. I mean I can leave anyway, but where am I going to go? Look at me! I've got dresses and wine and cigars and money. And I won't do this forever. You see the carriages go by with the rich folks? Half those women started like me, Nate!" She spoke very earnestly, then laughed when she saw his unhappiness. "Now listen. Take off that sword, sit down proper, and tell me about the Legion. Make me real happy and tell me Ethan has shot himself. You know that son of a bitch took my Ma's ring? The silver ring?"

"I'll get it back for you."

"No!" She shook her head. "Ma wouldn't want that ring in this place, but you can get it for Pa." She thought for a second, then smiled wanly. "He loved my Ma, you know, he really did."

"I know. I saw him at her grave."

"Course you did." She took a crystalized cherry and bit it in half, then tucked her legs up onto the chair. "So why did you call yourself a preacherman? I often wondered about that."

So Starbuck told her about Boston and the Reverend Elial Starbuck and the big dark brooding house on Walnut Street that always seemed filled with the dangerous silences of parental anger and the smell of wax and wood oil and Bibles and coal smoke. Darkness fell over Richmond, but neither Starbuck nor Sally moved to light a candle, instead they talked of childhood and of broken dreams and how love always seemed to trickle through the fingers when you thought you had a grasp of it.

"It was when Ma died that everything went wrong for me," Sally said, then she gave a long sigh and turned in the darkness to look at Starbuck. "So you reckon you'll stay here? In the South?"

"I don't know. I think so."

"Why?"

"To be near you?" He said it easily, like a friend, and she laughed to hear it. Starbuck leaned forward, his elbows propped on his long legs and wondered about the real truth of his answer. "I don't know what I shall do," he said softly. "I know I'm not going to be a preacher now, and I don't really know what else I can be. I could be a schoolteacher, I guess, but I'm not really sure I want to do that. I'm no good at business, at least I don't think I am, and I don't have the money to become a lawyer." He paused, drawing on his third cigar of the evening. Delaney had been right, it was soothing.

"So what are you going to sell, honey?" Sally asked ironically. "I've been taught real good what I have to sell, so what about you? No one looks after us for nothing, Nate. I learned that. My Ma might have done that for me, but she's dead, and my Pa." She shook her head. "All he wanted was for me to be a cook and a hog slaughterer and a fowl keeper and a farmer's woman. But that ain't me. And if you ain't a lawyer or a preacherman or a teacher, then what in hell's name are you going to be?"

"That." He gestured at the discarded saber that was propped in its cheap scabbard against the windowsill. "I'm going to be a soldier. I'm going to be a very good soldier." It was strange, he thought, but he had never said this before, not even to himself, but suddenly it all made such sense. "I'm going to be famous, Sally. I'm going to ride through this war like a, like a …" He paused, seeking the right word, then suddenly a bout of thunder cracked overhead, shaking the very house, and at the same instant a bolt of lightning sizzled through the Richmond sky like white fire blazing. "Like that!" Starbuck said. "Just like that."

Sally smiled. Her teeth looked very white in the darkness, and her hair, when the sheet lightning blanched the night, reflected like dark gold. "You won't get rich being a soldier, Nate."

"No, I guess I won't at that."

"And I'm expensive, honey." She was only half teasing him.

"I'll find the money somehow."

She stirred in the dark, stubbing out her cigar and stretching her slen-der arms. "They've given you tonight. I don't know why, but I guess Mis-ter Delaney likes you, right?"

"I think he does, yes." Starbuck's heart was thumping in his chest. He thought how very naive he had been about Delaney, then how much he owed Delaney, and then how little he knew about Delaney. How blind he had been, he thought, how trusting. "Does Delaney own this place?" he asked.

"He has a bit of it, I don't know how much. But he's given you tonight, honey, all night, right till breakfast, and after that?"

"I said I'll find the money." Starbuck's voice was choked and he was trembling.

"I can tell you how to earn it forever. For as long as you and I still want it." Sally spoke soft in the darkness and the rain drummed on the street and on the roof.

"How?" It was a miracle Starbuck could speak at all, and even so the word came out like a croak. "How?" He said it again.

"Kill Ethan for me."

"Kill Ethan," Starbuck said as though he had not heard her correctly, and as though he had not spent these last days persuading himself that Ethan was his enemy and fantasizing a young man's dreams of how he would destroy his enemy. "Kill him?" he asked in dread.

"Kill that son of a bitch for me. Just kill him for me." Sally paused. "It ain't that I mind being here, Nate, in fact it's probably the best place for me, but I hate that son of a bitch for telling me lies, and I hate that he thinks he got away with telling me lies, and I want that son of a bitch dead and I want the last thing he hears on this earth to be my name so he don't ever forget why he's gone to hell. Will you do that for me?"

Dear God, Starbuck thought, but how many sins were here brought into one foul bundle? How many entries would the Recording Angel be making in the Lamb's Book of Life? What hope of redemption was there for a man who would contemplate murder, let alone commit it? How wide the gates of hell gaped, how searing the flames would be, how agonizing the lake of fire, and how long would all eternity stretch if he did not stand now, fetch his sword, and walk out from this den of iniquity into the cleansing rain. Dear God, he prayed, but this is a terrible thing, and if you will just save me now then I will never sin again, not ever.

He looked into Sally's eyes, her lovely eyes. "Of course I'll kill him for you," he heard himself saying.

"You want to eat first, honey? Or later?"

Like a slash of lightning, white across the sky, he would be marvelous.

PART THREE

9

Orders came from Richmond that directed the Legion to the rail junction at Manassas where the rails of the Orange and Alexandria met the Manassas Gap line. The orders did not arrive till three days after Washington Faulconer had returned from Richmond, and even then the permission seemed grudging. The order was addressed to the commanding officer of the Faulconer County Regiment, as though the Richmond authorities did not want to dignify Washington Faulconer's achievement in raising the Legion, but at least they were allowing the Legion to join General Beauregard's Army of Northern Virginia as Faulconer had requested. General Lee had enclosed a curt note regretting that it was not in his power to attach the "Faulconer County Regiment" to any one particular corps in Beauregard's army, indeed he took care to note that, because the regiment's availability had been made known to the authorities at such short notice and because the regiment had undertaken no brigade training of any kind, he doubted whether it could be used for anything other than detached duties. Washington Faulconer rather liked the sound of such duties until Major Pelham dryly noted that detached duties usually meant serving as baggage guards, railroad sentries or prisoner of war escorts.

If Lee's note was calculated to pique Washington Faulconer, it succeeded, though the Colonel declared it was no more than he expected from the mudsills in Richmond. General Beauregard, Faulconer was certain, would prove more welcoming. Faulconer's greatest concern was to reach Manassas before the war ended. Northern troops had crossed the Potomac in force and were said to be slowly advancing toward the Confederate Army, and rumor in Richmond claimed that Beauregard planned to unleash a massive encircling move that would crush the northern invaders. The rumors added that if such a defeat did not persuade the United States to sue for peace, then Beauregard would cross the Potomac and capture Washington. Colonel Faulconer dreamed of riding his black charger, Saratoga, up the steps of the unfinished Capitol Building and in the fulfillment of that dream he was willing to swallow the worst of Richmond's insults, and thus the day after the arrival of the churlish order the Legion was woken two hours before dawn with orders to strike the tent lines and load the baggage wagons. The Colonel anticipated a swift march to the rail depot at Rosskill, yet somehow everything took much longer than anyone expected. No one seemed entirely certain how to disassemble the eleven giant cast-iron camp stoves that Faulconer had bought, nor had anyone thought to order the Legion's ammunition to be fetched out of its dry storage at Seven Springs.

News of the move also provoked the mothers, sweethearts and wives of the soldiers to bring one last gift to the encampment. Men who were already laden down with haversacks, weapons, knapsacks, blankets and cartridge boxes were given woolen scarves, coats, capes, revolvers, bowie knives, jars of preserves, sacks of coffee, biscuits and buffalo robes, and all the time the hot sun rose still higher and the camp stoves were still not disassembled, and one of the wagon horses cast a shoe, and Washington Faulconer fumed, Pecker Bird cackled at the confusion and Major Pelham had a heart attack.

"Oh, good Christ!" It was Little, the bandmaster, who had been complaining to Pelham that there was not enough wagon space for his instruments when suddenly the elderly officer made an odd clicking noise in his throat, gasped one huge, despairing breath inward, then toppled from his saddle. Men dropped whatever they were doing to gather round the thin motionless body. Washington Faulconer spurred toward the gawking spectators and waved them back with his riding crop. "Back to your duties! Back! Where the hell's Doctor Danson? Danson!"

Danson arrived and stooped over the still form of Pelham, then declared him dead. "Out like a candle!" Danson struggled to his feet, putting his trumpet-stethoscope back into a pocket. "Damned good way to go, Faulconer."

"Not today, it isn't. Damn you! Back to work!" He pointed his riding crop at a staring soldier. "Go on, away with you! Who the hell's going to tell Pelham's sister?"

"Not me," Danson said.

"Goddamn it! Why couldn't he have died in battle?" Faulconer turned the horse. "Adam! Duty for you!"

"I'm supposed to be going to the Rosskill depot, sir."

"Ethan can go."

"He's fetching the ammunition."

"Damn Rosskill! I want you to go to Miss Pelham. My best regards to her, you know what to say. Take her some flowers. Better still, fetch Moss on your way. If a preacher isn't any good with the bereaved, then what the hell use is he?"

"You want me to go to Rosskill afterward?"

"Send Starbuck. You tell him what to do." Starbuck had not been in the Colonel's best books since the night in Richmond when he had stayed out till well past breakfast and had then refused to say where he had been. "Not that you need to be told what he's been doing," the Colonel had grumbled to his son that morning, "because it stands out a mile, but he might have the decency to tell us who she is."

Now Nate was ordered to ride to the Rosskill depot of the Orange and Alexandria Railroad and tell the depot manager to prepare for the Legion's arrival. Faulconer, who was a director of the railroad, had already sent a letter that, in anticipation of the orders from Richmond, had required two trains to be prepared for the Legion's journey, but someone now had to ride to the depot and order the engineers to fire up their boxes and so raise steam. One train would consist of the railroad director's car, which was reserved for Faulconer and his aides, and sufficient second-class passenger cars to carry the Legion's nine hundred and thirty-two men, while the second train would consist of boxcars for supplies and horses, and open wagons for the Legion's wagons, cannon, limbers and caissons. Adam handed Starbuck a copy of his father's letter and a copy of the written orders that had been dispatched to the depot manager at dawn. "Roswell Jenkin's company is supposed to be there by eleven, though God knows if they'll be ready by then. They're going to make ramps."

"Ramps?"

"To get the horses into the wagons," Adam explained. "Wish me luck. Miss Pelham is not the easiest of women. Dear God."

Starbuck wished his friend good luck, then saddled Pocahontas and trotted her out of the chaotic encampment, through the town and down the Rosskill road. The town, which held the nearest railroad depot to Faulconer County, was twice the size of Faulconer Court House and had been built where the foothills finally gave way to the wide plain that stretched to the distant sea. It was an easy downhill ride. The day was hot and the cows in the meadows were either standing under shade trees or else up to their bellies in the deep cool streams. The roadside was bright with flowers, the trees heavy with leaf, and Starbuck was happy.

He had a letter to Sally in his saddlebag. She had wanted him to send her letters and he had promised to write as often as he could. This first letter told of the last days of training and of how the Colonel had given him the mare, Pocahontas. He had kept the letter simple, the words short and the letters big and round. He had told Sally how he loved her, and he guessed that was true, but it was a strange kind of love, more like a friendship than the destructive passion he had felt for Dominique. Starbuck was still jealous of the men Sally would lie with, as any man surely should be

jealous, but Sally would have none of his jealousy. She needed his friendship as he needed hers, for they had come together in the thunder-riven
night like two lonely children needing comfort, and afterward, lying happily in the bed where they had smoked cigars and listened to the dawn
rain, they had agreed to write, or rather Starbuck had agreed to write and
Sally had promised she would try to read his letters and one day she
would even try to write back so long as Starbuck promised on his honor
not to laugh at her efforts.

He stopped at the Rosskill post office and sent the letter, then rode
on to the depot, where the manager was a plump, sweating man named
Reynolds. "There are no trains," Reynolds greeted Starbuck in his small
office next to the telegraph room.

"But Mister Faulconer, Colonel Faulconer, specifically requested two
sets of cars, both with locomotives—"

"I don't care if God Almighty ordered the cars!" Reynolds was a
plump man, sweating in his woolen railroad uniform, who was clearly
tired of the exigencies that wartime had imposed upon his careful
timetable. "The whole railroad's only got sixteen locomotives and ten of
those have gone north to move troops. We're supposed to do things railroad fashion, but how can I keep order if everyone wants locomotives? I
can't help you! I don't care if Mister Faulconer is a director, I don't care if
all the directors were here begging for cars, I can't do anything!"

"You have to help," Starbuck said.

"I can't make cars, laddie! I can't make locomotives!" Reynolds
leaned across his table, sweat dripping down his face into his ginger beard
and mustaches. "I am not a miracle worker!"

"But I am," Starbuck said, and he took out the big Savage revolver
from the holster at his waist, pointed it just to one side of Reynolds and
pulled the trigger. Smoke and noise filled the room as the heavy bullet
smashed through the timber wall to leave a ragged, splintered hole. Starbuck holstered the smoking gun. "I am not a laddie, Mister Reynolds," he
calmly told the gaping, astonished manager, "but an officer in the army of
the Confederate States of America and if you insult me once again I shall
put you against that wall and shoot you."

For a second Starbuck thought that Reynolds was going to follow
Major Pelham into an early grave. "You're mad!" the railroad man finally
said.

"I think that's probably true," Starbuck agreed placidly, "but I shoot
better when I am mad than when I am sane, so let us now decide how you
and I are going to move the Faulconer Legion north to Manassas Junction, shall we?" He smiled. It was Sally, he decided, who had released this
confidence in him. He was actually enjoying himself. Goddamn it, he
thought, but he was going to be a good soldier.

Yet Reynolds suspected there were no available passenger cars within fifty miles. All he had in the depot were seventeen old house cars. "What are house cars?" Starbuck asked politely, and the frightened manager pointed through his window at a boxcar.

"We call them house cars," he said in the same nervous voice that he had used to reassure the telegraph operator and two assistants who had run to his office to enquire about the shooting.

"How many men can we fit into a house car?" Starbuck asked.

"Fifty? Sixty maybe?"

"Then we have just enough." The Legion had not reached Faulconer's target of one thousand men, but over nine hundred had volunteered, making it into a formidable regiment. "What other cars do you have?" Starbuck asked.

There were just two gondola cars, which were simple open wagons, and that was all. One of the gondola cars and eight of the boxcars were in desperate need of repair, though Reynolds thought they could be used, but only at the slowest possible speed. There were, he said, no locomotives available, though when Starbuck put a hand toward the big Savage revolver, Reynolds hastily remembered that a locomotive was expected to pass through the depot on its way to Lynchburg, where it was going to collect a train of platform cars loaded with cut timber that was being carried to the coast to build artillery revetments.

"Good!" Starbuck said. "You'll stop the locomotive and turn it round."

"We don't have a roundhouse here."

"The engine can travel backward?"

Reynolds nodded. "Yes, sir."

"And how far is it to Manassas?"

"A hundred miles, sir."

"Then we shall go to war backward," Starbuck said happily.

Washington Faulconer, when he led the Legion's cavalry unit into the depot at midday, was furious. He had expected two trains to be waiting, one of them with the director's private car attached, but instead there was just a mutinous engineer with a single backward-facing locomotive and tender that was attached to seventeen boxcars and two gondola cars, while the telegraph operator was attempting to explain to Lynchburg why the locomotive would not be arriving, and Reynolds was trying to clear the track northward past Charlottesville. "For God's sake, Nate," the Colonel exploded, "why is everything such a mess?"

"Wartime, sir?"

"Damn it! I gave you simple enough orders! Can't you do the simplest thing?" He spurred off to abuse the grumbling engineer.

Adam looked at Starbuck and shrugged. "Sorry. Father's not happy."

"How was Miss Pelham?"

"Awful. Just awful." Adam shook his head. "And soon, Nate, there'll be scores of women getting that same news. Hundreds." Adam turned to look down Rosskill's Depot Street where the first of the Legion's infantry-men had come into sight. The marching column was flanked by twin ragged processions of wives, mothers and children, some of whom were carrying knapsacks to relieve their men of their equipment's weight. "Dear God, this is chaos," Adam said. "We were supposed to have left three hours ago!"

"I'm told that in war nothing ever goes to plan," Starbuck said hap-pily, "and that if it does, you're probably being whipped. We have to get used to chaos, and learn to make the best of it."

"Father's not good at that," Adam confessed.

"Then it's a good job he's got me." Starbuck smiled benignly at Ethan Ridley, who had ridden in with the approaching Legion. Starbuck had decided he would be very pleasant to Ridley from now until the end of Ridley's life. Ridley ignored him.

The Colonel had originally supposed that the Legion would be entrained in comfort by ten that morning, yet it was not till five in the evening that the single train limped slowly north. There was enough room for the infantrymen, three days' supply of food and all the Legion's ammunition, but precious little else. The officers' horses and servants were put into the two gondola cars. The Colonel would travel in the caboose, which had arrived with the locomotive, while the men were given the boxcars. The Colonel, mindful of his duties as a director of the line, gave strict orders that the cars were to arrive at Manassas Junction undamaged, but no sooner had he spoken than Sergeant Truslow found an axe and smashed a hole in the side of a boxcar. "A man needs light and air," he growled at the Colonel, then swung the axe again. The Colonel turned away and pretended not to notice the orgy of destruction as the Legion began its enthusiastic ventilation of the wooden boxes.

There was no room on the train for the Legion's cavalry, which had to be left behind, along with the two six-pounder guns, their caissons and limbers, the cast-iron camp stoves and all the wagons. The Legion's tents were slung into the boxcars at the last moment and Bandmaster Little took his instruments, claiming they were medical supplies. The Legion's colors were almost left behind in the confusion, but Adam saw the twin leather flag cases abandoned on a gun caisson and stowed them in the caboose. The depot was chaotic as women and children sought to say goodbye to their men, and as the men, exhausting the water in their can-teens, tried to fill the small round bottles from the outflow of the depot's stilt-legged water tank. Faulconer was shouting last-minute instructions for the cavalry, artillery and wagon train, which would now travel north by road. He reckoned they should take three days to make the journey while the train, even with its damaged axle boxes, should make it in one. "We'll see you in Manassas," the Colonel told Lieutenant Davies, who was to be in charge of the convoy, "or maybe in Washington!"

Anna Faulconer, driving her small cart, had arrived from Faulconer Court House and insisted on handing out small Confederate flags that she and the servants at Seven Springs had embroidered. Her father, impatient at the delay, ordered the engineer to sound the whistle to summon the men back to the boxcars, but the sound of the shrieking steam frightened some of the horses in the gondola cars and one Negro servant had his leg broken when Captain Hinton's mare kicked back. The servant was carried off the train and, in the delay, two men from E Company decided they did not want to fight and deserted, but three other men insisted on being allowed to join the Legion there and then and so climbed aboard.

Finally, at five o'clock, the train began its journey. It could go no faster than ten miles an hour because of the broken axle boxes and so it limped north, its wheels clanking across the rail joints and its bell clanging a mournful sound over the water meadows and green fields. The Colonel was still furious at the day's delays, but the men were in high spirits and sang cheerfully as their slow train chugged away from the hills, its smoke drifting among trees. They left the convoy of wagons, guns and cavalry behind and steamed slowly into the night.

The train journey took almost two days. The crowded cars spent twelve hours waiting at the Gordonsville Junction, another three at Warrenton, and endless other minutes waiting while the tender was fueled with cordwood or its water tank charged, but at last, on a hot Saturday afternoon, they reached Manassas Junction where the Army of Northern Virginia had its headquarters. No one in Manassas knew the Legion was coming or what to do with them, but finally a staff officer led the Legion north and east from the small town along a country road that wound through small steep hills. There were other troops camped in meadows, and artillery pieces parked in farm gates, and the sight of those other troops gave the Legion an apprehensive feeling that they had joined some massive undertaking that none of them truly understood. Till now they had been the Faulconer Legion, safe in Faulconer Court House and led by Colonel Faulconer, but the train had abruptly brought them to a strange place where they were lost in an incomprehensible and uncontrollable process.

It was almost dark when the staff Captain pointed to a farmhouse that lay to the right of the road on a wide, bare plateau. "The farm's still occupied," he told Faulconer, "but those pastures look empty, so make yourselves at home."

"I need to see Beauregard." Faulconer sounded irritable, made so by the evening's uncertainty. He wanted to know where exactly he was, and the staff officer did not know, and he wanted to know precisely what was expected of his Legion, but the staff officer could not tell him that either. There were no maps, no orders, no sense of direction at all. "I should see Beauregard tonight," Faulconer insisted.

"I guess the general will be real pleased to see you, Colonel," the staff officer said tactfully, "but I reckon you'd best still wait for morning now. Say at six o'clock?"

"Are we expecting action?" Faulconer asked pompously.

"Sometime tomorrow, I guess." The staff officer's cigar glowed briefly. "The Yankees are up that a way," he gestured vaguely eastward with his lit cigar, "and I guess we'll be crossing the river to give them a howdy, but the general won't be giving his orders till morning. I'll tell you how to find him, and you be there at six, Colonel. That'll give you boys time to have yourselves a prayer service first."

"A prayer service?" Faulconer's tone suggested the staff officer was touched in the head.

"Tomorrow's the Lord's Day, Colonel," the captain said reproachfully, and so it would be, for the next day would be Sunday, July 21, 1861.

And America would be broken by battle.

By two o'clock on Sunday morning the air was already stiflingly hot and breathlessly calm. The sun would not rise for another two and a half hours yet, and the sky was still star bright, cloudless and brilliant. Most of the men, even though they had lugged their tents the long five miles from the rail junction to the farm, slept in the open air. Starbuck woke to see the heavens like a brilliant scatter of cold white light, more beautiful than anything found on earth.

"Time to get up," Adam said beside him.

Men were waking all around the hilltop. They were coughing and cursing, their voices made loud by nervousness. Somewhere in the dark valley a set of harness chains jangled and a horse whinnied, and a trumpet called reveille from a far encampment, its sound echoing back from a distant dark slope. A cockerel crowed from the farmhouse on the hill where dim lights showed behind curtained windows. Dogs barked and the cooks banged skillets and kettles.

"'The armorers'"—Starbuck still lay on his back, staring up at the sharp-edged stars—"'accomplishing the knights, with busy hammers closing rivets up, give dreadful note of preparation.'"

Adam would normally have taken pleasure in capping the quotation, but he was in a silent, subdued mood and so said nothing. All along the Legion's lines the smoky fires were being coddled into life to throw a garish light on shirt-sleeved men, stands of rifles and the white conical tents. The thickening smoke shimmered the stars.

Starbuck still gazed upward. "'The cripple tardy-gaited night,'" he quoted again, "'who like a foul witch doth limp so tediously away.'" He was delivering the quotations to disguise his nervousness. Today, he was thinking, I shall see the elephant.

Adam said nothing. He felt that he had come to the brink of a terrible chaos, like the abyss across which Satan had flown in *Paradise Lost*, and that was exactly what this war meant for America, Adam thought sadly—the loss of innocence, the loss of sweet perfection. He had joined the Legion to please his father, now he might have to pay the price of that compromise.

"Coffee, Massa?" Nelson, Faulconer's servant, brought two tin mugs of coffee from the fire he had tended all night behind the Colonel's tent.

"You're a great and good man, Nelson." Starbuck sat up and reached for the coffee.

Sergeant Truslow was shouting at Company K, where someone had complained that there was no bucket with which to fetch water and Truslow was bellowing at the man to stop complaining and go steal a damned bucket.

"You don't seem nervous." Adam sipped the coffee, then grimaced at its harsh taste.

"Of course I'm nervous," Starbuck said. In fact the apprehension was writhing in his belly like snakes boiling in a pit. "But I have an idea that I might be a good soldier." Was that true, he wondered, or was he just saying it because he wanted it to be true? Or because he had boasted of it to Sally? And was that all it had been? A boast to impress a girl?

"I shouldn't even be here," Adam said.

"Nonsense," Starbuck said briskly. "Survive one day, Adam, just one day, then help make peace."

A few minutes past three o'clock two horsemen appeared in the regiment's lines. One man was carrying a lantern with which he had lit his way across the hilltop. "Who are you?" the second man shouted.

"The Faulconer Legion!" Adam called back the answer.

"The Faulconer Legion? Jesus wept! We've got a Legion on our goddamned side now? The damned Yankees might as well give up." The speaker was a short balding man with intense, button-black eyes that scowled from an unwashed face above a dirty black mustache and a ragged spade beard. He slid out of his saddle and paced into the firelight to reveal skeletally thin legs bowed like razor clam shells that looked entirely inadequate to support the weight of his big belly and broad, muscled torso. "So who's in command here?" the strange man demanded.

"My father," Adam said, "Colonel Faulconer." He gestured at his father's tent.

"Faulconer!" The stranger turned toward the tent. He was wearing a shabby Confederate uniform and was clutching a brown felt hat so battered and filthy that it might have been spurned by a sharecropper.

"Here!" The Colonel's tent was lit within by lanterns that cast grotesque shadows every time he moved in front of their flames. "Who is it?"

"Evans. Colonel Nathan Evans." Evans did not wait for an invitation but pushed through Faulconer's tent flap. "I heard troops arrived here last night and I thought I'd say howdy. I've got half a brigade up by the stone bridge and if the bastard Yankees decide to use the Warrenton Pike then you and I are all that stands between Abe Lincoln and the whores in New Orleans. Is that coffee, Faulconer, or whiskey?"

"Coffee." Faulconer's voice was distant, suggesting he did not like Evans's brusque familiarity.

"I've my own whiskey, but I'll have a coffee first and thank you kindly, Colonel." Starbuck watched as Evans's shadow drank the Colonel's coffee. "What I want you to do, Faulconer," Evans demanded when the coffee was drained, "is move your boys down to the road, then on up to a wooden bridge here." He had evidently opened a map that he spread on Faulconer's bed. "There's a deal of timber around the bridge and I guess if you keep your boys hidden then the sons of bitch Yankees won't know you're there. Of course we may all end up being about as much use as a pair of balls on a shad-bellied priest, but on the other hand we may not."

Evans's staff officer lit a cigar and gave Adam and Starbuck a desultory glance. Thaddeus Bird, Ethan Ridley and at least a score of other men were openly listening to the conversation inside the tent.

"I don't understand," Faulconer said.

"It ain't difficult." Evans paused and there was a scratching sound as he struck a match to light a cigar. "Yankees are over the stream. They want to keep advancing on Manassas Junction. Capture that and they've cut us from the valley army. Beauregard's facing them, but he ain't the kind to wait to get hit, so he plans to attack on their left, our right." Evans was demonstrating the moves on his map. "So Beauregard's got most of our army out on the right. Way over eastward, two miles away at least, and if he can get his pants buttoned before noon he'll probably attack later today. He'll hook round the back of the bastards and kill as many as he can. Which is dandy, Faulconer, but suppose the sons of bitches decide to attack us first? And suppose they ain't as dumb as northerners usually are and instead of marching straight into our faces suppose they try to hook around our left? We're the only troops to stop them. In fact there's nothing between us and Mexico, Faulconer, so what if the pox-ridden bastards do decide to have a go at this flank?" Evans chuckled. "That's why I'm right glad you're here, Colonel."

"Are you saying I'm attached to your brigade?" Faulconer asked.

"I ain't got orders for you, if that's what you mean, but why the hell else were you sent here?"

"I have an appointment with General Beauregard at six in the morning to discover just that," Faulconer said.

There was a pause as Evans evidently uncapped a flask, pulled at it, then screwed the cap back into place. "Colonel," he finally said, "why in hell's name were you put out here? This is the left flank. We're the last sons of bitches that anyone thought to position. We're here, Colonel, in case the goddamned Yankees attack up the Warrenton Pike."

"I have not yet received my orders," Faulconer insisted.

"So what are you waiting for? A choir of goddamned angels? For Christ's sake, Faulconer, we need men on this flank of the army!" Nathan Evans's temper had plainly snapped, but he made an effort to explain matters calmly again. "Beauregard plans to push north on our right, so what if the shit-faced Yankees decided to push south on theirs? What am I supposed to do? Hurl kisses at them? Ask them to delay the war while you fetch your damned orders?"

"I shall fetch those orders from Beauregard," Faulconer said stubbornly, "and no one else."

"Then while you're fetching your goddamned orders why don't you move your goddamned Legion to the wooden bridge? Then if you're needed you can march to the stone bridge over the Run and give my boys a hand."

"I shall not move," Faulconer insisted, "until I receive proper orders."

"Oh, dear God," Adam murmured for his father's obduracy.

The argument went on two minutes more, but neither man would shift. Faulconer's wealth had not accustomed him to taking orders, and least of all from diminutive, ill-smelling, bow-legged, coarse-tongued brutes like Nathan Evans, who, abandoning his attempts to snare the Legion into his brigade, stormed out of the tent and hauled himself into his saddle. "Come on, Meadows," he snarled at his aide, and the two men galloped off into the darkness.

"Adam!" Faulconer shouted. "Pecker!"

"Ah, the second in command is summoned by the great leader," Bird said caustically, then followed Adam into the tent.

"Did you hear that?" Faulconer demanded.

"Yes, Father."

"So you understand, both of you, that whatever that man may order, you ignore. I shall bring you orders from Beauregard."

"Yes, Father," Adam said again.

Major Bird was not so obliging. "Are you ordering me to disobey a direct command from a superior officer?"

"I am saying that Nathan Evans is a lunkhead addicted to stone-jug whiskey," the Colonel said, "and I did not spend a damned fortune on a fine regiment just to see it thrown away in his drink-sodden hands."

"So I do disobey his orders?" Major Bird persisted.

"It means you obey my orders, and no one else's," the Colonel said. "Damn it, if the battle's on the right then that's where we should be, not stuck on the left with the dregs of the army. I want the Legion on parade in one hour. Tents struck, fighting order."

The Legion paraded at half past four by which time the hilltop was bathed in a ghostly twilight and the farther hills were dark shapes receding ever more obscurely until, at last, there was nothing but an opaque darkness in which dimly mysterious points of red light suggested far-off camp fires. There was just enough gray half-light to see that the nearer countryside was littered with carts and wagons, giving the scene an odd resemblance to a camp meeting site on the morning after the preaching had ended, except that among these wagons were the satanic shapes of limbers, portable forges and cannon. The smoke of the dying camp fires clung in the hollows like mist beneath the last fading stars. Somewhere a band was playing "Home, Sweet Home" and a man in B Company tunelessly sang the words until a sergeant told him to be silent.

The Legion waited. Their heavy packs, blankets and groundsheets had been piled with the tents at the rear of the band so that the men would simply carry their weapons, haversacks and canteens into battle. Around them, mostly unseen, an army took up its positions. Pickets gazed across the stream, gunners sipped coffee beside their monstrous guns, cavalrymen watered horses in the dozen streams that laced the pastureland, and surgeons' assistants tore up lint for bandages or sharpened flesh knives and bone saws. A few officers galloped importantly across the fields, vanishing into the farther darknesses on their mysterious errands.

Starbuck sat on Pocahontas just behind the Legion's color party and wondered if he was dreaming. Was there really to be a battle? The short-tempered Evans had hinted as much and everyone seemed to expect one, yet there was no sign of any enemy. He half-wanted the expectations to be true, and was half-terrified that they would come true. Intellectually he knew that battle was chaotic, cruel and bitter, yet he could not rid himself of the belief that it would turn out to be glorious, plumed and oddly calm. In books, stern-faced men waited to see the whites of their enemies' eyes, then fired and won great victories. Horses pranced and flags whipped in a smokeless wind beneath which the decorous dead lay sleeping and the pain-free dying spoke lovingly of their country and of their mothers. Men died as simply as Major Pelham had died. Oh sweet Jesus, Starbuck prayed as a sudden burst of terror whipsawed through his thoughts, but don't let me die. I regret all my sins, every one of them, even Sally, and I will never sin again if you will just let me live.

He shivered even though he was sweating under his thick woolen uniform coat and trousers. Somewhere to his left a man shouted an order, but the sound was small and faraway, like a voice heard from a sickbed in a distant room. The sun had still not risen, though the eastern horizon was now suffused with a rosy brilliance and it was light enough for Colonel Faulconer to make a slow inspection of his Legion's ranks. He reminded the men of the homes they had left in Faulconer County, and of their wives, sweethearts and children. He reassured them that the war was not of the South's making, but of the North's choosing. "We just wanted to be left alone, is that so terrible an ambition?" he asked. Not that the men needed the Colonel's reassurance, but Faulconer knew that a commanding officer was expected to rouse the spirits of his men on the morning of battle, and so he encouraged his Legion that their cause was just and that men fighting for a just cause need not fear defeat.

Adam had been supervising the piling of the Legion's baggage, but now rode back to Starbuck's side. Adam's horse was one of the best beasts from the Faulconer stud—a tall, bay stallion, glossily beautiful, a disdainful aristocrat among beasts just as the Faulconers were lords among common men. Adam nodded toward the small house with its dimly glowing windows that stood silhouetted on the hill's flat top. "They sent a servant to ask us whether it would be safe to stay there."

"What did you say?"

"How could I say anything? I don't know what will happen today. But do you know who lives there?"

"How on earth would I know that?"

"The widow of the *Constitution*'s surgeon. Isn't that something? Surgeon Henry, he was called." Adam's voice sounded very stilted, as though it was taking all his self-discipline to contain his emotions. He had put on a soldier's coat for his father's sake, and worn a captain's three metal bars on his collar because to do so was simpler than wearing a martyr's sackcloth, but today he would pay the real price of that compromise, and the thought of it was making him sick to his stomach. He fanned his face with his wide-brimmed hat, then glanced to the east where the cloudless sky looked like a sheet of beaten silver touched with a shimmer of lurid gold. "Can you imagine how hot it will be by midday?" Adam asked.

Starbuck smiled. "'As they gather silver, and brass, and iron, and lead, and tin, into the midst of the furnace, to blow the fire upon it, to melt it; so will I gather you in mine anger and in my fury, and I will leave you there, and melt you.'" He imagined himself writhing in a blast of furnace heat, a sinner burning for his iniquities. "Ezekiel," he explained to Adam, whose expression betrayed that he had not placed the text.

"It isn't a very cheering text for a Sunday morning," Adam said, then shuddered uncontrollably as he imagined what this day might bring. "Do you really feel you might make a good soldier?" he asked.

"Yes." He had failed at everything else, Starbuck thought bitterly.

"At least you look like a soldier." Adam spoke with a touch of envy.

"How does a soldier look?" Starbuck asked, amused.

"Like someone in a Walter Scott novel," Adam answered quickly, "*Ivanhoe*, maybe?

Starbuck laughed. "My grandmother MacPhail always told me I had the face of a preacher. Like my father." And Sally had said he had her father's eyes.

Adam put his hat back on. "I suppose your father will be preaching damnation on all slaveholders this morning?" He was simply wanting to make conversation, any conversation, just noise to divert his thoughts from the horrors of war.

"Perdition and hell fire will indeed be summoned to support the northern cause," Starbuck agreed, and he was suddenly assailed by a vision of his comfortable Boston home where his younger brothers and sisters would just be waking up and readying themselves for early morning family prayers. Would they remember to pray for him this morning? His elder sister would not. At nineteen Ellen Marjory Starbuck already had the pinched opinions of crabbed middle age. She was betrothed to a Congregational minister from New Hampshire, a man of infinite spite and calculated unkindness and, instead of recommending Nathaniel to God's protection, Ellen would doubtless be praying for her older brother James, who, Starbuck supposed, would be in uniform, though for the life of him he could not imagine stuffy, punctilious James in battle. James would be a good headquarters man in Washington or Boston—making fussy lists and enforcing detailed regulations.

The younger children would pray for Nathaniel, though perforce their entreaties would necessarily be silent lest they provoked the wrath of the Reverend Elial. There was sixteen-year-old Frederick George, who had been born with a withered left arm, fifteen-year-old Martha Abigail, who most resembled Nathaniel in looks and character, and last of all was twelve-year-old Samuel Washington Starbuck, who wanted to be a whaling captain. Five other children had died in infancy.

"What are you thinking?" Adam asked abruptly, out of nervousness.

"I was thinking of family history," Starbuck said, "and how congestive it is."

"Congestive?"

"Limiting. Mine, anyway." And Sally's, he thought. Maybe even Ridley's too, though Starbuck did not want to indulge in pity for the man he would kill. Or would he? He glanced across at Ethan Ridley, who sat motionless in the dawn. It was one thing to contemplate a killing, Starbuck decided, but quite another to perform the deed.

A flurry of far musket shots rattled the last shadows of receding dark. "Oh, God." Adam spoke the words as a prayer for his country. He stared eastward, though not so much as a leaf moved in the far wooded hollows where, at last, the creeping light was showing vivid green among the dying grays. Somewhere in those hills and woods an enemy waited, though whether the firing was the first flicker of battle or merely a false alarm, no one could tell.

Another bout of terror rippled through Starbuck. He was frightened of dying, but he was far more terrified of displaying his fear. If he had to die he would prefer it to be a romantic death with Sally beside him. He tried to recall the sweetness of that thunder-laden night when she had lain in his arms and, like children, they had watched the lightning scratch the sky. How could one night change a man so much? Dear God, Starbuck thought, but that one night was like being born again, and that was as wicked a heresy as any he could dream of, but there was no other description that so exactly fitted what he had felt. He had been dragged from doubt into certainty, from misery into gladness, from despair to glory. It was that magical conversion, which his father preached and for which he had so often prayed, and which at last he had experienced, except it was the devil's conversion that had swamped his soul with calmness, and not the Savior's grace that had changed him.

"Are you listening, Nate?" Adam had evidently spoken, but to no avail. "There's Father. He's beckoning us."

"Of course." Starbuck followed Adam to the Legion's right flank beyond Company A where Colonel Faulconer had finished his inspection. "Before I go and find Beauregard," Faulconer spoke awkwardly, as though he was unsure of himself, "I thought I'd make a reconnaissance that way." He pointed northward, out beyond the army's left flank. The Colonel's voice sounded like that of a man trying to convince himself that he was a real soldier on a real battlefield. "Would you like to come? I need to satisfy myself that Evans is wrong. No point in staying here if there's no Yankees out in these woods. Do you feel like a gallop, Nate?"

Starbuck reflected that the Colonel must be in a better mood than he appeared if he called him Nate instead of the colder Starbuck. "I'd like that, sir."

"Come on, then. You too, Adam."

The father and son led Starbuck down the hill to where a tree-shaded stone house stood beside a crossroads. Two artillery pieces were creaking and jangling eastward along the turnpike, dragged by tired horses. The

Colonel galloped between the two guns, then swerved onto the road that led north from the crossroads. The road climbed a long hill between shadowed pastureland, rising to a wooded crest where the Colonel reined in.

Faulconer unholstered and extended a leather-bound telescope, which he trained north toward a far hill crowned by a simple wooden church. Nothing disturbed the fleeting shadows of darkness on that far hill, nor indeed anywhere else in the gentle landscape. A white-painted farm lay in the distance and leafy woods all around, but no soldiers disturbed the pastoral scene. The Colonel stared long and hard at the distant church on its hill, then collapsed the telescope's short tubes. "According to that lunkhead Evans's map, that's Sudley Church. There are some fords beneath there, and no Yankees in sight. Except for you, Nate."

Starbuck took the last words as a pleasantry. "I'm an honorary Virginian, sir. Remember?"

"Not any longer, Nate," Faulconer said heavily. "This isn't a reconnaissance, Nate. The Yankees will never come this far north. I brought you here instead to say goodbye."

Starbuck gazed at the Colonel, wondering if this was some kind of elaborate jest. It seemed not. "Goodbye, sir?" He managed to stammer the iteration.

"This isn't your quarrel, Nate, and Virginia isn't your country."

"But, sir ..."

"So I'm sending you home." The Colonel overrode Starbuck's feeble objection with a firm kindness, just as he might speak to a useless puppy which, despite its potential for amusement, he was about to put down with a single shot to the skull.

"I have no home." Starbuck had meant the words to be defiant, but somehow they came out as a pathetic bleat.

"Indeed you do, Nate. I wrote to your father six weeks ago and he has been good enough to reply to me. His letter was delivered under a flag of truce last week. Here it is." The Colonel took a folded paper from a pouch at his waist and held it out to Starbuck.

Starbuck did not move.

"Take it, Nate," Adam urged his friend.

"Did you know about this?" Starbuck turned fiercely on Adam, fearing his friend's betrayal.

"I told Adam this morning," the Colonel said, intervening. "But this is my doing, not Adam's."

"But you don't understand, sir!" Starbuck appealed to the Colonel.

"But I do, Nate! I do!" Colonel Faulconer smiled condescendingly. "You're an impetuous young man, and there's nothing amiss with that. I was impulsive, but I can't allow youthful impetuosity to lead you into rebellion. It won't do, upon my soul it will not. A man should not fight against his own country because of a youthful mistake. So I have determined your fate." The Colonel spoke very firmly, and once again pushed the letter toward Starbuck who, this time, felt obliged to grasp it. "Your brother James is with McDowell's army," the Colonel continued, "and he's enclosed a laissez-passer that will see you safe through the northern lines. Once past the pickets you should seek out your brother. I fear you'll have to give me your sword and pistol, but I'll let you keep Pocahontas. And the saddle! And that's an expensive saddle, Nate." He added the last words as a kind of enticement that might reconcile Starbuck to his unexpected fate.

"But, sir …" Starbuck tried to articulate his protest again, and this time there were tears in his eyes. He felt bitterly ashamed of the tears and tried to shake them away, but still one drop brimmed from his right eye and ran down his cheek. "Sir! I want to stay with you! I want to stay with the Legion."

Faulconer smiled. "That's kind of you, Nate, truly kind. I'm obliged, so I am, for your saying as much. But no. This isn't your quarrel."

"The North might think otherwise." Starbuck now attempted defiance, suggesting that the Colonel might be making a fearful enemy in thus sending him away.

"And so they might, Nate, so they might. And if you're forced to fight against us, then I'll pray you live to be reunited with your Virginia friends. Ain't that so, Adam?"

"Indeed it is, Father," Adam said warmly, then held out his hand for Starbuck to shake.

Starbuck did not respond. The sting of the insult was not that he was being ejected from the Faulconer Legion, but that the Colonel held such a low opinion of him, and so he tried to explain his burgeoning hopes of becoming a good soldier. "I really do feel, sir, that soldiering is a profession I can master. I want to be useful to you. I want to return your hospitality, your kindness, by showing what I can do."

"Nate! Nate!" The Colonel interrupted him. "You are not a soldier. You're a theology student who was caught in a snare. Don't you see that? But your family and friends are not going to let you throw your life away because of one conniving woman. You've been taught a hard lesson, but now it's time to go back to Boston and accept your parents' forgiveness. And to make your new future! Your father declares you must abandon your hopes of the ministry, but he has other plans for you, and whatever you do, Nate, I'm sure you'll do well."

"That's true, Nate," Adam said warmly.

"Let me just stay one more day, sir," Starbuck pleaded.

"No, Nate, not even one more hour. I can't brand you traitor in your family's eyes. It wouldn't be a Christian act." The Colonel leaned toward Starbuck. "Unbuckle the sword belt, Nate."

Starbuck obeyed. In everything he had ever done, he thought, he had failed. Now, with his military career a shambles before it had even begun, he unbuckled the clumsy sword and unclipped the heavy pistol in its worn leather holster and handed both weapons back to their rightful owner. "I wish you'd reconsider, sir."

"I have given this matter my weightiest consideration, Nate," the Colonel said impatiently, then, in a less irritated tone, "you're a Boston man, a Massachusetts man, and that makes you a different creature from us southerners. Your destiny doesn't lie here, Nate, but in the North. You'll doubtless be a great man one day. You're clever, maybe too clever, and you shouldn't waste your cleverness on war. So take it back to Massachusetts and follow your father's plans."

Starbuck did not know what to say. He felt belittled. He so desperately wanted to be in control of his own life, but he had always needed someone else's money to survive—first his father's, then Dominique's, and now Colonel Faulconer's. Adam Faulconer was equally as dependent on family as Starbuck, but Adam fitted into his society with a practiced ease, while Starbuck had always felt awkwardly out of place. He so hated being young, yet the chasm between youth and adulthood seemed so wide as to be unjumpable, except that in the last few weeks he had thought he might make a good soldier and thus forge his own independence.

The Colonel pulled Pocahontas's head about. "There are no northern troops out here, Nate. Keep on the road till you come to the fords by the church there, then cross the streams and follow the road toward the rising sun. You'll not find any Yankees for a good few miles, and you'll be coming from their rear, which means you shouldn't run too much risk of being shot by a nervous sentry. And take the coat off, Nate."

"I must?"

"You must. Do you want the enemy to think you're a southerner? You want to be shot for nothing? Take it off, Nate."

Starbuck peeled off the gray frock coat with its single metal bar, which denoted his second lieutenancy. He had never really felt like an officer, not even a lowly second lieutenant, but without the uniform coat he was nothing but a failure being sent home with his tail tucked between his legs. "Where will the battle be fought, sir?" he asked in a small boy's voice.

"Way, way across country." The Colonel pointed east where the sun was at last touching the horizon with its incandescent furnace glow. It was back there, far off on the Confederate right flank, that Washington Faulconer hoped to join the attack that would crush the Yankees. "Nothing's going to happen over here," Faulconer said, "which is why they put that no-good rascal Evans on this flank."

"Allow me to wish you good fortune, sir?" Starbuck sounded very formal as he held out his hand.

"Thank you, Nate." The Colonel managed to sound truly grateful for the wish. "And would you do me the kindness of accepting this?" He held out a small cloth purse, but Starbuck could not bring himself to accept the gift. He desperately needed the money, but he was far too proud to take it.

"I shall manage, sir."

"You know best!" The Colonel smiled and withdrew the purse.

"And God bless you, Nate," Adam Faulconer said vigorously to his friend. "I'll guard your traps and send them on when the war's over. By year's end, certainly. To your father's house?"

"I suppose so, yes." Starbuck shook his best friend's outstretched hand, wrenched the horse's head about and plunged his heels hard back. He went quickly so the Faulconers would not see his tears.

"He took it hard," Colonel Faulconer said when Starbuck was out of earshot, "damned hard!" Faulconer sounded astonished. "Did he really think he might be a success at soldiering?"

"He said as much to me this morning."

Colonel Faulconer shook his head sadly. "He's a northerner, and in times like these you trust your own, not strangers. And who knows where his allegiance lies?"

"It was with us," Adam said sadly, watching Nate canter away down the slope toward the far woods beneath the church. "And he is an honest man, Father."

"I wish I shared your confidence. I can't prove Nate danced a jig with our money, Adam, but I'll just feel happier without him. I know he's your friend, but we were doing him no favors by keeping him away from home."

"I think that is true," Adam said piously, for he genuinely believed Starbuck needed to make peace with his family.

"I had hopes of him," the Colonel said sententiously, "but these preachers' sons are all the same. Once off the leash, Adam, they go hog wild. They commit all the sins their fathers couldn't, or wouldn't or dared not. It's like being brought up in a fancy-cake shop and being told never to touch the candy, and it's no wonder they plunge in up to their snouts the moment they're free." Faulconer lit a cigar and blew a stream of smoke into the dawn. "The whole truth of this matter, Adam, is that blood signifies, and I fear your friend has unreliable blood. He won't stay the course. That family never has. What were the Starbucks? Nantucket Quakers?"

"So I believe, yes." Adam sounded reserved. He was still unhappy at what had happened to Starbuck, even though he recognized it was the best thing for his friend.

"And Nate's father abandoned the Quakers to be a Calvinist, and

now Nate wants to flee the Calvinists to be what? A southerner?" The
Colonel laughed. "It won't do, Adam, it just won't do. My Lord, he even
let that *Tom* company whore run him ragged! He's too unsteady. Altogether too unsteady, and good soldiers need to be steady." The Colonel
gathered his reins. "Sun's up! Time to unleash the hounds!" He turned
and spurred his horse southward, back to where the Confederate army
readied itself for battle beside a small stream called Bull Run that lay
twenty-six miles west of Washington, D.C., near the town of Manassas
Junction in the sovereign state of Virginia that had once formed a part of
the United States of America, which was now two nations, divided under
God, and gathering for battle.

Starbuck rode wildly down the long slope to the far woods where he
swerved off the dirt road and into the shade of the deep woodland. He
yanked too hard on the curb and Pocahontas protested at the pain as she
slowed to a stop. "I don't care, damn you," Starbuck growled at the horse,
then kicked his right foot out of the stirrup and swung himself down from
the saddle. A bird screeched at him from the undergrowth. He did not
know what kind of bird it was. He could recognize cardinals, blue jays,
chickadees and seagulls. That was all. He had thought he knew what an
eagle looked like, but when he had spotted one at Faulconer Court House
the men in Company C had laughed at him. That was no eagle, they said,
but a sharp-shinned hawk. Any fool could tell that, but not Second Lieutenant Starbuck. Christ, he thought, but he failed at everything.

He looped the horse's reins about a low branch, then slid down the
trunk of the tree to sit in the long grass. A cricket chattered at him as he
took the creased papers from his pocket. The rising sun was drowning the
treetops in light, filtering green brilliance through the summer leaves.
Starbuck dreaded reading the letter, but he knew his father's wrath must
be faced sooner or later, and better to face it on paper than in the musty,
book-lined Boston study where the Reverend Elial hung his canes on the
wall like other men hung fishing poles or swords. "Be sure your sin will
find you out." That was the Reverend Elial's favorite text, the threnody of
Starbuck's childhood and the constant anthem of his frequent beatings
with the hook-stemmed sticks. Starbuck unfolded the stiff sheets of paper.

The Reverend Elial Starbuck to Colonel Washington Faulconer, of
Faulconer County, Virginia.

My dear Sir.

I am in receipt of yours of the 14th, and my wife unites with me in a
Christian appreciation of the sentiments expressed therein. I cannot hide from
any man, least of all from myself, my keen disappointment in Nathaniel. He is

a young man of the most inestimable privilege, raised in a Christian family, nurtured in a Godly society, and educated as best our means would allow. God granted him a fine intelligence and the affections of a close and intimate family, and it had long been my prayerful wish that Nathaniel would follow me into the ministry of God's word, yet alas, he has instead chosen the path of iniquity. I am not insensible to the high feelings of youth, but to abandon his studies for a woman! And to fall into the ways of a thief! It is enough to break a parent's heart, and the pain Nathaniel has given to his mother is exceeded only, I am sure, by the sadness he has offered to our Lord and Savior.

Yet we are not unmindful of a Christian's duty to the remorseful sinner, and if, as you suggest, Nathaniel is ready to make a full confession of his sins in a spirit of humble and genuine repentance, then we shall not stand in the way of his redemption. Yet he cannot ever again hope that we might rekindle the kind affections we once felt for him, nor must he believe himself worthy for a place in God's ministry. I have repaid the man Trabell of the monies stolen, but will now insist that Nathaniel repay me to the full, to which purpose he must earn his bread by the sweat of his labors. We have secured for him a place with my wife's cousin's practice of law in Salem where, God willing, Nathaniel will reward the liberality of our forgiveness by a diligent attention to his new duties.

Nathaniel's elder brother, James, a good and Christian man, is now with our army embarked upon its present sad duties, and he will, God willing, undertake to see that this missive reaches you safe. I doubt if you and I can ever agree on the tragical events that are presently rending our nation, but I know you will unite with me in reposing a continued hope in the Giver of All Good, the One God, in whose Holy Name we shall yet, I pray, avert fratricidal conflict and bring to our unhappy nation a just and *honorable* peace.

I render you more thanks for your manifold kindnesses to my son, and pray fervently that you are right in describing his earnestness for God's forgiveness. I pray also for all of our sons, that their lives may be spared in this most unhappy of times.

Respectfully yours,

the Reverend Elial Joseph Starbuck.
Boston, Mass. Thurs. June 20, 1861.

Post scriptum. My son, Captain James Starbuck of the United States Army, assures me he will enclose a "pass" allowing Nathaniel through our army's lines.

Starbuck unfolded the enclosed laissez-passer, which read:

Allow the Bearer Free Ingress
into the Lines of the United States Army,
authorized by the undersigned,
Captain James Elial MacPhail Starbuck,
sous-adjutant to Brigadier General Irvin McDowell.

Starbuck smiled at the pompous subscription to his brother's signature. So James had become a staff officer to the commander of the northern army? Good for James, Starbuck thought, then supposed that he should not really feel any surprise, for his elder brother was ambitious and diligent, a good lawyer and an earnest Christian; indeed James was everything his father wanted all his sons to be, while Starbuck was what? A rebel kicked out of a rebel army. A man who fell in love with whores. A failure.

He rested the two sheets of paper on the grass. Somewhere far away there was a sudden flurry of musketry, but the sound was muffled by the day's close warmth and seemed impossibly remote to ex-Second Lieutenant Nathaniel Starbuck. What did life hold now, he wondered? It seemed he was not to be a minister of the gospel, nor a soldier, but a student lawyer in the offices of cousin Harrison MacPhail of Salem, Massachusetts. Oh dear God, Starbuck thought, but was he to be under the tutelage of that dry, grasping, uncharitable stick of moral rectitude? Was that grim fate what the whisper of illegitimate petticoats could do to a man?

He stood, unlooped Pocahontas's reins, and walked slowly northward. He took off his hat and fanned his face. The horse followed placidly, its hooves falling heavily on the dirt road, which ran gently downhill between unfenced woodland and small pastures. The shadows of the trees stretched hugely long on the summer-bleached meadows. Way off to Starbuck's right was a white farmhouse and a huge hayrick. The farm appeared deserted. The sound of rifle fire faded in the heavy air like a brushfire dying, and Starbuck thought how happy he had been in these last weeks. They had been healthy outdoor weeks, playing at soldiers, and now it was all over. A wave of self-pity engulfed him. He was friendless, unwanted, useless; a victim, just as Sally was a victim, and he thought of the promise to revenge Sally by killing Ridley. So many stupid dreams, he thought, so many stupid dreams.

The road climbed into more woods, then dropped to an unfinished railway embankment beyond which lay the twin Sudley Fords. He mounted Pocahontas and crossed the smaller stream, glanced up at the white-boarded church on the hill above, then turned east across the wider deeper Bull Run. He let the horse drink. The water flowed fast across rounded pebbles. The sun was in his eyes, huge, brilliant, blinding, like the fire of Ezekiel that would melt metal in the furnace.

He urged the horse out of the stream, across a pasture and into the welcome shadow of more woods where he slowed his pace, instinctively rebelling against the life of propriety that his father's letter described. He would not do it, he would not do it! Instead, Starbuck decided, he would join the northern army. He would enlist as a private in some regiment of strangers. He thought of his promise to Sally, that he would kill Ethan, and he was sorry that the promise could not now be kept, and then he imagined meeting Ridley in battle and stabbing forward with a bayonet to pin his enemy to the ground. He rode slowly on, imagining himself a northern soldier, fighting for his own people.

The sound of musketry had changed subtly. The noise had been fading on the summer air, but now the sound became louder again, and more rhythmic and harder edged. He had not given the change any real thought, being too immersed in his own self-pity, but as he turned a slight bend in the road he saw that the new sound was not the sound of musketry at all, but the noise of axes.

Soldiers' axes.

Starbuck stopped the horse and just stared. The axemen were a hundred paces ahead of him. They were stripped to their waists and their axe blades shattered the sunlight into brilliant reflections as chips of wood skittered bright from the blades' hard strokes. They were working on a tangled barricade of felled trees that completely blocked the narrow road. Half the roads of northern Virginia had been so barricaded by patriots trying to impede the northern invasion, and for a moment Starbuck supposed he had come across local men fashioning just such another obstacle, then he wondered why makers of a barricade would assault it with axes? And behind the axemen were teams of horses harnessed with drag chains to pull the sectioned tree trunks off the road, and behind those horse teams and half-hidden by the deep shadows, was a throng of blue-uniformed men above whom a flag showed bright in a slanting shaft of newly risen sunlight. The flag was the Stars and Stripes, and Starbuck suddenly realized these were Yankees, northerners, on a road where there were not supposed to be any northerners, and they were not just a few men, but a whole host of blue-uniformed soldiers who patiently waited for their pioneers to clear the narrow road.

"You there!" A man in officer's braid shouted at Starbuck from behind the half-dismantled barricade. "Stop where you are! Stop, you hear me?"

Starbuck was gaping like a fool, yet in truth he comprehended all that was happening. The northerners had fooled the South. Their plan was not to advance dully on Manassas Junction, nor to wait for the southerners to attack their left flank, but rather to attack here in the undefended Confederate left, and thereby to hook deep into the belly of the secessionist army and so rip it and tear it and savage it that all the vestiges of southern rebellion would die in the weltering horror of one Sabbath day's bloodletting. This, Starbuck grasped instantly, was Brigadier General McDowell's version of Thermopylae, the grand encircling surprise that would give the Yankee Persians victory over the Confederate Greeks.

And Starbuck, understanding all, understood that he no longer needed to become a northern soldier nor break his promise to a southern whore. He was saved.

10

"Faulconer should be here." Major Thaddeus Bird scowled eastward into the rising sun. Bird might have his sharp opinions about how soldiering should be managed, but left alone in notional command of the Faulconer Legion, he was not entirely certain he wanted the responsibility to enact those ideas. "He should be here," he said again. "The men need to know their commanding officer is with them, not lollygagging on his horse. Your future father-in-law," he spoke to Ethan Ridley, "is altogether too fond of excursions by quadruped." Major Bird found this remark amusing, for he raised his angular head and uttered a bark of laughter. "Excursions by quadruped, ha!"

"I presume the Colonel is making a reconnaissance," Ethan Ridley protested. Ridley had watched Starbuck ride away with the Faulconers and was jealous that he had not been invited. In two months Ridley would become Washington Faulconer's son-in-law, with all the privileges that kinship implied, yet still he feared that some other person might usurp his place in the Colonel's affections.

"You presume the Colonel is making a reconnaissance?" Major Bird scoffed at the supposition. "Faulconer's lollygagging, that's what he's doing. My brother-in-law lives under the misapprehension that soldiering is a sporting occupation, like hunting or steeplechasing, but it is mere butchery, Ethan, mere butchery. Our responsibility is to make ourselves into efficient butchers. I had a great uncle who was a pork butcher in Baltimore, so I feel that soldiering might well be in my blood. Do you have any such fortunate ancestry, Ethan?"

Ridley sensibly made no answer. He was sitting on his horse beside Bird who, as ever, was on foot, while the Legion was lounging on the grass watching the night shadows shrink and fade in the far countryside and wondering what this day would bring. Most of the men were confused. They knew they had spent two days traveling, but where they had come to, or what they were expected to do now that they had arrived, they did not know. Ethan Ridley, seeking answers to the same troubling questions, had sought enlightenment from Thaddeus Bird.

"I doubt anyone knows what will happen today," Thaddeus Bird answered. "History is not marshaled by reason, Ethan, but by the idiocies of lethal fools."

Ethan struggled to elicit a sensible answer. "They reckon we've got twenty thousand men, is that right?"

"Who are 'they'?" Major Bird asked serenely, intentionally infuriating Ridley.

"How many troops do we have, then?" Ridley tried again.

"I have not counted them," Bird said. The rumors at Manassas Junction said that Beauregard's Army of Northern Virginia numbered slightly less than twenty thousand men, but no one could be sure.

"And the enemy?" Ethan asked.

"Who knows? Twenty thousand? Thirty? As the sands of the sea, maybe? A mighty host, perhaps? Shall I guess twenty thousand, will that make you happy?" Again, no one knew how many northern troops had crossed the Potomac into Virginia. Rumor put the number as high as fifty thousand, but no American had ever led an army even half that size so Thaddeus Bird distrusted the rumor.

"And we are attacking on the right? Is that what you hear?" Ridley would normally have avoided Thaddeus Bird altogether, for he found the pedantry of the ragged-bearded schoolteacher annoying in the extreme, but the nervousness that accompanied the anticipation of battle had made even Bird's company acceptable.

"That is the prevailing rumor, yes, indeed." Bird was not inclined to make life easy for Ridley, whom he considered a dangerous fool, so he did not add that the rumor made a good deal of sense. The Confederate right wing, which was the bulk of Beauregard's army, guarded the direct road from Washington to Manassas Junction. If the federal army captured the rail junction then all of Northern Virginia was lost, so common sense suggested that General Beauregard's best hopes of victory lay in forcing the enemy away from the vulnerable railroads, just as the enemy's best hopes of a swift triumph would seem to be a quick capture of the vital junction. Neither eventuality precluded something cleverer, like a flank attack, but Bird, out on the flank, could see no evidence that either army was risking anything as sophisticated as an attempt to encircle the other, and so he assumed both armies planned to attack in the same place. He jerked his head back and forth at the pleasing notion of two armies mounting simultaneous assaults and of the northern left wing blundering into the advancing rebel right wing.

"But if there is a battle," Ridley said, struggling manfully to keep the discussion within the bounds of sanity, "then our present position is a long way from where it will be fought?"

Bird nodded vigorous assent. "God, if there is such a being, has been merciful to us in that regard. Indeed we are about as far from the army's right wing as it is possible for a regiment to be and still be a part of the army, if indeed we are a part of the army, which we don't seem to be, not unless my brother-in-law receives orders more to his liking than those brought to him by the noxious Evans."

"The Colonel just wants us to take part in the battle." Ethan defended his future father-in-law.

Bird looked up at the mounted Ridley. "I often wondered whether it was possible for my sister to marry beneath herself intellectually, and astonishingly she succeeded." Bird was enjoying himself. "If you want the truth, Ethan, I do not think the Colonel himself knows what he is doing. My own belief is that we should have embraced Evans's orders on the grounds that by staying here on the left we are less likely to risk an heroic death on the right flank. But what does my opinion count? I am merely a humble schoolteacher and a notional second in command." He sniffed.

"You don't want to fight?" Ridley asked with what he hoped was utter scorn.

"Of course I don't want to fight! I shall fight if I have to, and I trust I shall fight intelligently, but the most intelligent desire, surely, is to avoid a fight altogether? Why would any sane man want to fight?"

"Because we don't want the Yankees to win today."

"Nor do we, but neither do I wish to die today, and if I am presented with a choice of becoming worm fodder or else of being governed by Lincoln's Republicans, why then I do believe I would choose to live!" Bird laughed, jerking his head backward and forward. Then, spotting movement in the valley, he abruptly checked the idiosyncratic motion. "Has the great Achilles returned to us?"

Two horsemen had appeared on the Warrenton Turnpike. The sun had not risen high enough to slant its light into the valley and so the two riders were still in shadow, but Ridley, whose eyes were younger and sharper than Bird's, recognized the Faulconers. "That's the Colonel and Adam."

"But where is Starbuck, eh? Do you think he has become a casualty of a reconnaissance, Ethan? You'd like it if young Starbuck was a casualty, wouldn't you? What is it about Starbuck that you dislike so? His good looks? His wits?"

Ethan refused to dignify the cackling questions with any reply, instead he just watched as father and son held a moment's conversation at the crossroads, then parted company. The Colonel ignored his men on the hilltop and rode south, while Adam trotted his horse uphill. "Father's gone to find Beauregard," Adam explained when he reached the plateau where the Legion waited. His horse shivered then nuzzled the nose of Ridley's mare.

"And before that?" Bird enquired. "Ethan claims you were making a reconnaissance, but I decided you were merely lollygagging."

"Father wanted to see whether there were any northerners on the Sudley Road," Adam explained awkwardly.

"And are there?" Bird asked in mock solicitude.

"No, Uncle."

"The saints be praised. We may breathe free again. Sweet land of liberty!" Bird raised a hand toward heaven.

"And Father wants you to discharge Nate," Adam continued in his stilted tone. He was carrying Starbuck's sword, pistol and uniform jacket.

"Your father wishes me to do what?" Bird demanded.

"To discharge Nate," Adam insisted. "From the books."

"I understand what the verb 'to discharge' means, Adam. And I will happily scratch Starbuck from the Legion's books if your father so insists, but you must tell me why. Is he dead? Am I to inscribe the name of Starbuck in the honored rolls of southern heroes? Do I enter him as a deserter? Has he expired of a sudden conniption? The demands of accurate bookkeeping require an explanation, Adam." Major Bird peered up at his nephew as he spoke this nonsense.

"He is discharged, Uncle! That's all! And Father would like his name taken off the Legion's books."

Major Bird blinked rapidly, rocked back and forward, then clawed his dirty fingernails through his long straggly beard. "Why do you discharge a man on the verge of battle? I ask merely so that I might understand the subtleties of soldiering?"

"Father decided the matter." Adam wondered why his uncle had to make such a fuss of everything. "He believed Nate should go home."

"Now? Today? At this very instant? Home to Boston?"

"Yes, indeed."

"But why?" Bird insisted.

Ridley laughed. "Why not?"

"A perfectly good question," Bird mocked, "but twice as complicated as mine. Why?" he demanded again of Adam.

Adam said nothing, but just sat with Nate's erstwhile coat and weapons held awkwardly on his saddle's pommel, and so Ethan Ridley chose to fill the silence with a mocking answer. "Because you can't trust a northerner in these days."

"Of course Nate could be trusted," Adam said irritably.

"You are so very loyal," Ridley said with a barely disguised sneer, but added nothing more.

Bird and Adam both waited for Ridley to clarify his sneer. "Beyond complimenting my nephew," Bird finally spoke with heavy sarcasm, "can you elucidate why we should not trust Starbuck? Is it merely the accident of his birth?"

"For the Lord's sake!" Ridley said as though the answer was so obvious that he demeaned himself by even bothering to mention it, let alone explain it.

"For my sake, then?" Bird persisted.

"He arrives in Richmond just as Fort Sumter falls. Does that not indicate something? And he uses your friendship, Adam, to gain the Colonel's trust, but why? Why should a son of that son of a bitch Elial Starbuck come south at this time? Are we really expected to swallow the idea that a goddamn Starbuck would fight for the South? That's like John Brown's family turning against emancipation or Harriet Bitch Stowe attacking her precious niggers!" Ridley, having made what he believed to be an incontrovertible argument, paused to light a cigar. "Starbuck was sent to spy on us," he said, summarizing his case, "and your father's done a kind act in sending him home. If he hadn't, Adam, then we'd have doubtless been forced to shoot Starbuck as a traitor."

"That would have alleviated the boredom of camp life," Bird observed brightly. "We haven't had an execution yet, and doubtless the ranks would enjoy one."

"Uncle!" Adam frowned disapprovingly.

"Besides, Starbuck has nigger blood," Ridley said. He was not entirely sure this was true, but his group of cronies had developed the idea as yet another stick with which to beat the despised Starbuck.

"Nigger blood! Oh well! That's different! Thank God he's gone." Major Bird laughed at the absurdity of the charge.

"Don't be a fool, Ethan," Adam said. "And don't be offensive," he added.

"Damned nigger blood!" Ridley's temper drove him on. "Look at his skin. It's dark."

"Like General Beauregard's skin? Like mine? Like yours even?" Major Bird asked happily.

"Beauregard's French," Ridley persisted, "and you can't deny that Starbuck's father is a notorious nigger lover!"

Major Bird's frenetic rocking back and forth indicated the unseemly joy he was deriving from the conversation. "Are you suggesting that Starbuck's mother takes her husband's sermons only too literally, Ethan? That she plays the double-backed beast with contraband slaves in her husband's vestry?"

"Oh, Uncle, please," Adam protested in a pained voice.

"Well, Ethan? Is that indeed what you are suggesting?" Major Bird ignored Adam.

"I'm saying we're well rid of Starbuck, that's what I'm saying." Ridley retreated from his allegations of miscegenation to attempt another attack on Starbuck. "Though I just hope he ain't telling the Yankees all about our battle plans."

"I doubt that Starbuck or anyone else knows about our battle plans," Thaddeus Bird observed dryly. "The plans of this day's battle will be decided in the memoirs of the winning general when the fighting's long over." He cackled at his own wit, then pulled one of his thin dark cigars from a pouch at his belt. "If your father insists that I discharge young Starbuck, Adam, then so I will, but I think it's a mistake."

Adam frowned. "You liked Nate, Uncle, is that it?"

"Did I mention my tastes? Or affections? You never did listen, Adam. I was commenting on your friend's ability. He can think, and that is a distressingly rare talent among young men. Most of you believe that it is sufficient to merely agree with the prevailing sentiment which is, of course, what dogs and churchgoers do, but Starbuck has a mind. Of sorts."

"Well, he's taken his mind north." Adam curtly tried to end the conversation.

"And his cruelty," Major Bird said musingly. "We shall miss that."

"Cruelty!" Adam, who felt he had been insufficiently loyal to his friend all morning, now saw a chance to defend Nate. "He isn't cruel!"

"Anyone raised in the more zealous parts of your church has probably imbibed a God-like indifference to life and death, and that will endow young Starbuck with a talent for cruelty. And in these ridiculous times, Adam, we are going to need all the cruelty we can muster. Wars are not won by gallantry, but by assiduously applied butchery."

Adam, who feared exactly that truth, tried to check his uncle's obvious glee. "So you have frequently told me, Uncle."

Major Bird scratched a match to light his cigar. "Fools usually need repetition to understand even the simplest of ideas."

Adam gazed over the heads of the silent troops to where his father's servants tended a cooking fire. "I shall fetch some coffee," he announced loftily.

"You won't fetch anything without my permission," Major Bird said slyly, "or had you failed to note that in your father's absence I am the regiment's senior officer?"

Adam looked down from his saddle. "Don't be absurd, Uncle. Now, shall I tell Nelson to bring you some coffee?"

"Not unless he serves the men first. Officers are not members of a privileged class, Adam, but merely officials encumbered with greater responsibilities."

Uncle Thaddeus, Adam thought, could twist and convolute the simplest matter into a tangle of difficulties. Adam found himself wondering just why his mother had insisted on making her brother a soldier, then realized that of course it was to annoy his father. He sighed at the thought, then gathered his reins. "Goodbye, Uncle." Adam turned his horse away and, without seeking permission to leave and with Ridley for company, he raked his spurs back.

The sunlight was at last reaching down the hill's western slope to cast long shadows aslant on the grass. Major Bird unbuttoned his uniform jacket's breast pocket and took out a linen-wrapped *carte de visite* on which was mounted a photograph of Priscilla. Vanity had caused her to take off her spectacles to have the picture made and she consequently looked rather myopic and uncertain, but to Bird she was a paragon of beauty. He touched the stiff pasteboard with its awkward daguerreotype image to his lips, then very reverently wrapped the card in its scrap of linen and placed it back in his breast pocket.

A half mile behind Bird, on a flimsy tower made of lashed branches up which a precarious ladder climbed to a platform thirty feet high, two wig-waggers prepared for their duty. The wig-waggers were signalers who talked to one another with semaphore flags. Four such wig-wagging towers had been constructed so that General Beauregard could stay in touch with the wide-flung wings of his army. One of the wig-waggers, a corporal, uncapped the heavy, tripod-mounted telescope that was used to read the flags from the neighboring towers, adjusted the instrument's focus, then swept it toward the leafy hills that lay northward of the rebel lines. He could see the sun bright on the shingles of the pitched church roof on Sudley Hill and, just beyond it, an empty meadow with a flash of silver showing where the Bull Run stream ran between lush pastures. Nothing moved in that landscape, except for the small figure of a woman who appeared at the church door to shake a mat free of dust. The wig-wagger turned the glass back east to where the sun blazed low over a horizon hazed by the dying smoke of a myriad cooking fires. He was about to turn the glass on toward the next signal tower when he saw some men appear on the summit of a bare knoll that lay about a mile beyond the Run on the enemy's side of the stream. "You want to see some damn Yankees?" the corporal asked his companion.

"Not now, not ever," the second signaler answered.

"I'm looking at the bastards." The corporal sounded excited. "Goddamn! So they are there after all!"

And ready to fight.

The group of men, some on foot, some on horseback, some civilian and some military, stopped on the summit of the bare knoll. The rising sun marvelously illuminated the landscape before them, showing the wooded valleys, fenced pastures and bright glimpses of the stream beyond which the Confederate Army waited for its defeat.

Captain James Elial MacPhail Starbuck was at the center of the small group. The young Boston lawyer sat his horse like a man more accustomed to a leather padded chair than to a saddle, and indeed, if James had to pick the one aspect of soldiering that he most disliked it would be the ubiquitous presence of horses, which he considered to be large, hot, smelly, fly-ridden beasts with yellow teeth, scary eyes and hooves like ungoverned hammers. Yet if riding a horse were necessary to end the slaveholders' revolt, then James would willingly straddle every horse in America for, though he might lack his father's eloquence, he was just as fervent in his belief that the rebellion was more than a blight on America's reputation, but an offense against God himself. America, James believed, was a divinely inspired nation, uniquely blessed by the Almighty, and to rebel against such a chosen people was to do the devil's work. So on this Christian Sabbath, in these green fields, the forces of righteousness would advance against a satanic rabble, and surely, James believed, God would not permit the northern army to be defeated? He prayed silently, beseeching God for victory.

"You reckon we can walk down to the battery, Cap'n?" One of the civilians interrupted James's reverie, gesturing at the same time to an artillery battery that was arranging its complicated affairs in a field that lay beside the Warrenton Turnpike at the foot of the knoll.

"It is not permitted," James responded curtly.

"Ain't it a free country, Cap'n?"

"It is not permitted," James insisted in the authoritative voice that always proved so effective in the Commonwealth of Massachusetts's Court of Common Pleas, but which merely seemed to amuse these newspapermen. The civilians accompanying James were reporters and sketch artists from a dozen northern papers who had come to Brigadier General McDowell's headquarters the previous night and had been told to attach themselves to the general's *sous*-adjutant. James already had the responsibility of escorting a half-dozen foreign military attachés who had ridden from their countries' Washington embassies and who were now treating the impending battle as though it were a fine entertainment laid on for their benefit, but at least the foreign military officers treated James with respect while the newspapermen merely seemed to aggravate him.

"What in hell's name is a *sous*-adjutant?" a reporter from *Harper's Weekly* had asked James in the raw small hours after midnight when, all around them, the northern army had been stirring itself ready for its march into battle. "A kind of Indian fighter?"

"*Sous* is French for 'under.'" James suspected that the newspaperman who came from the self-proclaimed "Journal of Civilization" knew full well what *sous* meant.

"Does that mean you're a kind of inferior adjutant, Cap'n?"

"It means I am an assistant to the adjutant." James had managed to keep his temper, despite feeling distinctly out of sorts. He had managed but two hours sleep and had woken to a sharp attack of flatulence that he acknowledged to be entirely his own fault. Brigadier General McDowell was a famous trencherman who had last night encouraged his staff to eat well, and James, despite his conviction that ample nourishment was necessary for both spiritual and bodily health, wondered if a third helping of the general's beef pie had been a plateful too much. Then there had also been the hotcakes and custard, all consumed with the teetotal general's well-sugared lemonade. Such indulgence would not have mattered if James had been able to take a spoonful of his mother's carminative balsam before retiring, but his fool of a servant had forgotten to put James's medicine chest into the headquarters' baggage wagons and so James had been forced to field the inquisitive reporters' questions and, at the same time, hide the exquisite discomfort of a severe attack of indigestion.

The newspapermen, meeting James in the farmhouse at Centreville where he had spent his uncomfortable night, had demanded to know McDowell's intentions, and James had explained, as simply as he could, that the general envisaged nothing less than the wholesale destruction of the rebellion. An hour's march to the south of the Bull Run stream was the small town of Manassas Junction and, once that town was captured, the rail line that linked the two rebel armies in Northern Virginia would be severed. General Johnston could no longer come from the Shenandoah Valley to support Beauregard, so Beauregard's defeated rebel army, cut off from that reinforcement, must retreat to Richmond and there be captured. The war would then peter out as the scattered rebel forces were either defeated or gave up. James had made it all sound very predictable and rather obvious.

"But the rebels gave us a whipping four days ago. Doesn't that worry you?" one of the newspapermen had asked. He was referring to a large northern reconnaissance force that had approached the Bull Run four days before and, in an excess of zeal, had tried to cross the stream, but had instead provoked a withering and deadly hail of bullets from the rebels concealed among the thick foliage on the farther bank. James dismissed the repulse as trivial, and had even tried to gloss it with a coat of victory by suggesting that the accidental contact with the enemy had been designed to convince the rebels that any northern attack would fall in the same place, on their right flank, when in fact the real assault would hook deep around the Confederate left.

"So what's the worst that could happen today, Captain?" another of the newspaperman had wanted to know.

The worst, James conceded, was that General Johnston's forces might have left the Shenandoah Valley and be on their way to reinforce Beauregard's men. That, he admitted, would make the day's fighting much harder, but he could assure the newspapermen that the latest telegraph news from the northern forces in the Shenandoah was that Johnston was still in the valley.

"But if Joe Johnston's rebs do join up with Beauregard's," the newspaperman insisted, "does that mean we're whipped?"

"It means we must work somewhat harder to defeat them." James felt annoyed by the tone of the question, but calmly reiterated his assurance that Johnston was still trapped far to the west, which meant that the great issue of American unity must this day be decided by the men presently gathered either side of the Bull Run. "And it will be a victory," James had confidently predicted. He had taken repeated pains to tell the newspapermen that this northern army was the largest force of troops ever assembled in North America. Irvin McDowell led more than thirty thousand men, over twice as many as George Washington's army at Yorktown. It was, James assured the journalists, an overpowering force and proof of the federal government's resolve to crush the rebellion swiftly and absolutely.

The reporters had pounced on the word *overpowering*. "You mean we outnumber the rebs, Captain?"

"Not outnumber, exactly." In fact no one knew just how many men the rebels had mustered on the Bull Run's farther bank, the estimates ranging from ten thousand to a most unlikely forty thousand, but James did not want to make the northern victory sound like an inevitability brought about by sheer numbers. There had to be some room for northern heroism, and so he had hedged his answer. "We think," he said grandly, "that the rebels can muster numbers not unlike our own, but in this battle, gentlemen, it will be training, morale, and justice that shall prevail."

And justice would prevail, James still believed, not just to capture a rural railhead, but rather to so defeat and so demoralize the Confederate forces that the victorious northern troops could march unobstructed on to the rebel capital, which lay a mere hundred miles south. "On to Richmond!" the northern newspapers cried, and "On to Richmond!" was sewn in bright cloth letters on the standards of some federal regiments, and "On to Richmond!" the spectators had called to the troops marching across the Long Bridge out of Washington. Some of those spectators had done more than watch the troops leave, but had actually accompanied the army into Virginia. Indeed it seemed to James as though half of

Washington's polite society had come to witness the great northern victory for, as the sun now rose above the Bull Run, he could see scores of
civilian spectators already mingling with the federal troops. There were
elegant carriages parked among the gun limbers, and artists' easels and
sketch pads standing amidst the stacks of rifles and muskets. Fashionable
ladies sheltered under parasols, servants laid out rugs and picnic hampers,
while self-important congressmen, eager to share if not wholly capture
the glory of the hour, pontificated to whomever might listen on the
army's strategy.

"You reckon we'll make Richmond by Saturday?" the *Harper's Weekly*
reporter now asked James Starbuck.

"We devoutly hope so."

"And we'll hang Jefferson Davis on Sunday," the reporter said, then
gave a whoop of glee at that happy prospect.

"Not on Sunday, I think." James was too much of a lawyer to let such
a careless remark go unchallenged, especially in front of the foreign military attachés, who might conclude from the reporter's words that the
United States was not only a nation of Sabbath breakers, but also a pack
of uncivilized roughs who did not understand the need for strict legality.
"We'll hang Davis after due process," James said for the benefit of those
foreigners, "and only after due process."

"The Captain means we'll tie a good knot in the rope first," one of
the reporters helpfully explained to the military attachés.

James dutifully smiled, though in truth he found the ways of these
newspapermen shockingly dishonest. Many of these journalists had
already written their accounts of this day's battle, using their imaginations
to describe how the cowardly troops of the slave masters had fled at the
first sight of the Stars and Stripes, and how other rebel soldiers had fallen
penitent to their knees rather than open fire on the glorious old flag.
Northern cavalry had trampled their hooves red in the slavocracy's gore
and northern bayonets had become sticky with southern blood. James
might be shocked by the dishonesty, but as the stories merely reported an
outcome for which he most earnestly prayed, he did not feel comfortable
in expressing reproof lest he should be considered defeatist. Defeat, after
all, was unthinkable, for this was the day when the rebellion must be broken and the race to Richmond could begin.

There was a sudden flurry at the foot of the hill as the artillery horses
were freed from their gun and limber traces. The guns had been placed
behind a snake-rail fence and were aimed toward a handsome stone
bridge that carried the turnpike over the stream. The bridge was the key
to Brigadier General McDowell's hopes for, by persuading the rebels that
his main attack would be an assault straight down the turnpike, he hoped
to draw their forces forward in the bridge's defense while his secret flank-

ing column curled about their rear. Other northern troops would demonstrate against the enemy's right wing, but the vital achievement was to
hold the rebel left wing hard up against the stone bridge so that the
northern flank attack would sweep unopposed and undetected into the
Confederate rear. The rebels had thus to be deceived into believing that
the feigned attack on the bridge was the main attack of the day, and to
add verisimilitude to that deception a massive piece of artillery had been
brought forward to open the fake assault.

That artillery piece was a thirty-pounder Parrott rifle with an iron
barrel more than eleven feet long and weighing nearly two tons. The
gun's metal-rimmed wheels stood as high as a man's shoulders, and the
huge weapon had needed nineteen horses to drag it forward during the
last hours of darkness. Indeed its slow progress had held up the advance of
the whole federal army, and some northern officers thought it madness to
maneuver such a giant piece of fortress artillery into the army's forward-
most positions, but every soldier who saw the cumbersome gun roll pon-
derously past in the first light of dawn reckoned that the beast would be a
battle winner all by itself. The bore of the rifled barrel was over four
inches across, while its iron-banded black breech was now crammed with
nearly four pounds of black powder onto which a conical shell had been
rammed. The shell was filled with black powder and was designed to burst
apart in a killing explosion of flame and shattering iron that would tear
and splinter and flense the rebels on the Bull Run's far bank, though
presently the dawn's early light was hardly revealing much in the way of
targets on that rebel side of the stream. Once in a while a Confederate
officer spurred a horse across a distant field, and some few infantrymen
were scattered on a hill that lay at least a mile beyond the stone bridge,
but otherwise there was small evidence that the rebels were present in
any force.

A friction primer was shoved through the Parrott's touchhole and
deep into the canvas bag of black powder. The primer was a copper tube
filled with finely mealed gunpowder. The topmost section of the tube
held a small charge of fulminate and was pierced by a serrated metal
crosspiece, which when pulled hard by its lanyard would scrape violently
across the fulminate and, just like a match head scratched by a file, would
detonate the fulminate with friction. A gunner sergeant now grabbed the
lanyard's free end while the other crew members stood well clear of the
weapon's lethal recoil.

"Ready!" the gunner sergeant called. Some of the crewmen from the
other guns in the battery had assembled in a small group to listen to a
Bible reading and to say a prayer, but all now turned toward the giant Parrott rifle and covered their ears.

A mounted artillery officer consulted his watch. In the years to come he wanted to tell his children and grandchildren the exact moment at which his great gun had signaled the beginning of the rebellion's end. By his watch it was just approaching eighteen minutes past five in the morning, a mere twelve minutes since the sun had first burst its brilliance across the eastern horizon. The artillery officer, a lieutenant, had entered that moment of sunrise in his diary, though he had also meticulously noted that his watch was liable to gain or lose five minutes in any one day, depending on the temperature.

"Ready!" the gunner sergeant called again, this time with a touch of impatience in his voice.

The artillery lieutenant waited till the watch's hand exactly pointed to the speck that marked the eighteenth minute, then dropped his right hand. "Fire!"

The sergeant snatched the lanyard and the small crosspiece scraped violently across the fulminate. Fire flashed down the copper tube and the powder bag ignited to hurl the shell forward. The base of the shell was a cup of soft brass that expanded to grip the Parrott gun's rifled barrel and start the shell spinning.

The noise exploded violently across the landscape, startling birds up from the trees and thumping the eardrums of the thousands of men who waited for the orders to advance. The gun itself was hurled backward, its trail gouging the soil and its wheels bouncing a clear eighteen inches up from the ground and coming to rest a full seven feet back from where the gun had been fired. In front of the fuming barrel was a scorched patch of turf beneath a roiling cloud of dirty white smoke. Onlookers who had never heard a great gun fired gasped at the sheer fury of the sound, at the appalling crack of the cannon's firing, which promised a horrid destruction on the far side of the stream.

The crew was already feeding the monster's smoking maw with a soaking sponge that would douse the remnants of fire deep in the barrel before the next bag of gunpowder was rammed into the muzzle. Meanwhile the first shell screamed across the meadows, flashed above the bridge, crashed through the wood in a splinter of shattering twigs, then spun hard into the empty hillside beyond the trees. Inside the shell was an ordinary rifle's percussion cap that was fixed to the front of a heavy metal rod which, when the missile struck the hillside, was thrown violently forward to strike against an iron anvil plate in the shell's nose. The copper percussion cap was filled with a fulminate of mercury that was unstable enough to explode under such sudden pressure and which thus ignited the gunpowder crammed into the shell's casing, but the missile had already buried itself three feet into the soft ground and the explosion did little more than quake a few square paces of empty hillside and gout a sudden vent of smoky earth from the riven grass.

"Six and a half seconds." The mounted artillery officer noted the flight time of the shell aloud, then entered the figure into his notebook.

"You may report that the battle proper began at twenty-one minutes past five," James Starbuck announced. His ears were still ringing from the violence of the cannon's report and his horse's ears were still pricked nervously forward.

"I make it only a quarter past five," the *Harper's Weekly* man said.

"Eighteen minutes past?" The speaker was a French military attaché, one of the half-dozen foreign officers who were observing the battle with Captain James Starbuck.

"Too damned early, whatever the time," one of the newspapermen yawned.

James Starbuck frowned at the oath, then flinched as the heavy gun crashed its second shot toward the stone bridge. The percussive sound of the gun's firing thumped across the green countryside and seemed far more impressive than any effect the shell was having on the distant landscape. James desperately wanted to see havoc and maelstrom beyond the stream. He had thought when he had first seen the huge Parrott that a single shell fired from so massive a weapon might serve to panic the rebels, but alas, everything beyond the stream looked oddly calm, and James feared that lack of carnage might seem ridiculous to these foreign soldiers who had all served in Europe's wars and who, James thought, might therefore be supercilious about these amateurish American efforts.

"A very impressive weapon, Captain." The French attaché soothed all James's worries with the generous remark.

"Entirely manufactured in America, Colonel, at our West Point foundry in Cold Spring, New York, and designed by the foundry's superintendent, Mister Robert Parrott." James thought he heard one of the newspapermen making a birdlike noise behind him, but managed to ignore the sound. "The gun can fire common shell, case shot, and bolts. It has a range of two thousand two hundred yards at five degrees of elevation." Much of James's service had so far consisted of learning just such details so he could keep foreign attachés properly informed. "We would of course be happy to arrange an escorted tour of the foundry for you."

"Ah! So." The Frenchman, a colonel called Lassan, had one eye, a horribly scarred face, and a magnificently ornate uniform. He watched as the huge gun fired a third time, then nodded his approval as the rest of the federal artillery, which had been waiting for the third shot as their signal, opened fire in unison. The green fields to the east of the stream blossomed with smoke as gun after gun crashed back on its trail. A teamhorse, inadequately picketed, bolted in panic from the sky-battering noise, dispersing a group of blackberrying infantrymen behind the gun line. "I never enjoyed artillery fire," Colonel Lassan remarked mildly, then

touched a nicotine-stained finger to the patch over his missing eye. "This
went to a Russian shell."

"We trust the rebels are sharing your distaste, sir," James said with
heavy humor. The strike of the gunshots was now visible beyond the
stream where trees shook from the impact of shells and the soil of the farther hillsides was being flecked by ricocheting and exploding missiles.
James had to raise his voice to be heard above the loud cannonade.
"Once the flanking column reveals itself, sir, I think we can anticipate
swift victory."

"Ah, indeed?" Lassan enquired politely, then leaned forward to pat
his horse's neck.

"Two bucks says we'll have the bastards on the skedaddle by ten
o'clock," a reporter from the *Chicago Tribune* offered the assembled company, though no one took up the wager. A Spanish colonel, magnificent
in a red and white dragoon's uniform, unscrewed the cap from a flask and
sipped whiskey.

Colonel Lassan suddenly frowned. "Was that a train whistle?" he
asked Captain Starbuck.

"I'm sure I couldn't say, sir," James said.

"Did you hear a train whistle?" the Frenchman asked his companions,
who shook their heads.

"Is it important, sir?" James asked.

Lassan shrugged. "General Johnston's forces from the Shenandoah
Army, surely, would travel here by train, would they not?"

James assured Colonel Lassan that the rebel troops in the Shenandoah Valley were fully occupied by a contingent of northern soldiers and
could not possibly have arrived at Manassas Junction.

"But suppose General Johnston has given your covering forces the
slip?" Colonel Lassan spoke excellent English in a British accent which
James, whose indigestion had not improved with the passing hours, found
rather irritating. "You are naturally communicating with your troops in
the Shenandoah by telegraph?" Colonel Lassan continued with his
needling enquiries.

"We know General Johnston was fully engaged by our forces two days
ago," James assured Colonel Lassan.

"But two days is more than sufficient time to sidestep a covering force
and ride the trains to Manassas, is it not?" the Frenchman asked.

"I think it most unlikely." James tried to sound coolly dismissive.

"You will recall," Colonel Lassan persisted, "that our great victory
over Franz Joseph at Solferino was caused by the speed with which our
emperor moved the army by train?"

James, who did not know where Solferino was and knew nothing of any battle there and had never heard of the French emperor's railroad achievements, nodded wisely, but then gallantly suggested that the rebel forces of the Confederacy were hardly capable of imitating the achievements of the French army.

"You had better hope not," Lassan said grimly, then trained his field glasses on a far hill where a rebel telegraphist was sending a message. "You are confident, Captain, that your flanking force will be on time?" Lassan asked.

"They should be arriving at any moment, sir." James's confidence was belied by the lack of any evidence that fighting had indeed broken out in the rebel rear, though he consoled himself that the intervening distance would surely prevent any such evidence being visible. That proof would come when the Confederate forces defending the stone bridge began their panicked flight. "I've no doubt our flanking force is attacking at this very moment, sir," James said with as much certainty as he could muster, then, because he was so proud of Yankee efficiency, he could not resist adding two words, "as planned."

"Ah! Planned! I see, I see," Colonel Lassan responded gnomically, then shot a sympathetic glance at James. "My father was a very great soldier, Captain, but he always liked to say that the practice of war is much like making love to a woman—an activity full of delights, but none of them predictable and the best of them capable of inflicting grievous injury on a man."

"Oh, I like that!" The Chicago newspaperman scribbled in his notebook.

James was so offended by the tastelessness of the remark that he just stared speechless into the distance. Colonel Lassan, oblivious of the offense he had given, hummed a tune, while the newspapermen scribbled down their first impressions of the war which, so far, were disappointing. War was nothing but noise and smoke, though, unlike the journalists, the skirmishers on both banks of the Bull Run were learning just what that noise and smoke meant. Bullets whickered across the stream as rebel and federal sharpshooters sniped from the trees and edged the watercourse with a wispy lacework of powder smoke that was twitched aside by the screaming passage of the heavy shells that crashed into the timber to explode in gouts of sulfurous black smoke and whistling iron fragments. A branch was struck by a shell, cracked, and splintered down to break a horse's back. The beast screamed terribly while a drummer boy cried for his mother and feebly attempted to stop his guts spilling from the ragged shrapnel gash in his belly. An officer stared in disbelief at the spreading blood that filled his lap from the bullet wound in his groin. A bearded sergeant gripped the ragged stump of his left wrist and wondered how in

God's name he was ever to plough a straight furrow again. A corporal vomited blood, then slowly crumpled onto the ground. Gunsmoke sifted among the branches. The cannon were firing more quickly now to make a gigantic drumroll that rose to drown the music of the regimental bands, which still played their jaunting tunes behind the battle lines.

And farther behind the rebel battle line still, back at Manassas Junction, a plume of blue-white woodsmoke streamed back from a locomotive's blackened stack. The first of General Joseph Johnston's men had come from the Shenandoah. They had escaped the northern troops, and eight thousand more rebels had thus begun to reinforce the eighteen thousand that Beauregard had already assembled beside the Run. The armies had gathered, the guns were heating up, and a Sabbath Day's slaughter could begin.

11

"So you're our damned spy, are you?" Colonel Nathan Evans greeted Nathaniel Starbuck who, still mounted on Pocahontas, had his hands tied behind his back and was under the guard of two Louisiana cavalrymen who while scouting the country toward Sudley Church had found and pursued Starbuck, then captured and pinioned him, and now had fetched him back to their commanding officer, who was standing with his brigade staff a short distance behind the stone bridge. "Get the bugger off his horse!" Evans snapped.

Someone took hold of Starbuck's right arm and pulled him unceremoniously out of the saddle so that the northerner fell heavily at Evans's feet. "I'm not a spy," he managed to say. "I'm one of Faulconer's men."

"Faulconer?" Evans barked a brief, humorless noise that might have been laughter or was maybe a growl. "You mean that bastard who thinks he's too good to fight with my brigade? Faulconer doesn't have men, boy, he has white-livered fairies. Milksops. Mudsills. Black-assed, shad-bellied, shit-faced, pussy-hearted trash. And you're one of that scum, are you?"

Starbuck recoiled from the stream of insult, but somehow managed to persevere with his explanation. "I found northern troops in the woods beyond the Sudley Fords. A lot of them, and coming this way. I was on my way back to warn you."

"Bastard's lying like a rug, Colonel," one of the two Louisianan cavalrymen interjected. They were whip-lean, rough-bearded horsemen with weather-darkened faces and wild scary eyes, reminding Starbuck of Sergeant Truslow. They were outrageously armed, each man carrying a carbine, two pistols, a saber and a bowie knife. One of the two cavalrymen had a bleeding cut of freshly slaughtered pork hanging from his saddle bow, while the other, who had efficiently relieved Starbuck of his three dollars and sixteen cents, had two unplucked chickens hanging from his crupper strap by their broken necks. That man had also found the letter from Starbuck's father and his brother's laissez-passer, but, being illiterate, he had taken no interest in the papers which he had carelessly shoved back into Starbuck's shirt pocket. "He weren't weaponed," the laconic cavalryman continued, "and he didn't have no uniform on him. I reckons he's a spy, Colonel, sir. Just listen to the sumbitch's voice. He ain't no southron."

A shell thumped into the meadow a dozen paces in front of the small group. It exploded, jarring a seismic thump through the soil and rooting up chunks of red dirt. The sound, even muffled by the earth, was a violent, scary crack that made Starbuck wince with shock. A scrap of stone or metal whistled close to Evans's shabby brown hat, but the colonel did not even flinch. He just glanced at one of his orderlies who was mounted on a piebald horse. "Intact, Otto?"

"*Ja*, Colonel, intact."

Evans looked back to Starbuck, who had struggled to his feet. "So where did you see these federal troops?"

"Maybe a half mile beyond the Sudley Fords, sir, on a road that leads east."

"In the woods, you say?"

"Yes, sir."

Evans picked with an opened penknife at his teeth, which were dark and rotten from chewing tobacco. His sceptical eyes looked up and down Starbuck, and did not seem to like what they saw. "So how many federal troops did you see, cuffee?"

"I don't know, sir. A lot. And they've got cannon with them."

"Cannon, eh? I am frightened! Shitting in my pants, I am." Evans sniggered and the men around him laughed. The colonel was famous for the filth of his language, the depth of his thirst and the ferocity of his temper. He had graduated from West Point in 1848, though barely, and now ridiculed the academy's curriculum by claiming that what made a soldier was the talent to fight like a wildcat, not some prinking ability to speak French or to solve fancy problems in trigonometry or to master the complexities of natural philosophy, whatever the hell that was. "You saw the cannon, did you?" he now demanded fiercely.

"Yes, sir." In truth Starbuck had seen no northern guns, but he had watched the federal troops dismantling the barricade and he reasoned they would surely not waste their time clearing the road for infantry. An infantry column could have skirted the felled trees, but guns would need an unobstructed passage, which surely suggested that the concealed flank attack was bringing artillery.

Nathan Evans cut a new slice of tobacco that he plugged into one of his cheeks. "And just what in the name of God were you doing in the woods beyond Sudley Fords?"

Starbuck paused and another shell cracked apart in black smoke and a stab of red flame. The intensity of the explosion was extraordinary to

Starbuck, who again flinched as the percussive clap shivered the air, though Colonel Nathan Evans appeared entirely unworried by the sound apart from another enquiry of his mounted orderly that all was still well.

"Ja, Colonel. All is vell. Don't vorry yourself." The German orderly was a huge man with a woeful face and a curious stoneware barrel that was strapped like a rucksack on his broad back. His master, Colonel Evans, whom Starbuck had gathered from his captors was nicknamed "Shanks," did not look any more prepossessing by daylight than he had in the small hours of the morning; indeed, to Starbuck's jaundiced eye, Evans most resembled one of the bent-backed Boston coal heavers who scuttled with hundredweight sacks of fuel from the street to the kitchen cellars, and it was hardly surprising, Starbuck thought, that the fastidious Washington Faulconer had refused to put himself under the South Carolinian's command.

"Well? You ain't answered my question, boy." Evans glared at Starbuck. "What were you doing on the far side of the Run, eh?"

"Colonel Faulconer sent me," Starbuck said defiantly.

"Sent you? Why?"

Starbuck wanted to salve his pride and say that he had been sent to reconnoiter the woods beyond Bull Run, but he sensed the lie would never hold, and so he settled for the ignominious truth. "He didn't want me in his regiment, sir. He was sending me back to my people."

Evans turned to stare intently at the trees edging the Bull Run stream where his half-brigade was defending the stone bridge carrying the turnpike west from Washington. If the northerners did attack this section of the Run then Evans's defense would be desperate, for his brigade consisted only of a handful of light cavalry, four obsolete smoothbore cannon, an understrength infantry regiment from South Carolina and another, equally undermanned, from Louisiana. Beauregard had left the brigade thus thinly defended because he was certain that the battle would be fought far out on the Confederate right wing. So far, and fortunately for Evans, the northern assault on the brigade had been restricted to harassing rifle and artillery fire, though one of the enemy's cannon delivered a shell so monstrous that the sky seemed to tremble each time one passed overhead.

Evans watched the trees with his head cocked to one side as though he was judging the course of the fighting by the noise of battle. To Starbuck the rifle and musket fire sounded oddly like the fierce crackling of burning dry undergrowth, while above it boomed the artillery fire. The flight of the shells made a noise like ripping cloth, or perhaps bacon frying, except that every now and then the sizzling would swell into a sudden ear-hurting crash as a missile exploded. A few rifle bullets snickered close by Evans's small group, some of them making an eerie whistling. It was all very odd to Starbuck, who was aware of his heart thumping in his chest, yet, in all truth, he was not so frightened of the shells and bullets as he was of the fierce, bow-legged Shanks Evans, who now turned back to the prisoner. "Goddamn Faulconer was sending you to your people?" Evans asked. "What the hell do you mean?"

"My family, sir. In Boston."

"Oh, Boston!" Evans guffawed the name gleefully, inviting his staff to join his mockery. "A shit hole. A piss hole. A city of puling crap. Christ, but I hate Boston. A city of black-assed Republican trash. A city of interfering, hymn-singing, lickbelly women who are no damned good for anything." Evans spat a lavish gob of tobacco-laced spittle onto Starbuck's shoes. "So Faulconer was sending you back to Boston, was he, boy? Why?"

"I don't know, sir."

"Don't know, sir," Evans mimicked Starbuck, "or perhaps you're telling me lies, you miserable twist of shit. Maybe you're trying to drag my men away from the bridge, is that it, you shit-belly?" The Colonel's vehemence was terrifying, overwhelming, blistering, forcing Starbuck to take an involuntary backward step as the Colonel's harangue spattered him with spittle. "You're trying to sell me down the river, you cuffee bastard. You want me to open the pike so the northern bastards can swarm over the bridge and then we'll all be hanging from the trees come nightfall. Ain't that right, you son of a no-good bitch?" There was a few seconds' silence, then Evans repeated his question in a voice that was a high-pitched scream. "Ain't that right, you son of a cuffee bitch?"

"There's a column of northern troops in the woods beyond the Sudley Fords." Starbuck somehow managed to keep his voice calm. He gave his hands a futile jerk, trying to point to the north, but the pinion at his wrists was far too secure. "They're marching this way, sir, and they'll be here in another hour or so."

Another shell crashed into the pasture beyond the turnpike where Evans's two reserve artillery pieces stood waiting in the uncut grass. The resting gunners did not even look up, not even when one of the giant shells fell shorter than usual and tore a branch from a nearby tree before exploding forty yards away in a turmoil of dirt, leaves, iron fragments, and hot smoke.

"How's my barrelito, Otto?" Evans shouted.

"No harm, Colonel. Don't you vorry." The German sounded impassive.

"I vorry," Evans growled, "I vorry about lunkhead pieces of shit from Boston. What's your name, boy?"

"Nathaniel, sir. Nathaniel Starbuck."

"If you're lying to me, Nathaniel Shitface, I'll take you to the woodshed and cut your balls off. If you've got any balls. Have you got balls,

Nathaniel?" Starbuck said nothing. He was feeling relieved that this furious, foul-tongued man had not connected his surname to the Reverend Elial. Two more shells screamed overhead and an overshot rifle bullet made its odd whistling noise as it flicked past. "So if I move my men to face your column, fairy-shit"—Evans thrust his face so close to Starbuck that the Bostonian could smell the mephitic mix of whiskey and tobacco on the South Carolinian's breath—"I'll be letting the enemy across the bridge here, won't I, and then there'll be no Confederacy anymore, will there? And then the emancipating shitheads from Boston will come down to rape our women, if that's what the hymn singers from Boston do. Maybe they'd prefer to rape our men? Is that your taste, cuffee-boy? You'd like to rape me, would you?"

Again Starbuck said nothing. Evans spat derision of Starbuck's silence, then turned to see a gray-coated infantryman limping back along the turnpike. "Where in hell are you going?" Evans exploded in sudden fury at the soldier, who just stared back in blank astonishment. "You can still shoot a rifle, can't you?" Evans screamed. "So get back! Unless you want those black-assed Republicans fathering your wife's next bastards? Get back!" The man turned and limped painfully back toward the bridge, using his rifle-musket as a crutch.

A solid shot slapped dust from the turnpike, then ricocheted on without hitting anyone in Evans's headquarters group, but the wind of the shot's passing seemed to stagger the injured infantryman who swayed on his makeshift crutch, then collapsed at the roadside close by the two reserve six-pounder guns. Evans's other two guns were closer to the Bull Run, returning the enemy's fire with shrapnel shells that burst in the distant air like sudden small gray clouds from which fizzing white smoke trails spiraled crazily earthward. Whether the shells were finding their targets no one knew, but in truth Evans was merely firing to keep up his men's morale.

The reserve gunners bided their time. Most lay on their backs, apparently dozing. Two men tossed a ball back and forth while an officer, spectacles perched low on his nose, leaned on a bronze barrel and turned the pages of a book. A shirt-sleeved gunner with bright red suspenders sat with his back against the gun's offside wheel. He was writing, dipping his pen into an ink bottle that rested in the grass by his side. The men's insouciance did not seem out of place for, though the fighting was generating a carapace of noise and smoke, there was no great sense of urgency. Starbuck had expected battle to be more vigorous, like the newspaper accounts of the Mexican War that had told of General Scott's brave troops carrying the American flag through shot and screaming shell into the Halls of Montezuma, but there was almost an abstracted air about this morning's events. The gunner officer slowly turned a page, the letter writer carefully drained ink from his pen's nib before lifting it to the page, while one of the ball players missed a catch and laughed lazily. The wounded infantryman lay in the ditch, hardly moving.

"So what do I do with the sumbitch, Colonel?" one of the Louisiana cavalrymen guarding Starbuck asked.

Evans had been frowning toward the mist of smoke that hung above the stone bridge. He turned bad-temperedly back to announce his decision about Starbuck, but was interrupted before he could speak. "A message, sir." The speaker was the lieutenant who had accompanied Evans on his abortive visit to Faulconer's tent that morning. The lieutenant was mounted on a gaunt gray horse and carried a pair of field glasses with which he had been watching the semaphore station on the hill. "From the wig-wag, sir. Our left is turned." The lieutenant spoke without a trace of emotion.

There was a moment's stillness as one of the enemy's monstrous shells ripped overhead. The injured man beside the road was trying to stand, but seemed too feeble to rise. "Say that again, Meadows," Evans demanded.

Lieutenant Meadows consulted his notebook. "'Look out on your left, you are turned.' Those are the exact words, sir."

Evans swiveled fast to stare north, though nothing showed there except the heavy summer trees and a high hawk soaring. Then he turned back to Starbuck, his small eyes wide with shock. "I owe you an apology, boy. By God I owe you an apology. I'm sorry, so I am, sorry!" Evans blurted out the last word, then twisted again, this time to stare toward the stone bridge. His left hand twitched spasmodically at his side, the only evidence of the strain he was enduring. "This is a pretense. They ain't attacking here, they're just stroking our bellies, fooling us, keeping us still while the real attack comes up our backsides. Jesus!" He had been speaking to himself, but suddenly he snapped into a much louder voice. "Horse! Bring my horse! Get on your horse, boy!" This last was to Starbuck.

"Sir!" Starbuck yelped.

"Boy?"

"I'm tied up."

"Release the boy! Otto?"

"Ja, Colonel?"

"Give Boston some barrelito. One cup." It seemed that Evans had chosen the name "Boston" for Starbuck's nickname, just as the curious stone barrel on the German orderly's back was called "barrelito."

The big German rode his piebald horse close to Starbuck while another man, hurrying to obey Evans's orders, cut the rope at Starbuck's wrists. Starbuck began massaging the rope burns, then saw that the

impassive German orderly had reached behind his back to manipulate a
small wooden tap that was let into the base of the stoneware barrel. The
German drew a tin cup of liquid from the barrel, then solemnly handed
the cup down to Starbuck. "Trink! Come now, quick! I need the cup
again. Trink!"

Starbuck accepted the cup that was filled with what appeared to be
cold tea. He was thirsty as a dog and eagerly tipped the cup to his lips,
then half choked for the liquid was not tea, but whiskey; raw, hard, un-
diluted whiskey.

"Trink up!" Otto sounded bad-tempered.

"My horse!" Evans yelled. A shell screamed overhead, thumping into
the hill behind. At the very same moment a solid shot struck the
wounded man beside the road, killing him instantly and flinging his
blood ten feet into the air. Starbuck saw what he thought was the man's
severed leg spinning through the air, then instantly rejected the sight as
unreal. Another solid shot cracked into a tree, splitting a three-foot lance
of fresh wood from the trunk and showering leaves onto the raggedly torn
leg. Then Lieutenant Meadows, who had repeated the wig-wagger's
alarming message, suddenly gulped and widened his eyes. He was staring
at Starbuck and his eyes seemed to grow wider and wider as his hand
slowly strayed to his throat, where a bead of blood swelled and glistened.
His notebook slipped to the ground, its pages fluttering, as the bead of
blood grew and split, then suddenly he choked a flood of gore down his
tunic's front. He swayed, gargling blood, then his whole body twitched
violently as he slid out of the saddle and onto the grass. "I'll take Meadows's horse," Evans snapped, and grabbed the gray's reins. The dying
man's foot was caught in the stirrup. Evans jerked it free, then pulled
himself up onto the horse's back.

Starbuck drained the tin cup, gasped for breath, then reached for
Pocahontas's reins. He clambered awkwardly into the saddle, wondering
what he was supposed to do now that he was free.

"Boston!" Evans turned his horse toward Starbuck. "Will that bastard
Faulconer listen to you?"

"I think so, sir," Starbuck said, then, more honestly, "I don't know,
sir."

Evans frowned as a thought came to him. "Why are you fighting for
us, Boston? This ain't your fight."

Starbuck did not know what to say. His reasons were more to do with
his father than with America's destiny, still more to do with Sally than
with slavery, but this did not seem the time or the place to explain such
things. "Because I'm a rebel." He offered the explanation feebly, knowing
its inadequacy.

But it pleased Nathan Evans, who had just taken a mug of whiskey from his stern-looking orderly. He drained the mug. "Well, you're my rebel now, Boston, so find Faulconer and tell him I want his precious Legion. Tell him I'm moving most of my troops to the Sudley Road, and I want his Virginians up there too. Tell him to form on my left."

Starbuck, dizzied by the whiskey, his change of fortune and by the sense of panic whirling in the humid air, tried to insert a note of caution into Evans's planning. "Colonel Faulconer was determined to move to the right wing, sir."

"Damn what Faulconer wants!" Evans screamed so loud that the idling gunners across the turnpike were startled. "Tell Faulconer that the Confederacy needs him! Tell the bastard we have to stop the Yankees or else we'll all be doing Lincoln's rope dance tonight! I'm trusting you, boy! Get Faulconer and tell the bastard to fight, damn his eyes! Tell the damp-bellied bastard to fight!" Evans shouted the last words, then savaged his heels back, leaving Starbuck astonished and alone as the staff officers and orderlies streamed after Evans toward the men defending the stone bridge.

Bullets snicked and whimpered in the heavy air. Flies were gathering thick in the ditch to lay their eggs in the gobbets of flesh that had been a man just moments before. Lieutenant Meadows lay on his back with his dead eyes showing surprise and his blood-swilled mouth gaping wide open. Starbuck, the whiskey sour in his belly, gathered the reins, turned Pocahontas's head, and went to find the Legion.

The Faulconer Legion took its first casualty at around five minutes past eight in the morning. A shell came over the hill to the east, skipped once on the reverse slope, tumbled in the air with a horrid shrieking noise, then struck the ground a second time some twelve yards in front of A Company. The shell exploded there, driving a splinter of jagged iron into the skull of Joe Sparrow, the boy who had a scholarship to the university, but who now died as easy a death as any soldier could wish. One moment he was standing upright, grinning at a joke told by Cyrus Matthews, and the next he was on his back. He twitched once, felt nothing, died.

"Joe?" Cyrus asked.

The other men edged nervously away from the collapsed boy, all but his friend George Waters, who had been standing beside Sparrow in the second rank and who now dropped to his knees beside the body. Sparrow's cap had been tugged round by the force of the striking shell fragment and George now tried to pull it straight, but as he tugged at the cap's stiff visor a terrible wash of blood escaped from under the sweatband. "Oh, God!" George Waters recoiled from the horrid sight. "He's dead!"

"Don't be a lunkhead, boy. Skulls bleed like stuck pigs, you know that." Sergeant Howes had pushed through the ranks and now knelt beside Sparrow. "Come on, Runt, wake up!" He pulled the cap straight, trying to hide the blood, then slapped the dead boy lightly on the cheek. This was Blanche and Frank Sparrow's only boy, the pride of their lives. Blanche had tried real hard to persuade the boy not to march to war, but someone had left a scornful petticoat on their front porch, addressed to Joe, and young Joe had wanted to join the Legion anyways and so Blanche had relented, but now Joe was flat on his back in a field.

"Call the doctor! The doctor!" Paul Hinton, captain of A Company, slid out of his saddle and shouted the order.

Major Danson came running with his medical bag from the rear of the regiment where the band was playing "Annie Laurie," the saxhorn tubas embroidering a clever bass line in counterpoint to the plangent melody that was so popular with the men. Danson pushed through the ranks of A Company. "Give him air!" he shouted, which is what he usually shouted whenever he was called to a sick person. Invariably the field hands or the servants or the family members all crowded about the patient, and Danson could not stand working amidst a throng of onlookers all offering suggestions. If they were so knowledgeable, he often wondered, why did they need him? "Stand back, now. Who is it, Dan?"

"Blanche Sparrow's boy, doc," Hinton said.

"Not young Joe! Now come on, Joe, you'll be missing all the fun!" Doctor Danson dropped to his knees. "What's the matter, now? Got hit on the head, did you?"

"He's dead." George Waters had gone white with shock.

Major Danson frowned at this amateur diagnosis, then felt for Joseph Sparrow's pulse. He said nothing for a few seconds, then lifted off the blood-stained forage cap to reveal Joe's hair all soaked and matted red. "Oh, poor Blanche," the doctor said softly, "what are we to tell her?" He unbuttoned the collar of the dead boy's tunic as if to give him air.

Another ricocheted shell whipsawed overhead and crashed to earth a half mile beyond the regiment, its explosion lost in the dense foliage of a stand of trees. Adam Faulconer, who had been standing his horse on the hill crest to watch the cannonade ripple smoke and flame about the distant stream, now realized something was amiss within the Legion's ranks and spurred back to the regiment. "What's happened?" he asked Doctor Danson.

"It's Blanche's boy, young Joe."

"Oh, God, no." There was an awful pain in Adam's voice. The day was already bringing Adam the violence he had feared, and yet, he suspected, the battle had not really begun. The two sides had made contact and were hurling shells at each other, but neither seemed to have launched a real assault.

"Blanche will never live with this," Danson said, struggling to his feet. "I remember when Joe nearly died of the whooping cough and I thought she'd go with him to his grave. Dear God, what a terrible thing." Around him a ring of soldiers stared aghast at the dead boy. It was not that death was so strange to any of them; all had seen sisters or brothers or cousins or parents laid out in the parlor, and all had helped carry a casket into the church or had helped pull a drowned body from the river, but this was different; this was chance death, war's lottery, and it could just as easily have been themselves lying there all bloody and still. This was something they were not really prepared for, because nothing in their training had convinced them that young men ended up open-mouthed, flat on their backs, fly-blown, bloodied and dead.

"Carry him to the back, lads," Captain Hinton now said. "Lift him up! Careful now!" Hinton supervised the removal of the body, then walked back to Adam. "Where's your father, Adam?"

"I don't know."

"He should be here." Hinton gathered his horse's reins and hauled himself laboriously into the saddle.

"I suppose the general's keeping him," Adam suggested lamely. There was a glistening patch of blood beside Joe Sparrow's fallen cap on the grass. "Poor Blanche," Adam said. "We took Joe out of the color party because we reckoned he'd be safer in the ranks."

But Hinton was not listening. Instead he was frowning eastward to where a horseman had appeared on the brow of the hill. "Is that Starbuck? It is, by God!"

Adam turned and, to his astonishment, saw that it was indeed Starbuck who was galloping toward the Legion and, for a second, Adam thought he must be seeing ghosts, then he saw that it really was his friend who, not three hours before, had been dispatched back north to his own people, but who had now returned coatless, pale, hurried, and urgent. "Where's your father?" Starbuck shouted.

"I don't know, Nate." Adam had ridden to meet his friend. "What are you doing here?"

"Where's Pecker?" Starbuck's voice was curt, ungiving, out of tune with the melancholy mood of Sparrow's death.

"What are you doing here, Nate?" Adam asked again, spurring his horse after Starbuck. "Nate?"

But Starbuck had already kicked his horse down the front of the Legion to where Major Bird stood beneath the Legion's colors that hung limp in the windless air.

"Sir!" Starbuck reined in close to Bird.

Bird blinked up at the horseman. "Starbuck? I was told to discharge you! Are you certain you're meant to be here?"

"Sir." Nathaniel Starbuck sounded stilted and formal. "Colonel Evans sent me, sir. He wants us to advance on the Sudley Road. The enemy has crossed the stream by Sudley Church, and are marching this way."

Pecker Bird blinked up at the young man and noted that Starbuck had sounded remarkably calm, which calmness, he supposed, was a perverse symptom of the boy's excitement, and then Bird thought how astonishingly well everyone was playing their soldierly parts on this unlikely morning. "Aren't those orders more properly addressed to Colonel Faulconer?" Bird heard himself asking, and was amazed that his natural inclination was so to avoid taking the responsibility.

"If I could find the Colonel, sir, I'd tell him. But I don't think there's time, and if we don't move, sir, there won't be anything left of this army."

"Is that so?" Bird also sounded calm, but his hands were clawing through his beard with the stress of the moment. He opened his mouth to speak again, but no sound came. He was thinking that he too would have to play a soldierly part, now that fate had dropped this responsibility into his lap, and then he pusillanimously thought that a soldier's duty was to obey and Colonel Faulconer's orders had been very specific: that he was to ignore any instructions from Colonel Nathan Evans. Faulconer was even now attempting to have the Legion deployed southward to where Beauregard expected the main battle to be fought, but Colonel Nathan Evans wanted the Legion to march northward and was evidently claiming that the Confederacy's entire future depended on Bird's obedience.

"Sir!" Starbuck was evidently not so calm as he seemed for he was pressing Major Bird for a decision.

Bird waved Starbuck to silence. Thaddeus Bird's first impulse had been to avoid all responsibility by blindly obeying Washington Faulconer's instructions, but that very impulse allowed Bird to understand just why his brother-in-law had given in to Miriam's entreaties and appointed him as a major. It was because Washington Faulconer believed that Bird would never dare disobey him. The Colonel evidently dismissed Bird as a safe nonentity who would never detract from his glory. In fact, as Thaddeus Bird suddenly realized, no one was allowed to compete with Washington Faulconer, which was why the Colonel surrounded himself with dullards like Ridley, and why, when a man like Starbuck threatened to show some independence, he was so quickly ejected from the Colonel's entourage. Even Adam's scruples were acceptable to Washington Faulconer because they prevented Adam from rivaling his father. Washington Faulconer would surround himself with dull men just so that he could shine all the brighter, and as Thaddeus Bird understood that truth, so he was determined to thwart it. Damn Faulconer, because Major Thaddeus Bird would not be dismissed as a nonentity! "Sergeant Major Proctor!"

"Sir!" The dignified sergeant major marched stiffly from his place behind the color party.

"The Legion will advance on the crossroads at the foot of the hill, Sergeant Major, in columns of company. Then up the farther road," Bird pointed across the valley. "Give the orders, if you please."

The sergeant major, who knew exactly how much authority Major Bird was supposed to exercise in the Faulconer Legion, drew himself to his full and impressive height. "Are those the Colonel's orders, Major, sir?"

"They are the orders of your superior officer, Sergeant Major Proctor." Now that Bird had made up his mind he seemed to be enjoying himself, for his head was nodding back and forth and his thin mouth was twisted into a sardonic grin. "We shall advance along the Sudley Road, which is that dirt road beyond the crossroads." Bird pointed northward again, then looked at Starbuck for confirmation. "Is that right?"

"Yes, sir. And Colonel Evans requests that we form up on his left when we cross the farther hill." Starbuck guessed that was the exact place where Washington Faulconer had said farewell to him.

"Would it not be better, sir ..." Sergeant Major Proctor said, attempting to subdue Pecker Bird's lunacy.

"Do it!" Bird screamed in sudden rage. "Do it!"

Adam Faulconer had followed Starbuck to Major Bird's side and now intervened to calm things down. "What are you doing, Uncle?"

"The Legion will advance in column of companies!" Major Bird snapped in a surprisingly loud voice. "Company A will advance first! Companies! 'Shun!"

A very few men shuffled to attention, but most just stayed on the ground, supposing that Pecker had fallen off his perch as he had used to do in the schoolroom after he had been teased or otherwise goaded into a fury. Many of the Legion's officers were having difficulty in suppressing their laughter and some, like Ridley, were jerking their heads back and forth like feeding birds.

"Nate." Adam turned to his friend. "Will you please explain exactly what's happening?"

"The enemy has got round our rear," Nate explained loudly enough for the nearest companies to hear, "and Colonel Evans needs this regiment to help head off their attack. There's no one but us and Colonel Evans's men who can stop them, and if we don't move, the day's lost."

"Like shit." That was Ethan Ridley. "You're a goddamned Yankee and you're doing a Yankee's work. There's no enemy over there."

Adam put a hand on Starbuck's arm to restrain him. Then he stared north across the turnpike. Nothing moved there. Not even a leaf stirred. The landscape was heavy, somnolent, empty.

"I think we'd better stay here," Adam suggested. Sergeant Major Proctor nodded agreement, and Major Bird looked up at Starbuck, appeal in his eyes.

"I saw the northerners," Starbuck said.

"I'm not moving," Ridley announced, and a murmur of agreement supported his stand.

"Why don't we send an officer to have Evans's orders confirmed?" Captain Hinton suggested sensibly. Hinton, like a dozen other officers and sergeants, had come to join the discussion.

"Don't you have written orders, Nate?" Anthony Murphy asked.

"There wasn't time to put anything in writing," Starbuck said.

Ridley laughed sourly, while Thaddeus Bird looked uncertain, as though wondering if he had made the right decision.

"Where's Evans now?" Hinton asked.

"He's moving his men from the stone bridge to the Sudley Road." Starbuck was feeling increasingly desperate.

"Is that the Sudley Road?" Thomas Truslow's growl interrupted the proceedings.

"Yes," Starbuck said. Truslow had been pointing north across the shallow valley.

"And you saw Yankees out there?"

"Beyond the fords, yes."

Truslow nodded, but to Starbuck's disappointment said nothing more. Across the turnpike a small group of gray-clad horsemen galloped up to the far crest, their horses leaving dark hoofprints in the turf. The Legion's officers watched until the horsemen disappeared into the far trees. The horsemen were the only sign that anything might be happening beyond the army's left flank, but there were so few of the cavalry that their maneuver was hardly convincing evidence. "It means nothing," Adam said dubiously.

"It means we move to support Colonel Evans"—Bird had decided to stick to his decision—"and the next man to disobey my order will be shot!" Bird drew a Le Mat revolver, which he hefted in his thin right hand, then, as though unsure whether or not he could really carry out his threat, he passed the brutal-looking gun up to Starbuck. "You will shoot, Lieutenant Starbuck, and that is an order. You hear me?"

"Very clearly, sir!" Starbuck realized that the situation had gotten disastrously out of hand, but he did not know what he could do to restore sanity. The Legion was desperate for leadership, but the Colonel was missing and no one seemed adequate to step into his boots. Starbuck himself was a northerner, and a mere second lieutenant if he was anything at all, while Thaddeus Bird was a laughingstock, a country schoolmaster masquerading in a soldier's gaudy uniform, yet only Bird and

Starbuck understood what needed to be done, but neither man could impose his will on the regiment and Starbuck, holding the awkward pistol, knew he would never dare use it.

Major Bird took three formal paces forward. He appeared ludicrous as he paced the three giant steps, which he doubtless thought were solemn but which looked more like the gait of a clown clumping upstage on stilts. He turned and stood to attention. "The Legion will come to attention! On your feet!"

Gradually, reluctantly, the men stood. They pulled on their haversacks and lifted their rifles from the grass. Bird waited, then snapped his next orders. "The Legion will advance by column of companies. Company A! By the right! Quick march!"

Not one soldier moved. They had stood up, but they would not move away from their patch of hillside. Company A looked at Captain Hinton for a lead, but Hinton was clearly troubled by the order and made no attempt to enforce it. Thaddeus Bird swallowed hard, then looked up at Starbuck. The pistol felt hugely heavy in Starbuck's hand.

"Lieutenant Starbuck?" Major Bird's voice was a yelp.

"Oh, Uncle Thaddeus, please!" Adam appealed.

The men were on the edge of hysterical laughter, placed there by the ludicrous bathos of Adam's homely appeal, and it would have taken just one more syllable to trigger that laughter when a hard voice, as sudden and grim as the ripsaw sound of the passing shells, turned the Legion's mood into instant apprehension. "Company K! Shoulder arms!"

Truslow had paced back to the Legion's left flank and now shouted the order. Company K snapped to obey him. "On my mark!" he shouted. "Forward march!"

Company K crashed out of line, advancing down the hill. Truslow, squat and dark-faced, did not look left or right, but paced ahead with his deliberate, countryman's stride. Captain Roswell Jenkins, the company's commanding officer, galloped after the company, but his remonstrance to Truslow was utterly ignored. We came here to fight, Truslow seemed to be saying, so for God's sake, let us get off our butts and fight.

Captain Murphy, commanding D Company, looked questioningly at Starbuck. Starbuck nodded, and the simple confirmation was enough for Murphy. "Company D!" he shouted, and the men did not even wait for the order to advance, but just started after Truslow's men. The rest of the Legion edged forward. Sergeant Major Proctor looked wildly up at Adam, who shrugged, while Major Bird, at last seeing his orders obeyed, stirred the laggards into motion.

Ridley turned his horse wildly, looking for allies, but the Faulconer Legion was marching west, led by a sergeant, and the officers were left to catch up with their men. Starbuck himself, who had precipitated the move northward, now turned away to shout at Adam. "Where's my coat?"

Adam pushed his horse through the bandsmen, who were making a cacophony of thumps and squawks as they hurried to catch up with the advancing Legion. "Nate!" Adam sounded distressed. "What have you done?"

"I told you. The federals are coming round our rear. Do you know where my jacket is?" Starbuck had dismounted beside Joe Sparrow's dead body. He picked up Sparrow's rifle and tugged off the dead boy's belt with its canteen, cartridge box and cap box.

"What are you doing?" Adam asked.

"Arming myself. I'll be damned if I spend the rest of this day without a gun. People are killing each other here." Starbuck meant the words as a grim joke, but their flippancy made him sound hard.

"But Father sent you home!" Adam protested.

Starbuck turned a bitter face on his friend. "You can't dictate my loyalty, Adam. Work out your own, but leave me mine."

Adam bit his lip, then twisted in his saddle. "Nelson! Bring Mister Starbuck's coat and weapons!"

The Colonel's servant, who had been waiting beside the Legion's piled knapsacks, tents and baggage, brought Starbuck his old sword, pistol and coat. Starbuck nodded his thanks, pulled on the coat, then strapped on the sword belt with its heavy pistol. "I seem to be overweaponed," he said, looking at his own revolver, at Joe Sparrow's rifle and at Major Bird's Le Mat revolver. He threw down the rifle, then grimaced at the ugly Le Mat. "It's a nasty-looking brute, isn't it?" The revolver had two barrels, the upper one rifled for bullets, the lower a smoothbore barrel that took a shotgun cartridge. Starbuck broke the gun open and laughed, then showed Adam that the cylinder's nine chambers were all empty. The shotgun barrel was loaded, but the revolving hammer, by which the user could select which barrel to fire, had been twisted upward to fall on one of the empty chambers. "It wasn't loaded," Starbuck said, "Pecker was bluffing."

"He's not bluffing now!" Adam protested and gestured at his father's Legion, which was now halfway down the hill. "Look what you've done!"

"Adam! For Christ's sake, I saw the Yankees. They are coming straight toward us, and if we don't stop them then this war is over."

"Isn't that what we want?" Adam demanded. "One battle, you promised me, then we could talk."

"Not now, Adam." Starbuck had neither the time nor patience for his friend's scruples. He belted his saber and holster belt over his jacket and hauled himself into his saddle just as Ethan Ridley rode back to the hilltop.

"I'm going to find your father, Adam." Ridley ignored Starbuck.

Adam stared downhill to where his neighbors and friends were marching northward. "Nate? Are you sure you saw northerners?"

"I saw them, Adam. After I left you. They were beyond the Sudley

Fords and marching this way. They fired at me, Adam, they chased me! I didn't imagine it." The chase had been brief, confused by the woods, and his northern pursuers had given up five minutes before Starbuck had been captured by the two Louisianan cavalrymen who had refused to cross the fords to discover the truth of Starbuck's story for themselves.

"He's lying," Ridley said calmly, then blanched as Starbuck turned toward him.

Starbuck said nothing to Ridley. Instead he was thinking that he was going to kill this man, but not in front of Adam. He would do it in the chaos of battle where no witness could bring a charge of murder. "The Yankees are coming across at Sudley," Starbuck said, turning back to his friend, "and there's no one else who can stop them."

"But ..." Adam seemed wholly unable to grasp the enormity of Star-buck's news—that this left wing of the rebel army really was threatened, and that his confident, wealthy, assured father had been wrong.

"It's Thermopylae, Adam," Starbuck said earnestly, "think of it as Thermopylae."

"It's what?" Ethan Ridley demanded. Ridley had never heard of Ther-mopylae, where Xerxes's Persians had stolen a flank march on Leonidas's Greeks to snatch victory, nor how the three hundred Spartans had sacri-ficed themselves so that the other Greeks could escape. Nathan Evans seemed an unlikely Greek hero, but today he was playing the Spartan role and Adam, given a classical context to the emergency, instantly under-stood that his father's tenants and his father's neighbors had marched off to become heroes and he could not simply let them die alone. A Faulconer had to be there, and if his father was absent, then Adam must be present.

"We have to fight, don't we?" Adam said, though unhappily.

"You should go to your father!" Ridley insisted.

"No. I have to go with Nate," Adam said.

Ridley felt a pulse of victory. The crown prince was siding with the king's enemy, and Ridley would replace them both. Ridley turned his horse. "I'm going for your father," he called back as he spurred away past Joe Sparrow's body.

Adam looked at his friend and shivered. "I'm frightened."

"So am I," Starbuck said, and thought of the severed leg spinning across the road spilling its trails of blood. "But so are the Yankees, Adam."

"I guess they are," Adam said, then clicked his tongue to urge his horse forward. Starbuck followed more clumsily on Pocahontas, and thus the two friends rode down the hill to follow the Legion northward. Above them, in the clear summer air, a howitzer shell drew a trail of smoke across the sky, then fell to earth and exploded somewhere in the woods.

It was still not nine o'clock in the morning.

* * *

Advancing in column of companies had not been Major Bird's happiest inspiration, but he had thought it the quickest way to get the Legion moving and so he had ordered it. The formation demanded that the companies march in line abreast, four ranks deep, each rank comprising nineteen or twenty men depending on the company's strength, and the ten companies making a long, broad column with the color party at its center and the band and Doctor Danson bringing up the rear.

The problem was that the Legion had never really rehearsed maneuvers in anything but the flat pastureland at Faulconer Court House, and now they were advancing across a landscape that contained inconvenient ditches, rail fences, bushes, dips, knolls, blackberries, streams and impenetrable thickets of trees. They managed to cross the turnpike successfully enough, but the trees about the stone house and the rail fences of the pastures beyond caused the companies to lose all their cohesion and, naturally enough, the men preferred to use the road and so the column of companies became a long straggling line of men that jostled onto the dirt track before advancing toward the trees at the top of the farther hill.

But at least the men were cheerful. Most were glad to be moving, and happier still to have escaped the bare hillside where the overshot enemy shells fell so randomly, and somehow the morning took on a sportive atmosphere like the sylvan days of training back in Faulconer County. They joked as they climbed the hill, boasting what they would do to the Yankees they only half-expected to meet on the farther slope. Many of the men suspected that Pecker Bird had got everything plain bad wrong and that the Colonel would wring his damned neck as soon as he came back from his meeting with the general, but that was Pecker's problem, not theirs. No one expressed any such suspicions to Truslow, who had begun the whole march and who now stolidly led the Legion north.

Starbuck and Adam galloped their horses up the side of the column until they found Thaddeus Bird striding along with the color party. Starbuck leaned precariously from his saddle to offer Major Bird the big Le Mat revolver. "Your pistol, sir. Did you know it wasn't loaded?"

"Of course it wasn't loaded." Bird took the gun from Starbuck. "Did you really think I wanted you to shoot someone?" Bird chuckled, then turned to look at the straggle of men advancing in shambolic order up the dirt road and into the woods. So this was Washington Faulconer's elite force? Faulconer's Imperial Guard? The thought made Bird laugh aloud.

"Sir?" Starbuck thought Bird had spoken.

"Nothing, Starbuck, nothing. Except I have a suspicion that we should be advancing in more soldierly order."

Starbuck pointed ahead to where a patch of sky promised open country at the far side of the thick belt of woodland which crowned the ridge.

"There are fields over the hill crest, sir. You can shake the men into proper line there."

It occurred to Bird that Starbuck had ridden this road when the Colonel had tried to get rid of him. "Why didn't you go when Faulconer gave you the chance?" he asked Starbuck. "Do you really want to fight for the South?"

"I do, yes." But this was hardly the time to explain how quixotic that decision was, nor why the sight of the axemen in the woods had prompted his sudden decision. It was not, he knew, a rational choice, but rather a revulsion against his family, and Starbuck was suddenly amazed at the way in which life presented such choices, and the carelessness with which those choices could be taken even though the resultant decision might utterly change everything that would ever follow, right down to the grave itself. How much history, he wondered, had been made by such flip-pant choices? How many important decisions were taken from mere pride or from lust or even out of sloth? All Starbuck's religion, all his upbring-ing, had taught him that there was a plan to life and a divine purpose to man's existence, yet this morning he had taken a shotgun to that idea and had blasted it clean out of God's firmament, and it seemed to Starbuck that his world, as a result, was a better and clearer place.

"Since you are on our side," Thaddeus Bird spoke from beside Star-buck's left stirrup, "would you ride ahead and stop the men at the open land you promised me? I'd rather we didn't stream into battle like a flock of sinners scurrying for repentance." He waved Starbuck forward with a flourish of the Le Mat pistol.

By the time Starbuck reached the column's head Sergeant Truslow had already ordered his men off the road. Company K had reached the crest of the hill where Starbuck had been expelled from the Legion by the Colonel and where the trees gave way to a long, gentle slope of empty pastureland. Truslow was lining his men in two ranks just short of a zigzag rail fence that had been placed to keep cattle from straying out of the grassland and into the trees. K Company's commanding officer was nowhere to be seen, but Truslow did not need officers. He needed targets. "Make certain you're loaded!" he growled at his men.

"Sergeant! Look!" A man at the right flank of the company pointed to the open country where a horde of oddly dressed troops had suddenly appeared from among the trees. The strange troops wore baggy bright red shirts, voluminous black and white pantaloons tucked into white gaiters, and floppy red caps tipped with long blue tassels. It was a regiment in fashionable Zouave uniform that aped the famous light infantry of France.

"Leave 'em alone!" Truslow bellowed. "They're our clowns!" He had spotted the Confederate flag in the center of the weirdly uniformed troops. "Face front!" he shouted. More of the Legion's men were emerging

from the road to form on the right of Truslow's company, while the
Legion's officers, unsure exactly what was happening or who was commanding this sudden deployment, huddled excitedly at the edge of the
trees. Major Bird shouted at the officers to join their companies, then
looked to his right to see still more Confederate troops emerging from the
trees to fill the wide gap between the Legion and the brightly uniformed
Zouaves. The newcomers wore gray, and their arrival meant that a hasty
defensive line was forming at the wood's northern edge to face a long
wide stretch of open ground that fell softly away from the zigzag fence,
past a farmhouse and hayrick, to where a farther belt of woodland hid the
distant Sudley Fords. The long open slope seemed designed for the
defenders' rifles, a killing ground lit by a merciless sun.

Colonel Evans galloped on his borrowed gray horse to where the
Faulconer Legion was still forming its ranks. "Well done, Boston! Well
done!" He greeted Starbuck, then added gesture to the congratulations by
swerving his horse close by the northerner and slapping him hard on the
back. "Well done! Is Colonel Faulconer here?"

"No, sir."

"Who's commanding?"

"Major Bird. By the colors, sir."

"Bird!" Evans turned his horse hard, slewing soil and grass up from its
hooves. "We just have to hold the bastards here. We have to give the bastards hell." His nervous horse had stopped, blowing and shivering as
Evans stared northward down the long open slope. "If they're coming," he
added the words softly. His left hand was drumming nervously on his
thigh. The German orderly with the "barrelito" of whiskey reined in
behind the Colonel, as did a dozen staff officers and a mounted standard
bearer who carried the palmetto flag of South Carolina. "I've got two
guns coming," Evans told Bird, "but no more infantry, so what we've got
here will have to do the job until Beauregard wakes up to what's happening. Those gaudy thieves," he nodded toward the far Zouaves, "are
Wheat's Louisiana Tigers. I know they look like whores on a picnic, but
Wheat says they're mean sons of bitches in a fight. The nearer fellows are
Sloan's South Carolinians, and I know they'll fight. I've promised them
all Yankee meat for their supper. How are your rogues?"

"Eager, sir, eager." Major Bird, panting and hot after the fast pace of
the advance, took off his hat and pushed a hand through his long, thinning hair. Behind him the thirsty men of the Legion were draining their
canteens.

"We'll give the shit-eating bastards hell, so we will," Evans said, looking northward again, though nothing moved in that empty landscape, not
even a wind to stir the far trees where the road to the fords vanished under
the thick canopy of leaves. A small group of men, women and children

were standing by the Sudley Church on the hill to the left of the road, and
Evans guessed they must be worshipers come to the church only to discover that God's service had been overtaken by war. Behind Evans, dulled
by distance now, the sound of the northern cannonade thundered softly in
the hot still air. Evans had left just four understrength companies at the
stone bridge, a tiny force to hold off any determined Yankee attack down
the turnpike, and he suddenly felt a terrible fear that he had been
deceived and that this rumored flank attack was a feint, a cheat, a deception to strip the stone bridge of its defenders so that the damned Yankees
could end the war in one maneuver. And where the hell was Beauregard?
Or General Johnston's men, who were rumored to be arriving from the
Shenandoah Valley? Christ on his cross, Evans thought, but this was
agony. Evans had fought the Comanches in his years of soldiering, but he
had never been forced into taking a decision as momentous as the one he
had just made, a decision that had left the northern flank of the Confederate army stripped perilously thin. Would history mock him as the fool
whose stupidity had handed an easy victory to the northerners? "Boston!"
Evans twitched round in his saddle to glare at Starbuck.

"Sir."

"You didn't lie to me, boy, did you?" Evans remembered the wig-
wagger's message and tried to convince himself he had done the right
thing, but God in his heaven, just what had he done? Far behind him, out
of sight beyond the trees and the turnpike, the shells rumbled and crashed
on the empty land he had left virtually unguarded. "Did you lie to me,
boy?" he shouted at Starbuck. "Did you lie?"

But Starbuck did not answer. Starbuck was not even looking at the
fierce-eyed Colonel. Instead Starbuck was staring down the long pale
slope to where, out of the distant trees, the northerners were at last
appearing. Rank upon rank of men with the sunlight glinting from their
belt buckles and cap badges and rifle butts and saber scabbards and from
the polished muzzles of their artillery to make the mirrored lights of a
righteous army come to remake God's country.

For the northern trap was sprung. Four full brigades of infantry bol-
stered by the finest field artillery in North America had hooked into the
rebellion's ragged rear to where a scratch southern force led by a whiskey-
sucking foulmouth was the only obstacle left to victory. Now all the day
needed was one overwhelming charge and the slaveholders' rebellion
would become a mere footnote to history, a thing forgotten, a passing
summer's madness that would be gone and ended and vanished like
smoke in a sudden wind. "God bless you, Boston," Evans said, for Starbuck had not lied after all, and there was going to be a fight.

12

The Yankees came on quick. Their predawn flanking march had taken hours longer than their commanders had expected, and now their task was to thrust hard and fast into the rebel rear before the southerners had time to understand just what was happening.

Drums beat the pace as the first northern regiments spread into their attack lines and as cannon unlimbered at the attackers' flanks. Some guns were deployed on the dirt road, others in the farm at the foot of the slope from where they sent the first shells screaming up toward the wooded ridge where the thin line of Confederate forces waited. The advancing Yankees were confident. They had expected the Sudley Fords would be defended, then had half-feared that the southerners might have fortified an unfinished railway embankment just beyond the fords, but instead they had encountered no resistance as they had steadily advanced into the rebel rear. The surprise of their attack seemed to be total, the ineptness of the southern commanders complete, and all that now stood between the federal forces and victory was this contemptible line of rebel farmboys who edged a wood at the long hill's crest. "On to Richmond, boys!" an officer shouted as the attack started up the gentle slope, and behind the blue-coated infantry a regimental band swung into the tune "John Brown's Body," as though the ghost of that irascible old martyr was personally present to see the two leading regiments, both from Rhode Island, crack the rebel line apart.

More northern troops emerged from the woods behind the advancing Rhode Islanders. Men from New York and New Hampshire joined the attack as the flanking guns jetted clouds of gray white smoke. Swift fan-shaped patterns of compressed gases rippled the long grass under the guns' smoke as the shells seared up the slope. The explosions were mighty, ear splitting, terrible. Some shells, fired too high, crashed through the branches above the Confederate line, scaring birds out of the trees and showering twigs and leaves down onto the bandsmen and chaplains and servants and medical orderlies who crouched in the rear. A regiment of

regular U.S. Army troops marched out from the trees, deployed from column into line, fixed their bayonets, and advanced uphill with the New
Yorkers and New Englanders.

Colonel Evans had galloped back to his line's center where Colonel
Sloan's South Carolinians were crouching at the wood's edge to make
themselves into a difficult target for the enemy artillery. A few rebel skirmishers had advanced beyond the fence and were firing rifles at the
advancing Yankees, but Starbuck, watching from horseback at the trees'
edge, could see no sign that the rifle fire was causing any casualties. The
enemy came steadily on, driven by the music of the distant northern
bands and by the beat of the drummers advancing with the companies
and by the proximity of glorious victory that waited for the attackers at
the hill's crest where the first of Nathan Evans's two ancient cannon had
arrived. The gun was hurriedly unlimbered, turned, then fired a roundshot down the slope. The ball bounced on the turf, soared over the Rhode
Islanders and plunged harmlessly into the trees beyond. A northern shell
exploded short. The sound of the airburst was appalling, as though part of
the fabric of the universe itself had been suddenly cracked in two. The air
became crazy with smoke and sizzling fragments. Starbuck shuddered. The
artillery fire by the stone bridge had been scary, but this was much worse.
These gunners were aiming directly at the Legion and their shells
screeched like demons as they flashed overhead.

"Skirmishers!" Major Bird called in a cracked voice. He tried again,
this time achieving a firmer tone. "Skirmishers! Advance!"

A and K companies, the Legion's two flanking companies, clambered
awkwardly over the fence rails and ran into the pastureland. The men
were encumbered by their rifles, their sheathed bayonets, their bowie
knives and haversacks, and by the canteens, pouches and cap boxes that
hung from their belts. They made a loose formation a hundred paces
ahead of the Legion. Their task was first to deter the enemy skirmishers,
then to snipe at the main line of attackers. The riflemen opened fire,
enveloping each kneeling marksman in a small cloud of smoke. Sergeant
Truslow walked from man to man, while Captain Roswell Jenkins, still on
horseback, fired his revolver at the distant northerners.

"Make sure your weapons are loaded!" Major Bird called to the
remaining eight companies. It seemed slightly late to remember such
advice, but nothing seemed real this morning. Thaddeus Bird, schoolmaster, was commanding a regiment in battle? He giggled at the thought and
earned a disapproving look from Sergeant Major Proctor. The Yankees
were still five hundred paces away, but coming on at a smart pace now.
The northern officers carried drawn swords. Some carried the blades
upright in a stiff attempt at formal dignity, while others slashed at dande-
lions and thistles as though they were out on a Sunday afternoon stroll. A

few were mounted on nervous horses. One horse, scared by the gunfire, had gone out of control and was bolting with its rider across the face of the northern attack.

Starbuck, dry mouthed and apprehensive, remembered that his Savage pistol, which he had earlier returned to Colonel Faulconer and only just retrieved, was still unloaded. He pulled the heavy gun from its long clumsy holster, then released the cylinder lock to expose the empty chambers. He took six paper-wrapped cartridges from the pouch on his belt. Each cartridge contained a conical bullet and its powder charge. He bit the bullet off the first cartridge, tasting the bitter salty gunpowder on his tongue, then carefully poured the powder into one of the cylinder's chambers. Pocahontas, bitten by a horsefly, suddenly whinnied and shifted sideways, causing Starbuck to spill some of the powder onto his saddle.

He swore at the horse, which meant that the bullet in his lips slipped free, bounced on the saddle pommel and fell into the grass. He swore again, tipped the powder from the chamber, and bit off a fresh bullet. This time, as he began to pour the charge, he found his hand was shaking and there seemed to be two chambers under the lip of the torn paper instead of one. His sight was blurred, then he realized his hand was shaking uncontrollably.

He looked up at the advancing enemy. Above them, oddly clear in his otherwise smeared eyesight, was the Stars and Stripes, his own flag, and suddenly Starbuck knew that there were no easy decisions, no turnings in life that could be taken flippantly. He gazed at the distant flag and knew he could not fire on it. His great-grandfather MacPhail had lost an eye on Breed's Hill and later, fighting under Paul Revere at Penobscot Bay, had lost his right hand in the defense of that good flag, and suddenly Starbuck felt a catch in his throat. God, he thought, but I should not be here! None of us should be here! He suddenly understood all Adam's objections to the war, all Adam's unhappiness that this glorious country should find itself riven by battle, and he gazed longingly at the distant flag and was unaware of the first Yankee skirmishers' bullets whipping hard overhead, or of the shell that exploded just short of the fence, or of the hoarse shouts as the Rhode Island sergeants shouted at their men to keep their lines straight as they advanced. Starbuck was oblivious to it all as he sat in the saddle, shaken, his trembling hand dribbling gunpowder down his thigh.

"Are you all right?" Adam joined him.

"Not really."

"Now you understand, do you?" Adam asked grimly.

"Yes." Starbuck's hands trembled as he closed up the still-unloaded revolver. His whole life suddenly seemed trivial, wasted, gone to hell. He had thought this morning that war would prove a fine adventure, a defiance to toss into his father's face and an adventure story to describe to Sally, but instead it was proving to be something much more terrible and unexpected, as though a curtain in a frippery theater had lifted to reveal a glimpse of hell's horrors seething with twisted flames. My God, he thought, but I could die here. I could be buried at this wood's edge. "It was a girl," he blurted out.

"Girl?" Adam frowned with incomprehension.

"In Richmond."

"Oh." Adam was embarrassed by Starbuck's admission, but also troubled by it. "Father guessed as much," he said, "but I don't understand why you risk everything for ..." He stopped, maybe because he could not find the right words, or perhaps because a shell had smashed into a tree trunk and ripped a chunk of bright timber clean out of the wood and filled the shadows with its filthy sulfur-laden smoke. Adam licked his lips. "I'm thirsty."

"And me." Starbuck wondered why he had blurted out his confession. The Yankees were coming stolidly on. In minutes, he thought, just minutes, we have to fight. All the posturing and defiance has come to this warm meadow. He watched a northern officer stumble, drop his sword and fall to his knees in the grass. An enemy skirmisher ran forward five paces, knelt to take aim, then realized he had left his ramrod behind and went back to find it in the long grass. A riderless horse cantered across the slope. The drummers' rhythm was more ragged, but still the northerners came on. A bullet whistled close by Starbuck's head. One of the northern bands was playing "The Star-Spangled Banner" and the music prickled at Starbuck's eyes and conscience. "Do you not think about girls?" he asked Adam.

"No." Adam seemed not to be concentrating on the conversation but was staring down the slope. "Never." His fingers were twitching on the reins.

"Are you certain you two should be on horseback?" Major Bird strode over to join Adam and Starbuck. "I'd hate to lose you. You heard that young Sparrow died?" He asked this question of Starbuck.

"I saw his body, yes."

"He should have stayed at home with his mother," Major Bird said. His right hand was clawing at his beard, betraying his nerves. "Blanche was ridiculously overprotective of that boy, as I discovered when I insisted he was ready to imbibe logarithms. Oh, Christ!" Major Bird's imprecation was caused by a sudden volley loosed by the neighboring South Carolinians who were firing over the heads of their own skirmishers. "Actually he mastered logs very quickly," Bird went on, "and he was by far my best pupil for construing Greek. A clever boy, but prone to tears. Highly strung, you see? A waste though, a terrible waste. Why doesn't war take the illiterates first?"

A fresh artillery battery on the enemy's right wing had opened fire and one of its shells struck the slope a hundred paces in front of the Legion and ricocheted up into the trees. Starbuck heard the missile rip through the branches overhead. A second shell plunged into the ground close to the skirmish line and there exploded underground to heave the red soil up in a sudden eruption of brown smoke. Some of the skirmishers edged backward.

"Stand still!" Truslow bellowed, and not only the skirmishers, but the Legion's other eight companies froze like rabbits faced by a wildcat. The eight companies at the trees' edge were in two ranks, the formation suggested by the drill books that Major Pelham and Colonel Faulconer had used in the Legion's training. The books were American translations of French infantry manuals and recommended that riflemen open fire at long range, then sprint forward to finish off the enemy with bayonet thrusts. Major Bird, who had assiduously studied the manuals, believed they were nonsense. In practice the Legion had never proved accurate when firing their rifles at more than one hundred paces, and Bird did not understand how they were supposed to shake an enemy's composure with ill-aimed fire at twice that distance followed by a clumsy charge into the teeth of hostile artillery and rifle fire. The Colonel's airy answer had always been that the men's natural belligerence would overcome the tactical difficulties, but to Major Bird that seemed a problematical and overoptimistic solution.

"Permission to open fire?" Captain Murphy shouted from Company D.

"Hold your fire!" Bird had his own opinions about infantry fire. He was convinced that the first volley was the most destructive and should be saved until the enemy was close at hand. He accepted that he had no experience to bolster that opinion, which clashed with the professional doctrine that was taught at West Point and that had been tested in the war against Mexico, but Major Bird refused to believe that soldiering demanded that he entirely suspend the exercise of his intelligence, and so he looked forward to this morning's test of his theory. Indeed, as he watched the blue-coated ranks advance toward him through the patches of gunsmoke that hung above the meadow, he found himself hoping that Colonel Faulconer did not suddenly reappear to take back the Legion's command. Major Thaddeus Bird, against all his expectations, was beginning to enjoy himself.

"Time to open fire, Uncle?" Adam suggested.

"I'd like to wait, in fact I will wait."

The Yankees' attacking line was losing its order as the attackers paused to fire and reload, then hurried on again. The minié bullets from

the southern skirmishers were causing casualties, and the small round-
shots of the two southern guns were slapping horribly through the attackers' files to slash quick bloody swathes on the grass and leave wounded
men screaming and writhing in agony. The Yankee skirmishers were snip-
ing at their Confederate opposites, but the battle of skirmishers was a
sideshow, a mere sop to military theory that insisted that light infantry
range ahead of an attack to weaken the defenders with a galling fire. The
main northern attack was coming on too fast and in too much force to
need the help of a skirmish line.

Much of the northern artillery had become unsighted by their own
men and had fallen silent, though their howitzers, which fired their missiles high into the air, still lobbed shells over the attackers' files. Evans's
two guns carried on firing, but Starbuck noted a change in the sound the
guns were making and realized they must have changed their ammunition
to canister. Canister was a cylindrical tin crammed with musket bullets
that burst open at the cannon's muzzle to hurl a spreading cone of bullets
at the enemy, and Starbuck could see the effect of the tin cans by the
groups of wounded and dead men snatched backward onto the turf from
the attackers' lines. Drummers were still beating the attack onward and
the northerners were cheering as they advanced, their voices enthusiastic,
almost cheerful, as if this whole performance were a sporting contest. The
closest American flag was lavishly fringed with gold tassels and so heavy
that the standard bearer seemed to wade forward as though he walked in
water. The regiment of regular soldiers had caught up with the attack's
front line and now hurried forward with fixed bayonets for the honor of
being the first federal soldiers to break into the rebel defense.

"Fire!" a South Carolinian officer called, and the gray-coated infantry
fired a second volley. A ramrod wheeled through the air as the dirty bank
of smoke rolled away from the muskets. The Faulconer Legion's skirmishers were falling back to the regiment's flanks. The Rhode Islanders' bayonets looked wickedly long in the smoke-torn sunlight.

"Take aim!" Major Bird shouted, and the Legion's rifles went into
their shoulders.

"Keep your aim low! Keep it low!" Sergeant Truslow shouted from the
left flank.

"Aim for the officers!" Captain Hinton, falling back with his skirmishers, shouted.

Starbuck just stared. He could hear a northern officer shouting his
men forward. "On, on, on!" The man had long red side-whiskers and
gold-rimmed spectacles. "On! On!" Starbuck could now see the individ-
ual characters of the northern faces. The men's mouths opened as they
shouted, their eyes were wide. A man stumbled, almost dropped his rifle,
then regained his balance. The attackers were past the first dead bodies

left by the skirmishers. A gold-braided officer mounted on a gray horse dropped his sword to point it straight at the rebels. "Charge!" he shouted, and the attack line quickened into a stumbling run. The northerners were cheering as they came and the drummers lost all cohesion, simply beating their stricks in a frenzy of effort. A fallen color was picked up, its glorious silk stripes a dazzling patch of color in the gray smoke. "Charge!" the northern officer shouted again, and his horse pranced in the gunsmoke's skeins.

"Fire!" Major Bird screamed, then whooped with unfeigned glee as the Legion's whole front disappeared in a gout of filthy smoke.

The fusillade was like the crack of doom at the world's end. It was one sudden, violent, horrifying volley at lethally short range and the shouts and drumming of the attacking northerners were wiped into instant silence, or rather transmuted into screams and shouts.

"Reload!" Murphy shouted.

Nothing could be seen through the bank of powder smoke that twisted above the rail fence. A few enemy bullets whipped through the smoke, but too high. The Legion reloaded, ramming their minié bullets hard down onto powder and wadding.

"Forward!" Major Bird was shouting. "Take them forward! To the fence, to the fence!" He was jumping up and down with excitement and waving his unloaded revolver. "Forward! Forward!"

Starbuck, still lost in a daze, began to load his revolver again. He was not sure why he did it, or whether he could ever use the weapon, but he just wanted to be doing something, and so he fumbled the powder and bullets into the Savage's six chambers, then smeared the bullet cones with grease to seal each chamber and thus prevent the ignited powder in the firing chamber setting off the other charges. His hands still shook. In his mind's eye he could still see that gorgeous banner, all shining red and white, being lifted from the blood-streaked grass to wave again in the sunlight.

"Fire!" Sergeant Truslow shouted from the flank.

"Kill the bastards! Kill the bastards!" That was Major Bird who, only an hour before, had been ridiculing the idea that he wanted to be involved in the day's fighting.

"Aim low! Aim at the bastards' bellies!" That was Captain Murphy, who had abandoned his horse and was firing a rifle like his men. The smoke of the first volley thinned to show that the Yankee officer's gray horse was down in the grass. There were bodies there, puffs of smoke, knots of men.

Adam stayed back at the tree line with Starbuck. He was breathing hard, as though he had just run a race. One of Evans's small smoothbore cannon fired a barrel of canister down the meadow. A northern shell whistled fragments above the Legion's color party. A man reeled back from G Company, blood soaking his left shoulder. He leaned against a tree, breathing hard, and a bullet slapped into the trunk just above his head. The man cursed and pushed himself upright, then stumbled back toward the gun line. Adam, seeing the man's resolve, pulled his revolver from his holster and urged his horse forward.

"Adam!" Starbuck called, remembering his promise to Miriam Faulconer to keep Adam safe, but it was too late. Adam had taken his horse through the bank of bitter gunsmoke, over the fallen fence rails and into the smoke-free air where he was now calmly priming his revolver's chambers with percussion caps in apparent oblivion of the bullets that whipcracked around him. Some of the Legion's men shouted warnings that a man on a horse made a much choicer target than a foot soldier, but Adam ignored them.

Instead he leveled the revolver and fired its full cylinder into the enemy's bank of smoke. He looked almost happy. "Forward! Forward!" he shouted to no one in particular, but a dozen men of the Legion responded by advancing. They knelt close to Adam's horse and fired blindly at the scattered enemy. The Legion's first, overwhelming volley had torn the attackers into small groups of blue-uniformed men who stood in a crude line to exchange shots with the gray-clad southerners. The soldiers' lips were stained by black powder from biting cartridges and their faces were wild with fear or with rage or with excitement. Adam, his revolver empty, was laughing. Everything was in chaos, nothing but a whirl of smoke and stabbing flame and men screaming defiance. A second line of attackers was advancing up the slope behind the ravaged enemy front line.

"Forward!" Major Bird shouted, and groups of men darted a few paces forward, and the enemy edged a few paces backward. Starbuck had joined Adam and was spilling percussion caps from his right hand as he tried to prime the Savage's six cones. Beside him a man knelt and fired, stood up and reloaded. The man was muttering swear words at the northerners, cursing their mothers and their children, cursing their past and all their short futures. A Rhode Island officer waved his sword, urging his men on, and a bullet thumped into his belly, bending him over. Sergeant Truslow, grim-faced and silent, was loading his gun with buck and ball, a combination of a round bullet with three smaller buckshots that achieved something of a shotgun effect. He did not fire the charge blindly, but carefully sought a target then fired deliberately, making sure of his aim.

"Go home! Go home!" Adam was shouting at the northerners, the apparently mild words made almost ludicrous by the note of excitement in his voice. He leveled his revolver again, pulled the trigger, but either he had misloaded or forgotten to prime the gun, for nothing happened, but he went on pulling the trigger as he screamed at the invaders to go home. Starbuck, beside his friend, seemed unable to shoot at the flag he had known all his life.

"Come on, boys! Come on!" The shout came from the far right of the Confederate line where Starbuck saw the gaudily uniformed Louisiana Zouaves charging out of the powder smoke to carry their bayonet-tipped rifles at the enemy. Some of the Louisianans whirled bowie knives as huge as cutlasses. They advanced raggedly, screaming a terrible high-pitched scream that made Starbuck's blood run cold. My God, he thought, but the Zouaves would all be cut down, shot in the open field, but instead the northerners edged back and still farther back, and suddenly the Louisiana infantry were among the blue-coated skirmishers and the northerners were running for their lives. A bowie knife sliced round and a man fell with his skull streaming blood. Another northern skirmisher was pinned to the ground with a bayonet as the whole center of the federal attack line stumbled backward from the bloody Zouave attack, then the rearward movement became a sudden rout as the northerners fled to avoid the heavy blades. But there was only a handful of Louisiana infantry, and their flanks were open to fire, and suddenly a northern volley smashed into their ranks. Colonel Wheat went down, his baggy red shirt soaked with blood.

The Louisianans, hugely outnumbered, came to a halt as their enemies' bullets drove into them. Their gaudy bodies twitched as the bullets struck, but their mad charge had hurled the heart of the Yankee line a good hundred paces back down the hill. But now it was the Zouaves' turn to go backward and to carry their wounded Colonel toward the trees.

"Fire!" a southern artilleryman shouted and one of the smoothbore cannon belched a belly of canister at the northerners.

"Fire!" Major Bird shouted, and a score of Legion rifles crashed smoke and flame. A boy from Company D rammed a bullet onto a barrel already crammed with three charges of powder and bullets. He pulled the trigger, did not seem to notice that the gun had not fired, and started loading the musket yet again.

"Fire!" Nathan Evans screamed, and the South Carolinians smashed a volley across the fence, and in the pastureland the Rhode Islanders shuffled back to leave their dead and wounded bleeding in the grass.

"Fire!" A Louisiana chaplain, his Bible forgotten, emptied his revolver at the Yankees, pulling the trigger until the hammer fell on empty chambers, yet still he went on pulling, his face a rictus of exaltation.

"Fire!" Truslow shouted at his men. A sixteen-year-old screamed when a cartridge load of powder exploded in his face as he poured it into the hot barrel of his rifle. Robert Decker fired a shotgun into the smoke cloud. The grass of the meadow was flickering with small fires started by

the burning wads from the rifle barrels. An injured man crawled back
toward the tree line, attempted to clamber over the clutter of fallen fence
rails, and there collapsed. His body seemed to shiver, then was still. An
officer's horse lay dead, its body shuddering as northern bullets thudded
home, but the Yankee fire was sporadic as the Rhode Islanders, too frightened to stand still and reload properly, stepped backward. The rebels
screamed defiance and spat bullets into hot barrels, rammed the charges
hard home, pulled their triggers, then started the process again. Starbuck
watched the Legion fight its first battle and was struck by the atmosphere
of glee, of sheer release, of carnival enjoyment. Even their soldiers'
screams sounded to Starbuck like the mad whoops of overexcited children. Groups of men were darting forward, emulating the Zouaves'
charge, and driving the demoralized Rhode Islanders farther back down
the long slope where the first Yankee charge had been stopped cold.

Yet a second Yankee attack line was already halfway up the slope and
still more northern troops were coming from the Sudley Road. A U.S.
Marine regiment was there, together with three fresh regiments of New
York volunteers. More field guns appeared, and the first Yankee cavalry
galloped off to the left of their line as the fresh northern infantry marched
stoically into the open land to reinforce the ragged remnants of the first
attack, which had retreated two hundred paces back from the litter of
bodies and the line of slick bloody grass and scorched turf that marked
the high-tide line of their first failed assault.

"Form line! Form line!" The shout started somewhere in the center of
the Confederate formation, and somehow enough sane officers and
sergeants heard the order and echoed it, and slowly the screaming, maddened rebels were brought back to the fence line. They were grinning and
laughing, full of pride for what they had done. Every now and then a man
would whoop for no apparent reason, or else a man might turn around to
blast a bullet at the stalled northern attack. Insults were hurled down the
long slope.

"Go back to your mothers, Yankees!"

"Send some real men next time!"

"So how do you like a Virginia welcome, you yellow bastards!"

"Silence!" Major Bird shouted. "Silence!"

Someone began laughing, a hysterical mad laugh. Someone else
cheered. At the foot of the slope the northern guns opened fire again,
screaming their shells up to the ridge to blast apart in dark-flamed smoke.
The short-barreled northern howitzers had never ceased to fire, lobbing
spherical case shot high over the Rhode Islanders and New Yorkers to
crash raggedly about the edge of the woods.

"Back to the trees! Back to the trees!" The order was repeated down
the rebel line and the southerners retreated back into the shadows. In

front of them, where the powder smoke cleared slowly from the burnt
grass, a handful of bodies lay on either side of the remnants of rail fence
while beyond the fence, in the brighter sunlight, a scattering of dead
northerners was sprawled in the pasture. The officer with red side-
whiskers lay there with his mouth open and his gold-rimmed spectacles
half-fallen off his face. A crow flapped down to land near the man's body.
A wounded northerner pulled himself toward the trees, asking for water,
but no one in the Legion had any water. They had emptied their canteens
and now the sun was beating hotter and their mouths were dried by the
saltpeter in the gunpowder, but there was no water, and ahead of them
were yet more Yankees coming from the far trees to reignite the attack.

"We'll do it to them again, boys! We'll do it to them again!" Major
Bird shouted, and even though the chaos of the Legion's first fight had
not given him a chance to fully test his theory of musketry, he suddenly
knew he had achieved something far more valuable; he had discovered an
activity he utterly enjoyed. For all of his adult life Thaddeus Bird had
been faced with the classic dilemma of a poor relation, which was
whether to show an eternal deferential gratitude or to demonstrate an
independency of mind by cultivating a prickly opposition to every prevailing orthodoxy, which latter course had pleased Bird until, in the
smoke and excitement of battle, there had been no need to posture. Now
he paced behind his men, watching the new northern attack take shape,
and felt strangely content. "Load your guns," he called in a firm voice,
"but hold your fire! Load your guns, but hold your fire."

"Go for their bellies, boys," Murphy called aloud. "Put them down
hard and the rest will go home."

Adam, like his uncle, also felt as though a great weight had gone from
his soul. The awful noise of the battle spelt the death of all that he had
worked for in the months since Lincoln's election, but the terrible sound
also meant that Adam was no longer concerned with the great issues of
war and peace, of slavery and emancipation, of states' rights and Christian
principle, but only with being a good neighbor to the men who had volunteered to serve his father. Adam even began to understand his father, who
had never agonized over morality or wanted to weigh up the balance of his
actions in an earnest attempt to guarantee a favorable verdict on the Day
of Judgment. Once, when Adam had asked his father about the principles
by which he lived his life, Washington Faulconer had simply laughed the
question away. "You know your trouble? You think too much. I've never
known a happy man who thought too much. Thinking just complicates
affairs. Life's like jumping a bad fence on a good horse, the more responsibility you leave to the horse the safer you'll be, and the more you leave to
life the happier you are. Worrying about principles is schoolmaster's talk.
You'll just find you sleep better if you treat people naturally. It ain't prin-

ciple, just practicality. I never could stand listening to cant about principle. Just be yourself!" And Adam, in the sudden splintering chaos of a fire-
fight, had at last trusted the horse to take the jump, and discovered that all
his agony of conscience had evaporated in the simple pleasure of doing his
duty. Adam, in a meadow whipsawed by fire, had behaved well. He might
have lost the battle for his country, but he had won the war in his soul.

"Load your guns! Hold your fire!" Major Bird walked slowly behind
the Legion's companies, watching the Yankee horde gather for its next
attempt. "Shoot low when they come, boys, shoot low! And well done,
all of you, well done."

The Legion, in just five minutes, had become soldiers.

"Hey, you!" The voice shouted at Ethan Ridley from the top of the central wig-wag tower. "You! Yes, you! Are you a staff officer?"

Ridley, who had been lost in thought as he galloped his horse southward, reined in. Ridley suspected that being one of Washington
Faulconer's aides was not what the signal officer meant by a staff officer,
but Ridley was quick-witted enough to realize he needed some excuse to
be galloping alone in the rear areas of the Confederate army and so he
shouted the affirmative. "Yes!"

"Can you find General Beauregard?" The speaker, an officer wearing
captain's bars, clambered down the makeshift ladder. A hand-lettered sign
at the foot of the ladder read "Signalers ONLY" while another, in even
larger letters, read "KEEP OFF." The officer ran across to Ridley and held
up a folded sheet of paper secured by a wafer seal. "Beauregard needs that
quick."

"But ..." Ridley had been about to say he had no idea how to find
General Beauregard, but then decided such a disclaimer would sound odd
from a self-proclaimed staff officer. Besides, Ridley reckoned that Colonel
Faulconer would be wherever the general was, so by finding the Colonel
he would also discover Beauregard.

"I have wig-wagged the message to Beauregard, if that's what you're
about to suggest," the captain said peevishly, "but I'd like to send a written confirmation. You can never be certain a message gets wig-wagged
through, not with the fools they give me to work with. I need good men,
educated men. I wish you'd make that point to Beauregard for me. With
my respects, of course. Half the lunkheads they provide me never learned
to spell, and the other half didn't have brains to begin with. Now go on
with you, there's a good fellow, quick as you can!"

Ridley kicked back his heels. He was in the army's baggage area
where wagons, limbers, portable forges, ambulances and carriages were
parked so tightly that their upturned shafts looked like a winter thicket.
A woman shouted as Ridley galloped past, wanting to know what was

happening, but he just shook his head and spurred on past cooking fires, past groups of men playing cards and past a child playing with a kitten. What were all these people doing here? he wondered.

He breasted a rise and saw the smoke of battle lying like a river fog in the Bull Run valley to his left. That fog, where the great guns slammed their missiles across the stream, lay around the center and left of the rebel army, while in front of Ridley was the tangle of woods and small pastures that was the Confederate right wing and from where General Beauregard hoped to launch his own attack on the unsuspecting northerners. Colonel Washington Faulconer was somewhere in that tangle and Ridley rested his horse while he tried to make some sense of the landscape. He was tense and angry, fidgeting in his saddle, aware of the enormity of the gamble he was taking, but Ridley would take almost any gamble to fulfill his ambitions. For weeks now Ethan Ridley had played fast and loose with Washington Faulconer's money, but now, as the Legion divided along a line that separated the Colonel's admirers from those who despised him, Ridley would make his choice. He would side whole-heartedly with the Colonel and defeat Starbuck and Bird who, aided by Adam's pusillanimity, had forced the Legion to abandon its obedience to Faulconer.

The reward of loyalty was money, and money was Ridley's god. He had watched his father impoverish a family and seen the pity on his neighbors' faces. He had endured his half-brother's condescension just as he endured Anna Faulconer's cloying attentions, and all because he was poor. He was patronized for his skill with a pencil and paintbrush, as though he could always earn his living as a portrait painter or as an illustrator, but he had no more wish to earn his living as a painter than as a coal heaver or as a lawyer. Instead he wanted to be like Faulconer, to be the possessor of wide acres and fast horses and of a mistress in Richmond and a fine big country house. Of late, since Adam's return, Ridley had doubted that even being Faulconer's son-in-law would be enough to secure an adequate share of the Faulconer wealth, but now the god of battle had played into Ridley's hands. Colonel Washington Faulconer had left one firm order—that the Legion was to ignore Nathan Evans, and Ridley's rivals for the Colonel's gratitude had combined to disobey that order. It was time to betray that disobedience.

But first Ridley had to find Colonel Faulconer, which meant discovering General Beauregard, and so he spurred down from the hill into the undulating landscape of deep woods and small pastures. His horse cleared two fences, running as gamely as though she were following the hounds in the winter hills. He swerved left into a wide path that led under trees where a regiment of southern Zouaves in their distinctive red pantaloons and baggy shirts lolled at their ease. "What's happening?" one of the Zouaves shouted at Ridley.

"We whipping the bastards?" a sergeant called.

"You looking for us?" An officer ran into Ridley's path.

"I'm looking for Beauregard." Ridley curbed his horse. "You know where he is?"

"Go to the end of the wood, turn left, there's a road in your front, and like as not that's where he is. He was there a half hour ago, anyways. You got any news?"

Ridley had no news, so just cantered on, turning left to see a horde of infantrymen resting beside the road at the far end of the clearing. The soldiers were in blue coats and for a second Ridley feared he had galloped clean into the Yankee lines, then he saw the triple-striped Confederate flag over the troops and realized they were southerners in makeshift uniforms of northern blue. "Do you know where the general is?" he called to a blue-coated officer, but the officer just shrugged, then pointed a helpful hand vaguely to the north and east. "Last I heard he was at a farmhouse thataway, but don't ask me where the hell that is."

"He was here," a sergeant offered, "but he ain't here now. You know what's happening, mister? Are we whipping the sumbitches?"

"I don't know." Ridley carried on, coming at last to an artillery battery that was comfortably ensconced on the southern bank of the Bull Run behind a breastwork of wicker baskets filled with dirt.

"This here's Balls Ford," an artillery lieutenant said, taking a pipe from his mouth, "and the general sure was here an hour ago. Can you tell us what's happening out there?" He gestured westward from where the sound of cannon fire grumbled and crackled in the sultry air.

"No."

"Making enough noise about it, ain't they? I thought the war was being held over here, not over there?"

Ridley crossed Balls Ford to the enemy side of the Bull Run. The water came up to his horse's belly, making Ridley lift his boots and stirrups above the quick flow. A company of Virginian infantry lay in the shade on the far bank, waiting for orders. "You know what's happening?" a captain asked.

"No."

"Nor me. An hour back they said as we should wait here, but no one said why. I kind of think we're forgotten."

"Have you seen the general?"

"I ain't seen anything above a major for three hours now. But a sutler said as how we're attacking, mister, so maybe all the generals are that way." The man pointed north.

Ridley rode northward under tall trees, going slow so that his sweating horse did not break a leg in one of the savage ruts cut into the dirt road by artillery wheels. A quarter mile beyond the ford at the edge of a

trampled cornfield Ridley found a battery of heavy twelve-pounder cannon. The guns had been unlimbered and deployed to point their lethal
barrels across the growing corn, but the battery commander had no idea
why he was there or what he was expected to see emerge from the dark
green woods at the farther side of the cornfield. "You know what's making
all that damned noise?" The artillery major gestured toward the west.

"They seem to be firing at each other over the stream," Ridley said.

"I wish they'd give me something to fire at, because I don't know
what in hell's name I'm doing here." He gestured at the cornfield as
though it were the dark heart of equatorial Africa. "You're looking at
Beauregard's big attack, Captain. Trouble is there ain't no enemy here,
nor anyone else. Except maybe some boys from Mississippi who went up
the road a while, and God only knows what they're doing."

Ridley wiped the sweat off his face, pulled his slouch hat back on, and
spurred his tired horse up the road. He found the Mississippi infantry
sheltering under a break of trees. One of their officers, a major whose
accent was so thick Ridley could scarce understand him, said that the
Confederate advance had come to a halt here, under these cedar trees,
and he was not all of a piece sure why, but he was certain, or at least as
certain as a man from Rolling Forks could ever be certain, and that was
not altogether certain, but it was pretty certain, that General Beauregard
had gone back to the other side of the Bull Run, but by a different ford. A
ford farther to the east. Or maybe it was farther west. "So do you know
what's happening?" the Major asked before taking a bite out of a green
apple.

"No," Ridley confessed.

"Nor me!" The Major had a fine feather in his hat, a curved saber and
a lavish mustache that had been oiled into sleek elegance. "If you find
anyone who does know just what they're doing, mister, then you tell 'em
that Jeremiah Colby is right well eager to get this war over and done
with. Good luck to you, mister! Fine apples you boys grow here!"

Ridley turned his horse and rode back to the stream, then began
quartering the country between the Bull Run and the railroad. The guns
thundered in the distance, their bass sound punctuated by the brushfire
sound of rifles and muskets. The noise lent urgency to Ridley's quest,
except he had no idea how to expedite the urgency. The general, his staff
and hangers-on seemed to have been swallowed into this warm huge
countryside. He stopped his tired horse at a crossroads beside a small
wooden cabin. The vegetables in its trim garden had been torn out, all
but for a row of unripe squash. An elderly Negress, smoking a pipe,
watched him warily from her cabin door. "Ain't nothing to steal, massa,"
she said.

"You know where the general is?" Ridley asked her.

"Ain't nothing to steal, massa, all stolen already."

"Stupid cuffee bitch," Ridley said, then louder and slower, as though he were talking to a child. "Do you know where the general is?"

"All stolen already, massa."

"And damn you, too." A shell screamed far overhead, tumbling and wailing as it shrieked across an empty Sunday sky. Ridley swore at the woman again, then chose one of the roads at random and let his weary horse walk at its own slow pace. Dust drifted from the mare's hooves onto a drunken soldier sleeping beside the road. A few paces farther on a black and white farm dog lay dead in the road, shot in the head by some soldier who had presumably resented the dog worrying his horse. Ridley passed the dog by and began to worry that perhaps Beauregard, and Faulconer with him, had ridden north and west to where the battle sounded, for surely no general could stay in this somnolent, buzzing countryside while his men were dying just three miles away? Then, as his horse cleared the margin of a grove of trees, he saw another of the strange lattice signal towers standing beside a farmhouse, and beneath the tower a huddle of horses picketed by the farm's fence, and on the farm's verandah a group of men glinting with gold braid, and so Ridley gave his horse spurs, but, just as he kicked her into reluctant speed, so a single horseman mounted a tall black horse in front of the farm and galloped hard down the drive toward him. It was the Colonel.

"Sir! Colonel Faulconer!" Ridley had to shout to get the Colonel's attention. Washington Faulconer would otherwise have galloped clean past Ridley.

The Colonel glanced at the tired horseman, recognized Ridley, and slowed. "Ethan! It is you! Come with me! What on earth are you doing here? Never mind! I've got good news, wonderful news!"

The Colonel had spent a frustrating morning. He had discovered Beauregard shortly after six o'clock, but the General had not been expecting him and had no time to see him, and so Faulconer had been forced to cool his heels as the hours dragged by. Yet now, wondrously, he had received the orders he had craved. Beauregard, desperate to vivify his attack that had mysteriously stalled in the vacant countryside across the Run, had appealed for fresh troops and Faulconer had seen his chance. He had volunteered the Legion and received orders to march the men across to the right wing. General Johnston's newly arrived men from the Army of the Shenandoah could be left to buttress the rebel left wing, while Beauregard put new impetus into the right. "We need some enthusiasm," Beauregard had grumbled to Faulconer, "some push. It's no good playing kitty-bender on a battlefield, you have to show 'em a touch of whip and spurs." It was all Faulconer wanted; a chance to lead his Legion into a battle-winning charge that would write another glorious page of Virginia history.

"Come on, Ethan!" Washington Faulconer now called back. "We've got permission to attack!"

"But they've gone!" Ridley shouted. His tired horse was much slower than the Colonel's well-rested stallion, Saratoga.

The Colonel curbed Saratoga in, turned him and stared at Ridley.

"They've gone, sir." Ridley said. "That's what I came to tell you."

The Colonel swatted at a fly with his riding crop. "What do you mean, gone?" He sounded very calm, as if he had not understood the news Ridley had just fetched across the battleground.

"It was Starbuck," Ridley said. "He came back, sir."

"He came back?" the Colonel asked, incredulous.

"He claimed to have orders from Evans."

"Evans!" Faulconer pronounced that name sulfurously.

"So they marched off to Sudley, sir."

"Starbuck brought orders? What the hell did Pecker do?"

"He ordered the men to Sudley, sir."

"Under that ape Evans's command?" The Colonel shouted the question and his horse, unsettled, whinnied softly.

"Yes, sir," Ridley felt the satisfaction of delivering damning news. "That's why I came to find you."

"But there's no damned battle at Sudley! That's a feint! A lure! The General knows all about that!" The Colonel was goaded into a sudden and incandescent fury. "The battle will be here! Christ! On this side of the field! Here!" The Colonel slashed down with his riding crop, whistling the air and frightening an already nervous Saratoga. "But what about Adam? I told him not to let Pecker do anything irresponsible."

"Adam let himself be persuaded by Starbuck, sir." Ethan paused to shake his head. "I opposed them, sir, but I'm only a captain. Nothing more."

"You're a major now, Ethan. You can take Pecker's place. Goddamn Pecker, and goddamn Starbuck! Damn him, damn him, damn him! I'll kill him! I'll feed his guts to the hogs! Now come on, Ethan, come on!" The Colonel slashed his spurs back.

Major Ridley, following as fast as he could, suddenly remembered the wig-wagger's message for Beauregard. He pulled the wafer-sealed paper from his pocket and wondered whether he should mention its existence to the Colonel, but the Colonel was already pounding ahead, his horse kicking up dust, and Ridley did not want to be left too far behind, not now that he was a major and the Colonel's second in command, and so he threw the message away, then galloped after the Colonel toward the sound of the guns.

On the tree-lined crest where Evans's scratch brigade had repelled the first northern attack the battle had become a grim one-sided pounding

match. For the Yankee gunners it was little more than a session of unopposed target practice, for both of the small Confederate cannon had
been destroyed; the first thrown off its carriage by a direct hit from a
twelve-pounder roundshot, while the second had lost a wheel from
another plumb hit and, within minutes, another twelve-pound ball had
shattered the spokes of its replacement wheel. The two stricken cannon,
still loaded with unfired canister, lay abandoned at the edge of the wood.

Major Bird wondered whether there was anything he should be
doing, but nothing suggested itself. He tried to analyze the situation and
came up with the simple fact that the southern troops were holding off a
far greater number of northerners, but that every moment the southerners
spent at the tree line the more men they lost and that eventually, by a
process as ineluctable as a mathematical equation, there would be no living southerners left and the northerners would march across the rebel
corpses to claim the battle and, presumably, the war. Major Bird could not
stop that happening because there was nothing clever he could do; no
flank attack, no ambush, no manner of out-thinking the enemy. The time
had simply come to fight and die. Major Bird regretted it had come to
such a hopeless plight, but he saw no elegant way out, and so he was
determined to stay where he was. The odd thing was that he felt no fear.
He tried to analyze that lack and decided he was privileged by possessing
a sanguine temperament. He celebrated that happy realization by sneak-
ing a fond look at his wife's picture.

Nor was Adam Faulconer feeling fear. He could not say he was enjoying the morning, but at least the experience of battle had reduced life's
turmoil to simple questions, and Adam was reveling in that freedom. Like
all the other officers, he had abandoned his horse, sending it back among
the trees. The Legion's officers had learned that the enemy's rifle fire was
too high to be of much danger to crouching men, but not so high that the
bullets could miss a man on horseback, and so they had abandoned the
Colonel's precious orders to stay mounted and had become infantrymen.

Nathaniel Starbuck noted how some men like Truslow and, more surprisingly, Major Bird and Adam, seemed effortlessly brave. They went
calmly about their business, stood straight in the face of the enemy, and
kept their wits sharp. Most of the men oscillated wildly between bravery
and timidity, but responded to the leadership of the brave men. Each time
Truslow went forward to shoot at the northerners a dozen skirmishers
went with him, and whenever Major Bird stalked along the line of the
trees the men grinned at him, took heart from him and were pleased that
their eccentric schoolmaster was so apparently unmoved by the dangers.
Harness those middling men, Starbuck understood, and the Legion could
achieve miracles. There was also a minority of men, the cowards, who
huddled far back in the trees, where they pretended to be busy loading or

repairing their guns, but who were in fact just cowering from the eerie whistling sound of the minié bullets and the sizzling crack of the shellfire.

The bullets and shellfire had reduced Nathan Evans's Confederate brigade to a ragged line of men crouched in the shadows at the edge of the trees. Every now and then a group of soldiers would dash to the open ground, fire their shots, then scurry back, but the Yankees now had a horde of skirmishers in the pasture and every appearance of a rebel sparked a bitter flurry of rifle fire. The bravest rebel officers strolled at the wood's margin, speaking encouragement and making small jokes, though Adam, determined to be seen by his father's Legion, refused to walk in the shadow but strolled openly in the sunlight, calling aloud as he strolled to warn men not to fire as he passed in front of their guns. The men shouted at him to take cover, to get back in the trees, but Adam would have none of it. He flaunted himself, as though he believed his life was charmed. He told himself he feared no evil.

Major Bird joined Starbuck and watched Adam in the sunlight. "Do you note," Bird said, "how the bullets are going high?"

"High?"

"They're aiming at him, but are shooting high. I've been noting it."

"So they are." Starbuck would probably not have noticed if the Yankees had been firing at the moon, but now that Thaddeus Bird pointed it out he saw that most of the northern rifle fire was indeed clipping at the leaves above Adam's head. "He's a fool!" Starbuck said angrily. "He just wants to die!"

"He's making up for his father," Bird explained. "Faulconer ought to be here, but he's not, so Adam is sustaining the family honor, though if his father had been here, Adam would probably be having a fit of conscience. I've noticed how Adam usually benefits from Faulconer's absence, haven't you?"

"I promised his mother I'd keep him safe."

Bird yelped with laughter. "More fool you. How are you supposed to do that? Buy him one of those ridiculous iron breastplates that the newspapers advertise?" Bird shook his head. "My sister only charged you with that responsibility, Starbuck, to belittle Adam. I assume he was present?"

"Yes."

"My sister, you understand, married into a family of serpents and has been teaching them the secrets of venom ever since." Bird chuckled. "But Adam is the best of them," he allowed, "the very best. And brave," he added.

"Very," Starbuck said, and felt ashamed of himself, for he had done nothing brave in this morning's clash. The confidence that had so filled him in the railroad depot at Rosskill had evaporated, stolen by the sight of his country's flag. He had still not fired the revolver, nor was he sure that he could shoot at his own countrymen, but neither was he willing to desert his friends within the Legion's ranks. Instead he fidgeted at the wood's edge and watched the far-off gouts of smoke spitting from the Yankee guns. He wanted to describe the smoke to Sally and so he had watched it carefully, seeing that it was white at first and how it darkened rapidly into a grayish blue. Once, gazing intently down the slope, Starbuck had sworn he could see the dark trace of a missile in the smoky air, and seconds later he had heard a shell clatter destructively through the branches overhead. One of the northern guns had been placed beside a hayrick in the farmyard at the bottom of the slope and the flame of the gun's firing had set the hay alight. The flames leaped and curled furiously, pumping a darker smoke into the gun-fouled air.

"Did you hear that poor Jenkins is gone?" Major Bird said in the tone of voice he might have used to remark that the spring was early this year, or that the vegetable crop was looking good.

"Gone?" Starbuck asked, because the imprecision of the word had somehow suggested that Roswell Jenkins had simply walked away from the battlefield.

"Vanished. Hit by a shell. Looks like something left on a butcher's slab." Bird's words were callous, but the tone of his voice was regretful.

"Poor Jenkins." Starbuck had not particularly liked Roswell Jenkins, who had distributed bottles of whiskey to ensure his election as an officer and who had left the running of his company to Sergeant Truslow. "So who'll take over A Company?"

"Whoever my brother-in-law wishes, or rather whoever Truslow wants." Bird laughed, then turned the pecking motion of his head into a rueful shake. "If there's any point in anyone taking over at all? Because maybe there'll be no Legion left?" Bird paused. "Maybe there'll be no Confederacy left?" Bird involuntarily ducked as a shell fragment whipped overhead to smack into a tree just six inches above Starbuck's head. Bird straightened up and took out one of his dark cigars. "You'd like one?"

"Please." Since that night with Belvedere Delaney in Richmond, Starbuck had found himself smoking more and more cigars.

"Do you have any water?" Bird asked as he handed the cigar to Starbuck.

"No."

"We seem to have exhausted our water. Doc Billy wanted some for the wounded, but there isn't any and I can't spare anyone to find more. There's so much we overlooked." A crashing volley of musketry sounded to the north, evidence that more Confederate troops had come into action. Starbuck had seen at least two more southern regiments join the right flank of Nathan Evans's makeshift line, but for every fresh man from Alabama and Mississippi there were at least three northerners, and the reinforced Yankees were sending ever more troops up the slope to lay their weight of rifle fire at the thin-scraped rebel line. "It can't be long now," Major Bird said ruefully, "it can't be long."

A South Carolinian officer came running up the tree line. "Major Bird? Major Bird?"

"Here!" Bird stepped away from Starbuck.

"Colonel Evans wants you all to advance, Major." The South Carolinian had a powder-blackened face, a ripped tunic and bloodshot eyes. His voice was hoarse. "The Colonel's going to sound a bugle call, and he wants us all to make a charge." The man paused as though he knew that he was asking the impossible, then he tried a direct appeal to patriotism. "One last real good charge, Major, for the South."

For a second it looked as if Major Bird would laugh at such a naked appeal to his patriotism, but then he nodded. "Of course."

For the South, one last mad charge, one last defiant gesture.

Before the battle and the cause were lost.

The four companies that Shanks Evans had left guarding the stone bridge were forced away when northerners under a colonel called William Sherman discovered a ford upstream of the bridge and thus outflanked the tiny afterguard. The men fired a ragged volley, then retreated fast as Sherman's men advanced across the Bull Run.

A shell exploded above the abandoned bridge, then a blue-coated officer appeared on its far side and signaled its capture by waving his sword toward the northern gun batteries. "Cease fire!" a battery commander shouted. "Sponge out! Horses up! Look lively now!" The bridge was taken, so now the northern army could pour across the Bull Run and complete the encirclement and destruction of the rebel army.

"It is now safe for you gentlemen to advance to the battery position," Captain James Starbuck announced to the newspapermen, though his announcement was scarcely needed, for groups of excited civilians were already walking or riding toward the captured stone bridge. A congressman waved a smoking cigar at the troops, then stepped aside to let a battery of horse artillery clank and rattle by. "On to Richmond, boys! On to Richmond!" he shouted. "Give the yeller dogs a good whipping, boys! Go on, now!"

A battalion of gray-coated northern infantry followed the horse artillery. The 2nd Wisconsin Regiment wore gray because there had not been enough blue cloth available for their uniforms. "Just hold the good flag high, boys," their colonel had said, "and the good Lord will know we're not rebel scum." Once across the bridge the Wisconsin men swung off the turnpike to march north toward a distant haze of gunsmoke that showed where a stubborn Confederate line still resisted the federal flanking movement. Captain James Starbuck assumed the gray-coated Wisconsin troops would lead the assault on the exposed flank of those rebel defenders, crumpling and destroying them, and thus adding to the God-given victory that the North was enjoying. Almighty God, James thought piously, had been pleased to bless his country on this Lord's Day. God's vengeance had been swift, his justice mighty, and his victory overwhelming, and even the godless foreign military attachés were offering congratulations. "This is exactly what Brigadier General McDowell planned," James said, loyally ascribing God's doings to the northern general. "We anticipated an initial resistance, gentlemen, then a sudden collapse and a progressive destruction of the enemy positions."

The Frenchman, Colonel Lassan, alone seemed sceptical, wondering why there had been so little evidence of any Confederate artillery fire. "Perhaps they are saving their gunfire?" he suggested to James.

"I would rather suggest, sir," James bridled at the Frenchman's scepticism, "that the rebels lack the necessary professional skills to deploy their guns efficiently."

"Ah! That must be it, Captain, indeed."

"They're really farmers, not soldiers. Think of it, Colonel, as a peasants' revolt." James wondered if that was pitching it a bit strong, but anything that denigrated the rebels was music to James Starbuck's ears, and so he not only let the insult stand, but embroidered it. "It is an army of ignorant farmboys led by immoral slave owners."

"So victory is assured?" Lassan asked diffidently.

"Assured, guaranteed!" James felt the burgeoning happiness of a man who sees a difficult endeavor triumphantly concluded, and there was indeed a genuine elation of victory as yet more federal regiments crossed the stone bridge. Three northern divisions were crowding the road as they waited to cross the stream, a dozen bands were playing, women were cheering, the flags were flying, God was in his heaven, Beauregard's flank was turned and the rebellion was being whipsawed into bloody shreds.

And it was still not even midday.

13

"Fix bayonets!" Major Bird shouted the order, then listened as it was echoed out toward the Legion's flanks. The men pulled the heavy, brass-handled sword-bayonets from their scabbards and clicked them over their guns' blackened muzzles. Most of the Legion had never believed they would use the bayonets in an infantry charge, instead, when the war was over and the Yankees had been sent back north, they had thought they would take the bayonets home and use them for pig sticking or hay cutting. Now, though, behind the thinning veil of smoke that hung above the scorched and shattered fence rails, they fixed the bayonets onto the fiercely hot rifle muzzles and tried not to think of what waited in the sunlight.

For a horde of Yankees waited out there—men from Rhode Island, New York and New Hampshire, their volunteer ardor reinforced by the professional fighters from the U.S. Army and Marines. The northern attackers now outnumbered Nathan Evans's men by four to one, yet the Yankee attack had been held for more than an hour by the stubborn southern defense. Those defenders had now been whittled perilously thin and so Evans wanted one last effort to throw the northern attack into chaos and thus buy a few more minutes in which the remainder of the Confederate army could change its alignment to meet the flank attack. Evans would offer one last act of defiance before his rebel line disintegrated and the mighty northern assault rolled irresistibly on.

Major Bird drew his sword. He had still not loaded his Le Mat revolver. He gave the sword an experimental slash, then hoped to God he would not have to use it. To Bird's way of thinking last-ditch bayonet charges belonged in the history books or in romance novels, not in present day actuality, though Bird had to admit the Legion's bayonets looked foully effective. They were long slender blades with a wicked upward curve at their tips. Back in Faulconer County the Colonel had insisted the men practice with their bayonets, and had even hung a cow's carcass from a low branch to make a realistic target, but the carcass had rotted and the men could not be induced to attack it. Now, with the sweat making white channels through the powder stains on their faces, those same men readied themselves for a bout of real bayonet practice.

The northerners, encouraged by the lull in southern rifle fire, began advancing again. A fresh battery of southern artillery had reached the right flank of Evans's line and the newly arrived gunners cracked their canister and roundshot across the face of the federal attack, persuading the northerners to hurry. Three northern bands were now playing in rivalry, driving the heavy fringed flags forward through the smoke wraiths that hung above the meadow that had been so battered by shells and roundshot that the sulfurous stink of the powder smoke was laced with the sweeter smell of new cut hay.

Major Bird looked at his old-fashioned watch, blinked, and looked again. He held the watch to his ear, thinking it must have stopped, yet he could still hear it ticking steadily away. He had somehow thought it was afternoon already, but it was only half past ten. He licked his dry lips, hefted the sword and looked back to the approaching enemy.

The bugle called.

One false note, a pause, then it rang a clean, clear triple of notes, then another triple, a heartbeat's pause, and suddenly the officers and sergeants were shouting at the southern line to get up and go. For a second no one moved, then the gray line at the wood's shell-torn and bullet-stripped edge stirred into life.

"Forward!" Major Bird called, and he walked into the sunlight with his sword held shoulder high and pointing forward. He somewhat spoilt the heroic posture by stumbling as he crossed the fence rails, but he recovered and walked on. Adam had taken command of Company E whose captain, Elisha Burroughs, was dead. Burroughs had been a senior clerk in the Faulconer County Bank who had not really wanted to volunteer for the Legion, but had feared he might jeopardize his advancement in Washington Faulconer's bank if he had refused. Now he was a corpse, his skin darkening and thick with flies, and Adam had taken his place. Adam walked five paces ahead of E Company with his revolver in his right hand and his saber scabbard in his left. He needed to hold the scabbard away from his legs to stop it tripping him. Starbuck, walking alongside Bird, was having the same trouble with his own scabbard.

"I'm not sure it's worth wearing a sword," Bird commented. "I knew the horses were a bad idea, but it seems that swords are an equal encumbrance. My brother-in-law will be disappointed! I sometimes think his dream is to carry a lance into battle." Bird snuffled with laughter at the thought. "Sir Washington Faulconer, Lord of Seven Springs. He'd like that. I never did understand why our Founding Fathers abolished titles. They cost nothing and give fools a great deal of satisfaction. My sister would dearly love to be the Lady Faulconer. Is your revolver loaded?"

"Yes." Though Starbuck had yet to fire a single shot.

"Mine isn't. I keep forgetting." Bird slashed at a dandelion with his sword. To his right Company E was advancing in good order. At least two of the company's men had slung their rifles and were carrying their long bowie knives instead. Butchers' knives, Thaddeus Bird liked to call them, but the long ungainly blades seemed appropriate enough for this desperate venture. Northern bullets made their odd whistle as they whipped past in the warm air. The Legion's colors twitched as bullets slapped and tugged at the cloth. "Notice how the Yankees are still firing high?" Bird commented.

"Thank God for that," Starbuck said.

The bugle sounded again, urging the rebel line on, and Bird gestured with his sword to encourage the Legion to go faster. The men half-ran and half-walked. Starbuck skirted a patch of smoking earth littered with shell fragments where a mutilated skirmisher lay dead. The shell had ripped out most of the man's belly and half his rib cage, and what was left of him was thick with flies. The corpse had prominent teeth in a face that was already turning black in the heat. "I think that was George Musgrave," Bird said conversationally.

"How could you tell?" Starbuck managed to ask.

"Those rodent teeth. He was a wretched boy. A bully. I wish I could say I'm sorry to see him dead, but I'm not. I've wished him dead a hundred times in the past. A nasty piece of work."

A man in Company A was hit by a bullet and began uttering a succession of panting screams. Two men ran to help him. "Leave him be!" Sergeant Truslow snapped and the wounded man was left writhing on the grass. The Legion's bandsmen, sheltering at the edge of the wood, were the stretcher bearers, and two of them came hesitantly forward to collect the injured soldier.

A howitzer shell screamed down to bury itself in the meadow. It exploded, and was immediately followed by another shell. The northern infantry had stopped their steady advance and were reloading their rifles. Starbuck could see the ramrods rising and falling, and could see the powder-stained faces glancing up from the weapons to eye the approaching rebel line. There seemed so few southerners in the attack, and so many northerners waiting for them. Starbuck forced himself to walk calmly, to show no fear. Funny, he thought, but at this moment his family would be taking their pew in the tall, dark church and his father would be in the vestry, praying, and the congregation would be shuffling out of the sunlight, their pew doors clicking and creaking open beneath the high windows that were left open in the summertime so that the breezes from Boston harbor might cool the worshipers. The stink of horse manure in the street would permeate the church where his mother would be pretending to read her Bible, though in truth her attention would be solely on the gathering congregation; who was present and who absent, who looked well and who queer. Starbuck's older sister, Ellen Marjory, betrothed to her minister, would be ostentatiously displaying her piety by praying or by reading the Scripture, while fifteen-year-old Martha would be catching the eyes of the boys in the Williamses' box across the aisle. Starbuck wondered if Sammy Williams was among the blue-coated enemy waiting three hundred yards away in this Virginian meadow. He wondered where James was, and had a sudden pang as he thought of the possibility of his pompous but kindly older brother lying dead.

The bugle called again, this time more urgently, and the rebel line stumbled into a run.

"Cheer!" Major Bird shouted. "Cheer!"

It seemed to Starbuck that instead of cheering, the men began to scream. Or rather to yelp like the wounded man whom Truslow had left behind on the grass. The sound could have been translated as a screech of terror, except that in unison there was something in the noise that curdled the blood, and the men themselves sensed it and began to reinforce the weird ululating sound. Even Major Bird, running with his clumsy sword, echoed the eerie shriek. There was something bestial in the noise, something that threatened an awful violence.

And then the northerners opened fire.

For a second the whole summer sky, the whole heavy firmament itself, was filled with the wail and scream of the bullets, and the rebel yell hesitated before starting again, only this time there were real screams mingled with the shrill sound. Men were falling. Men were jarred back by the mule-kick force of the striking bullets. Some men staggered as they tried to keep walking. There was fresh blood on the grass. Starbuck could hear a clattering noise and realized it was the sound of northern bullets hitting rifle stocks and bowie knife blades. The southern charge had slowed and men seemed to be wading forward, as if the air had thickened into a resistant treacle in which the ordered lines of the rebel regiments had first broken and then coalesced into shattered groups. The men stopped, fired, then advanced again, but the advance was slow and hesitant.

Another volley came from the federals and more men were plucked back from the rebel charge. Major Bird was screaming at his men to charge, to run, to carry the day, but the Legion had been stunned by the ferocity of the northern counterfire and overwhelmed by the sheer quantity of gunfire that now crackled and flamed and whistled about them. The northern howitzer shells crashed down like thunderbolts, each shell spewing a barrowload of red earth high in the air.

Adam was ten paces ahead of E Company. He walked slowly forward, apparently unmoved by the danger. A sergeant called him back, but Adam, his revolver held low, ignored the call.

"Keep going! Keep going!" Major Bird screamed at his men. So far not one bowie knife nor one bayonet had been reddened, but the men could not keep going. Instead they fell back, silent, and the federals bayed a deep-noted shout of triumph and the noise seemed to spur the rebel retreat into a stumbling run. The Confederates were not panicking yet, but they were close. "No!" Major Bird was livid, trying to force his men back into the attack by sheer force of personality.

"Major!" Starbuck had to shout to make Bird hear. "Look to your left! Your left!" A fresh northern regiment had come up on the Legion's left and now threatened to wrap itself round the open flank of the Virginians. The new attack would not only drive back this failed bayonet attack, but would overlap the wood. Evans's defenders had been outflanked and out-fought at last.

"Goddamn!" Bird stared at the new threat. His oath sounded very unconvincing, like a man unused to cursing. "Sergeant Major! Take the colors back." Bird gave the order, but did not yet retreat himself.

"Come back, sir, please! Come back!" Starbuck pulled at Major Bird's sleeve, and this time the major began to withdraw. Bullets screamed in the air as Bird and Starbuck stumbled back, preserved from the northern marksmen by the fog of battle smoke that obscured proper aiming.

Only Adam would not retreat. He was shouting at his men to join him, that there was no danger, that all they had to do was push on to the far side of the meadow, but E Company had seen the retreat of the whole Confederate line, and so they edged backward themselves. Adam stopped and turned toward them, shouting at them to advance, but then he staggered and almost dropped his revolver. He opened his mouth to speak, but no sound came out. He somehow managed to hold his balance as, very slowly and very carefully, like a drunken man pretending to be sober, he pushed the revolver into its holster. Then, with an oddly puzzled look on his face, he fell onto his knees.

"You stupid bastard." Sergeant Truslow had seen Adam fall and now ran across the face of advancing northerners. The rest of the Legion was hurrying back toward the safety of the trees. The whole southern charge had failed utterly and the northerners were in full cry.

"It's my leg, Truslow," Adam said in a puzzled voice.

"Should have been your goddamn brain. Give me your arm." Truslow, even when rescuing Adam, sounded grimly hostile. "Come on, boy. Hurry!"

Adam had been struck in his left thigh. The bullet had hit like a hammer blow, but had not hurt much at the time. Now suddenly there was pain searing white hot from his groin down to his toes. He hissed with the agony and could not resist a half-scream. "Leave me here!" he gasped to Truslow.

"Shut your bleating, for Christ's sake." Truslow half-dragged and half-carried Adam back toward the trees.

Neither Major Bird nor Starbuck had seen Adam's plight. They were hurrying back toward the wood, or rather Starbuck was hurrying and Thaddeus Bird was strolling calmly. "Do you notice," Bird asked yet again, "just how many bullets go high?"

"Yes." Starbuck was trying to run and crouch at the same time.

"We should do something about that," Bird remarked purposefully. "Because we must have been firing high too, wouldn't you say?"

"Yes." Starbuck would have agreed with whatever propositions Bird wanted so long as the Major hurried.

"I mean how many hundreds of bullets have been fired on this pasture this morning," Bird went on, suddenly enthused by his new proposition, "and how many casualties have they caused? Remarkably few, really." He waved with his unblooded sword at the grass where maybe three score of bodies lay where the Legion's charge had failed. "We should look at the tree trunks to see where the bullet scars are, and I'll wager you, Starbuck, that most will be at least eight or ten feet above the ground."

"I shouldn't be surprised, sir. I really shouldn't." Starbuck could see the fence rails ahead now. Just another few paces and they would be among the trees. Most of the Legion was already safe in the woodland, or as safe as any men could be who were crouching among trees that were being shelled by a dozen federal howitzers.

"There, look! You see? Twelve feet up, fifteen. There's another, ten feet high if it's an inch. See?" Major Bird had now stopped altogether and was pointing with his sword at the interesting phenomenon of how high the bullet marks on the trees were. "That one's a little lower, I admit, but look, see? There, on that hickory, Starbuck? Not one bullet strike below ten feet and how many can you see above that height? Four, five, six, and that's just one trunk!"

"Sir!" Starbuck shoved Bird onward.

"Steady!" Bird protested, but did start walking again so that, at last, Starbuck could take shelter under the trees. He saw that most of the men had retreated farther among the trunks, instinctively seeking safety, though a few, the brave few, lingered at the trees' edge to keep steadily firing on the advancing Yankees.

"Go back, lads!" Major Bird realized the southern stand was beaten. "God knows where," he muttered under his breath. "Sergeant Major Proctor?"

"Sir!"

"Make sure the colors are safe!" How ridiculous, Bird thought, that he should think of such things, for what were the colors but two gaudy flags, stitched together from scraps of silk in his sister's bedroom? The northern bullets were ripping and tearing through the leaves. "Starbuck?"

"Sir?"

"Would you mind warning Doc Billy? Tell him we're retreating. He must rescue what wounded he can, and leave the rest. I guess the Yankees will treat them right?"

"I'm sure they will, sir."

"Be off with you, then."

Starbuck ran back through the woods. A shell cracked off to his left and a heavy branch splintered and tore down through the surrounding trees. Groups of men were flitting back through the trees, not waiting for orders, but just making off toward safety. They were abandoning bowie knives, blankets, haversacks, almost anything that might delay their flight. Starbuck found a chaotic press of men about the picketed horses and a corporal trying to lead Pocahontas free of the panicked rabble. "That's mine!" Starbuck shouted, and snatched the reins.

For a second the corporal looked as though he would contest the issue, then he saw Starbuck's grim face and fled. Captain Hinton ran past, shouting for his horse, followed by Lieutenant Moxey, whose left hand was dripping blood. Starbuck hauled himself onto Pocahontas's back and turned her toward the clearing where he had last seen Doctor Danson. Another rush of men ran past, shouting unintelligibly. A crackle of rifle fire sounded from the edge of the trees. Starbuck kicked Pocahontas's flanks. Her ears were pricked back, showing she was nervous. Starbuck ducked under a branch, then almost lost his seat as the mare leaped a fallen trunk. He galloped into the road, planning to turn south toward the casualty station, but suddenly a bullet slashed past his head and he saw a puff of flame-streaked smoke and a blur of blue uniforms in the opposite woods. A man shouted at him to surrender.

Starbuck wrenched the reins, half-falling off the horse. The mare turned, protesting, and Starbuck kicked his heels back. "Come on!" he shouted at her, then cringed as another bullet whipcracked past his head. He still held his heavy pistol and he used its barrel to hit Pocahontas's flank and suddenly the horse jerked forward, almost throwing Starbuck off, but he somehow held on with his left hand as she bolted back into the woods. Starbuck turned her back toward the hillcrest. There seemed no sense in trying to organize an orderly withdrawal of the wounded; instead he needed to find Bird and tell him that the Legion had been deeply outflanked. "Major Bird!" he shouted. "Major Bird!"

Thaddeus Bird had found Sergeant Truslow and was now helping

carry Adam back to safety. The three men were with the color party and
were the very last of the Legion left in the upper wood. Sergeant Major
Proctor was carrying one color, a corporal from Company C had the
other, but the heavy flags on their unwieldy staffs were difficult objects to
carry through the tangle of thorns and undergrowth. The rest of the
Legion, indeed the rest of Nathan Evans's brigade, seemed to have fled,
and Bird supposed that this battle was lost. He wondered how the histori-
ans would describe the southern revolt. A summer's madness? An aberra-
tion of American history to set alongside the Whiskey Rebellion that
George Washington had put down so savagely? A shell cracked through
the upper trees, showering the color party with leaves.

"Major Bird!" Starbuck shouted. He was galloping madly, blindly
through the trees. Fugitives were shouting all around him, but Starbuck's
world was a blur of sunlight and green shadow, of a panicked horse running, of sweat and thirst. He could hear a Yankee band off in the meadows and he turned the horse away from the sound. He shouted for Major
Bird again, but the only reply was a spatter of shots somewhere to his left.
Bullets whistled and slapped close to him, but the northerners were firing
in close woodland and could not aim properly. A shell crashed smoke and
sizzling fragments off to the right, then Starbuck was in a clearing and he
saw the flash of red and white that was the Faulconer Legion colors at the
far end of the open space and he turned his horse toward it. He thought
he saw Thaddeus Bird with about a dozen other men. "Major Bird!"

But Bird had disappeared into the farther trees. Starbuck hurried after
the color party, bursting through a skein of smoke that hung over the
clearing. Shots sounded in the woods, a bugle called, and still the Yankee
band was playing behind. Starbuck crashed into the trees at the far end of
the clearing and ripped through a tangle of low branches that slashed
painfully across his face. "Major Bird!"

Bird at last turned, and Starbuck saw Adam was there, dark blood on
his thigh. Starbuck was about to shout that there were Yankees on the
right flank, but he was too late. A squad of blue-coated men was already
running through the trees, coming from the dirt road, and it seemed
inevitable that the Legion's colors would fall and that Bird, Adam,
Truslow and the other men around the two flags would be captured.
"Look out!" Starbuck shouted, pointing.

The color party was running through the trees, desperate to get away,
but Bird and Truslow were hampered by Adam. The northerners were
shouting at them to stop and put their hands up, while Major Bird was
shouting at Sergeant Major Proctor to run. Adam, his leg jolted as he was
dragged through the trees, screamed.

Starbuck heard the scream and kicked back. The northerners were
whooping and hollering like boys playing games. A rifle fired, the bullet

slapping off into the leaves. Major Bird and Sergeant Truslow were staggering under Adam's weight. The northerners shouted again for their surrender and Truslow turned, ready to fight, then saw the bayonets coming straight for him.

And Starbuck struck. He had galloped the mare directly at the pursuing Yankees and now he screamed at them to back away, to leave Adam alone. The northerners swung their bayonet-weighted rifles toward him, but Starbuck was riding too fast. He was screaming at them, all self-control gone, his decision to fight at last made. The Yankees were not backing off but trying to aim their guns as Starbuck straightened his right arm and pulled the Savage's lower trigger, then the upper one, and the gun jarred hard back to his shoulder, smothering him with an instant of smoke that was there and gone. He whooped with joy as though, by firing the gun, he had released his soul to a dark desire. He heard a rifle fire, but no bullet struck him and he screamed defiance.

There were six Yankees in the squad. Five of the six scattered from Starbuck's crazy charge, but the last bravely tried to lunge with his bayonet at the maddened horseman. Starbuck pulled the revolver's lower trigger, revolving the cylinder, then thust the gun's barrel hard down at the man who was challenging him. He had a glimpse of bushy black side-whiskers and tobacco-blackened teeth, then he pulled the trigger and the man's face vanished in a spray of blood-streaked smoke, chips of bone and scarlet drops. Starbuck was keening a terrible sound, a scream of victory and a howl of fury as another Yankee was trampled down by Pocahontas's heavy hooves. A gun crashed terribly loud by his right ear and suddenly the mare was screaming and rearing, but Starbuck kept his balance and urged her on. He tried to fire at a blue-coated man, but the revolver jammed because he pulled both triggers simultaneously, but it did not matter. Major Bird, Adam and Truslow had escaped, the colors had gone safe into the green wood's shelter, and Starbuck was suddenly riding free and clear into a leaf-filled silence.

He was laughing. It seemed that he was filled with a most miraculous happiness, that he had experienced the second most exciting, wonderful moment of his life. He wanted to scream his joy at the heavens as he remembered the Yankee's face exploding away from the gun's muzzle. My God, but he had shown that bastard! He laughed aloud.

While in faraway Boston the dust motes danced and shifted in the shafts of sunlight that streamed down from the high church windows onto the Reverend Elial Starbuck who, his eyes closed and his strong face contorted with the agony of passion, beseeched Almighty God to protect and succor the righteous forces of the United States, to give them the spirit to endure all hardships and the strength to overcome the foul forces of unspeakable evil that had been spewed from the southern states. "And if the cause should come to battle, O Lord, then let thy will be done, and thy victory be gained, and let the blood of thine enemies soak the land and let their pride be trampled beneath the hoofbeats of the righteous!" His appeal was intense, his prayer echoing, his voice as hard as the New Hampshire granite from which the church was built. Elial let the echo of the prayer fade as he opened his eyes, but the congregation, somehow aware that their pastor's angry gray gaze was searching the pews for any evidence of faithlessness, kept their eyes tight shut and their fans quite still. Not one person moved, indeed they hardly dared breathe. Elial lowered his hands to grip the lectern. "In thy holy name we beseech it, Amen."

"Amen," the congregation echoed. Timid eyes opened, hymnals rustled, and Mrs. Sifflard pumped some humid air into the harmonium's bowels. "Hymn number two hundred and sixty-six." The Reverend Elial sounded like a man spent of sudden force, righteously weary. "'There is a fountain filled with blood, Drawn from Emmanuel's veins; And sinners, plunged beneath that flood, Lose all their guilty stains.'"

A loose horse galloped out of the brush and through a row of wounded southern soldiers who had been left to the mercy of the advancing Yankees. One man screamed and convulsed as a hoof struck his thigh. Another man was weeping, calling for his mother. A third man had lost his eyes to a shell's splinters and could not weep. Two of the injured men were already dead, their beards jutting skyward and their skins crawling with flies. The woods slowly filled with northern troops who stopped to rifle the pockets and pouches of the dead. The shellfire had finally stopped, though the fierce fires started by the explosions still burned and crackled in the undergrowth.

To the east of the woods the gray-clad 2nd Wisconsin Regiment, advancing on the Georgia regiment that now formed the right flank of the broken Confederate defense line, was mistaken for southern reinforcements. The northern flag, hanging limp in the windless air, looked very like the Confederate banner, and the Georgians allowed the Wisconsin men to come so close that every southern officer was killed or wounded by the Yankees' opening volley. The surviving Georgians stood for a desperate moment, then broke and fled, and so the last of the makeshift line that Nathan Evans had scraped together was finally vanquished. Yet the line had done its work. It had held an overwhelming attack long enough for a new defense line to be cobbled together on the flat wide summit of the hill where the Faulconer Legion had begun their day.

A battery of Virginian guns commanded by a lawyer turned gunner waited at the plateau's northern crest. The guns looked out across the valley where the men of Evans's shattered brigade now streamed back from the victorious Yankees. Behind the lawyer's guns was a Virginian brigade that had come from the Shenandoah Valley and was led by a godly man of eccentric views and grim demeanor. Thomas Jackson had been an unpopular lecturer at Virginia's Military Institute and afterward an unpopular commander of a militia brigade that he had trained and drilled, drilled and trained until the farmboys in his ranks were sick to the belly of his training and drilling, but now Thomas Jackson's farmboys were on a wide plateau waiting for a victorious Yankee army to attack them, and they were drilled, trained and ready to fight. They were eager for it too.

A second Confederate artillery battery came to the hilltop and deployed its weapons close to where the Faulconer Legion's baggage was piled. The battery commander was an Episcopal minister who ordered his second in command to check and recheck the battery's wormscrews, sponge covers, scrapers, handspikes, and rammers, while he himself prayed aloud that God would have mercy on the Yankees' guilty souls that he intended to send to a better world with his four big guns that he had named for the four evangelists. Thomas Jackson, expecting an enemy cannonade at any moment, ordered his men to lie flat so as not to make themselves a target for the enemy gunners, then he calmly sat in his saddle reading his Bible. He worried that his men might get confused in the smoke of battle, and so all his Virginians had strips of white cloth tied to their arms or tucked into their hatbands, and were under orders to shout a watchword as they fought. "Our Homes!" was their cry, and Jackson expected them to strike their breasts with their left hands as they shouted it. Captain Imboden, the lawyer turned gunner, had long decided that Jackson was mad as a March hare, but he was somehow glad that he was on Jackson's side and not having to face the madman in battle.

A mile to Imboden's right, at the stone bridge where more and more northern troops crossed the Bull Run to continue the crushing attack that had at last begun to roll the rebel army into chaos, General Irvin McDowell sat on his horse beside the turnpike and cheered on his men. "Victory, boys!" he called again and again. "Victory! On to Richmond! Well done, boys, well done!" McDowell was jubilant, ecstatic, so happy that he could forget the dyspepsia that had plagued him ever since his injudiciously large helpings of beef pie at supper the previous night. What did indigestion matter? He had won! He had led the largest army in the history of American warfare to a brilliant victory, and just as soon as the chore of cleaning up the rebel army was completed he would send a sheaf of captured colors back to Washington to be laid as trophies at the president's feet. Not that he had seen any captured colors yet, but he was certain they would soon come in abundance. "Starbuck!" He spotted his *sous*-adjutant surrounded by foreign attachés in their gaudy uniforms. McDowell had gone to college in France and was used to European military fashions, but now, seeing the bright uniforms amid the plain honest coats of his own army, he thought how ridiculously ornate the foreigners appeared. "Captain Starbuck!" he called again.

"Sir?" Captain James Starbuck had been happily beating time to the music of a regimental band that was playing opera selections to the advancing troops. Now he urged his horse closer to the victorious general.

"Scout across the bridge, will you?" McDowell requested genially. "And tell our fellows to send all captured colors back to me. Be sure of that, will you? All of them! And don't worry about your foreign fellows. I'll have a chat with them." The general waved to a passing artillery troop. "Victory, boys, victory! On to Richmond! On to Richmond!" A fat and drunken congressman from New York was riding a limber westward, and the general good-naturedly saluted the politician. The congressman was a rascal, but his good opinion could be useful to a victorious general's career when this short fighting season was done. "A great day, Congressman! A great day!"

"Another Yorktown, General! A veritable Waterloo!" A victorious general could also be of use to a congressman's career, and so the fat politician waved his beaver hat in affable salute to the portly McDowell. "On to glory!" the congressman shouted, and waved his hat so vigorously that he almost lost his balance on the narrow limber seat. ·

"And Starbuck!" McDowell called after his aide who was already forcing his passage across the crowded bridge. "Don't let too many civilians clutter up the rear. That fellow won't hurt, but we don't want any ladies injured by stray shots, do we?"

"No, sir!" James Starbuck went to hunt for flags.

Colonel Washington Faulconer was also seeking colors, his own, and he found them in the pastureland north of the turnpike. At first all he could find were the shattered remnants of his precious Legion; a succession of powder-stained, weary men who straggled from the trees, dragging their rifles and scarcely able to recognize their own Colonel. A few men were still in good order, held so by officers or sergeants, but the majority had abandoned their expensive equipment and had lost any idea of where their companies, their officers or even their friends were. Some had retreated with the South Carolinians, some with the Louisianans, just as some men from those regiments now walked back with the Virginians. They were a beaten force, exhausted and stunned, and the Colonel watched them in appalled disbelief. Ethan Ridley, who had at last caught up with Faulconer, dared not even speak for fear of triggering the Colonel's rage.

"This was Starbuck's doing," Washington Faulconer finally said, and

Ridley just nodded in mute confirmation. "Have you seen Adam?" the Colonel called to the Legion's survivors, but they just shook their heads. Some glanced up at the beautifully uniformed Colonel who sat his horse so elegantly then turned away to spit dry-mouthed at the meadow.

"Sir?" Ridley had glanced to his right and seen blue Yankee uniforms advancing from the wooden bridge that carried the turnpike across the small tributary of the Bull Run. "Sir!" he repeated more urgently.

But the Colonel was not listening because Faulconer had at last seen his color party emerge from the woods, and he galloped forward to meet them. He was determined that whatever else happened on this awful day, he would not lose the two flags. Even if the Confederacy went down in blazing defeat he would carry those twin colors back to Seven Springs and there hang the flags in his hallway to remind his descendants that their family had fought for Virginia. Ridley followed the Colonel, made silent by the enormity of the defeat.

At first the Colonel did not see Adam, who was now being helped by Sergeant Truslow and Sergeant Major Proctor. The Colonel only saw Thaddeus Bird, who was dragging the Faulconer coat-of-arms in the dirt. "What the hell did you do with my Legion!" Faulconer shouted at his brother-in-law. "What the hell have you done?"

Thaddeus Bird stopped and stared up at the angry Colonel. It seemed to take him a few seconds to recognize Washington Faulconer, but when he did, he just laughed.

"Damn it, Pecker! Damn it!" Faulconer very nearly slashed his riding crop across the schoolmaster's laughing face.

"Adam's wounded." Bird had abruptly ceased laughing and now spoke with an earnest intensity. "But he'll be all right. He fought well. They all fought well, or almost all. We have to teach them to aim low, though, and there are a host of other lessons we have to learn. But we didn't do badly for a first fight."

"Badly! You threw the Legion away! Goddamn you! You threw it away!" The Colonel spurred Saratoga on to where Truslow and Proctor were helping Adam. "Adam!" the Colonel shouted, and was astonished to see his son smiling almost happily.

"Be careful of the woods, Faulconer!" Sergeant Truslow growled. "They're full of goddamned Yankees."

The Colonel had intended to snap at Adam, to reprimand him for letting Bird disobey orders, but his son's bloody leg checked his anger. Then he looked up to see a last figure in gray uniform stagger out of the trees. It was Starbuck, and the sight of him made Washington Faulconer's anger surge up so intensely that he shuddered uncontrollably. "I'll come back for you, Adam," he said, then spurred Saratoga on toward Starbuck.

Starbuck was on foot, limping. After Pocahontas had screamed he had pulled her head to the left, raked her sore flanks with his heels and then galloped clear of the stunned and scattered Yankees. He had tried to follow the fleeing color party, but instead he had felt the mare stumble and he saw droplets of blood spraying from her mouth and nostrils. Her stride had faltered, she had blown a great bubbling breath, then half-collapsed onto her knees. Still she had tried to keep going, but the life was roaring out of her punctured lung and so she had fallen to her side, sliding through the leaf mold and thorns, and Starbuck had just managed to kick his feet free of the stirrups and hurl himself out of the saddle before the dying mare crashed into a tree and stopped. She shivered, tried to raise her head, whinnied once, then her hooves beat a dying tattoo on the ground.

"Oh, God." Starbuck was shaking. He was crouching, bruised and frightened, his breath coming in huge gasps. The horse shuddered and a great wash of blood split from her mouth. The bullet wound in her chest seemed very small. Flies buzzed loud, already settling on the dead horse.

The woodland seemed oddly silent. Flames or musketry crackled far away, but Starbuck could hear no footsteps close by. He clambered to his feet and hissed with pain when he put his weight onto his left ankle. His revolver had fallen into the litter of bloody leaves. He picked it up, shoved it into his holster and had been about to start limping away when he remembered how only that morning Colonel Faulconer had stressed how expensive the saddle was, and Starbuck was assailed by the ridiculous conviction that he would be in bad trouble if he did not rescue the saddle and so he had knelt at the belly of the dead horse and scrabbled to unbuckle the girth. Then, half-sobbing and half-panting, he had heaved the heavy saddle free and pulled the stirrups and girth out from under the deadweight of the mare's carcass.

He staggered through the woods, clumsy on his turned ankle and blundering under the weight of the saddle and the heat of the day. He had needed both hands to carry the saddle, so could not keep his sword from tangling in his legs. After the saber had tripped him a third time he stopped, unbuckled the scabbard slings and threw the wretched blade far off into the undergrowth. One small part of his conscious thoughts told him it was stupid to rescue the saddle and throw away the saber, but somehow the saddle seemed more important now. Voices shouted in the far woods, a bugle sounded, a man whooped in triumph and, fearing that he would be ambushed, Starbuck pulled out the revolver, worked the lower lever trigger, then held it in his right hand beneath the heavy saddle. He staggered on, at last emerging from the woodland into a wide pasture scattered with retreating rebels. Ahead of the southerners was the turnpike, then a steep hill climbing to the plateau where the Legion had started its day. He could see the small wooden house on the hilltop and, next to it, some cannon. He wondered if the guns belonged to the North or the South, to the enemy or to friends.

"You bastard!" The shout echoed across the pastureland and Starbuck turned his sweat-stung eyes to see Colonel Faulconer spurring toward him. The Colonel slewed to a stop beside Starbuck, his stallion's hooves slinging up clods of turf. "What in the name of Christ did you do to my Legion? I told you to go home! I told you to go back to your damned father!" And Colonel Faulconer, who was too angry to think what he was doing, or whether a mere second lieutenant could possibly have exercised the power he was now ascribing to Starbuck, brought back his whip hand and slashed it forward so that the riding crop slashed across Starbuck's face. Starbuck flinched, gasped at the pain, then fell as he twisted away. Blood ran salt from his nose.

"I brought your saddle," he was trying to say, but instead he was on all fours, blood dripping from his nose, and the Colonel raised his whip again. "You did your filthy northern work, didn't you? You broke my Legion, you bastard!" He slashed down a second time, then a third. "You bastard!" He screamed, then raised his hand to strike a fourth blow.

The first of the pursuing Yankees had appeared at the edge of the wood. One of them, a corporal, had been with the group of men charged by Starbuck and now, coming into the pastureland, he saw a mounted Confederate not fifty yards away and he thought of his dead comrade as he dropped to his right knee and brought his rifle into his shoulder and snapped off one fast shot. The smoke billowed to hide the Yankee's view, but his aim had been good and the bullet struck the Colonel on his raised right arm, splintering the bone and ricocheting down to score across his ribs and lodge in his belly muscles. Blood poured from his arm that had been thrown back by the bullet's force and his riding crop wheeled through the air. "Oh, God," Washington Faulconer said, astonished rather than hurt. Then the pain stabbed at him and he cried aloud as he tried to force the arm down and to comprehend the sudden mess of torn and blood-soaked cloth and sharp pain.

"Colonel!" Ethan Ridley galloped to the Colonel's side just as a volley of northern shots crackled at the wood's margin. Ridley ducked and hauled on his reins as the minié bullets screamed about his ears. The Colonel was turning away, spurs slashing back, screaming with pain while Ridley was staring down at Starbuck who had brought his right hand out to protect himself from the Colonel's beating. The Savage revolver was in Starbuck's hand and Ridley, seeing it, thought the northerner had tried to kill the Colonel. "You shot him!" Ridley screamed in shocked accusation, then pulled his own revolver free of its holster.

Blood dripped from Starbuck's nose. He was still shocked, still too dazed to understand what was happening, but he saw Ridley's face grimace and saw the revolver spurt smoke, and then the saddle which was still supported by Starbuck's left hand kicked as Ridley's bullet thumped into the wooden tree beneath the leather.

The kick of the bullet hitting the saddle woke Starbuck from his daze. Behind him the northerners were swarming from the trees and Ridley was already turning away, not out of fear of Starbuck but to escape the onrush of Yankees. "Ridley!" Starbuck shouted, but Ridley kicked back with his bloodied spurs as Starbuck raised the heavy gun. He had a promise to keep and just seconds to keep it and so he aimed the big Savage revolver and pulled the upper trigger. Sparks ripped away from the exploding per-cussion cap as the gun hammered back in Starbuck's hand.

Ridley screamed and arched his back. "Ridley!" Starbuck shouted again, and the air about him whistled with a volley of northern bullets and Ridley's mare reared up, screaming. Ridley was wounded, but he auto-matically kicked his boots free of the stirrups as he twisted to stare at Starbuck. "This is for Sally, you bastard!" Starbuck shouted hysterically, all sense gone. "For Sally!" He had promised that her name would be the last thing Ridley heard and he shouted it again as he worked the Savage's lower trigger, then pulled the top one again.

Ridley twitched as the second bullet struck and as he fell to earth. He and his horse were both screaming now, but the horse was trying to limp away while Ridley thumped onto the grass.

"You bastard, Ridley!" Starbuck was on his feet, pointing the revolver. He fired again, but his third bullet just drove scraps of soil up from the ground beside the fallen Ridley whose wounded horse was limp-ing away. The Colonel was fifty yards off, but had turned to stare in hor-ror at Starbuck. "This is for Sally," Starbuck said and fired his last bullet into his enemy's body, and suddenly the whole ground in front of Star-buck erupted in dirt and flying blood as a Confederate shell crashed into Ridley's dying body, eviscerating the twitching flesh and throwing up a screen of bloody scraps to hide Starbuck from the retreating Legion.

The warm and bloody blast of the shell threw Starbuck back and soaked his gray tunic with Ridley's blood. More shells screamed across the valley to crack black and red on the meadow where the advancing north-erners had appeared from beneath the trees. The crest of the far hill grew a low cloud that pulsed as more smoke poured from the artillery. Starbuck had fallen to his knees again, while Ridley was nothing but a butcher's mess on the grass. Ahead of Starbuck the beaten Confederates were retreating across the turnpike and climbing the farther hill with its crown of gray-white, flame-streaked smoke, but Starbuck stayed in the meadow, staring at the mess of flesh and blood, of white ribs and blue guts, and he knew he had committed murder. Oh dear sweet forgiving Christ, he tried to pray, shivering in the heat, but suddenly a rush of northerners swept past him and one man kicked the revolver out of Starbuck's nerveless fingers and then a brass-bound rifle butt smacked the back of his head and he pitched forward as a northern voice snarled that he should lie still.

He lay facedown in the sweet-smelling grass and remembered Ridley's final despairing backward glance, the whites of his eyes showing, the terror on his dying face the gift of a girl he had betrayed in Richmond. It had taken a second, one short second, to commit murder. Oh God, Starbuck thought, but he could not pray because he felt no remorse. He felt no sense of sin. He just wanted to laugh for Sally's sake, for he had kept her faith and killed her enemy. He had done a friend's duty, and that thought made him start to laugh.

"Over!" A man stirred Starbuck with his bayonet. "Turn over, you crazy bastard!"

Starbuck rolled over. Two bearded men went through his pouches and pockets, but found nothing worth stealing except his cartridge box with its handful of Savage revolver cartridges. "Thinner pickings than a starved dog," one of the two men said, then grimaced at the awful gory mess that had been Ethan Ridley. "You want to search that pile of blood, Jack?"

"Shit, no. On your feet." He prodded Starbuck with the bayonet. "Over there, rebel."

A score of prisoners was assembled at the edge of the trees. Half were from the Legion, the rest were either South Carolinians or Louisianan Zouaves. The Confederate prisoners sat disconsolate, watching as the northern regiments massed on the lower slopes of the opposite hill. More and more northern regiments were appearing from the Bull Run and marching to reinforce the gathering attack. More and more guns wheeled off the turnpike and were aimed toward the Confederate defenders. "What's to happen to us?" one of the Legion prisoners asked Starbuck.

"I don't know."

"You'll be all right," the man spoke resentfully. "You're an officer, they'll exchange you, but not us. They'll keep us right through harvest time."

A Yankee sergeant heard the exchange. "You shouldn't have rebelled then, should you?"

An hour after midday the prisoners were marched down to the red fieldstone house that stood by the crossroads. The northern soldiers were still readying themselves for the attack that would break the last vestiges of southern resistance and, while they gathered themselves, the artillery of each side screamed their shells overhead, battery firing at battery from opposing hilltops and causing a constant trickle of wounded men who limped, staggered or were carried to an aid post that had been established inside the stone house.

Starbuck, limping from his twisted ankle and with his uniform soaked from Ridley's blood, was pushed toward the kitchen door of the house. "I'm not wounded," he protested.

"Shut your mouth, get inside, do what you're told," the sergeant snapped, then ordered the unwounded prisoners to look after the dozen wounded men who had been brought into the open air to recover from their surgery. Inside the house Starbuck found still more men from the Faulconer Legion; one from K Company had lost a leg from a shell burst, two had lungs punctured by bullets, one had been blinded and another had a minié bullet lodged in his lower jaw that now dribbled a mixture of blood and spittle.

A red-bearded doctor was working at a table that had been shoved into the sunlight coming through the kitchen window. He was amputating a man's leg, and his bone saw made a grating noise that set Starbuck's teeth on edge. The patient, a northerner, groaned horribly and the doctor's assistant dripped more chloroform onto the pad he was holding against the man's nose and mouth. Both the doctor and his assistant were dripping with sweat. The room was foully hot, not just with the day's natural warmth, but also because a fierce fire in the kitchen range was being used to boil water.

The doctor discarded the saw and picked up a long-bladed scalpel with which he finished the amputation. The bloody leg, still clad in a boot and sock, thumped to the floor. "A change from treating the pox," the doctor said happily, wiping his forehead with his sleeve. "That's all we've done for the last three months, treat the pox! You southerners needn't have bothered raising an army, you could have just sent all your whores north, then you could have poxed us all to death and saved us a heap of trouble. He's still with us, is he?" This last question was to the assistant.

"Yes, sir."

"Give him a whiff of ammonia, let him know he ain't knocking at the pearly gates yet." The red-bearded surgeon was probing with forceps for the arteries that needed tying off. He had filed the bone stump smooth and now, with the arteries tied, he let the flesh compress over the bone's cut end before drawing the flap of skin round the patient's thigh. He put quick stitches in the newly formed stump, then untied the tourniquet that had constricted the thigh's blood supply during the operation. "Another hero," he said dryly to mark the procedure's end.

"He won't come round, sir." The assistant was holding an open bottle of ammonia spirits next to the patient's nose.

"Give me the chloroform," the doctor ordered, then took a scalpel to the patient's torn trousers and cut back the tattered, bloody cloth to reveal the man's genitals. "Behold a miracle," the doctor announced and poured a trickle of chloroform onto the unconscious man's testicles. The man seemed to go into instant spasm, but then opened his eyes, bellowed with pain and tried to sit up. "Frozen balls," the doctor said happily, "known in the profession as the Lazarus effect." He stoppered the chloroform bottle and stepped away from the table, looking to his unwilling audience for appreciation of his wit. He spotted Starbuck, sheeted with blood from head to foot. "Christ, but why aren't you dead?"

"Because I'm not even wounded. It's someone else's blood."

"If you're not wounded, then get the hell out of here. Go and watch your damned dreams being broken."

Starbuck went into the yard where he leaned against the house wall. The sun shone cruelly bright on a desolate scene of rebel defeat. To the north, where Evans had led his forlorn companies to stem the triumphant Yankee advance, the meadows were empty, all but for a littering of dead men and broken horses.

The battle had swept across those fields and, like a vast wave pushed by a storm surge, now climbed the hill toward the Henry House, where the attacking line seethed against the second Confederate defense. Nathan Evans had constructed the first barrier out of a flimsy line of men that had stalled the federal attack long enough for Thomas Jackson to make this second line, which the Yankees now set about dismantling. Newly arrived northern cannon were being dragged to the hill's crest while long blue columns of fresh infantry climbed past the guns to reinforce their comrades who were already assaulting the hill's top. The rebel guns that had originally lined the crest had been pushed back by the Yankees' advance. Starbuck, slumped disconsolate beside the kitchen step of the stone house, saw an occasional Confederate round overshoot the plateau and draw a trail of smoke across the sky. Such wasted rounds were evidence that the rebel army still fought, but the turnpike was now so crowded with northern guns and infantry that Starbuck did not see how the fight could ever be sustained.

"What the hell are you doing here?" the officious sergeant demanded of Starbuck.

"The doctor sent me out here."

"You shouldn't be here. You should be over there, with the other prisoners." The sergeant gestured toward the farthest corner of the yard where a small group of unwounded rebels sat under guard.

"The doctor said I should wash this blood off," Starbuck lied. He had just noticed a well beside the road and he hoped the lie would serve to get him a drink of water.

The sergeant hesitated, then nodded. "Hurry, then."

Starbuck crossed to the well and drew up its wooden bucket. He had meant to wash his face clean before drinking, but he was too thirsty to wait and, gripping the pail with both hands, he greedily tipped the water to his face and gulped down great cool mouthfuls. The liquid poured down his face and his bloodied tunic and trousers, and still he drank, slaking a dry thirst stoked by the hours of powder smoke and heat.

He rested the bucket on the well's edge, panting, and saw a blue-eyed, pretty face watching him. He gaped back. A woman. He must be dreaming. A woman! And a pretty woman, an angel, a vision, a clean, crisp, pretty woman in a lacy white dress and a pink-trimmed bonnet shaded by a white fringed parasol, and Starbuck just stared, wondering if he was going mad, when suddenly the woman, who was sitting in a carriage in the road just beyond the yard's fence, burst out laughing.

"Leave the lady alone!" the sergeant barked. "Back here, rebel!"

"Let him stay!" the woman demanded imperiously. She was sitting with a much older man in an open carriage drawn by two horses. A Negro driver sat on the carriage's box, while a federal lieutenant was attempting to turn the carriage back. They had come too far, the young officer explained to the woman's companion, there was danger here, they should not have crossed the bridge.

"Do you know who I am?" The man was a middle-aged dandy in a colored vest, tall black hat and white silk tie. He carried a gold-topped cane and had a small gray beard elegantly cut to a jutting point.

"Sir, I don't need to know who you are," the northern officer said, "you should not have crossed the bridge, and I must insist—"

"Insist! Lieutenant! Insist! I am Congressman Benjamin Matteson, of the great State of New Jersey, and you do not insist with me."

"But it's dangerous here, sir," the lieutenant protested weakly.

"A congressman can go wherever he finds the Republic endangered," Congressman Matteson answered with lordly scorn, while the truth was that he, like so many others from Washington's society, had merely followed the army so that he could claim a share of the victory's credit and collect some trifling keepsakes like spent rifle bullets or a rebel's bloodstained cap.

"But the woman, sir?" The lieutenant tried again.

"The woman, Lieutenant, is my wife, and a congressman's wife can share any danger." The woman laughed at her husband's absurd compliment, and Starbuck, still dazzled by her, wondered why so young a beauty would marry so pompous a man.

Mrs. Matteson's eyes, blue as the flag's field of stars, were full of mischief. "Are you truly a rebel?" she asked Starbuck. She had bleached gold hair, very white skin and her lace-trimmed dress was smudged with red dust from the summer road.

"Yes, ma'am." Starbuck stared at her as a man dying of thirst might look on a cool, shadowed, clear pool of water. She was so unlike the earnest, plain-spoken, obedient girls who worshiped at his father's church. Instead, this congressman's wife was what the Reverend Elial Starbuck would have called a painted lady, a Jezebel. She was, Starbuck realized, the very image and model of all Sally Truslow wanted to be, and all he himself wanted a woman to be, for his father's biblical austerity had put a taste for just such forbidden fruit into Nathaniel Starbuck. "Yes, ma'am," he said again, "I'm a rebel." He tried to sound defiant.

"Secretly," the woman confided to Starbuck in a voice that carried clean above the cacophony of shells and musketry to reach every prisoner in the yard, "I'm a Lincoln killer too."

Her husband laughed too loudly. "Don't be absurd, Lucy! You're from Pennsylvania!" He gave his wife a reprimanding tap on her knee with his gloved hand. "From the great State of Pennsylvania."

Lucy pushed his hand away. "Don't be obnoxious, Ben. I'm a Lincoln killer through and through." She looked at her driver's stolid back. "Aren't I a rebel, Joseph?"

"You are, missus, you are!" The driver laughed.

"And when we win I shall enslave you, Joseph, won't I?"

"You will, missus, you will!" He laughed again.

Lucy Matteson looked back to Starbuck. "Are you hurt bad?"

"No, ma'am."

"What happened?"

"My horse was shot, ma'am. It fell. I was captured."

"Did you," she said, beginning a question, colored slightly, then a half smile flickered on her face. "Did you kill anyone?"

Starbuck had a sudden memory of Ridley falling backward off his horse. "I don't know, ma'am."

"I feel like killing someone. We slept in the most uncomfortable farm kitchen at Centreville last night, and the Lord only knows where we'll rest tonight. If we rest at all, which I doubt. The rigors of war." She laughed, showing small very white teeth. "Is there a hotel at Manassas Junction?"

"I don't know of one, ma'am," Starbuck said.

"You don't sound like a southerner," the congressman interrupted with a sour note in his voice.

Starbuck, unwilling to explain, merely shrugged.

"You are mysterious!" Lucy Matteson clapped her gloved hands, then held out a cardboard box filled with scraps of tissue paper. "Have one," she said.

Starbuck saw there were pieces of crystallized fruit nestling in the tissues. "Are you sure, ma'am?"

"Go on! Help yourself." She smiled as Starbuck took a piece of the fruit. "Will they send you back to Washington, do you think?"

"I don't know what they plan for the prisoners, ma'am."

"I'm sure they will. They're going to have a mighty victory parade, all honking bands and congratulations, and the prisoners will be marched at gunpoint before being slaughtered in the grounds of the White House."

"Don't be absurd, Lucy. I do beg of you not to be absurd." The Honorable Benjamin Matteson frowned.

"So maybe they'll parole you instead," Lucy Matteson smiled at Starbuck, "and then you'll come to supper. No, Benjamin, don't argue, I'm quite decided. Give me a *carte de visite*, quick!" She held out her hand until her husband, with obvious reluctance, surrendered a pasteboard card which, with a smile, she passed down to Starbuck. "We rebels shall exchange war stories while these cold northerners frown at us. And if you need anything in prison, you are to ask me. I wish I had something more than scraps of fruit to give you now, but the congressman ate all our cold chicken because he said it would go bad once the pounded ice melted." There was a pure venom in her words that made Starbuck laugh.

The lieutenant who had originally tried to turn the congressman's carriage around now reappeared with a major whose authority was considerably greater. The major would not have cared if half the U.S. Congress had been in the carriage, it still had no business blocking the turnpike in the middle of a battle and so he touched his hat to Lucy Matteson and then insisted that the driver turn the carriage round and take it back across the Bull Run.

"Do you know who I am?" Congressman Matteson demanded, then half ducked as a rebel shell exploded a hundred yards away and a piece of shrapnel rustled overhead and cracked harmlessly against the stone house.

"I don't care if you're the emperor of France. Get the hell out of here! Now! Move!"

Lucy Matteson smiled at Starbuck as the carriage jerked forward. "Come and see us in Washington!"

Starbuck laughed and stepped back. Above him the hill smoked like a volcano and the shells cracked and the rifle fire splintered and the wounded limped back to the crossroads where the prisoners waited for jail and the Yankees waited for victory and the dead waited for burial. Starbuck, ignored now by the sergeant who no longer seemed to care whether he joined the other prisoners or not, sat with his back against the sun-warmed stone of the house and closed his eyes and wondered what his future held. He supposed the whole southern rebellion was being beaten to death in these hot fields, and he thought how much he would regret the premature ending of this war. He had seen the elephant, and he wanted to see more of it. It was not the horror that attracted him; not the memory of the severed leg spinning across the road, nor the man's face disappearing in powder smoke and gore, but rather the rearrangement of all creation that appealed to Starbuck's soul. War, Starbuck had learned this day, took everything that was, shook it, and let the pieces fall where they might. War was a gigantic game of chance, a huge gamble, a denial of all predestination and prudence. War would have saved Starbuck from the fate of family respectability, while peace was duty. War had relieved him of obligation, but peace offered dullness, and Nathaniel Starbuck was young enough and self-confident enough to hate dullness above all other things in the world.

But now he was a prisoner and the battle hammered on while, warmed by the sun and wearied by the day, Starbuck slept.

14

The remnants of the Faulconer Legion had stumbled uphill to where, in a tangle of small woods and fields behind Jackson's Virginia Brigade, the survivors of Nathan Evans's force recovered. The men were exhausted. At Evans's insistence they made a crude line that faced toward the Bull Run, but they were on the flank of the reconstituted southern defense and far enough from the turnpike to be spared the renewed federal attacks. The men sat on the grass, dull-eyed and thirsty, wondering if there would be any food or water.

Doctor Danson extracted the bullet from Adam Faulconer's leg, working fast and without chloroform, "You're lucky, Adam. No major blood vessels hit. You may even have a slight limp to attract the ladies, but that's all. You'll be dancing with the ladies in ten days." He poured lunar caustic into the wound, bandaged it, and moved on to the Colonel. He worked just as swiftly to extract the bullet from Washington Faulconer's belly muscles, sewed up the mangled flesh of his arm, then splinted the broken bone. "You're not quite as lucky as your son, Washington"—the doctor could still not get used to treating his neighbor as a superior officer—"but in another six weeks you'll be back to rights."

"Six weeks?" Colonel Faulconer was still furious that his precious Legion had been decimated under Thaddeus Bird's command and at Nathaniel Starbuck's bidding. He wanted his revenge, not on Bird, whom he had always known was a fool, but on Starbuck, who had become the Colonel's personification for the Legion's failure. Instead of marching to glorious victory under Washington Faulconer's personal command the regiment had been thrown away in some miserable skirmish at the wrong end of the battlefield. The Legion had lost all its baggage and at least seventy men. No one knew the full total, though the Colonel had established that Starbuck was himself among the missing.

Doctor Danson had heard that Starbuck had been captured by the pursuing Yankees, or maybe worse. "A boy in B Company thought Starbuck might have been shot," he told the Colonel as he bandaged the splinted arm.

"Good," the Colonel said with a savagery that might have been excusable in a man suffering from the pain of a newly broken arm.

"Father!" Adam nevertheless protested.

"If the damned Yankees don't shoot him, we shall. He killed Ridley! I saw it."

"Father, please." Adam pleaded.

"For God's sake, Adam, must you always take Starbuck's side against me? Does family loyalty count for nothing with you?" The Colonel shouted the hurt words at his son who, appalled by the accusation, said nothing. Faulconer flinched away from the splints that Danson was trying to put on his upper arm. "I tell you, Adam," Faulconer went on, "that your damned friend is nothing but a murderer. Christ, but I should have known he was rotten when he first told us that tale of thieving and whores, but I trusted him for your sake. I wanted to help him for your sake, and now Ethan's dead because of it and, I promise you, I'll snap Starbuck's neck myself if he has the gall to come back here."

"Not with that arm, you won't," Doctor Danson said dryly.

"Damn the arm, Billy! I can't leave the Legion for six weeks!"

"You need rest," the doctor said calmly, "you need healing. If you exert yourself, Washington, you'll invite the gangrene. Three weeks of exertion and you'll be dead. Let's fashion a sling for that arm."

A thunderous crash of musketry announced that Jackson's Virginians were greeting the enemy. The battle was now being fought on the plateau about the Henry House, a flat hilltop edged with flame and thunder. The waiting Confederate guns tore great gaps in the advancing federal lines, but the northern infantry outflanked the batteries and forced them back, and northern guns unlimbered to take the rebel cannon in the flank. To Captain Imboden, the lawyer turned gunner, the ground around his out-numbered cannon looked as though it was being truffled by a horde of hungry hogs. The northern shells burrowed deep before exploding, but some were finding more solid targets. One of Imboden's limbers exploded from a direct hit and one of his gunners screamed in brief, foul gasps as his guts were sliced open by a jagged-edged scrap of shell casing. More gunners dropped to the marksmanship of northern sharpshooters. Imbo-den was serving one of his guns, ramming a canister down on top of a roundshot, then stepping back as the lanyard was pulled and the lethal missiles flensed through a northern regiment of infantry that was advanc-ing through the smoke and stench.

The flags were bright squares of color in the gray. Stars and Stripes came forward while the three stripes of the Confederacy edged backward, but then stopped where Thomas Jackson, his well-thumbed Bible safe in his saddlebag, had decreed they would stop. Jackson's men stood hard in the smoke and discovered that the hated hours of drill were transmuted by battle into the unconscious motions of efficiency, and that somehow, despite the flail of northern canister and musketry, and despite the terror of men surrounded by the screaming of the wounded, the sobbing of the dying, the horrors of shattered flesh and of disemboweled friends, their hands still kept ramming bullets and charges, kept feeding percussion caps onto cones, kept aiming, kept firing. Still kept fighting. They were terrified, but they had been trained, and the man who had trained them glowered at them, and so they stayed like a stone wall built across a hilltop.

And the northern attack broke on the wall.

Jackson's Virginians should have been beaten. They should have been swept away like a sand ridge struck by a sea, except they did not know the battle had been lost and so they fought on, even edged forward, and the northerners wondered how you were supposed to beat these bastards, and the fear lodged in the northern hearts and the southerners edged another pace forward over dry grass scorched by burning cartridge wadding. The federals looked behind for reinforcements.

Those northern reinforcements came, but the southerners were being reinforced too as Beauregard at last realized that his whole plan of battle had been wrong. It had been about as wrong as any plan could be wrong, but now he was making amends by plucking men from his unbloodied right and hurrying them toward the plateau about the Henry House. Irvin McDowell, irritated that such a stubborn defense was delaying the sweet moment of victory, was busy ordering more men up the slope and into the sights of Captain Imboden's cannon and into the ghastly carnage of Matthew, Mark, Luke and John's canister, and into range of General Thomas Jackson's rifle-muskets.

And thus the day's real dying had begun.

It began because a battle of motion, of outflanking, advance and retreat, had become a standoff fight. The hilltop was bare of trees, devoid of ditch or wall, just an open space for death, and death grasped at it greedily. Men loaded and fired, fell and bled, cursed and died, and still more men filed onto the plateau to extend death's grip. Twin lines of infantry were stalled just a hundred paces apart and there tried to blast the guts out of each other. Men from New York and New Hampshire, Maine and Vermont, Connecticut and Massachusetts shot at men from Mississippi and Virginia, Georgia and the Carolinas, Maryland and Tennessee. The wounded crawled back to collapse in the grass, the dead were hurled aside, the files closed on the center, the regiments shrank, yet still the firing went on beneath the bright flags. The northerners, firing again and again at the Confederate lines, knew that they only needed to break this small army, capture Richmond, and the whole conceit of a Southern Confederacy would collapse like a rotten pumpkin, while the southerners, returning bullet for bullet, knew that the North, once bloodied, would think twice before they dared invade the sovereign and sacred soil of the South again.

And so, for their twin causes, men fought beneath the colors, though, in the windless heat, the real trophies of the day were the opposing guns, for the side that could silence their enemy's guns was the side likeliest to win the struggle. None of the guns was emplaced behind earthworks, for none of the generals had planned to fight on this bare plateau, and so the gunners were vulnerable to infantry fire because there was not room on the hilltop for men to stand off at a distance. This was a belly-to-belly brawl, a murderous gutter fight.

Men charged at open guns, and the guns, crammed with lethal canister, left swaths of attackers dead in front of their muzzles, yet still the men charged. Then, as the sun passed its dazzling height, a Virginia regiment dressed in blue coats, which had been the only uniforms available to their colonel, came to reinforce the Confederate left and saw a northern battery in front of them. They marched forward. The gunners saw them and waved at them, believing them to be northerners, and in the still, hot smoky air the triple stripes of the Confederate flag hung red, white and blue like the Stars and Stripes. The northern gunners, stripped to their waists and sweating white stripes through powder stains and cursing as they burned their hands on the blazing hot barrels of their guns, did not give a second glance to the blue-coated infantry that marched, as the gunners supposed, to give them support against the infantry in front.

"Take aim!" A whole battalion of Virginia infantry had come to close pistol range on the flank of a northern battery. The rifle muskets went onto blue-uniformed shoulders. There was no time to turn the field guns and so the gunners threw themselves flat, wriggled under their guns and limbers, then covered their heads with their arms.

"Fire!" The flames ripped through the gray smoke and the Virginian officers heard the rattle as hundreds of musket balls beat home on iron gun barrels or wooden limber boxes, and then they heard the screams as forty-nine of the fifty battery horses died. The gunners who had survived the volley turned and fled as the Virginians charged with fixed bayonets and bowie knives. The battery was captured, its guns splashed with blood.

"Turn the guns! Turn the guns!"

"Charge!" More southerners ran forward, bayonets bright in the smoky gloom. "Our homes! Our homes!" they called, and a crash of musketry greeted them, but the northerners here were falling back. A shell exploded somewhere between the lines, streaking the smoke with flame. "Our homes!"

The northerners counterattacked. A regiment swept over the captured guns, forcing the Virginians back, but the recaptured guns were of
no use to the federals for the gunners had been shot or else slaughtered by
bayonets, and the horse teams were so much dead meat, so the cannon
could not even be taken away. Other gunners in other batteries were
killed by sharpshooters, and slowly the Confederates edged forward and
the northerners heard the strange wailing scream as the rebel line
attacked. The shadows lengthened and still more men climbed the hill to
enter the stubborn horror.

James Starbuck came to the hilltop. He no longer searched for trophies that his victorious general could lay before the president's feet,
instead he came to discover just what had gone wrong on the smoke-
wreathed plateau. "Tell me what's happening, Starbuck," Irvin McDowell
had ordered his aide. "Off you go!" McDowell had sent six other men on
similar errands, but had not thought to visit the plateau himself. In truth
McDowell was swamped by the noise and the uncertainty and simply
wanted an aide to come back with good news of victory.

James urged his horse up the shell-scarred hillside to where he found
hell. His horse, devoid of guidance, ambled slowly forward to where a
New York regiment, newly ordered to the hilltop, marched with fixed
bayonets toward the enemy line, and it seemed to James that the whole
southern army suddenly flowered in flame, a great fence of flame which
turned to a rolling bank of smoke, and the New Yorkers just shuddered to
a stop, and then another southern volley came from their flank and the
New Yorkers stepped backward, leaving their dead and dying, and James
saw the ramrods working as the men tried to return the fire, but the New
York regiment had attacked alone, without flank support, and they had
no chance against the southern volleys that enfiladed and confronted and
decimated them. James tried to cheer them on, but his mouth was too dry
to make words.

Then James's world obliterated itself. His horse literally jumped
beneath him, then reared up its head to scream as it collapsed. A southern shell had exploded dead under its belly, eviscerating the beast and
James, stunned, deafened and screaming for help, sprawled clumsily off
the collapsing mass of guts and blood and flesh and hooves. He scrambled
away on all fours, suddenly throwing up the contents of his distended
belly. He stayed on all fours, retching foully, then managed to stagger to
his feet. He slipped in a puddle of his horse's blood, then stood again and
staggered toward the wooden house that lay at the center of the federal
battle line and seemed to offer a kind of refuge, though, as he got closer,
he saw how the little building had been splintered and riven and
scorched by bullets and shells. James leaned on the springhouse in the
yard and tried to make sense of his world, but all he could think about

was the welter of horse's blood into which he had fallen. His ears still rang from the explosion.

A Wisconsin soldier, his face a mask of white, was sitting beside him, and James slowly became aware that the man's head was half-severed by a shell fragment and his brains exposed. "No," James said, "no!" Inside the house a woman was wailing while somewhere in the distance it sounded as though a whole army of women was wailing. James pushed away the springhouse and staggered toward a regiment of infantry. They were Massachusetts men, his own people, and he stood close beside their colors and saw the heap of dead that had been thrown up behind the flags, and even as he watched, another man crumpled down. The flags were a target for enemy marksmen, a bright-starred invitation to death, but as soon as the color bearer fell another man plucked up the staff and held the standards high.

"Starbuck!" a voice shouted. It was a major whom James knew as a dour and canny attorney in Boston, but for some reason, although James must have met the man every week at the Lawyer's Club, he could not place his name. "Where's McDowell?" the major shouted.

"Down by the turnpike." James managed to sound reasonably coherent.

"He should be here!" A shell screamed overhead. The major, a thin and gray-haired man with a neatly clipped beard, shuddered as the missile exploded somewhere behind. "Damn them!"

Damn who, James wondered, then was astonished that he had used the swear word, even silently in his thoughts.

"We're fighting them piecemeal!" The Boston attorney tried to explain the northern army's predicament. "It won't do!"

"What do you mean?" James had to shout to make himself heard over the constant crash of gunnery. What was this man's name? He remembered how the attorney was a terrier in cross-examination, never letting go of a witness till he had shaken the evidence free, and James remembered how, famously, the man had once lost his temper with Chief Justice Shaw, complaining in open court that Shaw was intellectually and judicially costive, for which contempt Shaw had first fined him, and had then purchased him supper. What was the man's name?

"The attacks should coincide! We need a general officer to coordinate affairs." The major stopped abruptly.

James, who was always made uncomfortable by criticism of constituted authority, tried to explain that General McDowell was undoubtedly aware of what was happening, but then he stopped talking because the major was swaying. James put out a hand, the major gripped it with a demonic force, and then opened his mouth, but instead of speaking he just voided a great flow of blood. "Oh, no," the major managed to say, then he slumped down to James's feet. James felt himself shaking. This was a nightmare, and he felt a most terrible, abject and shameful fear. "Tell my dear Abigail," the dying major said, and he looked pathetically up at James, and James still could not remember the man's name.

"Tell Abigail what?" he asked stupidly, but the major was dead, and James shook the corpse's hand away and felt a terrible, terrible sadness that he was going to die without ever knowing the pleasures of this world. He would die and there was no one who would really miss him, no one who would truly mourn him, and James stared at the sky and howled a self-pitying cry, then he managed to fumble his revolver from its stiff-leather holster and he aimed it vaguely in the direction of the Confederate army and pulled its trigger time and again to spit its bullets into a smoke cloud. Each single shot was a protest and a revenge for his own cautious nature.

The Massachusetts regiment stumbled forward. They were no longer in line but had coalesced into small groups of men that now sidled between the dead and dying. They talked to one another as they fought, cheering one another on, offering praise and small jests. "Hey, reb! Here's a lead pill for your sickness!" a man shouted, then fired.

"You all right, Billy?"

"Gun's all choked up." The minié bullets expanded in the barrels as their hollowed-out backs were swollen by the powder gases to grip the rifling and so give the missile a deadly accurate spin. The friction of the expanded bullet scraping through the barrel was supposed to clean the fouled powder deposits from the rifling, but the theory did not work and the harsh deposits still accreted to make the guns terribly hard for a tired man to load.

"Here, reb! Here's one for you!"

"Christ! That was close."

"No use ducking, Robby, they've gone past before you hear 'em."

"Anyone got a shot? Someone give me a cartridge!"

James took comfort from the quiet words and edged closer to the nearest group of men. The commanding officer of the Massachusetts regiment had started the day as a lieutenant and now shouted at the survivors to advance, and so they tried, shouting a harsh defiance from their raw throats, but then two Confederate six pounders took the regiment's open flank with barrel loads of canister and the musket balls whipped along the survivors, decimating their groups and bloodying the slippery turf with still more blood. The Massachusetts men stepped back. James reloaded his revolver. He was close enough to see the dirty faces of the enemy, to see their eyes showing white through the powder stains on their skin, to see their unbuttoned coats and loose shirts. He saw a rebel fall down, clutching at his knee, then crawl away to the rear. He saw a rebel officer with long fair mustaches screaming encouragement at his men. The man's coat hung open and his trousers were belted with a length of rope. James took careful aim at the man, fired, but his revolver's smoke obscured the effect of his shot.

The rebel guns crashed back, bucking on their trails, smashing down on their wheels, sizzling as the sponges cleaned out their barrels, then firing again to feed the cloud of smoke that thickened like a Nantucket fog. More guns came from Beauregard's right wing. The rebel general sensed that disaster had been averted though it was none of his doing, but rather because his farmhands and college boys and store clerks had withstood the northern assault and were now counterattacking everywhere along Jackson's makeshift line. Two amateur armies had collided and luck was running Beauregard's way.

General Joseph Johnston had brought his men from the Shenandoah Valley, but, now that they were here, he had no duties except to watch them die. Johnston outranked Beauregard, but Beauregard had planned this battle, knew the ground, while Johnston was a stranger, and so he was letting Beauregard finish the fight. Johnston was ready to take over if Beauregard were hit, but till then he would stay silent and just try to understand the flux of the huge event that had come to its terrible climax on the hilltop. Johnston understood clearly enough that the North had wrong-footed Beauregard and turned his flank, but he also saw how the southern forces were fighting back hard and could yet scrape through to victory. Johnston also understood that it was Colonel Nathan Evans, the unregarded South Carolinian, who had probably saved the Confederacy by planting his feeble force across the path of the northern flank attack. Johnston sought out Evans and thanked him, then, working his way back to the east, the general came to where the wounded Washington Faulconer lay on the ground with his back propped against a saddle. Faulconer had been stripped to the waist and his chest was swathed in bandages while his right arm was in its blood-stained sling.

The general reined in and looked sympathetically down at the wounded Colonel. "It's Faulconer, isn't it?"

Washington Faulconer looked up to see a dazzle of yellow braid, but the smoke-diffused sun was behind the horseman and he could not make out the man's face. "Sir?" he answered very warily, already rehearsing the arguments he would use to explain his Legion's failure.

"I'm Joseph Johnston. We met in Richmond four months ago, and of course we had the pleasure of dining together at Jethro Sanders's house last year."

"Of course, sir." Faulconer had been expecting a reprimand, yet General Johnston sounded more than affable.

"You must be feeling foul, Faulconer. Is the wound bad?"

"A six-week scratch, sir, that's all." Faulconer knew how to sound suitably modest, though in truth he was desperately readjusting himself to the wonderful realization that General Johnston was not full of recrimination. Washington Faulconer was no fool, and he knew that he had behaved badly or, at the very least, that it might be imputed that he had behaved unwisely by leaving his Legion and thus not being in place to save them from Starbuck's treachery and Bird's impetuosity, but if Johnston's friendliness was any guide then maybe no one had noticed that dereliction of duty?

"If it hadn't have been for your sacrifice," Johnston said, pouring the balm of Gilead onto Faulconer's self-esteem and making the Colonel's happiness complete, "the battle would have been lost two hours back. Thank God you were with Evans, that's all I can say."

Faulconer opened his mouth to respond, found nothing whatever to say, so closed it.

"The federals had Beauregard completely bamboozled," Johnston went on blithely. "He thought the thing would be decided on the right flank, and all the time the rascals were planning to hit us here. But you fellows got it right, and thank God you did, for you've saved the Confederacy." Johnston was a pernickety, fussy man and a professional soldier of long experience who seemed genuinely moved by the tribute he was paying. "Evans told me of your bravery, Faulconer, and it's an honor to salute you!" In fact Shanks Evans had paid a tribute to the bravery of the Faulconer Legion and had not mentioned Colonel Washington Faulconer's name at all, but it was a simple enough misunderstanding and not one that Washington Faulconer thought needed to be corrected at this moment.

"We merely did our best, sir," Faulconer managed to say, while in his mind he was already rewriting the whole story of the day—how he had, in fact, known all along that the rebel left lay dangerously exposed. Had he not reconnoitered toward the Sudley Fords at daybreak? And had he not left his regiment well placed to meet the enemy's thrust? And had he not been wounded in the subsequent fighting? "I'm just glad we could have been of some small service, sir," he added modestly.

Johnston liked Faulconer's humility. "You're a brave fellow, Faulconer, and I'll make it my business to let Richmond know who are the real heroes of Manassas."

"My men are the real heroes, sir." Just ten minutes ago the Colonel had been cursing his men, especially the bandsmen who had jettisoned two expensive saxhorn tubas, a trumpet and three drums in their desperate efforts to escape the northern pursuit. "They're all good Virginians, sir," he added, knowing that Joseph Johnston was himself from the old dominion.

"I salute you all!" Johnston said, though touching his hat specifically to Faulconer before urging his horse on.

Washington Faulconer lay back and basked in the praise. A hero of
Manassas! Even the pain seemed diminished, or maybe that was the mor-
phine that Doctor Danson had insisted he swallow, but even so, a hero!
That was a good word and how well it sat on a Faulconer! And maybe six
weeks in the Richmond town house would not come amiss, so long, of
course, that this battle was won and the Confederacy survived, but
granted that proviso, surely a hero stood a better chance of promotion if
he dined regularly with the rulers of his country? And what a rebuke to
the mudsills like Lee who had been so niggardly in their attitude. Now
they would have to deal with a hero! Faulconer smiled at his son. "I think
you've earned yourself a promotion, Adam."

"But …"

"Quiet! Don't protest." The Colonel always felt good when he could
behave generously, and this moment was made even better by the burgeoning hopes that his new status as a hero of Manassas made credible.
He could surely attain general rank? And he could surely find the time to
perfect his Legion, which could then become the jewel and heart of his
new brigade. Faulconer's Brigade. That name had a fine ring, and he
imagined Faulconer's Brigade leading the march into Washington, presenting arms outside the White House and escorting a conqueror on
horseback into a humbled land. He took a cigar from the case beside him
and jabbed it toward Adam to emphasize the importance of what he said.
"I need you to be in charge of the Legion while I'm convalescing. I need
you to make sure Pecker doesn't run wild again, eh? That he doesn't frit-
ter the Legion away in some piddling skirmish. Besides, the Legion should
be in family hands. And you did well today, son, very well."

"I did nothing, Father," Adam protested hotly, "and I'm not even
sure—"

"Now, now! Quiet!" Washington Faulconer had seen Major Bird
approaching and did not want Thaddeus to witness his son's prevarica-
tions. "Thaddeus!" The Colonel greeted his brother-in-law with an unac-
customed warmth. "The general asked me to thank you. You did well!"

Major Bird, who knew full well that the Colonel had been furious
with him until just a moment before, stopped dead in his tracks then
looked ostentatiously about, as though searching for another man called
Thaddeus who might be the object of the Colonel's praise. "Are you talking to me, Colonel?"

"You did marvelously well! I congratulate you! You did precisely what
I would have expected of you, indeed, exactly what I wanted of you! You
held the Legion to its duty till I arrived. Everyone else thought the battle
would be on the right, but we knew better, eh? We did well, very well. If
my arm wasn't broken I'd shake your hand. Well done, Thaddeus, well
done!"

Thaddeus Bird managed to hold his laughter in check, though his head did jerk nervously back and forth as if he was about to burst into a fit of devilish cackles. "Am I to understand," he finally managed to speak without laughing, "that you are also to be congratulated?"

The Colonel hid his anger at his brother-in-law's effrontery. "I think you and I know each other well enough to dispense with an exchange of admiration, Thaddeus. Just be assured I'll put your name forward when I'm in Richmond."

"I didn't come here to offer you admiration," Thaddeus Bird said with tactless honesty, "but to suggest we send a work party to find some water. The men are parched."

"Water? By all means, water. Then you and I should put our heads together and decide what's needed for the future. Mr. Little tells me we've lost some band instruments, and we can't afford to lose as many officers' horses as we did today."

Band instruments? Horses? Thaddeus Bird gaped at his brother-in-law, wondering if the broken bone had somehow drained Faulconer of his wits. What the Legion needed, Thaddeus Bird decided as the Colonel meandered on, was a McGuffey's *Reader* in elementary soldiering, a child's primer in rifle-fire and drill, but he knew it would be no good saying as much. Faulconer's huge complacency had been puffed up by some fool's praise, and he was already seeing himself as the conqueror of New York. Bird tried to sober the Colonel with a small dose of reality. "You'll want the butcher's bill, Faulconer?" He interrupted the Colonel. "The list of our dead and wounded?"

Washington Faulconer again had to hide his irritation. "Is it bad?" he asked guardedly.

"I have nothing with which to compare it, and sadly it's incomplete. We misplaced a lot of men in the course of your brave victory, but we know for sure that at least a score are dead. Captain Jenkins is gone, and poor Burroughs, of course. I assume you'll write to the widow?" Bird paused, but received no answer, so just shrugged and carried on. "Of course there can be other dead ones still out there. We know of twenty-two wounded fellows, some of them atrociously bad—"

"Twenty-three," the Colonel interrupted, and offered Thaddeus Bird a modest smile. "I count myself a member of the Legion, Thaddeus."

"So do I, Faulconer, and had already numbered you among its heroes. As I said, twenty-two, some of them grievously. Masterson won't survive, and Norton has lost both his legs so ..."

"I don't need every detail," Faulconer said peevishly.

"And there still appear to be seventy-two men missing," Bird continued stoically with his bad news. "They aren't necessarily lost to us forever; Turner MacLean's boy staggered in five minutes ago having spent the best part of two hours wandering around the battlefield, but he never did have an ounce of sense. Others are probably dead and gone. I hear Ridley was killed."

"Murdered," the Colonel insisted.

"Murdered, was he?" Bird had already heard the story, but wanted to provoke the Colonel.

"He was murdered," the Colonel said, "and I witnessed it, and you will enter that in the regiment's books."

"If we ever find the books," Bird remarked happily. "We seem to have lost all the baggage."

"Murdered! You hear me?" Faulconer thundered the accusation, sending a stab of pain through his wounded chest. "That's what you will enter. That he was murdered by Starbuck."

"And Starbuck's missing," Bird went blithely on, "I'm most sorry to say."

"You're sorry?" There was something very dangerous in the Colonel's voice.

"You should be too," Bird said, ignoring the Colonel's tone. "Starbuck probably saved our colors, and he certainly prevented Adam from being taken prisoner. Didn't Adam tell you?"

"I've been trying to tell you, Father," Adam said.

"Starbuck is gone," the Colonel said flatly, "and if he was here you would be required to arrest him for murder. I saw him shoot Ridley. I saw him! Do you hear that, Thaddeus?" In fact half the Legion could hear the Colonel, whose indignation soared as he remembered poor Ridley's death. Good God, Faulconer thought, but did none of these men believe him when he said he had seen Starbuck fire the shots that murdered Ridley! The Colonel had turned in his saddle and watched him fire the revolver! And now Pecker Bird wanted to make out that the Bostonian was some kind of hero? Christ, the Colonel thought, but he was the hero of Manassas! Had not General Johnston said as much? "You say we lost poor Roswell Jenkins?" he asked, deliberately changing the subject.

"He was quite obliterated by shellfire," Bird confirmed, then obstinately changed the subject back. "Are you really ordering me to arrest Starbuck for murder?"

"If you find him, yes!" the Colonel shouted, then winced as a lance of pain shot down his arm. "For God's sake, Thaddeus, why do you always have to make such a damn fuss about things?"

"Because someone has to, Colonel, someone has to." Bird smiled and turned away while behind him, on a plateau edged with fire, the battle came to its breaking point at last.

James Starbuck never quite understood why the northern lines broke, he just remembered a desperate panic suddenly overtaking the federal troops until, all order gone, there was nothing but panic as McDowell's army ran.

Nothing they had done had moved the southern regiments off the plateau. No assault gained enough ground to let supporting troops reinforce success, and so the northern attacks had been beaten back again and again, and each repulse had whelped its litter of dead and dying men who lay in rows like tidal wrack to mark the limits of each federal assault.

Ammunition had run short in some northern regiments. The southerners, pushed back toward their own baggage, were distributing tubs of cartridges to their troops, but the northern supplies were still east of the Bull Run and every wagon or limber or caisson had to be brought through the traffic jam that developed around the stone bridge and too often, even when ammunition was brought to the hilltop, it proved to be the wrong kind and so troops armed with .58 rifles received .69 musket ammunition and, as their rifles fell silent, they retreated to leave a gap in the northern line into which the gray rebels moved.

On both sides the rifles and muskets misfired or broke. The cones through which the percussion cap spat its fire into the powder charge broke most frequently, but as the southerners pressed forward they could pick up the guns of the northern dead and so keep up the slaughter. Yet still the northerners fought on. Their rifle and musket barrels were fouled with the clinker of burnt powder so that each shot took a huge effort to ram home, and the day was hot and the air filled with acrid powder smoke so that the mouths and gullets of the weary men were dry and raw, and their shoulders were bruised black from the recoil of the heavy guns, and their voices hoarse from shouting, their eyes were smarting with smoke, their ears ringing with the hammer blows of the big guns, their arms aching from ramming the bullets down the fouled barrels, yet still they fought. They bled and fought, cursed and fought, prayed and fought. Some of the men seemed dazed, just standing open-eyed and open-mouthed, oblivious to their officers' shouts or to the discordant din of bullets, guns, shells and screams.

James Starbuck had lost all sense of time. He reloaded his revolver, fired and reloaded. He scarce knew what he was doing, only that every shot could save the Union. He was terrified, but he fought on, taking an odd courage from the thought of his younger sister. He had decided that Martha alone would mourn him and that he could not disgrace her affection and it was that resolve which held him to his place where he fought like a ranker, firing and loading, firing and loading, and all the while saying Martha's name aloud like a talisman that would keep him brave. Martha was the sister whose character was most like Nathaniel's, and as James stood amid the litter of wounded and dead, he could have wept that God had not given him Martha and Nathaniel's brazen daring.

Then, just as he manipulated the last of his small percussion caps onto his revolver's cones, a cheer spread along the southern line and James looked up to see the whole enemy front surging forward. He straightened his aching bruised arm and pointed the revolver at what looked like a vast rat-gray army scorched black by powder burns that was charging straight toward him.

Then, just as he muttered his sister's name and half-flinched from the noise his revolver would make, he saw he was utterly alone.

One moment there had been a battle, and now there was rout.

For the federal army had broken and run.

They pelted down the hill, discipline gone to the wind. Men threw away rifles and muskets, bayonets and haversacks, and just fled. Some ran north toward the Sudley Fords while others ran for the stone bridge. A few men tried to stem the charge, shouting at their fellow northerners to form line and stand firm, but the few were swamped by the many. The panicked troops flooded the fields on either side of the turnpike on which a limbered cannon, its horses whipped into a frantic gallop, ran down screaming infantrymen with its iron-shod wheels. Other men used battle standards as spears with which to fight their way toward the stream.

The rebel pursuit stopped at the plateau's edge. A spattering of musket fire hurried the northerner's retreat, but no one on the rebel side had the energy to pursue. Instead they reveled in the slow realization of victory and in the scurrying defeat of the panicked horde beneath them. The rebel gunners brought their surviving cannon to the hillcrest and the southern shells screamed away into the afternoon warmth to explode in bursts of smoke along the crowded turnpike and in the farther woods. One of the shots burst in the air plumb above the wooden bridge that carried the turnpike over the deep tributary of the Run just as a wagon was crossing. The wagon's wounded horses panicked and tried to bolt, but the fatal shell had torn off a front wheel and the massive vehicle slewed round, its broken axle gouging timber so that the heavy wagon body was jammed immovably between the bridge's wooden parapets, and thus the northern army's main escape road was blocked and still more shells screamed down to explode among the fleeing northerners. The federal guns, carriages, limbers and wagons still on the Bull Run's western bank were abandoned as their teamsters fled for safety. A shell exploded in the stream, spouting tons of water. More shells smacked behind, driving the panicked mass of men in a maddened scramble down the steep slippery bank and into the Run's quick current. Scores of men drowned, pushed under by their own desperate comrades. Others floundered across the deep stream and somehow pulled themselves free and then ran toward Washington.

Nathaniel Starbuck had watched the rout spill over the plateau's edge. At first he had not believed what he saw, then disbelief turned to amazement. The sergeant guarding the prisoners had taken one look at the hillside, then ran. A wounded northerner, recuperating in the yard, had limped away, using his musket as a crutch. The red-bearded doctor came to the door in his blood-spattered apron, took one incredulous look at the whole scene, then shook his head and went back inside to his patients.

"What do we do now?" one of the rebel prisoners asked Starbuck, as if an officer might know the etiquette of handling victory in the middle of a defeated rabble.

"We stay real quiet and polite," Starbuck advised. There were north-erners fleeing past the house and some were looking angrily at the south-ern prisoners. "Stay sitting, don't move, just wait." He watched a north-ern field gun retreating off the plateau. The gun captain had somehow managed to assemble a team of four horses which, whipped bloody by their frightened drivers, were galloping recklessly down the shell-scarred slope so that the gunners perched on the narrow limber seat were clinging grimly to the metal handles. The horses were white-eyed and scared. The gun itself, attached behind the limber, bounced dangerously as the rig splashed through a streamlet at the hill's foot, then the driver pulled on his reins and the panicked horses turned too fast onto the turnpike and Starbuck watched in horror as first the cannon, then the limber, tipped, rolled and slid hard across the road to crash sickeningly into the trees at the edge of the yard. There was a moment's silence, then the first screams tore the humid air.

"Oh, Christ." A wounded man turned in horror from the carnage. A horse, both rear legs broken, tried to scramble free of the bloody wreck-age. One of the gunners had been trapped under the limber and the man clawed feebly at the splintered timbers that impaled him. A passing infantry sergeant ignored the wounded man as he cut the traces of the one uninjured horse, unhooked its chains, then scrambled onto its back. A roundshot from the spilt limber trundled across the road and the wounded horses went on screaming like the dying gunner.

"Oh God, no." One of the prisoners in the tree-shaded yard was a tidewater Virginian who now recited the Lord's Prayer over and over again. The awful screaming went on until a northern officer walked over to the wounded animals and fired into their skulls. It took five shots, but the animals died, leaving only the shrieking, gasping, writhing gunner who was impaled by the mangled spokes of the limber's wheel. The officer took a breath. "Soldier!"

The man must have recognized the tone of authority for he went still for just a second, and that second was all the officer needed. He aimed the revolver, pulled the trigger and the gunner fell back silent. The northern officer shuddered, tossed away the empty revolver then walked away weeping. The world seemed very quiet suddenly. It stank of blood, but it was quiet until the tidewater boy said the Lord's Prayer one more time, as though the repetition of the words could save his soul.

"Are you boys safe?" A gray-coated officer galloped his horse down to the crossroads.

"We're safe," Starbuck said.

"We whipped 'em, boys! Whipped 'em good!" the officer boasted.

"You want an apple, mister?" A South Carolina prisoner, released now, had been searching among the knapsacks that had spilled from the fallen gun limber and now plucked some apples from among the bloody wreckage. He tossed the jubilant officer a bright red apple. "Go whip 'em some more!"

The officer caught the apple. Behind him the first southern infantry was advancing toward the Bull Run. Starbuck watched for a while, then turned away. War's lottery had freed him yet again, and he had one more promise yet to keep.

Tired men collected the wounded, those they could find. Some of the injured were in woodland, and doomed to slow and forgotten deaths in the undergrowth. Thirsty men looked for water while some just drank the fouled liquid in the cannon's sponge buckets, gulping down the gunpowder debris along with the warm, salty liquid. The small wind was brisker now, stirring the camp fires that men made from shattered musket stocks and fence rails.

The rebels were in no state to pursue the federal troops, and so they stayed on the battlefield and stared in dazed astonishment at the plunder of victory—at the guns and wagons and caissons, at the mounds of captured stores and at the hordes of prisoners. A fat congressman from Rochester, New York, was among those prisoners; he had been found trying to hide his vast belly behind a slim sapling and had been brought to the army headquarters where he blustered about the importance of his position and demanding to be released. A rail-thin Georgian soldier told him to shut his damned fat mouth before he had his damned fat tongue cut out to be cooked and served with an apple sauce and the congressman fell instantly silent.

At dusk the rebels crossed the Run to capture the thirty-pound Parrott field rifle that had signaled the federal attack that dawn. The northerners had abandoned twenty-six other guns, along with nearly all their army's baggage. Southern soldiers found full-dress uniforms carefully packed ready for the triumphant entry into Richmond and a North Carolinian soldier paraded proudly about in a Yankee general's finery, complete with epaulettes, sword, sash and spurs. The pockets of the dead were rifled for their pitiful haul of combs, playing cards, testaments, jackknives and coins. A lucky few found wealthier corpses, one with a heavy watch chain hung with golden seals, another with a ruby ring on his wedding finger. Daguerreotypes of wives and sweethearts, parents and children were tossed aside, for the victors were not looking for mementoes of shattered affections, but only for coins and cigars, silver and gold, good boots, fine shirts, belts, buckles or weapons. A brisk market in plunder established itself; fine officers' field glasses were sold for a dollar, swords for three, and fifty-dollar Colt revolvers for five or six. Most prized of all were the posing photographs showing New York and Chicago ladies out of their clothes. Some of the men refused to look, fearing hell's fires, but most passed the pictures around and wondered at the plunder that would come their way if ever they were called upon to invade the rich, plump, soft North that bred such women and such fine rooms. Doctors from North and South worked together in the farm hospitals of the scorched, torn battlefield. The wounded wept, the amputated legs and arms and hands and feet piled in the yards, while the dead were stacked like cordwood for the graves that must wait for morning to be dug.

As evening drew on, James Starbuck was still free. He had hidden himself in a stand of trees, and now he crawled in the bottom of a deep ditch toward the Bull Run. His mind was in chaos. How had it happened? How could defeat have happened? It was so bitter, so terrible, so shameful. Was God so careless of the right that he would allow this awful visitation upon the United States? It made no sense.

"I wouldn't go a foot farther, Yankee," an amused voice suddenly spoke above him, "because that's poison ivy just ahead of you, and you're in enough trouble like it is."

James looked up to see two grinning lads whom he rightly suspected had been watching him for the last few minutes. "I'm an officer," he managed to say.

"Nice to meet you, officer. I'm Ned Potter and that's Jake Spring, and this here's our dog, Abe." Potter gestured at a ragged little mongrel that he held on a length of rope. "We ain't none of us officers, but you're our prisoner."

James stood and tried to brush the dead leaves and stagnant water from his uniform. "My name," he said in his most officious manner, then stopped. What would happen to Elial Starbuck's son in southern hands? Would they lynch him? Would they do the terrible things his father said all southerners did to Negroes and emancipators?

"Don't care what your name is, Yankee, only what's in your pockets. Me, Jake and Abe are kind of poor right now. All we captured so far is two boys from Pennsylvania and they didn't have nothing but cold hoe cakes and three rusty cents between 'em." The musket came up and the grin widened. "You can give us that revolver for a begin-nings."

"Buchanan!" James blurted out the name. "Miles Buchanan!"

Ned Potter and Jake Spring stared uncomprehendingly at their pris-oner.

"An attorney!" James explained. "I've been trying to remember his name all day! He once accused Chief Justice Shaw of being costive. Intel-lectually costive, that is …" His voice died away as he realized that poor Miles Buchanan was dead now, and Abigail Buchanan was a widow, and he himself was taken prisoner.

"Just give us the revolver, Yankee."

James handed over the blackened revolver, then turned out his pock-ets. He was carrying over eighteen dollars in coin, a New Testament, a fine watch on a seal-heavy chain, a pair of folding opera glasses, a box of pen nibs, two notebooks and a fine linen handkerchief that his mother had embroidered with his initials. Ned Potter and Jake Spring were delighted with their luck, but James felt only a terrible humiliation. He had been delivered into the hands of his bitterest enemies and he could have wept for his country's loss.

One mile away from James, Nathaniel Starbuck searched a meadow that was pockmarked with shell fire and scored with hoofprints. The Yan-kees were long gone and the meadow was empty except for the dead. It was the pasture where Washington Faulconer had struck him with his rid-ing crop, the place where Ethan Ridley had died.

He found Ridley closer to the tree line than he remembered, but he supposed all his recollections of the battle were confused. The body was a horror of blood and bone, of torn flesh and blackened skin. The birds had already begun their feasting, but flapped reluctantly away as Starbuck walked up to the corpse that was beginning to stink. Ridley's head was recognizable, the small pointed beard being oddly clear of blood. "You son of a bitch," Starbuck said tiredly and without real anger, but he was remembering the scar on Sally's face, and the child she had lost, and the rapes and beatings she had endured just so that this man could be free of her, and so some insult seemed fitting to mark the moment.

The sick-sweet stench of death was thick and nauseous as Starbuck crouched beside the corpse and steeled himself. Then he reached out for what was left of his enemy. There but for the grace of God, he thought, and he pulled the neck of Ridley's jacket to free the remnants of the gar-ment from the bloody corpse, and something deep in the body made a gurgling sound that almost made Starbuck retch. The jacket would not come clear of the bloody mess and Starbuck realized he would have to undo the leather belt that was somehow still in place around the eviscer-ated mess. He plunged his fingers into the cold, jellylike horror, and found the buckle. He undid it, heaved, and a portion of the corpse rolled away to reveal the revolver that Ridley had fired at Starbuck.

It was the pretty, ivory-handled English gun that Washington Faulconer had shown to Starbuck in his study at Seven Springs. The gun was now choked with Ridley's blood, but Starbuck wiped it on the grass, cuffed more of the blood away with his sleeve, then pushed the beautiful weapon into his empty holster. He then unthreaded the cap box and the cartridge case from Ridley's belt. There were a dozen dollar coins in the case, which he pushed into one of his own blood-soaked pockets.

Yet he had not come here simply to loot his enemy's body, but rather to take back a treasure. He wiped his fingers on the grass, took another deep breath, then went back to the bloody remnants of the gray jacket. He found a leather case which seemed to have held a drawing, though the paper was now so soaked with blood that it was impossible to tell just what the drawing might have shown. There were three more silver dollars in the pocket and a small, blood-wet leather bag, which Starbuck pulled open.

The ring was there. It looked dull in the fading light, but it was the ring he had wanted; the silver French ring that had belonged to Sally's mother and which Starbuck now pushed into his own pocket as he stepped back from the corpse. "You son of a bitch," he said again, then he walked away past Ridley's dead horse. Across the valley the smoke of the camp fires drifted away from the hill to veil the sunset.

Dark was falling as Starbuck climbed the hill to where the southern army made its weary bivouac. A few officers had tried to order their men off the hilltop and down to where the ground did not stink of blood, but the men were too tired to move. Instead they sat around their fires and ate captured hard tack and cold bacon. A man played a fiddle, its notes wondrously plangent in the graying light. The far hills were darkening and the first stars gleaming pale and sharp in a clean sky. A Georgia regiment held a service, the men's voices strong as they sang praises for their victory.

It took Starbuck an hour to find the Legion. It was almost full dark by then, but he saw Pecker Bird's distinctive face in the light of a fire made from a dozen fence rails which radiated out from the flames like spokes. Every man about the fire was responsible for a rail, nudging it into the fire as the rail burned down. The men around the fire were all officers who looked up astonished as Starbuck limped into the flame light. Murphy nodded a pleased greeting to see the Bostonian, and Bird smiled. "So you're alive, Starbuck?"

"So it seems, Major."

Bird lit a cigar and tossed it to Starbuck who caught it, sucked in the smoke, then nodded his thanks.

"Is that your blood?" Murphy asked Starbuck, whose uniform was still thick with Ridley's blood.

"No."

"But it's very dramatic," Bird said in gentle mockery, then twisted himself around. "Colonel!"

Colonel Faulconer, his shirt and jacket now wrapped around his wounded arm, was sitting outside his tent. He had made a huge commotion about the Legion's missing baggage and finally a reluctant search party had discovered Nelson, the Colonel's servant, still guarding as much of the Colonel's baggage as he had managed to carry away from the Yankee attack. Most of the baggage was gone, looted by successive waves of northerners and southerners, but the Colonel's tent had been salvaged and a bed of blankets laid down inside. Adam was lying on the bed while his father sat on a barrel in the tent's door.

"Colonel!" Bird called again, his insistence at last making Washington Faulconer look up. "Good news, Colonel." Bird could hardly keep from grinning as he made his mischief. "Starbuck is alive."

"Nate!" Adam reached for the makeshift crutch that a man had cut from a thicket nearby, but his father pushed him down.

Faulconer stood and walked toward the fire. A mounted staff captain chose that same moment to approach the fire from farther along the plateau, but the captain, who had a message for Colonel Faulconer, sensed the tension around the camp fire and checked his horse to watch what happened.

Faulconer gazed through the flames, flinching from Starbuck's horrid appearance. The northerner's uniform was dark with blood, stiff with it, black in the flame light with the blood that had soaked into every stitch and weave of the gray coat. Starbuck looked like a thing come from a nightmare, but he nodded pleasantly enough as he blew a stream of cigar smoke into the night. "Evening, Colonel."

Faulconer said nothing. Bird lit himself a cigar, then looked at Starbuck. "The Colonel was wondering how Ridley died, Starbuck?"

"Got hit by a shell, Colonel. Nothing left of him but a mess of bones and blood," Starbuck said, his voice careless.

"Is that what you want me to put in the book, Colonel?" Thaddeus Bird asked with a studied innocence. "That Ridley died of artillery fire?"

Still Washington Faulconer did not speak. He was staring at Starbuck with what seemed like loathing, but he could not bring himself to say a word.

Bird shrugged. "Earlier, Colonel, you ordered me to arrest Starbuck for murder. You want me to do that right now?" Bird waited for an answer and when none came he looked back to Starbuck. "Did you murder Captain Ethan Ridley, Starbuck?"

"No," Starbuck said curtly. He stared at Faulconer, daring the Colonel to contradict him. The Colonel knew he was lying, but he did not have the guts to make the accusation to his face. Men had come from the Legion's other camp fires to watch the confrontation.

"But the Colonel saw you commit the murder," Bird insisted. "What do you have to say to that?"

Starbuck took the cigar from his mouth and spat into the fire.

"I assume that expectoration signifies a denial?" Bird asked happily, then looked around the men who were crowding into the flame light. "Did anyone else here see Ridley die?" Bird waited for an answer as sparks whirled upward from the burning rails. "Well?"

"I saw the son of a bitch get filleted by a shell," Truslow growled from the shadows.

"And did Starbuck fire the fatal shell, Sergeant?" Bird asked in a pedantic voice, and the men around the fire laughed aloud at the major's mockery. Faulconer shifted his weight, but still kept his silence. "So I reckon, Colonel, that you were wrong," Bird went on, "and that Lieutenant Starbuck is innocent of murder. And I further reckon you'll be wanting to thank him for saving the Legion's colors, isn't that right?"

But Faulconer could take no more humiliation from these men who had fought while he had been swanning across the countryside in search of fame. He turned away without a word, only to see the staff captain watching him from horseback. "What do you want?" he snapped bitterly.

"You're invited to supper, Colonel." The staff captain was understandably nervous. "The president has arrived from Richmond, sir, and the generals are eager for your company."

Faulconer blinked as he tried to make sense of the invitation, then saw in it his chance of salvation. "Of course." He strode away, calling for his son. Adam had struggled to his feet and was now limping to welcome Starbuck back, but his father demanded his son's loyalty. "Adam! You'll come with me."

Adam hesitated, then gave in. "Yes, Father."

The two men were helped onto their horses and no one spoke much as they rode away. Instead the men of the Faulconer Legion fed their fires and watched the sparks fly high, but said scarcely a word until the Faulconers had ridden far beyond the flame light and were just two dark shadows silhouetted against the southern sky. Somehow no one expected to see Washington Faulconer back again in a hurry. Bird looked up at Starbuck. "I guess I'm in command now. So thank you for saving our colors, and more important, for saving me. So now what do I do with you?"

"Whatever you want, Major."

"Then I think I shall punish you for whatever sins you undoubtedly

committed today." Bird grinned as he spoke. "I shall make you Captain
Roswell Jenkins's replacement, and give you Sergeant Truslow's company.
But only if Sergeant Truslow wants a miserable Boston-bred overeducated
beardless preacher's son like yourself as his commanding officer?"

"I reckon he'll do," Truslow said laconically.

"So you feed him, Sergeant, not me," Bird said, and raised a dismissive hand.

Starbuck walked away with Truslow. When the two men had gone
beyond the earshot of the soldiers gathered around the officers' fire, the
sergeant spat a stream of tobacco juice. "'So how does it feel to murder
someone?' You remember asking me that? And I told you to find out for
yourself, so now you tell me, Captain."

Captain? Starbuck noted, but said nothing of the unwonted respect.
"It felt most satisfying, Sergeant."

Truslow nodded. "I saw you shoot the son of a bitch, and I was kind of
wondering why."

"For this." Starbuck took the silver ring from his pocket and held it
out to the small, dark-bearded Truslow. "Just for this," he said, and
dropped the ring into the powder-blackened palm. The silver glinted for
an instant in the blood-stinking smoke-darkened night, and then
Truslow's hand closed on it fast. His Emily was in heaven, and the ring
was back with him where it belonged.

Truslow had stopped dead in the darkness. For a second Starbuck
thought the sergeant was weeping, but then he realized it was just the
sound of Truslow clearing his throat. The sergeant began walking again,
saying nothing, but just gripping the silver ring as if it was a talisman for
all his future life. He did not speak again until they were a few yards from
the fires of A Company, and then he put a hand on the blood-hardened
cloth of Starbuck's sleeve. His voice, when he spoke, was unwontedly
meek. "So how is she, Captain?"

"She's happy. Surprisingly happy. She was treated badly, but she came
through it and she's happy. But she wanted you to have the ring, and she
wanted me to take it from Ridley."

Truslow thought about that answer for a few seconds, then frowned.
"I should have killed that bastard myself, shouldn't I?"

"Sally wanted me to do it," Starbuck said, "so I did. And with much
pleasure." He could not keep himself from smiling.

Truslow was still for a long, long time, then he thrust the ring into a
pocket. "It's going to rain tomorrow," he said. "I can smell it in the air.
Most of these bastards have lost their groundsheets and blankets so I
reckon in the morning you should let us scavenge a while." He led Starbuck into the light of his company's fires. "New captain" was Truslow's

only introduction. "Robert? We'll have some of that fat bacon. John? Break that bread you're hiding. Pearce? That whiskey you found. We'll take some. Sit down, Captain, sit."

Starbuck sat and ate. The food was the most wonderful he had ever tasted, nor could he have asked for better company. Above him the stars shimmered in a sky of dissipating smoke. A fox called from the distant woods and a wounded horse screamed. Somewhere a man sang a sad song, and then a gunshot sounded in the lost darkness like a final echo of this day of battle in which a preacher's son, far from home, had made himself a rebel.

HISTORICAL NOTE

The first battle of Manassas (or Bull Run as northerners call it) was fought much as described in *Rebel*, though the novel ignores some tough but scrappy fighting that filled the gap between the retreat of Nathan Evans's half-brigade and the first engagement of Thomas Jackson's Virginia Brigade, and it ignores the presence of Jeb Stuart's cavalry on the battlefield, though in this battle, as in most of the big set-piece engagements to come in the War between the States, the cavalry was unimportant to the outcome. First Manassas was won by infantrymen, and it was Shanks Evans, who really did have a "barrelito" of whiskey on constant tap, whose timely maneuver saved the Confederacy, though it was "Stonewall" Jackson whose name became famous that day and whose statue still dominates the hilltop where he earned his nickname. Around nine hundred men died on July 21, 1861, and at least ten times as many were wounded.

The battlefield has been marvelously preserved by the National Park Service. The visitor center on the Henry House hill offers a splendid introduction to a site that is well signposted and explained, and is an easy drive from Washington, D.C. There is no Faulconer County in Virginia, nor was there a Faulconer Legion in the state's service.